DAMAGE

JOHN LESCROART

DAMAGE

DUTTON

DUTTON
Published by Penguin Group (USA) Inc.
375 Hudson Street, New York, New York 10014, U.S.A.
Penguin Group (Canada), 90 Eglinton Avenue East, Suite 700, Toronto, Ontario M4P 2Y3,
Canada (a division of Pearson Penguin Canada Inc.); Penguin Books Ltd, 80 Strand, London
WC2R 0RL, England; Penguin Ireland, 25 St Stephen's Green, Dublin 2, Ireland (a division
of Penguin Books Ltd); Penguin Group (Australia), 250 Camberwell Road, Camberwell,
Victoria 3124, Australia (a division of Pearson Australia Group Pty Ltd); Penguin Books India
Pvt Ltd, 11 Community Centre, Panchsheel Park, New Delhi–110 017, India; Penguin Group
(NZ), 67 Apollo Drive, Rosedale, North Shore 0632, New Zealand (a division of Pearson New
Zealand Ltd); Penguin Books (South Africa) (Pty) Ltd, 24 Sturdee Avenue, Rosebank,
Johannesburg 2196, South Africa

Penguin Books Ltd, Registered Offices: 80 Strand, London WC2R 0RL, England

Published by Dutton, a member of Penguin Group (USA) Inc.

 REGISTERED TRADEMARK—MARCA REGISTRADA

ISBN 978-0-525-95176-6

Printed in the United States of America
Set in ITC Berkeley Old Style Medium
Designed by Carla Bolte

To my consiglieri Al Giannini, and to my bride,
Lisa Marie Sawyer, always and forever

The total amount of suffering per year in the natural world is beyond all decent contemplation.

—RICHARD DAWKINS

Life is a cheap thing beside a man's work.

—ERNEST HEMINGWAY

DAMAGE

PROLOGUE

Felicia Nuñez saw him standing up against a building across the street from the stop where she normally got off her streetcar. With her heart suddenly pounding in her ears, she turned away from the streetcar door as it opened and sat down on one of the side-facing benches just at the front across from the driver.

As the car started up again, passing him, she caught another glimpse of him out of the corner of her eye.

Or maybe it was him. It looked very much like him. His hair maybe a little different, longer, from the last time she'd seen him in the courtroom, but the same attitude in the way he stood. He had one boot propped up against the building, his strong white arms crossed over his chest.

She knew why he was there. He was waiting. Waiting for her.

Back then she used to see him everywhere, even when her mind had known that he could not find her. She'd been in witness protection. No one even knew where she'd lived. So there was no way in reality that it could happen. And yet for a year or two, she thought she saw him every day.

But today?

This time it was *exactly* him. Most of the other times, whoever she saw reminded her of him—the hair, the arms, the set of the body. But today was all him, not a collection of similar parts that, in her terror, she could imagine into the monster that he was.

At the next stop she descended out into the neighborhood and heard the streetcar's door close behind her and then the brakes release and then the scraping sound as it moved ahead and left her standing alone at the curb.

She did not like to spend extra money and knew she could make a cup of coffee for free at home, but he might still be there lurking and if he saw her, he might, or he would . . .

She could not imagine.

No. She *could* imagine.

She went into the Starbucks and ordered a coffee—half an hour's work at the cleaners where she was lucky to have a job, but she needed to sit quietly and to think, and also to give him time to leave if he was really waiting there to see her.

How could he have found her?

She took a seat at the front window where she could see him if he suddenly appeared among the pedestrians passing by.

The first sip scalded her tongue and the pain seemed to break something within her. She put her paper cup down and blinked back the wave of emotion that threatened now to break over her.

Bastardo! she thought. The life-destroying bastard.

In her mind, she was eighteen again.

———

The sun shines in her eyes as she leaves the school building where the Curtlees were letting her take the English classes two times a week, paying for her tuition as part of their deal. She comes all this way to work for them, they provide documentation and help her learn the language. She is going to become a citizen one day in the U.S., where her children can grow up educated and free.

It is almost too much for her to believe, after her poverty in Guatemala and then her mother's death, leaving Felicia an orphan at seventeen. But now it is actually happening. She has been here for five months now and in spite of her initial fears of slavery and bad treatment, nothing bad has happened.

The son with greedy hands is someone to avoid, but the Curtlees are clearly just what they seem—good people, wealthy beyond mea-

sure, who bring young Latinas here to work for them out of the goodness of their souls.

And God for some reason had led their man in Guatemala to Felicia.

Now she walks with her eyes down against the sunlight. It is a warm autumn evening and she wears a white cotton dress and red rope shoes that are so comfortable to walk in, especially on the hills here in San Francisco. She says good-bye to the last of her classmates, and turns uphill again and enters the forested area they call Presidio that she has to cross to get to the house.

She is halfway through when he steps out from behind a bush in front of her. Here in the trees it is darker than the street, but light enough still to see that he is confident and smiling as he steps up to her.

"Hola," she says, with a tiny false smile, hoping he will leave her alone, and she goes to move around him.

But he steps to the side with her.

"You are so beautiful," he says. Still smiling, he is breathing very hard. He makes some motion with his head that makes her look down and she sees that he has let himself out of his pants.

"No, por favor," she says. She repeats it. "Por favor."

And always smiling, though his eyes are deadly cold, he moves quickly now, both hands at her waist, pulling her toward him, holding her against him.

"Don't fight," he rasps out. "Don't fight me. I'll kill you."

She struggles and he slaps her face hard, never letting go of her dress with his other hand. He now grabs her by the throat with the one free hand he'd slapped her with. Up against her, he pushes her back and back until she falls and then he is on top of her, holding her throat, opening her legs under him, forcing himself against and against and against and finally inside her and she screams out and he covers her mouth with one hand and tells her again that he will kill her and she believes him with all her heart. And she takes it in silence.

And then it is over and he stands up and smiles down at her, tucking himself in, and tells her that he likes her shoes and he's glad that she kept them on for him—that was sexy, he says, the fact that she couldn't even wait to take them off she wanted it so bad—and then he tells her that he will see her around and maybe they will do this again.

———

Her coffee had gone cold. She'd been sitting here now for twenty-five minutes. Outside, the fog advanced in bleary wisps.

If he was waiting for her, he would be very cold by now. She would wrap her coat up tightly and walk by at the end of the block to see if he was still there, and if he was, she would keep going and decide where she would hide.

But when she got there, he was gone.

She crossed the street and continued past until the next corner. She came up around the block and at it from the opposite direction.

He was gone.

Still, she kept herself bundled into her coat, her head down and the collar up as she passed first one building and then the next, darting quick looks into the doorways where he might be hiding. At her apartment's front door recess, she stopped to make sure that the door was locked. It was.

Turning around, she chanced another look out to the street. The asphalt shimmered in light rain. Seeing her name, NUÑEZ, clearly labeled under the mailboxes as the resident in number six, she clicked her tongue.

Not careful enough.

Inside the door, she began the trudge up the three steep flights of stairs, finally making it to the top and through her door to safety—a bedroom, a tiny living room, a kitchen.

She closed the door and threw the dead bolt. Going to the front window, she again looked down at the rain-glistening street. Turning, she wondered if she had pulled the bedroom door closed behind her this morning. She didn't specifically remember doing that.

But then finally she allowed herself a small smile. It might not even have been him to begin with. She'd let herself get all worked up again over something that had happened so very long ago. The paranoia, the memories, the relived fear had happened before and would happen again.

She couldn't let it dominate her life.

She had to get over it. Maybe there was still time to change and not live in the shadow of that one moment of horror and despair. People had survived worse and gone on to do great things.

She let out a long breath and crossed the three steps over to the bedroom door. Gently, gently, she kicked it open.

See? she told herself. No one is here. Her apartment door was locked when she came in just now. The front door was locked downstairs.

What could he possibly want with her out of all the women in the world anyway?

She was no longer the beauty she'd been at eighteen. She didn't want to be pretty and mostly avoided the temptation of trying to be.

Pretty had ruined her life.

She walked through the bedroom door.

1

On the morning of what was going to be his first day at his new job, a good-looking, well-built man with his hair trimmed to just over his ears stood in front of his bedroom closet in a pair of Jockey shorts. He pulled a T-shirt from the top of a large pile of them on their special shelf. Putting it on, he checked himself in the dresser's mirror, sucked in an imagined gut, then turned around with a small flourish. The T-shirt read: SHOTGUN WEDDING: A CASE OF WIFE OR DEATH.

"No." His girlfriend sat up against the bed's headboard. "Absolutely not."

"I like it," he said.

"Wes, you like them all."

"True. It's a foolish man who buys a shirt he doesn't like."

"It's a more foolish man who goes to work as the district attorney of San Francisco wearing a shirt that can only be misinterpreted, and will be."

"By who?"

"Everybody. And all for different reasons."

"Sam." Wes walked across the room, sat on the bed, and put a hand on her thigh. "Nobody's going to see it. It's not like I'm wearing it outside with my tie. And besides, if I have a heart attack and they have to rip open my dress shirt and somebody sees it, so what? It's not exactly inflammatory. It's just a pun, for God's sake."

"It's not just a pun. It's a political statement."

"Saying what?"

"That you're in favor of shotgun weddings. That getting married isn't sacred. That you don't think women are equal. Pick one. That you're not sensitive enough in a general way."

"Well, we already know that."

"You laugh, but it's nothing to laugh at. Everything you do, innocent or not, is going to be a political statement from now on. Don't you see that? I thought you would have learned that during the election."

"Nope. I guess not. And, might I remind you, I won."

Sam made a face. "Wes, you won by ninety votes out of three hundred and fifteen thousand after your opponent died the week before the election."

"As though it's a bad thing. No, listen. It's proof that God wanted me to win. He wouldn't have taken Mr. Dexter back into His bosom if He didn't want me to win. It's self-evident. Maybe even cosmic."

"It's hopeless."

"Well, I hope not that. It's only my first day. I'm sure I'll be way more hopeless as time goes by." He got up and crossed back to the closet. "But if you really think it's going to matter," he said, "I'll consider going with tomorrow's T-shirt instead."

"You're wearing one tomorrow, too?"

"Sam, I wear a T-shirt every day. It provides clues to my secret persona."

"Not so secret. The press is going to start wanting to see it if word gets out."

"Good. That'll just make me more *je ne sais quoi*. Quirky and lovable. But if you want, for the inaugural, I'll trade out this one with tomorrow's." He turned and held out the next shirt on the pile: HEAVILY MEDICATED FOR YOUR SAFETY.

"Much better. No, really, I mean it." Her head fell forward and she sighed. "Never mind," she said. "Never, never, never mind."

"Hey, Sam," he said. "If you can't have fun with all this, what's the point?"

———

Four days later, the fun part wasn't much in evidence.

Wes Farrell's office on the third floor of the Hall of Justice looked more like a janitor's space. A couple dozen unpacked moving boxes lay stacked by the windows that looked out on Bryant Street. His predecessor's comfortable and elegant furnishings were gone. Meanwhile, Farrell had commandeered a desk and several chairs from some offices down the hall. He'd also brought the Nerf ball basket from his old office and mounted it on the bookshelf.

Sitting in two of the folding chairs across from Farrell, Cliff and Theresa Curtlee had already congratulated him on his election victory. Now they exchanged glances with each other. Owners of San Francisco's number-two newspaper, the *Courier*, the Curtlees had a lot of experience getting what they wanted in several different businesses—waste management, towing, import/export—and their tag-team approach had a long history of success. For this current campaign, their expectations were high because they had been large donors to Farrell's campaign. Additionally the *Courier* had run some flattering profiles of him before the election and in the end had endorsed him.

Farrell had done as much homework as he could. The Curtlees' son, Ro, had spent the past nine years in prison serving a twenty-five-to-life term for the rape and murder of one of their housekeepers, Dolores Sandoval. On the day before Farrell's election, the U.S. Supreme Court had refused to review the decision of the federal Ninth Circuit Court of Appeal that had sent the case back to San Francisco for a new trial. The Ninth Circuit had reversed the conviction, overruling both the California Court of Appeal and the California Supreme Court.

Cliff evidently gave Theresa the green light to begin. Her face, rigid with Botox, twitched in a semblance of a smile, and she cleared her throat. "We wanted to talk to you about our son, Roland, as you may have already guessed."

Farrell grinned to make himself look amicable. "I thought that might be what it was."

"What it is"—Cliff came forward for emphasis—"is that he's innocent."

"This whole thing has just been such a travesty of justice," Theresa added, "and we were hoping that with someone new at the helm here, together we could find a way to make up for some of the time we've all lost over his case and possibly give us all a chance for the healing to begin."

"I can appreciate that," Farrell said, "but I don't think too much of what happens next is within my power."

"But it is," Theresa said. "You don't have to try him again. That's within the DA's discretion."

"Yes, well, but . . . I hope you both understand that I can hardly do that. The victim's family alone . . ."

Theresa's voice was low pitched, almost soothing. "But she wasn't *his* victim, Wes. That's the point. He didn't hurt her in any way. If you could make the family understand—"

Cliff huffed and interrupted, "What family? You'd have to find them first wherever the hell they're hiding out in Guatemala, and good luck with that. There's no family to concern yourself over. But there is my son."

Farrell cleared his throat. "I understood that the appeal wasn't based on the evidence presented at the trial." Farrell was referring to the two other women who testified they'd been raped by Ro.

Farrell knew that the successful appeal had been based on the fact that several members of the victim's family had worn a button with a picture of a smiling Dolores Sandoval on it in the courtroom during the trial. This, the Ninth Circuit had ruled, must have hopelessly prejudiced the jury against the defendant. It was as wacky a decision as Farrell had ever heard, even from a court renowned for its bizarre rulings.

Cliff Curtlee waved off Farrell's objection. "The evidence won't hold up in a new trial. You read the old transcript, you'll see. The two other so-called victims. Who are they? They shouldn't have been allowed to testify at all. And Ro admits he had sex with the girl, but she wanted it, too. There's no case anymore. There wasn't any to begin with."

"Well . . ."

Theresa cleared her throat again. "But whatever you decide on the trial, and I'm sure you'll come to the right decision, at the very least you can recommend a bail figure."

Here Farrell shook his head. "I don't want to seem unsympathetic to your son's situation, but I can't do that. There's no bail in a special circumstances case."

"Ah." The muscles in Theresa's face couldn't get traction and—perhaps to compensate for the lack of expression—she held up her index finger. "But that's the whole point. It's not a special circumstances case. It's never been one."

Farrell showed his confusion. "I'm sorry?"

"It was Sharron Pratt's one concession to us. After all we'd done for her." Cliff obviously didn't harbor any warm feelings for the former DA who'd prosecuted their son.

Well practiced, possibly even rehearsed, Theresa picked up the thread. "The charges were rape and murder, not murder in the commission of rape."

Farrell noted the logical impossibility. If her son did it, the crime had to be rape/murder. But evidently this hadn't bothered Sharron Pratt. "So it wasn't special circumstances," Wes said.

In other words, it wasn't a no-bail case.

Theresa bared her teeth slightly. "Exactly. So he was eligible for bail, and will be again this time."

"And last time, was he in fact released on bail?"

"No," Cliff said. "That fascist Thomasino"—a highly respected superior court judge—"denied the bail anyway."

"He was prejudiced against Ro," Theresa added. "All through the trial, every decision he made, it was obvious to everybody."

"And so this time . . . ?"

"This time," Cliff said, "since bail is legally permissible, we'd just like to make a personal appeal to you, Wes, to step in if you catch wind of any early sign of judicial activism. At the very least, keep it away from Thomasino. Or maybe even put the word out that you'll allow a reasonable bail before the matter even gets inside a courtroom."

"It wouldn't have to be a public statement," Theresa said. "The important thing is the result." And then, shifting into a less strident tone, she added, "Now that he's out of prison, Wes, we'd just love to have our boy back with us at home."

Farrell's own personal idea of hell was to have any of his own three grown children come and stay with him and Sam for more than a long weekend, but here was a chance to sound cooperative, if not conciliatory, and maybe bring this uncomfortable interview to a close. "I understand how you can feel that way," he said. "And I promise you I'll review the case closely and do everything I can to address your concerns."

Which, he knew, would be precious little.

But the finality in his tone conveyed his intended signal. Theresa smoothed her skirt and stood up. "That's all we ask, Wes. Really."

Cliff stared disconcertingly into Farrell's eyes for another second or two—threatening?—but then he, too, got to his feet. "It's good to know who your friends are," he said. "And you know that the *Courier*'s been good friends with a lot of politicians in this town."

"Well, I'm not much of a politician, as the election made pretty clear," Wes said. "But I do hope I can keep trying to do the right thing."

Theresa took his proffered hand and gave him a prim little nod. "That's all we can ask for. Thanks for sharing so much of your valuable time."

"My pleasure. To both of you. My door's always open."

———

Just down the hallway from his own office, Farrell knocked on the open door of his chief assistant, Amanda Jenkins.

Despite a long history together—or maybe because of it—theirs was an awkward relationship. The conflict might have been purely endemic—Jenkins was historically prosecution and Farrell was dyed-in-the-wool defense. More personally, in the sensational murder case that had made his bones in the city, Farrell had gone head-to-head against Jenkins and beaten her in court, getting a clean acquittal for his client.

Then last year, Jenkins had been considering a run for district attorney herself. But the powers that had eventually settled on Wes Farrell as their candidate made it clear that they felt that she was a bit too much a one-trick pony—her issues were women's issues, period. She was insufficiently left wing in other respects, believing, for example, that a period of house arrest was probably not the answer to violent crime. But in the immediate aftermath of Farrell's victory, those same power brokers had promoted Jenkins' cause as chief assistant—she had the prosecutorial chops, the administrative experience, the in-depth familiarity with the DA's office personnel, and at least in feminist circles the correct politics. So now they were four days into their respective new jobs, and this was the first time Farrell had seen her since his inauguration ceremony.

Jenkins looked up from the pile of work surrounding her on her desk and straightened in her chair. "Sir?"

Farrell half turned as though looking around behind him. "There's no 'sir' here, Amanda. It's just me, Wes. I was 'Wes' when we were colleagues at the bar. And even running against each other. Remember?"

"Yes, sir."

"Yes, Wes."

She took a breath. "Okay. Wes."

"Good. At ease." He came into the room. "Got a sec? Mind if I get the door?"

Jenkins was a career prosecutor, always professionally turned out with the possible exception of the trademark short skirts she wore to accentuate her truly show-stopping legs. Now she threw a slightly harried look at her new boss and shrugged, indicating her workload, but then pushed her chair back a bit and linked her hands on her lap. At his service. "What's up?"

Farrell closed the door and pulled a chair around. "I just had a chat with the Curtlees. Both of them."

"That was fast," she said, her eyes suddenly alive. "And let me guess. They wanted you to decline to retry Ro and, failing that, then let him out on bail."

"You got a bug in my office?"

Jenkins was deaf to humor. "I hope you told them to take a flying."

"Not in so many words. I said I'd look into the matter and try to do the right thing."

"There's nothing to look into. Their boy, Ro, is a monster."

Farrell held up a hand, waiting while she huffed out a breath or two. "I've already done some looking. Since you prosecuted that case, I thought you could catch me up quicker than reading the transcript all the way through."

Jenkins, smoldering, blew out again. "You see what they let him out on, those lunatics? The victim's family wore badges with her picture on it, so quote federal constitutional error must have permeated the proceedings unquote. Have you ever heard such horseshit? I mean, even for the Ninth Circus, this is out there."

Farrell let her rave.

And she went on, "I hope one of those judges has a daughter

and Ro gets out and finds her and . . . no. No, I don't hope that. But Jesus Christ. The guy's got to stay in jail. What did you tell them? The Curtlees?"

"Nothing, really. I wanted to get your take."

"My take." She sat back, closed her eyes briefly. "Keep him in jail. Get him back at trial as soon as you can. This is a no-brainer, Wes. The guy raped at least eight women, beat three of them, and finally succeeded in killing one."

"Eight?"

"At least eight, Wes. At least. All housekeepers brought up from Guatemala or El Salvador by the company who screened the Curtlee family's entire workforce. All of them here on a work visa. All who originally said they'd testify, and then six of them got bought off to the tune of like a hundred grand each."

"You know this for a fact?"

"One hundred percent. They were honest about it. In our lovely state, you know you can't make a rape victim testify if she doesn't want to. She can just refuse to get on the stand. And all these women preferred to take the hundred grand. There was nothing we could do."

"And all these women reported rapes with Ro?"

Jenkins' mouth closed down to a thin line. "These were women who *were raped* by Ro, Wes."

"I don't doubt it." Farrell kept his tone nonconfrontational. "But I was asking if any of these women had reported these rapes when they happened."

No answer.

"Amanda?"

Her eyes flashed. "They were scared to death of Ro, Wes. To say nothing of the Curtlees, who had absolute power over their lives. Plus, they didn't think anyone would believe them."

"So I'm taking that as a 'no.' Nobody reported. Is that right?"

Jenkins gave Farrell the thousand-yard stare, her face set in stone. "I really hoped we wouldn't be having this kind of conversation."

"What kind of conversation?"

"Temporizing over violent crime just because of the political climate."

This criticism knocked Farrell back in his chair. Shaking his head, adjusting his bearings, he came back at her. "So I ask one question to clarify if these women reported their rapes and suddenly I'm the enemy?"

"I spoke to these women, Wes. I know them. No question they were raped."

"All right," Farrell said. "Fine. Let's all agree on that."

"Let's also all agree, since we're being honest here, that the Curtlees were pretty big fans of yours all through the campaign, and that maybe you feel you might owe them a little . . . cooperation."

"That's just not true, Amanda. I made no promises of any kind to the Curtlees. As far as I know, Ro's in custody and should stay there until he gets his new trial. Certainly I'm not planning to do anything that'll let him get back on the street. That's the truth, Amanda. And regardless of what you might think, I don't take orders from the Curtlees or anybody else. Except sometimes Sam." He took a breath to calm himself, shaken at how far this had already gone, and with so little warning. "That's just not how I operate, all right? I'm a pretty up-front guy, actually."

She took a long beat, pursing her lips now. "They've hated me since I sent their fair-haired little boy off to prison. It's a miracle I have any kind of a career left after all they've tried to do to me."

"And yet here you are at number two, appointed by the very guy they supported. So who's the winner in that picture?"

"Number two isn't number one."

"True. But it's not hardly a dead career, either, is it? And you've got more years left on the planet than I do, so I wouldn't give up hope. And if I were you, I certainly wouldn't get mad at your boss for something he's not going to do."

She hung her head for another second. "I didn't believe you'd be able to resist them, or even want to. I'm sorry. I was out of line."

"This one time only," Farrell said, "I'll forgive you."

―――

Farrell had a gap in his appointment schedule, providing time for him and his administrative assistant, Treya Glitsky, to unpack more boxes. Treya was a strong, attractive woman of mixed ethnicity—mostly black with a hint somewhere of an Asian bloodline. She was married to the city's head of homicide, Abe Glitsky, and had three children—Raney off at college and Rachel and Zachary, six and three, at home.

Farrell sat on the edge of his desk, not being particularly helpful on the moving front. "No, I'm serious," he was saying. "I really shouldn't be here. I'm not cut out for this job. Maybe I ought to resign before I do too much damage."

Treya stopped moving books from the packing boxes onto his bookshelf and turned around, looking at her watch. "That could be a record. I think it took Clarence a week before he thought he ought to quit." She was referring to Farrell's immediate predecessor and her own previous boss, Clarence Jackman. "And he wound up staying nine years."

"That's not me," Farrell said. "I only ran for this thing to keep the Nazis from taking over, mostly as a favor to Sam and her women friends."

"And the Latinos, and the gays."

"Okay, some of them, too. And don't forget those crucial votes from a hundred straight old white guys. My margin of victory." Farrell swung his legs, kicked his heels back against the side of his desk. "Is that true? Clarence really wanted to quit, too?"

"At first, every day, for a couple of months. But don't worry. You still hold the record for least days in office before expressing the famed desire to retire."

"That's a relief. But why didn't he quit, then? Clarence."

Treya paused. "He got addicted to the naked wielding of power."

"No, really."

"You asked me. That's my answer. Power."

Farrell chortled. "Well, that's not me. That couldn't be further from me."

"No." Treya chortled right back at him. "No, of course not." She leaned over and grabbed another stack of books.

"That 'of course not' sounded a little sarcastic."

"It's the acoustics in here." Placing the books on their shelf, she half turned back to him. "So would you like me to go talk to Amanda?"

"No. I think we got it worked out. I'm not going to stab her in the back on this Ro Curtlee thing. Or anything else. That ought to be clear enough."

"Let's hope," Treya said.

2

OUR TOWN

By Sheila Marrenas

Justice took a big leap forward in San Francisco yesterday when Roland Curtlee, the son of this newspaper's publishers, was released on bail. Mr. Curtlee, whose conviction had been reviewed and reversed by the Ninth Circuit Court of Appeal, has served nine years in prison for the rape and murder of a housekeeper from his parents' home, Dolores Sandoval. During the trial, many of the victim's family members, and their supporters, had appeared daily in the courtroom, sporting large buttons with Sandoval's smiling face. It was an effective and, as the Court has ruled, illegal technique to elicit sympathy for the victim at the expense of Mr. Curtlee.

During the trial, Mr. Curtlee never denied that he was involved in a relationship with Ms. Sandoval. This explained the DNA evidence taken from Ms. Sandoval's body after her death. But never explained were allegations that Ms. Sandoval had a large "dance card" of suitors who were never pursued by police.

Although he was legally entitled to his freedom via bail during his last incarceration before his trial nine years ago, Mr. Curtlee had been denied bail by Judge Oscar Thomasino, a conservative judicial activist whose decision was

19

widely decried in legal circles. "Mr. Curtlee," said one Stanford professor, "was denied due process in the bail proceedings and was subject to a prejudicial review by Judge Thomasino that assumed his guilt and denied his basic civil rights."

In a hearing today at the Hall of Justice, Superior Court Judge Sam Baretto set bail for the recently remanded Mr. Curtlee at $10 million. Though this figure is on its face exorbitant, the Curtlee family had no serious objections: "Any amount that allows our innocent son to reclaim some of his life as a normal citizen is worth whatever it might cost," said Mr. Curtlee's mother, Theresa, after the bail figure was announced. "We are looking forward to his second trial, and are confident that this time, justice will prevail, and Ro will walk away a free man."

————

Amanda Jenkins was talking to her lunch partner and boyfriend, an investigator for the DA's office named Matt Lewis. "Farrell loves to play the aw-shucks-I'm-not-a-politician game, but he knew damn well that if he didn't put some pressure on Baretto that there was no avoiding bail. Look. I'm not saying he should have back-channeled Baretto and threatened to challenge him out of the building, but we both know elected officials in this town who would have done exactly that. At the very least, Farrell should have been in court and stood on counsel's table and screamed if he had to so Baretto got the message loud and clear. Instead, it was the Curtlees and all their power against a lowly assistant DA, me. Who did Farrell think was going to win that fight?"

"Still," Lewis said, "ten mil."

"It's ten mil only if Ro skips, and that's never going to happen. They just put up their house as a property bond, written before they left the building."

"So Farrell lied to you?"

"At least he deliberately misled me. Also," Jenkins went on, "Farrell's leaving out that we're talking a couple of years here before Ro gets his new trial. If even then."

"A couple of *years*?"

"Who's going to be pushing for it?" she asked. "Ro's lawyers don't want it, for obvious reasons. Farrell isn't going to press since none of the victim's family is around anymore. So this way, he can keep the Curtlees happy so they can write nice articles about him. That fucking Sheila Marrenas. Which leaves guess who as the only party interested in putting this scumbag back on trial within the decade? Well, maybe there are two of us."

"Who's the other one?"

"Glitsky. Perhaps."

"Well, if you've got to have an ally, you could do worse. Especially with his wife just outside Farrell's office."

"I don't know. Maybe. Maybe."

Lewis reached a hand and rested it palm side up on the white tablecloth. After a moment of silence, Jenkins put her own hand on top of his. "Farrell doesn't understand how bad they can be," she said. "These guys, the Curtlees, not just Ro, although he is in a class by himself. They are truly evil. The thought of going up against them again, it scares the shit out of me. And might Glitsky, for that matter."

"Hey, you both already did it once."

"And barely survived." At his skeptical look, she went on, "If that's an exaggeration, it's a small one. You know why I got yanked off trying homicides all those many years ago? Was it because I wasn't good at them? No. It was because I *succeeded* with Ro. I put him down and his parents spent the next few years trying their damnedest to ruin my reputation. I drank too much. I slept around. I withheld evidence. In the end, Pratt had to send me down 'for the good of the team.' You probably read all about it."

Trying to lighten it up, Lewis asked, "That was you?"

But Jenkins wasn't laughing. "And Glitsky, too."

"Amanda, he's head of homicide and used to be deputy chief. Nobody's ruined his career."

"They came close. You know what he was doing before he got appointed deputy chief? This was after he had already been head of homicide. Give up? Payroll. Head of homicide to payroll. The trajectory there isn't up."

"So what happened? How'd he get back?"

"Frank Batiste became chief of police, that's how. He and Glitsky go way back. But without Batiste, Glitsky was done. And he was done because the Curtlees, and Marrenas, never let up behind the scenes. I don't think even he knows exactly how far they went. But he must have seen at least some of the articles. As head of homicide, Glitsky tolerated sloppy detective work; that was the real reason we had the worst conviction rate in the country. He routinely told his men to plant evidence, his guys kept and/or sold the dope they found serving their warrants. You name it. If it was bad, he did it. Oh, and my favorite, he actually took part in the ambush that killed Barry Gerson." A previous head of homicide. "Glitsky maybe even killed him himself."

"Yeah, but nobody believed that."

"Still, the *Courier* printed it. And don't kid yourself. People did believe it. People believe anything. Obama wasn't born in the U.S. We never landed on the moon."

"Well," Lewis said, smiling again, "everybody knows those."

Jenkins blew out. "Well, you see what I'm saying. The Curtlees print whatever lies they find convenient, and some significant percentage of the lunatic fringe—which in this town is very large, as you know—believes it all. So I'm stuck down in crimes against women instead of homicide and Glitsky works ten years to get back to where he was when he arrested Ro all these many years ago." She drank off what remained of her cranberry juice. "And so, thanks to Mr. Farrell and the Ninth Circuit, here we are back again with Glitsky and me the only ones trying to get Ro back to trial. I'll tell you what, Matt, I don't know if I'm going to have the guts to do it. I don't know if the Curtlees won't try to stop me physically. Or Ro himself might."

"They've never done anything like that before, have they?"

"Hey, you don't have to believe me. Maybe I'm paranoid. But I know what they're capable of. And I'll tell you something else." She lowered her voice and leaned across the table. "I almost hope they try something."

"No, you don't."

"Yes, I do. You notice I'm carrying a larger purse? For the first time in my career, since Ro's out, I am packing heat."

———

Amanda Jenkins did not know that she had another ally besides Abe Glitsky in her quest to get Ro Curtlee back behind bars.

Sam Duncan was sitting at her kitchen table at about eight thirty when she heard the front door open and the sound of Farrell's voice as he entered their house on the periphery of Buena Vista Park. He was talking to their dog, a yellow Labrador named Gert, in a gentle singsong voice that bore no resemblance to the way he talked most of the time. "I know it's a long, long day, baby, but you're doing so good. So, so, so good. That's a good girl. That's the best girl. Yes, okay, you're my very favorite girl."

Man and dog got to the kitchen and Farrell stopped, straightening up. "Actually," he whispered as Gert jumped across the room to greet Sam, "she's my second favorite girl. But she gets jealous if I don't tell her it's her." Following the dog, he leaned over and kissed Sam on the cheek. "You're my very favorite."

No response.

"Female," Wes added. "Gert's only three years old so I call her a girl, which seems appropriate, even if she is a dog, whereas you are a mature and lovely human woman whom I would never under any circumstances call a girl."

She looked up at him. "I can't believe you let Ro Curtlee out on bail."

Farrell stopped halfway to shrugging out of his coat. "'And you're my favorite male,'" he said with a little lilt, meant to mimic Sam. "'Human male, I mean. And how was your day, honey?'" He got the coat off and draped it over one of the kitchen chairs. "Actually," he said, "I didn't let Ro Curtlee out on bail. Judge Baretto did that."

"You were supposed to tell him not to."

"I did. My chief assistant made the argument. Maybe you didn't get that memo."

"How could you not go down yourself and argue against bail? You've told me yourself Baretto was gutless. Why didn't you pass the word that you'd challenge him off every criminal case for the rest of his life if he granted bail?"

"How do you know I didn't?"

"Did you?"

"No." Farrell backed a step away. "Silly me. I thought that Baretto, being a superior court judge and all, might have reached his own conclusion about whether or not bail was appropriate. And it looks as though he did. Which, for the record, wasn't the conclusion I wished he'd gotten to."

"But you could have stopped him. Or at least headed him off."

"Actually, probably not, Sam."

"But you don't know for sure because you didn't try."

Farrell stalled for a little time, pulling one of the kitchen chairs out, turning it around, and straddling it. "Listen, Sam. This thing started back with Sharron Pratt, who in her wisdom decided to charge Ro with rape and murder, but not rape in commission of a murder." He held up a hand. "And I know, if he did one, he did the other. The charge made no sense, but that didn't stop Pratt. What it did do was leave it up to the courts to decide on bail. The last judge, Thomasino, denied it. Good choice. Baretto, not so much. Now, could I have threatened him somehow? Yes, but it would have been unethical and he would have only resented the intrusion into what is properly his domain. And I've got to work with these guys, the judges, for the next four years. I thought it might be a good idea not to antagonize them in my first month."

"So now we've got a convicted rapist out on the streets?"

"Sad to say, Sam, we've got a lot more than one. Rape's a bailable offense, as we have seen. It sucks, but what am I going to do? I'm supposed to enforce the laws, not write 'em."

Sam fixed him with a flat, disgusted glare. "I don't know how this whole district attorney thing with you is going to work out. You know that?"

"I'm starting to get an idea," Farrell replied.

3

Since they'd been kids, Janice and Kathy had worked harmoniously together in the kitchen. Today they were in Kathy's home in Saint Francis Wood, which was quite a bit more upscale than Janice's crowded three-bedroom stucco twenty blocks north, in the Avenues. But to hear the two women talking, gossiping, joking, occasionally breaking into song, only the keenest observer might sense that the disparity between their homes and kitchens was a little bit hard to bear for Janice.

Janice Durbin was, after all, the elder by four years, the better educated, the harder working, the more beautiful. Nevertheless, Janice often had to stifle the pang of envy that would lance her heart when she found herself confronted anew, as she was today, by her sister's material possessions—the newly redecorated island kitchen, the Tuscan tile work, the huge Sub-Zero refrigerator, the Viking stove, brushed stainless steel everywhere you looked.

In her darker moments, much more frequent of late, Janice sometimes found herself wondering why Kathy had gotten all this, what she'd done to deserve it. Could it all be a matter of luck?

And it wasn't just the *stuff*. Although to be sure there was plenty of that—furnishings, clothes, jewelry. Beyond that, Kathy's life was so smooth, so effortless, so serene. And why wouldn't it be? She'd gotten it exactly right in making the single most important choice of her life—the man she had married. Chuck Novio, tenured professor of American history at San Francisco State University, was one of the most effortlessly gifted men Janice had ever met. Kathy had snagged him soon after he transferred here from back East. Whip-smart, tall, trim, athletic, and funny, he also possessed a calm strength and sensitivity that seemed to rub off on Kathy and on their well-behaved twelve-year-old twin daughters, Sara and Leslie.

It was only because of this comparison that Janice sometimes let herself sink into self-pity that in turn primed the pump of her recurrent bouts of self-loathing. She knew about these things, about how they worked—after all, she was a psychiatrist. In reality, in real life, she was not any kind of a loser herself—she knew that. And neither were her husband, Michael, or any of their own three children, Jon, Peter, and Allie. It's just that Michael ran his own business, a UPS franchise on Union Street, and the stress of that took its continual toll, making him sometimes seem much older than his forty-one years. And add to that, the kids were all in high school now at the same time. Three teenagers in the home did not generally equate to much serenity.

Janice stood in front of the sink with the cold water running over her hands and into the colander of peeled potatoes. Through the window, Chuck and Michael and the boys were playing touch football in the late-afternoon sunlight. She went still and sighed.

"Janice? Is everything all right?"

"Fine," she told her sister. "Everything's fine. Just looking at them playing out there. They grow up so fast, the boys, don't they?"

"That's funny." Kathy came over and stood next to her. "You see your sons growing up and I see our husbands staying young, still boys themselves in a lot of ways."

"That's probably a healthier way to look at it."

"I don't know about healthier. It's just how I see it."

"It's healthier, trust me." She turned off the running water and put her hands on either side of the sink, leaning her weight into them.

Kathy touched her arm. "Are you sure you're okay?"

Janice shook her head. "It's just been a long week." Now she straightened up. "I'm sorry. I'm just so glad we're here, getting this break out of our house. And Sunday night dinner is always great. I don't mean to be a downer."

"You're not."

"Well, I'm not exactly Pollyanna, either." She glanced outside again. "I should be happy Michael's even out there with Chuck and the boys at all. This whole past week it's almost like he's been paralyzed. And in our house, with everybody on top of one another, moods tend to pile on up. So everybody's been a little snappy." She broke a brittle laugh. "Did I say *a little* snappy? I mean I know why it's smart we don't keep guns in the house."

"Janice. Come on."

"Well, not really, of course." Janice dried her hands on a dish towel, then handed it to her sister. Crossing over to the island, she pulled out a stool for Kathy, then sat on one herself. "But let's just say it's good for us all to be here and out from under each other's feet for a few hours."

"What's Michael been paralyzed about? Work?"

"No. Work's been good. Christmas was way better than anybody predicted. Crazy busy but good."

"So. What? Not you guys?"

"Well." Janice paused. "We've been better, I suppose, but I don't think it's that, either. Does the name Ro Curtlee ring a bell?"

Kathy scrunched her face in concentration for a second. "No. I don't think so. Who is he?"

"Remember the jury Michael was on, like, ten years ago?"

"Vaguely. Although ten years ago I had two-year-olds and everything was pretty much a blur. Michael was the jury foreman or something, right?"

"Right. And they found Ro guilty and sent him away."

"Good. Right. I remember now. But then his parents came after you, something like that."

"Exactly like that." The memory was still all too clear to Janice Durbin: When the newspapers did interviews with the other jurors after the trial, it came out that Michael had played a prominent role in getting the guilty verdict. The jury had started out at only 50 percent for conviction, but Michael kept at them in the deliberations and finally got the other six to go along with him and vote guilty.

When the Curtlees realized this, they set out to destroy her husband, and nearly succeeded. At the time, he'd worked for one of the city's big law firms as a word processing supervisor, a daytime job that left him time for his painting. The Curtlees had connections with the people he worked for and Durbin got accused of a lot of mischief—stealing supplies from the storeroom, using the firm's computers for his own work—until he got fired. He received no severance after seven years of employment and was told he was lucky they weren't prosecuting him criminally.

Finally, after a *Courier* article on Durbin the hypocrite vigilante and now thief who'd railroaded Ro Curtlee into jail, he found himself blackballed in the legal firms and couldn't get work for almost a year. Couldn't find the heart to get back to his painting.

Janice sighed. "I think having to abandon the painting was the hardest thing."

"That was a bad time," Kathy said. "I'd almost forgotten all about it. And his painting."

"Well, Michael hasn't. He's never really come to grips with having to quit that."

"Three kids," Kathy said.

"I know. But still . . ." Her mouth tightened at the memory. "It's a miracle he eventually got the UPS franchise, somehow under the Curtlees' radar. At least we thought they were more or less forever out of our lives."

"They're not?"

"They might be. We hope so. But maybe not."

"Why not?"

"Because last week some idiot judges let Ro out of prison on appeal, and another moron of a judge here in town gave him bail while he's waiting for a retrial, and now he's out. Ro, the convicted murderer, walking around free as a bird. And Michael's thinking it's all going to start again, that everything he went through, everything *we* went through, was all just in vain. And the idea, as I said, just paralyzes him. If Ro's out again, then Michael's stand with the jury basically made no difference. It was all just a big cosmic joke."

Out in the street, Michael Durbin took the hike from his younger boy, Peter.

When they'd been choosing up sides, Durbin had almost as a matter of course chosen Peter to be his teammate against Uncle Chuck and Jon. Both boys were athletic, but Jon had an indefinable special something as well as—much as he tried to deny and even hide it—a special place in Durbin's heart. Though he loved both of his sons and tried to treat them exactly equally, Durbin and his firstborn shared a natural simpatico and deep connection that Durbin knew might prove hurtful to his very sensitive younger son if he let down his guard and inadvertently revealed his instinctual favoritism.

It was a lifelong struggle.

So whenever he got the chance—as here choosing who would be his teammate—Durbin leaned over backward to pick his younger son over his older. He knew that Jon intuitively understood why Durbin did this, why he almost always appeared to favor Peter. The insecure younger boy needed the overt signs, the trappings of his father's love and approval. Jon did not. It wasn't something he and his dad had to talk about. They simply "got" each other.

Now Durbin faded to his left with the football as his brother-in-law, Chuck, started counting to five at the scrimmage line and

Peter raced down the street, cutting first right, then left, trying to shake his brother Jon's coverage. When Durbin saw Peter cut back again, gaining a step on Jon, he threw a high arching spiral that led his younger boy perfectly.

Or almost perfectly.

Jon jumped and with a cry of jubilation came down with the ball. Putting a move on Peter, he shook him and then sprinted up the street, yelling for Chuck to "block him, block him, block him," meaning Durbin.

But Durbin feinted right, left, right again and broke around Chuck, then got enough in front of Jon to slow him down a step, which in turn allowed Peter to come up from behind Jon and get him just as Durbin reached him, too. Even though they were playing touch football, Durbin threw his arms around his beloved son and held him in a hug for a full second, maybe two.

Contact.

_____

All the kids having dispersed to the television room at the other end of the house, the adults found themselves sitting around the Novios' now-cleared dining room table, everyone drinking Frangelico out of snifters.

"You really think he still cares?" Chuck was asking.

"He's done ten years in the slammer," Michael said. "That's a long time to think about getting back at who put you there."

Chuck sipped and nodded. "It's also a hell of a long time to hold a grudge, don't you think?"

Michael shrugged. "I don't think there's a statute of limitations on grudges."

"Yes, but," Kathy said, "it seems to me that these Curtlees did what they did back when all this was fresh in their minds and Ro just recently convicted, but now that he's out of prison, who cares about anybody who helped send him there? You're not a threat to him anymore."

Janice threw a look at her husband across the table. "That's what I told him, too."

Michael looked from one sister to the other. "And I hope you're both right. But even if you are right about his parents, there's still Ro himself."

Chuck was shaking his head. "I don't see that. He's not going to do anything except be a good boy while he waits for his new trial."

Michael swirled the liqueur in his glass. "I don't think so. He can't be a good boy. He doesn't know how."

"Michael," his wife said, "how can you know that?"

"I can know it because I heard him testify at his trial. I mean, here's this serial rapist on the witness stand trying to convince us that he was in fact in a normal relationship with the woman he killed. They were having consensual sex. What was the big deal?"

"Maybe they were," Kathy said.

"They were not, I promise. She's eighteen, just off the boat, scared to death, and she's living under his roof on a work visa that the Curtlees can pull anytime they want. Then Ro wants to have sex with her? So whatever it was, it wasn't consensual."

"Still," Chuck said, "it might not necessarily have been rape, right? I mean, she could have been coerced, but felt she had to."

"Chuck," Kathy said, "that's still rape."

"I'm just saying, maybe not technically, legally."

Michael nodded. "Don't tell that to the other two ex-housekeepers who testified. Who said that Ro had a thing about them keeping their shoes on."

"That's just weird," Kathy said.

"Why did he have them do that?" Chuck asked.

Michael shook his head. "Nobody knows. He's a nutcase. But they both said it."

"And this means?" Chuck asked.

"It means Ro's guilty as hell if Dolores Sandoval was naked except for her shoes. And she was. So it wasn't consensual sex. It was a rape and then when she started screaming, he had to shut her up. There's no other way to interpret it."

"What about the other two women?" Kathy asked. "The ones who did testify?"

"What about them?"

"I mean, what did he say about them, their testimony?"

"He just said they were lying. He'd never had sex with either of them, much less raped them. He was just being set up. Why? Who knew? By whom? He didn't know. There was just a lot of prejudice out there in the world against people who had money."

"But," Chuck came in again, "my point is, Michael, this guy Ro isn't going to come after you. You're no part of his new trial, right?"

"Right. If the new trial ever happens."

"Well, even if it doesn't, what kind of threat are you to him?"

Michael nodded. "Maybe you're right."

"I think I am. Why would he come after you? You've been put in your place after last time. You're not trying to get him thrown back in jail. I'd be surprised if he knew or cared if you were still alive."

Janice added, "I think Chuck's right, here, Michael. We don't have to worry about them anymore. They took their best shot at you, and it wasn't enough."

"But pretty darn close," Michael said. "Pretty darn close."

4

At 5:05 on a Friday afternoon almost three weeks later, the man who ran San Francisco's homicide detail picked up the telephone at his desk within the first half of the first ring. At the same time, he pulled his pad over in front of him, tucked the phone at his ear, and grabbed a pen. "Glitsky."

"Lieutenant." The female voice was metallic and without inflection. "We've got a female body at a probable arson fire scene at four twenty Baker, nearest cross street is Oak. Apartment number six. Fire is contained. Arson's taking jurisdiction, but local squad units, precinct captain, CSI, and paramedics are en route."

"Roger that." Glitsky was writing down the essentials. "I'll get a team rolling out there. Four twenty Baker, number six."

"That's it."

Hanging up, Glitsky pushed back from his desk.

Fifty-seven years old, he stood six foot two and weighed 210 pounds. During college, he had been a tight end for San Jose State at the same weight. Though his eyes were blue, his skin was dark, his nose prominent and slightly hooked. His father, Nat, was Jewish; his mother, Emma, long deceased, had been African American. His short Afro had by now gone mostly gray. A thick scar bisected his lips top to bottom at an acute angle. Today, as most days on the job, he wore civilian clothes—black cop shoes, dark blue khaki slacks with a thin black belt, a light brown ironed shirt, and black tie. No one had ever called him a snappy dresser.

On a whiteboard hanging on the wall directly across from his chair, he daily kept track of the twelve inspectors in the detail—their assignments and active cases. Today, that board was filled. It had been a busy winter for homicides in San Francisco.

Glitsky was around his desk, heading for the door out to the large room that held the inspectors' desks, when he stopped for a moment to glance at the whiteboard. He knew it by heart, of course, but now it struck him anew. Each of Glitsky's six homicide teams and his one solo inspector were currently working at least two murders. He needed more people, but what with budget issues, he knew he was lucky to not have had his staff cut by the morons, sycophants, and cretins who controlled these things.

His second wife, Treya, had worked since she'd met him, to no avail, to persuade Glitsky to try to temper somewhat his default expression, a flat, deathless, and menacing stare. He wasn't interested; the look had served him well at work, even if it sometimes terrified small children, even his own. Glitsky thought this was a reasonable trade—besides, it didn't hurt children to have a bit of a healthy fear of their father. Glitsky's large intelligent brow jutted over intense blue eyes. When he was thinking or daydreaming or actively scowling—all regular occurrences—the scar between his lips stood out in relief.

When people weren't calling him a snappy dresser, they often at the same time weren't calling him a sweetheart.

———

By the time Glitsky made it out to the fire scene through rush hour traffic, dusk had just about settled into night. This is not to say that it was dark in the immediate vicinity. Between the flashing red and blue police-car lights, the lamps on the firemen's helmets, the streetlights, and the kliegs from the several TV vans that had converged on the block, the place was lit up like a movie shoot.

Glitsky parked in the middle of Baker Street next to one of the fire trucks. Getting out of his city-issued car, he caught a gust of bitter, cold wind, heavily laden with the smell of smoke. He flashed his badge and signed into the scene with the cop who was controlling access to the area.

A man wearing a white fire helmet, the incident commander, stood talking with another man in civilian clothes on the sidewalk in front of a stoop that led up to a three-story Victorian.

As Glitsky walked over to check in with them, his shoes squished in the still-wet street. Stopping to zip his heavy leather jacket up against the cold, he noticed that several pairs of uniformed precinct cops were standing around by their squad cars, aimless. He was tempted to go over and personally motivate them to get back in their cars and on patrol, where they were supposed to be, working. But indulging this fantasy, he knew, would only come back to bite him—hard-ass homicide lieutenant lording it over the serfs, taking his job too seriously.

But that he had the fantasy at all served as a wake-up call: He was seething. The feeling had snuck up on him full-blown. It was a Friday night and he should by now be home with his wife and children. He didn't resent the overtime, never had, but he did when the idiocy of the bureaucrats and politicians gave him no choice—when he didn't have enough staff or the budget to get the job done, so he had to step in and do it himself. And he knew that he could have simply assigned an already overworked homicide team to take this case, but that wasn't leadership, and it wasn't his style.

Fifty feet on down the street, somebody was giving an interview to one of the TV stations, and that had attracted its own small crowd. Looking up at the obvious site of the blaze, Glitsky saw that the fire itself was out; teams of firemen were rolling up hoses, sweeping the gutters, cleaning up. Moving forward, Glitsky crunched along over debris and broken glass. Closer now, he recognized the incident commander in the white helmet as Norm Shaklee and the man with whom he was talking, the city's chief arson inspector attached to the Bureau of Fire Investigations, Arnie Becker.

Putting his anger in its secret place, he arranged his face and said hello to the men, both of whom knew him and greeted him cordially.

And then Becker said, "So they're sending out the big guns on homicides now?"

Glitsky kept it loose. "I sent myself. I was the only one in the office." He shrugged. "What are you going to do? So what do we have?"

"Pretty definitely arson. Started on the third floor, luckily, and even better luck, the neighbor across the hall smelled it early and called it right in. There'll be water damage and the usual mess, but the residents can probably move back in in a week or so. We only got a total loss on the one apartment out of six."

"What about our victim?"

"We don't know too much about her yet. The apartment was rented by a woman named Felicia Nuñez."

Glitsky's brow clouded briefly. "Do I know that name?"

Becker shrugged. "I'd bet there's more than one of them. It's common enough. Anyway, that's probably who she is, but we don't know that absolutely, and nobody's going to identify her from what we got up there, that's for sure. We'll probably have to wait for dentals." Becker's eyes, which in his career had already seen it all, went a little dull. "You should know that whoever set the apartment on fire, set her on fire first. It looked like she was probably naked or close to it when he poured whatever it was on her genitals and lit her up. And it spread from there."

"So. Rape?"

"Probably, I'd guess. And I'd imagine he killed her first, although that'll be the ME's call. That and how he did it. Nobody heard any screams or struggling, and there were people right below and across from her in the building. We may never really know about the rape. I'd be surprised if they get DNA from her. She's burned up pretty bad."

Glitsky swallowed against his revulsion. "And nobody saw an assailant?"

"Nothing, Lieutenant. Nobody saw a thing. I've got a crew working the neighborhood, but we've already talked to everybody in the building and the guy was lucky or careful, or both, and seems to have just disappeared. It's a pisser."

"Tell me about it." He turned to Shaklee. "Are my crime scene people here?"

The incident commander nodded. "I sent 'em up. Faro and his gang. But from what Arnie here has been telling me, they're going to have their work cut out for them."

"What else is new?" Glitsky looked up at the black holes where the upper story windows had been. Flashlight beams crisscrossed one another in the darkness. He drew a heavy breath. "You mind if I go up now?"

The incident commander has absolute control over access to a fire scene, which was why Glitsky asked. Now Shaklee nodded and turned to his partner. "If Arnie's got no objection."

"No," Becker said. "In fact, I'll go with you."

5

Abe and Treya Glitsky had planned on going out to an early movie that night, but he hadn't gotten home from the arson murder scene until nearly nine, so that got ruled out. Still, they had Rita, their housekeeper, staying late to babysit anyway, so they decided they'd just go out and drive around until fate led them to a destination, which in this case happened to be David's on Geary. Not really so random, if one knew Glitsky's love of Jewish delicatessens like Treya did.

Now Glitsky's eyes were focused out across the counter, far away from the liverwurst and onion on pumpernickel the waitress had just set down in front of him. "I *know* I know that name," he said.

Treya was just picking up her hot pastrami and Swiss on rye, and the half she held was far bigger than she could get into her mouth in one bite. So she stopped midway. "Maybe one of your old paramours?"

"None of my paramours were old. In fact, now that I think of it, you are my oldest paramour ever. And even you're not that old."

"Well, thank you, I think. Did I mean 'former' instead of 'old' and by chance misspoke? Imagine my chagrin."

"Imagine it," Glitsky said, "but she wasn't a former paramour. She's just in my brain—her name, anyway—rattling around. Felicia Nuñez."

"She'll show up."

"Her and Christmas." Glitsky bit into his sandwich, chewed

with a distracted air. "Sorry," he said after he'd swallowed. "I know the rule is no work on dates."

"So you're sure she's work related? The one you used to know, as opposed to the homicide victim you saw tonight?"

"Pretty sure."

"Well, I've bent the no-talking-about-work rule on occasion," she said. "I can give you one."

"I appreciate that, but I don't know if I want to talk about work in general. In fact, I'm pretty sure I don't. Starting with the fact that I've got no inspectors free to handle this latest case, so I've got to go down and do it myself on a Friday night when we've got a date planned. That's the kind of thing, I start talking about it, I could get myself worked up. And I'm betting this won't be the last homicide we see before too many of the others get cleared, so this is just an ongoing problem that's only going to get worse because of the incredibly misguided priorities of the idiots who get elected in this city. And why don't they seem to learn?"

"Good," Treya said. "You really don't want to talk about that. I can tell."

"I don't."

"I know. So we'll leave that part out. So, now, how about Felicia Nuñez?"

"The current one or the one I think I remember?"

"Maybe she's both. Maybe you arrested her before?"

"No. I don't think so. I remember people I've arrested."

"Okay, then, maybe she was a victim?"

Glitsky, his sandwich forgotten, was shaking his head. "Arnie Becker says it's a common name, but I don't think that's it."

"Maybe another cop, maybe somebody you interviewed for a job? Or, how about this? On a case, maybe a witness?"

Suddenly Glitsky's head went still. He brought his hand up to his mouth and covered it, his startling blue eyes scanning the corners of the ceiling.

Treya knew to leave him alone. He'd picked up the scent.

"Oh dear Lord," he half whispered through his fingers. Glitsky rarely used profanity, and only then under the greatest duress, and his calling upon the Lord in this context underscored the degree of his concern.

"What is it? Abe?"

He lowered his hand with an exaggerated calm. "Ro Curtlee."

"No." This was a name she didn't want to hear, since it was so thoroughly continuing to roil the waters at the DA's office. "What's she got to do with him?"

"She was a witness against him at his first trial and was going to be one of the central witnesses at the next one. But now obviously she isn't going to play much of a role, being dead and all."

Treya finally said, "This is just going to cream Wes."

"I've got to call him."

"Maybe Ro didn't have anything to do with this Felicia Nuñez," Treya said.

Glitsky, already punching numbers into his cell phone, rolled his eyes.

In the middle of a speech he was giving at the Immigrant Resource Fair on Valencia in the Mission District, Wes Farrell felt his cell phone buzz at his belt and silently cursed himself for bringing the damn thing with him at all. He didn't need distractions from the work at hand, and he didn't think of himself as one of the great natural orators of history, in any event. Nevertheless, this speech, he thought, was a pretty good one about something he truly cared about—protecting crime victims in San Francisco's immigrant community.

"What we've got to avoid," he was saying, "is the appearance and, even more important, the reality, that immigrant crime victims do not fall under the protection of law enforcement. If you're the victim of a crime in San Francisco, the status of your immigra-

tion is not, repeat, not going to be a factor. A visit by this city's
police enforcement arm is not a visit from the U.S. government's
immigration agencies."

In the meeting hall of the Centro del Pueblo, the crowd broke
into applause. Farrell, pumped up by the response, hazarded a
glance over at his girlfriend, heartened to see that she was taking
part in the ovation. He and Sam hadn't yet figured out how his new
job was going to fly within their relationship, and he'd take any
sign he could that it could still work out. The past few weeks—
from the day of Ro Curtlee's bail hearing forward—had been chilly
between them, and maybe this applause marked the beginning of
a thaw.

Glancing down at his notes, he picked up where he'd left off.
"We take very seriously our status as a City of Sanctuary for immigrants, and nowhere should that commitment to immigrant
rights be more forcefully implemented than when immigrants are
victims of crimes. And it is the policy of my administration that
the immigration status of crime victims will never—never ever—
be questioned in the course of a criminal investigation. That is
simply not going to be on the table. If you're the victim of a crime,
you must feel free to call the police and report the crime, and rest
secure knowing that nothing bad is going to happen to you because of your immigration status."

Another wave of applause broke over the room. But Farrell really had no time to enjoy the brief flutter of popularity because
he took the moment to sneak a look at his phone. Glitsky's name
there creased his face with a sudden concern. If Glitsky was calling his private number after nine o'clock, something was up. And
if it could have waited until morning, then Glitsky would have
waited.

Which meant it couldn't wait.

So, accepting the congratulations of the multitude, he thanked
his way off the podium and walked out into the hall, where he

could hear himself think. He touched the cell phone screen to connect him to the head of homicide.

Without preamble, Glitsky said, "Do you know where Ro Curtlee is?"

"How would I know that?"

"So you don't? You don't have a secret tail on him? Anything like that?"

"No, of course not. What's happened?"

"Felicia Nuñez got herself killed tonight. Maybe raped first, then set on fire. You know who Felicia Nuñez is, right?"

"Yeah. Sure."

"We've got to get this guy off the streets. Like yesterday."

"Oh. Okay. Let's do that." Sarcasm dripped into the connection. "You got an idea how that gets accomplished? You got anything implicating him at the scene?"

"No. Everything was burned up. Ro never occurred to me until I placed the woman's name. I'm going to go rattle his cage."

"Don't do that, Abe. Really. Anything remotely smacking of harassment—and that would—and we're sued from here to Denmark. If you arrest him, even if you get him back downtown just to talk, he's back out in a day or two anyway."

"That's two days he can't kill anybody else."

Glitsky was just venting and Farrell knew it, but he still felt he had to make his point. "No, listen. It's going to be hard enough to get his new trial on the docket, even without muddying the waters with harassment and a false arrest." Farrell drew a breath. "So. Has the press got ahold of this yet? The connection?"

"There were TV vans at the fire. I don't know if anybody's put this Nuñez woman together with Ro yet. But that's only a matter of time, and probably not too much of that. I've got to go talk to him."

"And then what? You think he won't have an alibi? You think he'll invite you in to have a nice talk? You think you can get a warrant to search his place? I can tell you right now, the answer's no to all of the above."

"Wes, the guy's got to be back in jail."

"I hear you, but I don't know how to make that happen."

"Rescind his bail."

"I can't do that. You need to find some evidence on this new one."

"At a fire scene? The place is gutted."

"Maybe there'll be his DNA on the victim."

"I thought of that, too, but not a chance. You didn't see her. There's no place to get swabs from. I didn't even know for sure that she was a woman. Arnie Becker says we'll be lucky to get a positive ID from dental records."

Farrell took a moment. "You're saying you're not even sure it was Nuñez?"

"It was her apartment, Wes. She was the only one in it."

"But if it's not, in fact, her, then there's no connection to Ro."

"Give me a break, Wes. You and I both know it's her, which means it's Ro. It's got to be Ro."

"I know, I know. I'm just thinking about containment."

"It's not a containment issue."

"Well, at least part of it is. Anyway, it could give us both some breathing room."

"And meanwhile, he kills his last remaining witness."

"Maybe not. Hopefully not. Who is she?"

"Another former Curtlee domestic servant, smack in the middle of the profile. Gloria Gonzalvez."

"Do we know where she is?"

"Not yet, but I intend to find out. Meanwhile, speaking of that, what's the problem with getting his new trial on the docket? Get him back behind bars that way."

"I'm working on that, Abe. Believe me. But his lawyer—you know Denardi?—needs to get up to speed on the facts of the case.

He told Baretto it's going to take him six months at least, and over my strenuous objections he thought that seemed reasonable and continued the goddamn thing until August, and that's just to set a trial date."

"Lord," Glitsky said. "The man's a menace in his own right." A beat. "So, what happens next? We can't just let this go on."

Farrell scratched his jaw with his cell phone. "Somebody around the fire might still have seen or heard something. Tell Arnie Becker what this might be about, and he can go back and recanvass the neighborhood. Talk to your crime scene people. Locate some DNA somewhere. You get anything real, Abe, bring Ro in and I'll take the flak and hold him. But get ready, and make sure it's real, 'cause there will be beaucoup flak."

6

The Curtlee mansion and its grounds took up the last third of Vallejo Street on the uphill side in the last block before it abutted into the abundant greenery of the tamed forest that was the Presidio.

Glitsky sat in his city-issued Taurus, driver's side window down, and stared across the street at the imposing structure. Set back about sixty feet from the curb, but otherwise surprisingly open to the street, the vast white block of stucco rose three stories up into the trees on the escarpment behind it. The driveway and its land-scaping blocked an unimpeded view of the ground floor, but on the two upper floors, lights shone in six of the sixteen windows. From where he sat, Glitsky could only just make out some flickering light and occasional movement behind the enormous bay window through the well-tended shrubbery on the house's right side.

He didn't know precisely why he was there. He might have told himself that he was investigating a murder in which a resident of this house, recently released from prison, was already his prime suspect, and this was true as far as it went. But it was also true that everything Wes had told him was probably correct—he had neither evidence nor a warrant to search for it. Ro would have an alibi and would probably refuse to talk to him in any event. The Curtlees were not only wealthy, they were by now experienced in dealing with, and frustrating the efforts of, law enforcement. They would have a lawyer down here the minute Glitsky showed his face, and he would wind up having nothing to show for all of his trouble.

But he didn't care.

He wanted them—the whole family—to know that he knew. And to remind them that in spite of their money and power, he'd won last time, and that he would win again. And that this time— with the Nuñez murder rather than the retrial of Ro for murdering Dolores Sandoval—he would get his special circumstances, and maybe even succeed in putting Roland Curtlee on death row, where he belonged.

It was juvenile, undisciplined, visceral, and Glitsky was acutely aware of, even somewhat embarrassed by, all that, but basically, at bottom, he wanted to put this dangerous and irresponsible family on notice that the damage they'd done to his career had not broken him. And that, in fact, he had resurrected himself to the relative eminence he had enjoyed before. In spite of the Curtlees' best efforts to ruin him through slander, libel, and innuendo, he was back at his job in homicide.

He opened his car door, and as the inside light came on, he checked his watch. It was ten fifteen, much later than a San Francisco policeman was authorized to pay a call on a citizen who was not actively involved in a crime or its aftermath either as perpetrator or victim. Glitsky knew that by ringing their doorbell, he was giving the Curtlees ammunition to claim that he was harassing them. But he had a ready response: The circumstances surrounding Felicia Nuñez's death, along with the role she had been about to play in Ro's new trial, necessitated a swift, early police interrogation, if for no other reason than to eliminate Ro as a suspect. He could argue that, if anything, he was doing them a favor.

In a cathedral of old-growth cypress, he stepped out of his car and into the hushed and imposing street.

———

The servant who opened the door was new since the last time Glitsky had been to the Curtlees' home. Ten years ago, they hadn't had a formal butler, but now it seemed that had changed. This guy was impressive, with the build of a wrestler. He looked to be in his late forties, with a full head of perfectly groomed salt-and-pepper hair. In a dark gray business suit and black tie, the man exuded a quiet and cold-blooded competence. His frankly Aztec face betrayed neither curiosity nor concern at Glitsky's arrival, his request to talk to the Curtlees if they were home, or the badge he proffered.

He spoke with an exaggerated politeness, in an exceptionally deep, unaccented voice. "Do you have an appointment?"

"No. As I said, I'm with the police department."

"Yes. I understand. Do you have a warrant?"

"No. I hope to get a few words with one of the Curtlees to apprise them of a situation that has come up."

"Can you give me the message?"

"I'd prefer to speak to one of them personally."

The man took a long moment, deciding. "And the name again?"

"Lieutenant Glitsky. San Francisco homicide."

"Yes, sir. One moment, please. I'll see if one of them is available."

Gently but firmly, he closed the door on Glitsky's face.

Glitsky turned around and distracted himself by looking down the driveway to the street beyond. There was no gate. He'd been able to walk unimpeded up to the front door. For the first time, this struck him as unusual, and he wondered what, if anything, it said about this family, about its arrogance and its culture. True, this block didn't get much foot traffic, and what there was of it wasn't particularly threatening in the mold of, say, the Tenderloin district; but every other domicile on this block had its fence and its gate. Maybe the Curtlees figured first that everyone would know who lived here and second that no one would dare disturb them because to do so would be to invite the family's wrath and retribution.

So a fence wasn't necessary; neither was a gate. The psychic barrier was enough.

When he heard footsteps approaching from back inside the mansion, Glitsky turned back and was facing the door when it opened on Ro Curtlee.

The young man had filled out some in the years he'd been away, but with the milky blue eyes and the weak jawline, he still had a bit of the look of a sullen child. His light blond hair had grown out in the weeks that he'd been out on bail. Somewhere he'd acquired a scar that began high on his forehead and disappeared into his hairline. The white tank top he wore tucked into his slacks revealed all of his arms, now with well-defined biceps; he'd clearly spent a lot of time working out in prison.

Seeing Glitsky, he let out a scornful note of laughter, shaking his head in mock disbelief. "Ez said it was you out here disturbing our peace so late on a weekend night, and I told him you knew better than that. So I had to come see for myself, and here you are, in the flesh. You got yourself a giant set of balls, I'll give you that, showing your face around me again. So what the fuck do you want this time?"

"I hoped to try to eliminate you as a suspect in a murder that happened today."

"Sure you did. Who got herself killed?"

Glitsky paused. "Who said it was a female?"

Ro's face went blank for an instant before a cracked smile flittered back. "Oh. Ouch! Got me with a little zinger there right out of the gate. Nice work. I better get my lawyer down here before I incriminate myself. You got your tape recorder going?"

"Nope."

Ro clucked. "That's a shame. You could have used that moment in court."

"I still can."

"Okay, you got me shakin' now, and especially if it turns out it was a woman got killed."

"You want to guess?"

"I don't suppose I do. Especially if I got it right. How would that look? You know what I'm saying?"

"Yeah. You're way too smart for a silly trick like that, Ro. But what I'm really here for, maybe you can tell me where you were this afternoon and who, if anyone, you were with."

"Maybe I don't have to tell you dick."

"That's right, you don't. But you could save us both some trouble if you did."

"That's my goal, Sergeant. Save you some trouble."

"It's lieutenant now. I got promoted."

"No shit! Well, congratulations on that one. I thought I heard your career had kind of gone in the toilet after my trial, arresting the wrong guy and all."

Glitsky's lips turned up a fraction of an inch. "Actually not so much. You getting convicted and all. You know? So?"

"So what?"

"Today. This afternoon. Where were you?"

"Out. Taking a drive."

"Alone?"

"You bet. Enjoying my freedom."

"Where'd you go?"

"Up to Napa, across to Sonoma, back down here by dinnertime."

"You stop anywhere?"

"I got a burger and a milkshake at Taylor's Refresher in Napa. You know that place? Awesome food. None of that fancy shit they serve everyplace else up there."

"Yeah," Glitsky said. "It's a good spot. What kind of milkshake?"

"Chocolate."

"Well, there you go. You think anybody up there, maybe working at Taylor's, would recognize you?"

"I got no idea."

"How about your car?"

"How about it?"

"What were you driving?"

"The Z-Four. The Beemer, you know. Top down."

"What color is it?"

"Purple."

"So it's pretty visible?"

"People notice it, yeah. It's bitchin' wheels. That what you wanted to know?"

"It's a good start."

"So who got killed?"

Glitsky looked at his watch. "It ought to be on the news right about now. You can check it out yourself."

"Ro." A female voice from upstairs. The mother, Theresa. "Who's there at this time of night?"

Ro Curtlee hesitated about a second before he allowed himself another dismissive half smile and looked Glitsky straight in the eye. "Nobody," he said.

And closed the door.

———

Glitsky could have—perhaps should have—gone back home. But his blood was racing and he knew he'd keep Treya up if he stayed in the living room and simply paced, or even sat.

So he drove back downtown, parked in the city lot, and ascended back to the self-contained little universe that was his office. Switching on his lights, he crossed over to his desk.

High on his left-hand wall, five grimed-over identical windows provided a tenuous connection to the real world outside, although when the room lights weren't on, even in the daytime, his office was almost too dark to read in. Under his framed personal photographs and departmental honors—Glitsky had been San Francisco Policeman of the Year in 1987, among other accomplishments— low shelves filled with bric-a-brac, memorabilia (his patrolman's hat, a football signed by his old teammates at San Jose State), and random case files half filled his right-hand wall. Behind him a floor-to-ceiling bookshelf sported an array of reading material, eclectic for a policeman: hundreds of paperbacks; a complete collection of Patrick O'Brian's seagoing novels along with their obscure reference volumes; a set of the *Encyclopedia Britannica*; an abridged but still enormous *Oxford English Dictionary*; the *Compendium of Drug Therapy*; a couple of dozen sports books; the translated librettos of *The Barber of Seville* and *Tosca* (one of Glitsky's older sons by his first marriage, Jacob, was a rising baritone in the opera world); the California Penal Code; and many other legal tomes.

But tonight, Glitsky saw none of it.

He'd already considered and rejected the idea of going directly to the night magistrate on duty somewhere down in the lower floors of this building and asking for a search warrant based on Ro's obvious knowledge that today's murder victim was female. Though Glitsky took some solace in the fact that if it ever came to trial, he would indeed be allowed to testify to the exchange and Ro's slip of the tongue, for the moment, it was essentially nothing as far as evidence was concerned. It did, however, perhaps irrationally, remove all doubt in Glitsky's mind that Ro had killed Nuñez.

Glitsky pulled over a legal pad and scribbled some notes: He had to find Gloria Gonzalvez, the last remaining witness in Ro's trial, before the rapist-killer could get to her. He needed to assemble a couple of identification six-packs—mug shots of five other people and Ro—to show around.

Other notes: How had Ro found Nuñez? Had he made an appointment with her? Might he have conceivably phoned her? Had one of his lawyers? Had she lived in the same apartment the last time she'd testified against him?

Now, putting aside his legal pad, he checked his Rolodex, picked up the phone, and punched up Arnie Becker's cell phone number. The arson inspector picked up on the second ring, in spite of the late hour, giving no sign that he was anywhere near turning in. He knew who was calling him and started right in. "Abe. You got something?"

"Couple of somethings, maybe. Including a suspect."

"That was fast."

"You still at the fire?"

"Just getting started, really. Your crime scene just left. I'll be here all night."

"So has anybody put together who Nuñez was?"

"No. Other than she's dead."

"She was also a witness in a murder trial and was going to be one again before too long for the same guy."

"Who's that?"

"Ro Curtlee."

"The guy Farrell let out on bail?"

"Actually it was Baretto, but yeah, him."

"Shit. And he went and killed her."

"That's my bet."

A long sigh. Then, "Why do they let these fuckers out anyway?"

"That's a great question, Arnie. Something to do with justice and the right to appeal. Ask your congressman or somebody."

"Assholes."

"Yeah, well, the point is he might have been driving a purple BMW Z-Four convertible and parked it somewhere nearby when he went upstairs. Somebody might have seen it. Also, I'm making up a six-pack you can show around the neighborhood tomorrow. Anybody saw him, we at least take him down here and grill him, maybe even get a warrant to take his house apart. You get anything at all down there?"

"Maybe." Becker paused. "I don't want to get your hopes up, but there might be a small something."

"Go ahead, get my hopes up," Glitsky said. "Small is good."

Again, Becker hesitated. "Well, it might not be conclusive, and I don't know what it means, if anything, but there were two almost identical burned-up pieces of what looks like rubber or plastic— I'll know by tomorrow—down by her feet."

Glitsky's heart did a little flip in his chest. He'd already had one heart attack several years before, and though this didn't feel the same at all, now he moved his hand over his chest and sucked in a quick breath. "She was wearing her shoes when he killed her," he said. It was not a question.

"That's what it looks like. Maybe. Does that mean anything to you?"

Glitsky still was finding it difficult to draw a breath. "That's what Ro Curtlee did to his rape victims. He made sure they kept their shoes on."

"Why?"

"God only knows, Arnie. Why anything?"

———

"Sorry about the time, Wes, but I wanted you to know first. I say they verify the shoes, we get a warrant."

Farrell breathed into the mouthpiece on his end. "Can't do it, Abe. We don't even know it was Nuñez, for Christ's sake. And we may never know for sure whether or not it's her if she never went to a dentist in this country, which I hear is a reasonable likelihood. And without at least that ID, we've truly got nothing a jury could even chew on. Did any of that shoe stuff get admitted in his last trial?"

"I don't know, Wes, but you can find out easy enough. Meanwhile, though, I went and talked to these women before they got bought off, his rape victims, all of them. They all said the same thing about the shoes. It's what he did."

"I believe you. But he didn't kill any of them, the others, did he?"

"He killed one. He beat up three."

"Okay, but the dead one, Sandoval, she was outside, found in the park, am I right?" He kept going over Glitsky's silence. "So, my point is, he didn't burn anybody. Not ever. That's new, right? It's not his old MO, so where's the argument that this has to be him?"

"I know it's him. Somebody in prison told him it was a good idea when you rape somebody and kill her, then you burn up the place and the evidence with it."

"Which is why, what you got from Becker earlier, we're not even going to get proof that this Nuñez woman was sexually molested, are we?"

"Not likely, no."

"Okay, so we've got nothing putting Ro in her apartment, no witnesses . . ."

"So far."

"All right, so far. But still. Then no proof of a sexual attack. So we've got a woman who died in a fire. We don't even know cause of death yet, do we? I mean, was she strangled, shot, stabbed? Tell me."

"We might not get that either, Wes. She's burned up pretty bad."

"That's what I'm saying, Abe. She might . . . or no, the evidence might not prove a damn thing. She might have been carrying a candle on her way to the bath and had a heart attack and fell down and it set her and then the place on fire."

"That didn't happen."

"I don't think so, either. For the record, I think you're probably right. But *probably* isn't close to what we need and you know it."

"So what are we going to do?"

"I don't know, Abe. Hope he screws up."

"You mean while he's killing his next victim?"

"No," Farrell said. "Before that."

7

Farrell thought that the furnishing of his office was coming along pretty well. It was a large area that didn't remotely resemble the workspace of his predecessor and never would. That's what happens when you replace extremely high-end conservative furnishings for your basic Goodwill/garage–sale style.

Farrell had long eschewed the tyranny of the desk in the middle of the room and preferred a foosball table with room to play cleared all around it. Up by the door and then again behind the foosball table were two seating areas, both of them anchored by a sofa in front of a coffee table, with armchairs facing the couch at the corners. One area was leather and chrome; the other fabric and wood.

His "working" desk was in fact a blond library table against the Bryant Street windows, with a computer, printer, phone, and fax machine covering its entire surface. Another table against the long wall featured a fifty-two-inch television set, with folding chairs arranged in front of it. These could, of course, also be moved to augment the seating around either of the couches. The finishing touch, on the shelf underneath his Nerf ball basket and law books, was a bar of sorts with a Jura espresso machine, cups and glasses, utensils, a wicker basket filled with sweeteners, and half a wall of spirits of varying quality.

Now, at ten forty-five on the Saturday morning after Felicia Nuñez had died, Farrell sat on one end of the leather sofa. Across from him, Amanda Jenkins and Abe Glitsky filled the corner chairs. "So I'm at a loss," Farrell was saying. "On the one hand, I agree with both of you. I think it's likely that Ro killed the Nuñez woman. On the other, we're stuck with probable cause. I don't really see a way out of that, and don't believe either of you want to go that route, either."

"I'd consider it," Glitsky said.

Farrell shrugged that off and continued, "But the main thing is that I can't have either of you thinking you don't have my support, because you do. I'll be happy to entertain any concrete suggestions from either of you, which is why I called you both down here, but I can't just pull the guy in off the street for no reason."

Jenkins, sitting back with her legs crossed, said, "Yeah, you can. He gets pulled over and appears to be drunk. He's acting suspicious in a high narcotics neighborhood, he spits on the sidewalk, we haul him in. Any cop worth his or her salt can find ten reasons to arrest anybody they need to before breakfast. Isn't that right, Abe?"

"Generally."

"Generally is good." She nodded at Glitsky and came back to Farrell. "But specifically, Wes, Matt says he'll go out and bring Ro in on anything we decide on anytime you want. Anything. Anytime. We've talked about it."

"I'm glad for you. But who's Matt?"

Jenkins just barely did not roll her eyes. "Matt Lewis," she said with exaggerated patience. "One of our DA inspectors. Not to mention my long-standing boyfriend, not that that's important."

Farrell looked chagrined. "I guess the politician in me should have remembered that," he said. "Or known it in the first place. But I'm just naturally hopeless at that stuff. I can't help it. Matt Lewis. I'll remember from now on." Then, with a smile, "What's he look like?"

"Clark Kent," Jenkins deadpanned, "without the glasses. But the point is he'll bring Ro in on any charge we want and there you go."

"No, there we don't go." Farrell was shaking his head back and forth. "Guys, so we hold him ten minutes and look stupid in the process. Besides which, we'd get crucified in the press. But that's not the point either. Bottom line, we don't do that. It's not happening. End of discussion. You're going to need . . . no, we're going to need a real offense."

"Murder ought to do it," Glitsky said.

Farrell sighed. "Get me *any* evidence, and it's done, Abe. I promise."

Glitsky looked over at Jenkins and she took the lead. "Wes, hear me out, okay? This is where you've got discretion. You can make this call on your own."

Farrell suddenly showed his fatigue, bringing his hand up to his head and rubbing his eyes before he pressed his fingers to his temple. In fact, feeling more than a degree of responsibility for Felicia Nuñez's murder, he hadn't slept much after Glitsky's call the night before. "How do I do that, Amanda? Make that call?" he asked.

"You have Abe bring him in on the Nuñez murder. That's not harassment. That's a real charge that (a) he's guilty of, and (b) a vast percentage of the public will buy."

"Yes, maybe, but . . ."

"No 'buts.' Listen. You're worried because in the normal course of events, there's nowhere near enough to bring him to trial. Right?"

"Try *nothing.*"

"Well, not exactly nothing. But even so . . . so what? That's not the point."

"It's not. Then what is?"

"The point is that it doesn't matter if you've got enough to get him on Nuñez. You're never going to have to get to Nuñez. At least we've got him upstairs behind bars while his lawyers gear up for the retrial, however long that is. Meanwhile, Ro's off the street and nobody else gets killed."

Farrell slumped, sitting back, and let his head rest on the cushion behind him. He sighed again. "Did I actually expend energy to get elected to this job?" he asked. "And can either of you tell me why if I did?" Then, abruptly he sat up. "It's a lovely idea, Amanda, but we've got this old-fashioned notion called probable cause, without which Mr. Curtlee's out again in forty-eight hours, and P.S., Lieutenant Glitsky here gets sued for false arrest."

"I think we've got probable cause," Jenkins said.

Farrell gave her the bad eye. "All right, let's be wildly imaginative and say you do. Next up, as you know, is a preliminary hearing. Maybe you've heard of it? A guy gets arrested, charged by this office, makes it over the probable-cause hurdle, then there's a hearing in ten days to look at the evidence. If it's not there, he walks."

"Wes, come on." Jenkins came forward in her chair. "How many PXs"—preliminary hearings—"have you seen where they let the guy go? Zero, am I right? Maybe one in a decade. It never happens. Standard of proof is again only probable cause, 'a strong suspicion . . .'"

Farrell patiently held up a hand. "Please, spare me. I know the law. The law reads that probable cause is defined as 'a strong suspicion in the mind of a reasonable person that the offense was committed and that the defendant committed it.'"

"So, think about it," Jenkins continued. "We've got Ro's past conviction, the connection to Nuñez, the threat of Nuñez coming up at his retrial, the shoes . . . my point, though, is that any reasonable person—which includes most of our judges—is going to strongly suspect Ro did Nuñez, and that's all we need. It's a simple call, Wes, and it's all yours."

"It's an unacceptable risk," Farrell said.

"It's a small risk," Jenkins countered. "Insignificant. Less than crossing the street. But if it's beyond your comfort level, you've still got the grand jury."

Farrell knew that this was true, and in fact had already contemplated it, though it, too, of course, had risk associated with it. If he went and sold his weak case and got a grand jury indictment on Ro in the Nuñez murder, then he could avoid the possible pitfall of a preliminary hearing. A grand jury indictment obviated the need for a preliminary hearing; by itself, it was authority enough to bind a defendant over to trial. But if Farrell went that way, Ro's attorneys, as was their right, would demand the trial begin within sixty days, and there would be no continuance. Farrell could ask the court to join the cases for trial, but the way things were going with Baretto, that motion might well be denied. Under those circumstances—that is, if Wes prosecuted Ro for the Nuñez murder only—a San Francisco jury would never convict him. He'd be freed again. Within two or three months. Making his retrial for the rape and murder of Sandoval—already hugely problematic— logarithmically more difficult.

"But the grand jury," Glitsky said, "you're still looking at ten days, two weeks before they could even get to the indictment. Ro could do a lot of damage in that time."

"Which is why our vote's for an arrest and indict before the prelim," Jenkins said. "Short and sweet. Take him out."

——

When the meeting broke up, Glitsky went back upstairs to his office with a couple of ideas rattling around in his brain, both of them having to do with Arnie Becker. He wanted the identification of the murder victim to be rock solid and also to be accomplished as soon as possible. If the dead person was not, in fact, Felicia Nuñez, then the theory that Jenkins and he were betting on would not fly—there had to be an immediate connection to Ro Curtlee, and they had to establish it quickly. Possible dental records were okay, but Glitsky knew that he could wait a very long time for dental records, to say nothing of the fact that finding the victim's dentist so that they even had a chance at a comparison might be flatly impossible. So they'd have to try to find another way to identify her.

But when he reached Becker—the man apparently didn't need to sleep—the arson inspector was at least a step ahead of him. The identification of the victims of fires was one of the inspector's most critical tasks. And over the years, Becker had picked up more than a few tricks. "It's her all right," he said. "Nuñez. When she cooked, her hands closed up into fists like they do. You noticed that, I'm sure."

"Sure," Glitsky lied.

"So I had the morgue pry 'em open, and as I'd hoped, we got four just-about-perfect fingerprints, two on each hand. So I had 'em run them in the INS database . . ."

"On a Saturday morning?"

"I got a pal I called in records. So anyway, he loads in the prints and, bingo, up pops Felicia Nuñez."

"You ever want a job in homicide," Glitsky said, "just give me a call."

"I'll keep it in mind, thanks. But I'm happy where I am."

"I can see that. Getting to sleep in on the weekends and all like you do."

"Sleep's overrated," Becker said. "You said there were two things?"

"The shoes. Or maybe the shoes."

"What about 'em?"

"Do we know that the rubber or plastic near her feet came from her shoes?"

"Oh yeah. When you told me last night they might be important, I brought 'em home to my own lab and checked 'em out this morning. They're the soles from an Adidas tennis shoe, the Honey Low, retails around fifty-five bucks. Size seven, by the way. The top burned away completely."

———

The fire scene was on Farrell's way driving back home from work.

He passed by once without really seeing it, although the yellow police tape must have stuck somewhere in his preoccupied brain, because half a block beyond the apartment building, the location registered. He checked his rearview in a double take, hung a U-turn at the next intersection, and drove back down, parking across the street in a space cleared by the tape.

Glitsky and Jenkins had kept at him for nearly an hour, until in the end he had run out of arguments. Which was not to say he'd made any decision, other than to go home for the afternoon and lie around the house in comfortable clothes before he had to go out this evening and give yet another speech somewhere about something important. Maybe even get in a little sack time with his girlfriend—stranger things had happened.

Now, at a few minutes past noon, the weather had turned foul with a gusty wind blowing around a gauzy drizzle that might as well have been rain. Farrell rolled his window down and looked at the shattered glass in what used to be the windows of the upper left-hand apartment.

Try as he might, he couldn't get the place to speak to him.

He didn't go to crime scenes. He was a lifelong defense attorney, and that was a job for the police and the prosecution.

And yet here he was, a prosecutor and top law enforcement person in the city of San Francisco. The job was bunching at him from every direction like an ill-fitting suit.

Although before he'd actually run for DA, he had been notorious for his oft-stated belief that all defendants were factually guilty of whatever crime they'd been charged with, his professional life had always been about getting these people off. Or more commonly getting them a plea bargain they could accept. In the working defense attorney's world, the objective rarely was to get your client off. Mostly you tried to reduce a charge or a sentence or a bail. Because it happened so infrequently, if at all, no one gave much thought to the idea that a client might actually be innocent.

So the fact that Ro Curtlee probably killed this Nuñez woman didn't make the impression it might have on Farrell. He'd worked with murderers before as clients. He would probably draw the line at saying that they were nice people in general, but he'd formed a sort of attachment with several of them based on their common humanity. They often had relatives they cared about—mothers, girlfriends, children. They sometimes felt bad about why they'd done what they did. They were not all irredeemable souls.

So the tectonic plate of Farrell's natural-born inclination and culture was slamming up against that of Glitsky and Jenkins. Talking with them this morning, trying to be accommodating and receptive to their arguments, he could not help but be aware of the Everest looming between them.

To Farrell, the law was a set of inflexible, impersonal, and objective rules that society adopted to settle disputes. There was little room for discretion; what you usually did was what you always did. Morality didn't much play into it. And the law was specifically not a tool that you used selectively to arrest some people but not others who did the same thing.

Both Glitsky and Jenkins apparently had no trouble being creative within the rules to get Ro Curtlee back into a cell. Farrell believed that if it couldn't be done in the normal course of business, then by definition it was wrong. And yet Glitsky and Jenkins clearly thought that they had the law and, more important, morality on their side.

And this Farrell knew to be a very slippery slope, and very disturbing.

While he was losing sleep last night over the degree of responsibility he bore for the release of Ro Curtlee and the subsequent death of Felicia Nuñez, he'd finally come to terms with his conscience because he knew that he had respected the law and applied it fairly. That was what he'd been elected to do. That was his job.

But what about this suggestion that he use one of the legal tools at his command—the grand jury or a preliminary hearing—to get Ro back behind bars? Surely that would be worthwhile, but would it be right? The man had already been convicted of rape and murder, and his successful appeal to the Ninth Circuit never even addressed the actual fact of his guilt for those crimes, which was never really in doubt. And if he had come from a poor family, Farrell knew that he never would have been able to make his $10 million bail, and he would still be in jail awaiting his retrial.

The crux was that Farrell *knew* that Glitsky had no physical evidence on Curtlee for the Nuñez murder. He had a great motive, true, and probably no good alibi, but Farrell didn't believe he could charge Ro or go to a grand jury on those issues alone. Forget whether they could adequately prove probable cause—Jenkins was correct that this was an often elastic criterion; evidence or no, her suggestion could work. That would get Ro back into the system, true, and it might keep him in jail until his retrial, or close to it. But it would be cynically playing the system and that was, to Farrell's mind, where the morality came into it.

Farrell knew he was not a saint. He was flawed in many ways. Ask his ex-wife and his grown and mostly far-flung kids. But he was *not* a hypocrite. He had sworn to uphold the law as he believed it to be, and that's what he was going to do, come what may.

Looking back up a last time at the empty shell of Felicia Nuñez's apartment, he unconsciously set his jaw and put the car back into gear.

8

Ro Curtlee turned north off Lake and pulled his BMW into a parking spot at the curb of a short dead-end street that, like his own much more high-end block, ended at the Presidio. On both sides of this street, near-identical two-story duplexes sat tight up against one another. A row of garage doors fronted the sidewalk, and next to each garage door, a walkway led first to a side door on the flat at the ground level, and then to a flight of stairs that led to the upper unit.

Ro got out of his car. He was wearing jeans and hiking boots and a heavy green slicker of some kind that he'd buttoned against the weather. His head was bare.

Checking the address numbers on the fronts of the duplexes, he started up the block, walking with a purposeful stride. Down at the end, he found the address he wanted. It was the upstairs unit in the building, and he climbed twelve steps, stood for a moment in front of the door, then rang the doorbell.

A female voice called from inside. "Just a minute!"

Ro waited.

The door opened and he was facing an attractive black woman who was almost his own size. "Yes. Can I help you?"

Ro could not believe she simply opened the door and greeted him. If she'd looked through the peephole, he'd missed it. And there was no chain to offer even token resistance if he decided he was going to get himself inside.

He thought that this was either supreme confidence or idiocy.

She was wearing a purple sweat suit and tennis shoes. Just beside her, holding her hand, a young girl of about five or six stood looking up at him with an appraising and confident air that Ro thought she might have lifted wholesale from her father's playbook.

Ro gave the daughter a fast glance and a quick, shallow smile and then brought his eyes back to the mother. "I was hoping to talk to Lieutenant Abe Glitsky," he said.

"He's not home right now," she said. "I expect him in the next couple of minutes." For a tantalizing second, Ro got the impression that she was considering inviting him in to wait. Instead, she backed up a half-step and put her hand on the edge of the door, as though preparing to slam it, although nothing changed in her eyes, which remained friendly, inquisitive. "If you'd like to come back, maybe in a half hour or so, you'll probably catch him."

"That's all right. I'm sure I'll run into him downtown and I'll talk with him then. I was just in the neighborhood and thought I'd drop by unannounced and hope to reach him at home, the way he did with me last night."

"Last night?"

"Right." He gave her a smirk. "If you wouldn't mind telling him that Ro Curtlee stopped by, I'd appreciate it."

This time the woman's eyes narrowed and her face went slack. Instinctively she moved farther back away from him, pushing her child partially behind her as she did so. Her hand tightened on the edge of the door. "What are you doing here?"

It was all the reaction of fear and anger that he'd hoped for.

"Really just telling your husband that I know where he lives, you know. Like he did with me."

She pulled the door around in front of her. "You'd better leave right now," she said. "You've got no business coming here."

With an exaggerated expression of disappointment, he said, "And just when we were all getting along so well." He pointed down at the little girl. "That's a real pretty little daughter you've got there."

At this, the door slammed on him, and from behind it he heard, "I'm calling nine-one-one."

"You don't have to bother," he said through the door. "I'll be long gone."

He started back down the stairs toward the street and his waiting car.

———

Glitsky was sitting in Jenkins' cluttered office on the third floor, drinking a cup of tea and filling her in on Becker's information—the positive ID on Nuñez, the soles of the Adidas—when Treya's call came in on his cell. As he listened to the sound of her voice—quivering beneath the controlled, low-pitched, and calm recital of events—he realized how close to panic she was, how proximate the danger had been.

Without realizing it, he stood up and paced from the door and back to the desk while the scar between his lips grew more pronounced, an angry white line. He lowered a haunch onto Jenkins' desk and with his free hand pulled at the skin of his face.

"Abe?" Treya asked into the extended silence.

"I'm here. Is he gone?"

"Yes."

"You're sure?"

"I saw him drive away."

"And you've got both the kids with you?"

"Right. We're all okay. A little shaky, that's all."

Glitsky let out a breath. Another one.

"Abe?" she asked again.

"Still here. Thinking."

"You want to come home? That would be good. Rachel wants to say hi to you."

Before he could object, he heard his daughter's voice. "Hi, Daddy. Mommy's upset. Is everything okay?"

"Everything's fine. But that man who came to the house. He's not a good man."

"You should arrest him."

"I know. I think that's what's going to happen. Are you okay now?"

"Just worried. For Mommy. He really scared her. Are you coming home soon?"

"Real soon. Can I talk to your mom again?"

"Okay."

And then Treya: "Hey."

"Trey, I'm sending a squad car by."

"No. I don't think we need . . ."

"We'll negotiate about that when I get there. But meanwhile, I'm sending some men if for nothing else to take a report. I'll be right behind them. But when they knock, check the peephole and make sure it's really them first, okay? And keep the dead bolt on until then."

"I never thought, with Ro . . ."

"It's okay," Glitsky said. "You got away with it once. Now we know. We check the peephole, huh?"

"All right. We'll be waiting for you."

"I'll be home in half an hour. You just keep everybody close till then."

"Don't worry."

"I won't. I love you."

"I love you, too. Get home soon."

"I will."

When he closed the phone, he looked over at Jenkins. "You heard that."

"Ro came by your house?"

"Yes, he did." His shoulders sagged with the weight of this latest burden. "He made a point of saying that Rachel was a pretty little girl." Glitsky's eyes went to the corners of the room, then back down to Jenkins. He let out a breath and shook his head.

"What are you thinking?" she asked.

"About what you'd expect. Blow his head off."

"I wouldn't blame you, but you'd probably get caught and go to jail."

"Somebody's got to stop him."

"There's another way."

"It couldn't be better than popping him."

"No. Better for you though. Arrest him."

"Wes didn't seem too hot on that idea."

"Yeah, but we didn't have anything to charge him with then. And now we do."

"What?"

"Threatening an executive officer. That's you. Or any member of your family. Penal Code sixty-nine or four twenty-two, take your pick. Both felonies."

"Is that true?"

Glitsky should have been used to attorneys knowing sections of the Penal Code by heart, but every time he ran up against it, it impressed him. Jenkins, unoffended, spun in her chair, closed her eyes, and said, "Sixty-nine: 'Every person who attempts, by means of any threat or violence, to deter or prevent an executive officer from performing any duty imposed upon such officer,' blah blah blah. And here's four twenty-two: 'Any person who willfully threatens to commit a crime which will result in death or great bodily injury to another person, with the specific intent that the statement' blah blah 'is to be taken as a threat,' and this is the good part, *even if there is no intent of actually carrying it out*, which, on its face and under the circumstances in which it is made, is so unequivocal, unconditional, immediate, and specific as to convey to the person threatened, a gravity of purpose and an immediate prospect of execution of the threat, and thereby causes that person reasonably to be in sustained fear for his or her own safety or for his or her immediate family's safety,' et cetera."

"You've got a good memory," Glitsky said.

Jenkins shrugged. "Comes with the territory. You can't remember stuff, don't go to law school. Anyway, I think we go for four twenty-two."

"What about Wes?"

"Wes said if we got something real, he'd charge it. And that's what our boy just gave us. I'll be your witness to the fact that right now you are in a state of sustained fear for your safety and your family's. Is that about true?"

"True enough."

"There you go. So it's textbook. And it's a felony. Plenty to get him back inside."

Glitsky shifted himself off the desk. "Then what am I sitting around here for?"

"You're sitting around waiting for me to clear this with Wes. He's going to want you to get a warrant. And in fact, he'll want somebody else to take this. He'll think you're too close. I could call Matt and I'm sure he and a couple of his buddies would jump all over the opportunity. Now you're supposed to ask me who Matt is."

Glitsky stood by the door. "I think I vaguely remember, but I'm afraid that this has got to be a police matter, Amanda. This is a serious guy who threatened my family. He's going into custody as soon as I can get him there."

———

But Glitsky couldn't do anything about Ro until he knew where his suspect was. And more specifically that he was not still skulking around his own home. Treya had watched Ro apparently walk away, but that didn't mean he wasn't still parked nearby, perhaps waiting for Glitsky to show himself on his street, an easy target for ambush.

So he called the precinct house downstairs at the Hall and requested a team of patrolmen be sent to his home ASAP, where they would remain with Treya and the kids until Glitsky's arrival. On the way there, the team was to keep a lookout for a purple BMW Z4 parked in the neighborhood and report immediately to Glitsky if they saw one.

Glitsky had a patrol woman place a call to the Curtlee home. She identified herself as a clerk concerned with his bail bond and said that she needed to speak to Ro about his status at his earliest convenience. When Ro picked up with a "what the fuck is this about now?" the patrol woman told him she just needed to confirm his resident address, and having accomplished the call's primary objective, which was to determine if Ro was back home, she hung up.

Glitsky, still in a high and glowing rage, left her office at the word and, out in the hallway, broke into a jog.

———

There are three ways that law enforcement officers can make a valid arrest in California, and Glitsky had had a great deal of experience with all of them.

In the first instance, the grand jury issues an indictment. The court issues a warrant and a couple of officers are assigned to arrest the suspect and deliver him or her to the jail. In the second case, investigators conclude that they have enough evidence to satisfy the probable-cause requirement, and they bring this evidence to a magistrate (one of the rotating superior court judges), who then signs off on an arrest warrant, after which, again, a couple of officers go out to effect the arrest. The third type, the so-called no-warrant arrest, is both the most common and the most challenged because it almost always includes an element of subjectivity—an officer or team of officers makes a unilateral decision that the suspect must be taken into custody immediately for any number of reasons, usually because he was caught in the act, but perhaps to stop him from committing another crime or to keep him from fleeing the jurisdiction.

Glitsky didn't know offhand who was the presiding magistrate on this Saturday afternoon, but he did know two other things for sure: that the magistrate might be Sam Baretto, who would be very unlikely to sign off on a warrant; and that Ro Curtlee needed to be in jail right now. These were two possibly irreconcilable scenarios, and the second one, in Glitsky's mind, was non-negotiable.

So by the time he was on the elevator heading down to the lobby, Abe had made up his mind. Because of the overt threat to his own family, he believed he had plenty to justify a no-warrant arrest. Wes Farrell had already promised him that if he had anything substantive to bring Ro in on, the DA's office would back him up. Besides, in police work—as in so many other endeavors—it was always better to ask for forgiveness later than for permission before.

His duty was clear and Glitsky was going to do it.

———

On reflection, Glitsky knew Jenkins was right that it would be hard for him to make the arrest himself. He was just too close to the case. He also knew he couldn't go into any suspect's house without an arrest warrant, even for a felony. But what he could do was put a bunch of officers in surveillance around the house who would nail Ro Curtlee the first time he set foot outside.

It only took him a couple of minutes to explain the situation and to pick up two pairs of uniformed patrolmen and another squad car from Southern Station, the precinct that worked out of the ground floor of the Hall of Justice. They would take the initial shifts around the Curtlee home until Glitsky could call in some of the detectives from night investigations to take over the surveillance.

Now the five policemen had pulled up and parked at the curb

down the street from the Curtlee home, Glitsky in his city-issue and his troops behind him in their black-and-white patrol cars with the wire mesh between the front and back seats.

They got out of their cars and gathered near Glitsky's back bumper. The light drizzle continued and in the late afternoon limited visibility to about fifty yards. The weather didn't seem to bother or even much register with any of the men.

Glitsky liked the trim of these youngsters—solid guys, all probably under twenty-five, pumped up and eager to be working with the head of homicide. They all looked like they worked out with some regularity. The biggest white kid—his name tag read DALY— stood with his arms folded across his chest. His partner, Monroe, lean and dark black, kept his hands in his jacket pockets and shifted his weight from foot to foot, loose and easy. The two others might have been their cousins. All the men wore their belts—guns, batons, and handcuffs. Glitsky, in plainclothes, had no patrolman's belt, just his service weapon in a shoulder holster underneath a dark brown Gore-Tex jacket.

"What if he doesn't come out?" Daly asked.

Glitsky's mouth turned up a fraction of an inch, anticipating a smile that never quite materialized. "We wait till he does. The man's going to jail."

The patrolmen exchanged a glance, galvanized by the thought of real action.

"Oh," Glitsky added, "and there may be a butler, large gentleman, who has a carry permit and might want to make this an issue. He interferes in any way, we restrain him and bring him downtown as well, clear? No chances with either of these guys."

"Yes, sir," the four men said in unison.

"All right. Let's go."

Glitsky sent one of the squad cars beyond the house to the end of the block so that if Ro came out, whether he turned left or right, there would be someone to cut him off. In their enthusiasm, the officers in this car turned on their overhead flashing lights to drive the fifty yards down the street. Glitsky flinched. At least, he thought, they didn't turn on their sirens.

But it turned out that the red strobes were enough.

Glitsky turned and had only taken two steps back toward his car when Ro Curtlee emerged from the house, his drink in his hand, striding purposefully down the walk, looking up the street toward the patrol car with its lights flashing. Today he was wearing a gray hoodie with the top down, new jeans, new tennis shoes. "*I don't believe this shit,*" he yelled into the night. Still focused on the patrol car up the street, he never even noticed Glitsky until he and the other two patrolmen were almost upon him.

"You'd better believe it," Glitsky said. "Ro Curtlee, I'm placing you under arrest for threatening a police officer's family. You have the right to remain . . ."

Shaking his head, seemingly enjoying himself, Ro flipped Glitsky the bird and turned to head back toward his front door.

Daly, on Glitsky's left, blocked the line of escape, leaving Ro surrounded by police. But Ro hadn't spent eight years in prison for nothing. His face actually broke a smile. "Hey, easy," he said.

He held his hands up as though he posed no threat, giving up. Taking a step forward, he slashed out his right hand in a vicious karate chop that Daly only partially blocked before it hit him in the throat. Staggered, Daly slumped enough for Ro to block him into a tree by the drive. Still coming forward in the same movement, Ro got ahold of Daly's belt and brought his knee up into Daly's groin. When the officer bent over, Ro reached around him and got his hand on the butt of Daly's gun, holding on to and pulling it out of the holster as he pushed him away, then butted him with enough force to send him back out into Glitsky.

Ro came around with the gun, but Monroe was ready for the attack and came around with his nightstick, hitting Ro a solid crack on the elbow. Amazingly the blow had no apparent effect.

Ro swung at Monroe's face with Daly's gun, a blow that Monroe blocked with his own nightstick, then came down with a counterstrike on Ro's arm, following it with a full-on body slam.

Ro brought the gun up in Monroe's general direction and pulled the trigger, but Daly hadn't chambered a round, and nothing happened but a click.

This gave Monroe just time to jab Ro in the gut and to take a swing at his gun hand, connecting and sending the semiautomatic skittering over the flagstones. Monroe then backed away just enough to get room for another swing.

But Glitsky came up and blocked him, grabbing his suspect by his sweatshirt, throwing him to the ground. Ro went sprawling facedown onto the wet flagstones, then used his momentum to flip himself over, get upright, and kick out at Monroe's legs with a guttural grunt. The second cop let out a cry and went down.

But by now Glitsky had Daly's nightstick and he swung it once in a roundhouse backhand that Ro tried to block with his forearm. A crack as hard wood met bone, and Ro let out a yell of agony, and almost simultaneously Daly slammed into him with a football tackle, taking him down, holding on as Ro continued to kick at him. Monroe scrambled over a few feet, brought up his nightstick, and hit Ro in the head, the shoulders, and then in the head again.

Daly yelling, "I got him! I got him!" he tried to wrestle Ro's arms behind his back while reaching for his handcuffs. The suspect kept up the struggle under him, but by now Monroe had come over and pinned his upper body while Glitsky got down by his feet and held him there.

In a few more seconds, it was over.

The two patrolmen jerked Ro to his feet. He was bleeding from his scalp and his mouth, spewing invective all over Glitsky, who'd by now drawn his gun. "You broke my arm, you cocksucker! You broke my fucking arm!"

"And your nose, too," Daly said, hitting him in the face as hard as he could.

"I'm going to sue your asses," Ro screamed. "I'll have your badges."

"Tell somebody who gives a shit," Monroe said, jerking Ro around, Daly now on Ro's other arm, pulling him off into the street, Ro keeping up his abuse all the way.

Following them, Glitsky took one last look back at the house's open door, then sucking for a breath, he fell in behind his two limping officers and his prisoner. The whole thing had taken less than a minute. The other two officers joined them, and they manhandled Ro into the patrol car and slammed the door behind him.

9

By eight thirty P.M., the drizzle had turned into a steady cold rain.

Wes Farrell was not the only new elected official in San Francisco that year. The two-term previous mayor, Kathy West, had moved out and, by some accounts, up to the State Assembly in Sacramento. Her successor as mayor was a forty-five-year-old former public defender and supervisor named Leland M. Crawford. These two electoral changes also coincided with a changing of the guard in the police department—Chief Frank Batiste's retirement had become official on the day before Farrell and Crawford had been sworn in, and in his place, hired after a nationwide search that ignored many candidates from the city's own pool of veteran police officers, was Vi Lapeer, a forty-eight-year-old African American woman and the former assistant chief of police of Philadelphia, Pennsylvania.

After he'd received his call from the Curtlees before Ro had even made it down to San Francisco General Hospital—where they'd treated his injuries and where he was currently under guard—Mayor Crawford had ordered an emergency confab in his ornate city hall office. Now Crawford was going to get his first chance to assert his dominance and capacity for leadership. He stood about six foot four. His thick black hair was going gray at the temples. He might have been handsome but for an overly toothy smile and a continual battle with facial rosacea. Unlike Farrell, Crawford's general tendency was to use his enormous antique desk to separate himself from his visitors, but tonight that was not his intention. Instead, in shirtsleeves, he sat on the front of that desk in front of a semicircle of folding chairs, on which, left to right, sat Farrell, Lapeer, Glitsky, and Amanda Jenkins.

Crawford was not a pro-cop politician. Like Farrell—one of their few similarities—he was a lifelong member of the defense bar. He believed that excess and denial of due process was part of police culture, the rule rather than the exception. Now he had a prime example of it occurring only a few weeks into his administration and from the Curtlees' reaction, it looked as though he was going to be blamed for it, at least to a certainly not-insignificant percentage of the electorate.

He wasn't inclined to sit idly by and let that happen, so he'd called this meeting. "You're telling me, Lieutenant," he was saying to Glitsky, "that even knowing what we know now, you'd pursue the same course of action?"

"In a heartbeat," Glitsky said. "The man threatened my family. I'd do it again tomorrow if it came to it."

Crawford spoke up heatedly. "You'd do it again tomorrow? Without a warrant? After the district attorney told you not to, with no notice to your chief or my office. Are you completely insane, Lieutenant, or merely totally out of control?"

"Excuse me, sir," Vi Lapeer said, "but if Ro Curtlee hadn't come out drunk and attacked the officers, none of this would have happened. All the lieutenant was trying to do was to neutralize the threat while we went through the usual process."

"That's not what I understand." Crawford was prepared for this and answered in clipped tones. "From what the Curtlees explained to me, Ro didn't go over to the Glitskys' home to threaten anybody."

Jenkins barked out a laugh. "Right."

Crawford fixed his gaze on her. "It is right, Ms. Jenkins. Maybe you don't know that Lieutenant Glitsky had gone over to Ro's house the night before, apparently just to harass the man, and Ro just wanted the lieutenant to know how that felt."

Lapeer squirmed in her chair. Even if she did not think that her lieutenant had acted correctly, she would have felt compelled to stand behind him, at least until she got him alone. The fact that she actually agreed with the way he'd proceeded underscored her words with a low-key vehemence. "With all respect, Lieutenant Glitsky went over there last night to question the suspect about his whereabouts when one of the witnesses in his upcoming murder trial was killed. That was official police business."

Crawford was shaking his head. "That's not how the Curtlees see it. The lieutenant didn't record the conversation, barely asked any specific questions. And in fact, we've all just heard from Lieutenant Glitsky that the Curtlee boy didn't make any overt threat at his home, in so many words, at all."

Glitsky, fuming, not trusting himself to speak, looked to his left, and Jenkins got his message and spoke up. "Sir," she said, "a convicted murderer coming to a policeman's house and commenting on his children is, de facto, an overt threat. What would you have had him do?"

"Well, that's a good question, Ms. Jenkins, and here's a good answer. I'd have had him step back and let more objective people handle the situation. At the very least, I'd have had him notify his superiors and apply for a warrant. I'd have had him follow the goddamn rules!"

"And how about while he's following the goddamn rules, his family gets goddamn dead, sir?" Jenkins asked. "Then what?"

"That's melodramatic horseshit." Crawford showed off a lot of his teeth. "And frankly I'm just a little bit annoyed that we're all having a discussion about this convenient threat when it's entirely clear to me—and don't kid yourselves, it will be clear to most of the rest of the city tomorrow—that this is just an end run around the real issue here, which is that you, Ms. Jenkins," and here he pointed at her, "and you, Lieutenant," another point at Glitsky, "decided unilaterally between yourselves to subvert the court's decision to release Ro on bail after he got released on appeal."

Jenkins raised her chin. "With all respect, that's just purely untrue, Your Honor."

Crawford drew himself up straight. "It is hardly that, Ms. Jenkins. What it is, in my opinion, is prosecutorial and police excess in its most blatant form. It's a classic denial of due process and harassment, and I'm not going to stand for it. Not in my city. Do you know how much the Curtlees are threatening to sue the city for? Anybody want to take a guess?"

"It doesn't matter," Jenkins said. "They won't get whatever it is."

"Would you like to bet your job on that, Ms. Jenkins? Because that's what I have to do here. That's the position you've put me in. Now I have to bet we can beat a lawsuit for a hundred million dollars! Do any of you have any idea how much money that is?"

After a moment of silence, Glitsky found his voice. "The man's a convicted killer, Your Honor, and he threatened my family. He needs to be in jail."

"Well, that's sure as hell where you've got him now, Lieutenant. Against the express decision of the court. And given that, how long do you honestly think you're going to be able to keep him there?" Suddenly the mayor shifted his focus and settled on Farrell. "Wes, you've been curiously silent throughout all this. Are you really planning to charge this thing?"

Farrell, still in his raincoat, seething for his own reasons, was sitting back with his arms and feet crossed. After a small hesitation, he said, "I read Ro's visit to Abe's house as a threat. I think the court will agree with us at the arraignment on Monday. Abe did what he had to do. If Ro wasn't a Curtlee . . ."

Crawford could no longer restrain himself. "But he is a Curtlee, goddamn it! That's kind of the point here, don't you see?" He looked around the semicircle, face by unyielding face, then started back and stopped at his new chief of police. "At the very least, Chief, I'd expect that you'd want to remove Lieutenant Glitsky from an active investigating role in this latest murder, this Nuñez woman. Clearly he's far from objective on anything that's got to do with Ro Curtlee."

Lapeer drew in a quick breath, then released it. She was thinking she might be the shortest-lived chief of police in San Francisco history, but she really had no choice about what to say. "The lieutenant is head of the homicide detail, sir. I respect his decisions to assign investigators to cases, including himself, as he sees fit."

Now, stymied, Crawford turned back to Farrell. "And if they let Ro off on Monday, Wes, then what?"

"Then the courts will have spoken," Farrell said.

"And what about his injuries? Ro's?" Crawford asked.

Glitsky jumped in with the answer. "He resisted arrest," he said. "Strenuously. He also injured two of our patrolmen. We're charging him on that, too."

"Wonderful," Crawford said. "Just wonderful."

———

Farrell, Glitsky, and Jenkins had all come to the meeting in their separate cars and parked in the underground lot just across from city hall. Finally the meeting and dressing-down had ended, and having jogged across the street through the rain, they got to the parking lot's elevator, all shivering wet dogs, anxious to get to their cars and back home.

Glitsky, in the lead, went to push the elevator button.

But Farrell came up from behind, put his hand out, and blocked him. "Hold on a minute, Abe. Amanda. I'd like a word."

"It's a little late and a lot cold, Wes," Jenkins said. She was wearing her trademark short skirt and she had her arms crossed into her armpits. "Can it wait?"

"You know, actually"—Farrell was atypically brusque—"I don't think it fucking can." He squared around on them. "I got both of you here now and I want to tell you both how much I don't appreciate the spot you put me in back up there."

Glitsky and Jenkins shared a glance.

"What? You don't know what I'm talking about? Don't give me that. We talked about this very thing just this morning. I'm sure you both remember."

Glitsky started in. "That was before Ro came by . . ."

"Yeah, yeah, yeah. Your house. I get it. But here's the thing I don't get, Abe. What I don't get is, even assuming that it was a bona fide threat to your family, which I'm not sure I completely buy . . ."

"It sure as hell was," Jenkins said.

"Maybe. But why make the visit a threat? If he wanted to hurt you, why didn't he just do whatever it was he wanted to do when he was there? Treya answers the door, whammo. Nobody knows he's there. He hits and he's gone. But he doesn't. Why not? Anybody got an answer to that one?" In the small space, Farrell made a half turn in agitation, then came back at them. "And if it was a threat, okay, then why didn't you go get a warrant? Tell a judge; make it official. I'm willing to bet you could have found one down at the Hall, even here on a Saturday. Instead, you go flying off with a couple of starstruck rookies and basically just go in and kick some ass. Which is exactly what you, personally, Abe, wanted to do."

"I did not . . ."

"Don't bullshit a bullshitter, Abe. Don't even try. And meanwhile, you give the fucking Curtlees everything they could ever need to make their case that you're harassing their precious little prick of a son? Did I get any of that wrong?"

"He was . . . ," Glitsky began again.

But again Farrell cut him off. "So *I don't give a damn what Ro's doing!* Why can't you seem to get that? The mayor was absolutely right in there when he was talking about the way it's going to get reported, and not just in the fucking *Courier.* I'm going to predict that you're not going to get flattering coverage in the *Chron,* either."

"Come on, Wes," Jenkins said, "it's not about the papers."

"Okay, it's not about the papers, but I'll tell you what it is about. It's about both of you putting me in a position where I've got to back up what you've done, when we had already discussed it and decided you weren't going to do exactly what you did."

"Wait a minute, Wes." Glitsky was finally getting a little hot. "You told me if I had something, almost anything, I could arrest him and you'd support me."

"And I just did that upstairs, in the face of the mayor, don't forget." Farrell raised a finger. "But here's what I don't understand, and it really, really, *really fucking fries my ass,* Abe, if you must know"—Farrell in a true rage now, his voice ratcheting up—"is why in God's name you had this great reason to go and righteously arrest Ro, and you didn't see fit maybe to run the idea by me. And you know how that strikes my cynical mind? It strikes me that you didn't think your reason was good enough. You thought I'd say no, and you know, I might have.

"And why?

"'Cause it still wasn't enough, not given all the political ramifications and all the other bullshit we're now going to have to be dealing with for the next God knows however many months. And you knew it! You goddamn well knew it, and you just said, 'Well, fuck Wes.' That's what happened, and both of you were in on it, which is why when the first I heard about it is when fucking Cliff Curtlee calls me—oh yeah, he called me before he called Leland, demanding your badge, Abe, how 'bout that?—and I'm stuck defending both of you when I think you did just about everything completely backward and wrong, I'm just a little bit beyond pissed off."

Farrell did a full pirouette and came back at them for a last round. "Just for the record, I feel bushwhacked and betrayed by both of you, and I don't know what the fuck is going to happen on Monday. All I know is that if the court lets Ro out, we're in deep shit. And if it keeps him in jail, we're also in deep shit. And either way, I've made an enemy out of Leland Crawford, and I'd like to thank both of you for that, too. You've both put in a hell of a day's work."

Finally out of steam, Farrell did a kind of double take, reached over and went to push the button for the elevator, then stopped himself. "That's all right. Fuck it. I'll walk down to my car." And turning on his heel, he opened the door to the stairway.

———

Glitsky pushed open the door to his home at ten forty-five P.M. He had last called Treya from the hospital when he'd gotten the call three hours earlier from the mayor's office that he was expected immediately or sooner at City Hall, no excuses. At that time, he thought and told Treya he'd probably be home in about an hour. But then had come Farrell's outburst in the elevator lobby and another half hour of discussion with Amanda Jenkins after that. And now the original hour had turned to nearly three.

The house was dark.

He'd walked nearly four blocks from the nearest place he'd found to park. Now, closing the door behind him, he shrugged out of his soaking jacket and hung it on the hook on the wall. He stood still a moment, listening to the rain, then moved up to the front of his house, where the bay window through his plantation shutters overlooked the block. The streetlights reflected off the shining streets.

"What are you looking at?"

His wife's voice startled him. He had assumed that she was sleeping, but there she sat on the living room couch.

"Just the rain," he said. He stayed at the window. Then, the thought just occurring to him, "Where are the men who were watching you?"

"I sent them home after you told me you'd arrested Ro."

"Their orders were to stay."

"I told them they could go. In fact, I ordered them to go." Glitsky sighed.

"Did your cell phone break?" she asked.

He looked over at her. "Don't bust my chops, woman."

"I'm just saying . . ."

"All right. Noted. But don't. Please. I'm sorry. If I would have thought of it, I would have. But there was no opportunity."

She patted the couch next to her. "Come sit down."

He came over and lowered himself, as though his body ached, onto the couch.

"Have you eaten?" she asked.

"No. But don't get up." He took her hand. "You're all right?"

"We're all fine. It was just scary."

"He's in jail now."

"I know."

"The Curtlees want my badge. I think the mayor does, too."

"Well, he'll learn."

"And then there's your boss."

Beside him, he felt her go a little tense. "Wes? What about him?"

"He wouldn't have arrested Ro yet. He didn't think it was a real threat."

"He wasn't here."

"No. I know that. But he thinks I should have called him first, before I went to pick Ro up. And maybe I should have. Anyway, apparently I've put him in a squeeze."

"Poor Wes."

"He's really unhappy. Furious, even."

"Because you arrested Ro? It was a real threat, Abe. No doubt about it. I wasn't making anything up."

"Nobody thinks you were."

"Except maybe Wes."

"No. He just didn't think . . . he thinks I should have cleared it with him, or a judge. And I probably should have. I probably should have assigned somebody else to set up this arrest."

"I thought your whole team was overbooked."

"It is. But still . . ."

"You can't win."

"No. That's not true. You can win a few." He squeezed her hand. "I just don't want to get in the way of you and Wes."

"You won't."

"He was really upset. Like I've never seen him."

"It's the job," she said. "He's just getting into it and doesn't want to mess it up."

"More than that," Glitsky said, "he doesn't want somebody else to mess it up for him. And I might have just done that."

"You did what you felt you had to do, didn't you?"

"Yes."

"It wasn't illegal or wrong, was it?"

"No. It was legal and right, in fact."

"Well, there you go. How could it hurt you?"

"I don't know." Glitsky shook his head. "And I'm not sure I want to find out."

10

On the following Monday morning, Michael Durbin was driving downtown, having visions.

For reasons he did not fully comprehend, every time Durbin had gotten into his car and started driving lately—since he'd become aware of Ro Curtlee's release into the population—he'd found himself vicariously experiencing the drive that Tony Soprano took at the beginning of every episode of *The Sopranos*, complete with the soundtrack about getting yourself a gun. You got yourself a gun.

It was weird, he thought, but also incredibly realistic, as though he actually was making that drive through New Jersey, smoking a cigar, noting the passing neighborhoods of San Francisco through the side windows and the windshield as he headed out from his parking garage on Union, up through Pacific Heights (where the Curtlees lived), then over the hill into the semi-ghetto of the Western Addition, and finally out on Geary to the Avenues. The vision became especially acute when he turned the last corner before getting to his home. He felt himself inhabiting the guise of the Mafia boss, the determined look on his face, opening his car door and getting out, clearly with an eye to doing someone grave damage.

And once he was in that unbidden, I'm-driving-now mind-set, a host of fantasies seemed to come along for the ride. Killing Ro Curtlee, of course, was the first and originally strongest of them. He could, in fact, go out and get himself a gun. Although they'd never had one in the house, he could remedy that in a few days. And he did have a shotgun, packed back somewhere in his garage.

With either his new pistol or his shotgun, he could then drive up to the Curtlees after nighttime had fallen, wait for Ro to show his face, and simply blow him away.

Would anybody put it together that it had been him? A straight, white, middle-class small-business owner with no criminal record? He didn't see how. He could actually do it and end all of his worries on that score.

But the fantasy wasn't just confined to Ro Curtlee. As often as not, no sooner had he dispatched Ro in his make-believe scenario than the fantasy rotated on some axis and turned his attention to Janice. He found this disconcerting not only because in his conscious mind and stupid heart he loved his wife, but because she had been his rock and support during those difficult years after Ro's trial. She had held the family together, earned the lion's share of the home's income, counseled and stood by Michael as he worked through his transition from promising young portrait artist eking by with a succession of day jobs to established and successful small business owner. She had essentially guided him through the shoals of ego-bound, angst-ridden, artistic immaturity to the terra firma of real, honest work and grown-up responsibility.

Part of him, rather suddenly, hated her for that.

He didn't understand why the catalyst for these negative feelings had been Ro's release from prison, but that's what had started it. Michael had always tried to make himself believe—and he'd sold himself on the idea pretty well—that the suffering he'd endured because of the stand he'd made to the other jurors had been worth it because at least they'd removed the vermin that was Ro Curtlee from society. And all at once, that had changed. Now he clearly saw his idealistic righteousness back then as an empty, meaningless gesture that had accomplished no permanent good.

So why had he given up on his art? And how was that in any way the fault or influence of Janice?

Well, there was a reason.

Even back then, Janice could have been making enough money from her practice to keep them afloat. If she'd gone full-time. But she'd wanted, and *they'd* decided, that they didn't want day care for their children; they would split their time at home as parents.

This was why the loss of Michael's day jobs because of the Curtlees' meddling had posed such an unnecessary financial hardship. But the plain fact—and it had always been a giant elephant in their living room—was that they could have made it. Michael could have gone on painting, working his art, taking the occasional portrait commission, and gone the gallery route, growing his body of work. By now—he was certain that he had been good enough—the painting would have paid off. It might not have made him rich and famous, but he would at least have a name and a reputation. And he would be doing what he loved, what he had always felt he'd been born to do.

But Janice—subtly to be sure, but subtle was her métier—saw her opening and never let up on the pressure for Michael to keep bringing in at least a token income. Whatever it took to prove himself a competent provider, a good husband. So for six or so years, the prime of his life, he'd hauled and delivered loads as a part-time moving man, he'd painted houses; he'd worked as a bartender, a landscaper, a blow-and-go gardener. The art, his painting, had had to slide, until it no longer had been even a hobby.

And Janice had been his helpmeet during the transition, weaning him away from a commitment to his art until it finally seemed like his own idea to get her father to invest in his UPS franchise. And because Michael was smart, organized, and diligent, that business had succeeded and now thrived. And Janice had loved him because he'd become the man she'd always wanted him to be—dutiful, hardworking, mature.

And maybe, honestly, Michael thought, that would have been enough. Maybe he could continue to forgive her for that, to realize that this was the trade-off he'd bargained for and eventually agreed to—the woman he loved and the family she wanted in exchange for his earlier vision of himself as a creative person, an artist, and, in her estimation—implied but never stated—some species of flake.

He supposed, maybe even believed, that it would have all been worth it, worth sacrificing his art and his essential self, to keep Janice happy. Just like it would have been worth all his suffering at the hands of the Curtlees if Ro had stayed in prison.

It would have been worth it if Janice had stayed faithful to him.

Now it didn't seem as if it was because—he was sure—Janice was having an affair with one of her patients.

———

With the echoing refrain about getting himself a gun playing nonstop in his brain, Michael Durbin pulled into the lot across the street from the Hall of Justice—$20 A DAY/NO IN & OUT. Court wouldn't go into session for over an hour, but in spite of the early time, the parking lot was nearly full, the curb alongside Bryant Street packed two deep with police patrol cars and other official vehicles, and a caravan of local and national TV vans.

Durbin got out of his car, paid the attendant, and buttoned his raincoat against the continuing mist. Across the street, the gray stucco of the Hall of Justice showed as a deep bruised blue in the damp. He stopped at the edge of a decent and so far peaceful crowd of perhaps a hundred souls on the steps out front, many of them holding signs exhorting whoever it might be to FREE RO and LET RO GO and STOP POLICE BRUTALITY and so on. Somewhat more prosaically one sign read, SF COPS SUCK THE BIG ONE.

Free speech, Durbin thought. Ain't it grand?

Part of the crowd seemed happy to demonstrate outside, but others were moving toward the entrance to the building, albeit slowly. Reporters and anchorpeople with microphones were descending upon unwitting citizens all over the place. With a shock that felt like a blow to his solar plexus, Durbin recognized the woman he'd long ago nicknamed Heinous Marrenas on the crowd's periphery. And it suddenly occurred to him that these "protesters" had probably been bought and paid for by the Curtlees. Everywhere he looked, people were holding copies of the morning *Courier*, where Ro's arrest and demands for Glitsky's resignation dominated the front page.

Durbin wanted no part of Marrenas or any of them. So he got into the portion of the crowd that slowly was snaking its way into the building. Five minutes later, he had passed through the doors and then the metal detectors inside.

Now he stood in the cavernous lobby, his stomach churning with nerves and relief at having dodged Marrenas. Part of himself was still wondering why he'd felt the need to take the morning off and come down to see this spectacle for himself. Suddenly he turned and found himself looking at his brother-in-law. Chuck Novio had just turned his head and saw him at the same time, and he raised a hand in greeting.

Getting over to him, Durbin said, "Okay, Chuckie boy, I've got an excuse. For my peace of mind, I need to make sure they get Ro back in jail where he belongs. But what are you doing here?"

Novio wore his easy smile. "Hello? American history. This is what I do. And if this isn't history, I don't know what is. Besides, this is the kind of stuff my kids eat up. Makes 'em believe that history's happening all around them all the time. Which, of course, it is."

"This isn't history, Chuck. This is a scumbag."

Novio said, "Are you kidding? History is just one scumbag after another, muddling along in an endless chain. That's why it's so great."

"I admire your enthusiasm," Durbin said. "But you should have told me yesterday at dinner you were coming down for this. We could have driven together."

"I didn't really decide until I got up this morning and figured I really should. And I didn't know you were coming anyway."

"I didn't say so last night? Maybe I hadn't made up my mind by then, either." Durbin paused. "So how do you think it's going to go?" he asked.

"I think he stays in jail."

"I'm hoping."

"How can he not?"

Durbin cocked his head toward the rabble. "Check out the crowd. You ever hear of the Curtlees?"

Novio shrugged. "The guy's a convicted murderer who beat up a couple of cops while resisting arrest. Put any spin on it you want, no judge in the world lets him back out."

"Let's hope you're right."

"I'm right. Want to put some money on it?"

"No. I want you to be right."

"But if we bet and I'm wrong, then you win anyway. I'll give you two to one."

Durbin, weary, stuck out his hand. "Twenty," he said.

Novio reached for his hand and they shook. "Done."

———

Department 11 had hard theater-style seating for about eighty people, and Durbin and Novio, early as they were, stood in a long line and as it was barely made it inside. They took the only two seats left in the next-to-last row.

The story of Ro Curtlee's arrest had not just been front-page news in the *Courier* yesterday in the Sunday edition of the paper, but it had also made headlines in the *Chronicle* and been the lead feature on every television network news program throughout the day. One of these broadcasts had been the last thing Durbin had seen before going to bed last night, alone—Janice called out after they'd all gotten back from Sunday night dinner at the Novios to an emergency session with one of her patients. Durbin had a good guess which one it was, although not his exact identity.

So he'd watched the news and heard sound bites from the haggard, unkempt district attorney Wes Farrell, the outraged mayor Leland Crawford opining that perhaps it was time for a special commission to address the "culture of violence and disregard of due process" within the police department, and—of course—Cliff and Theresa Curtlee bemoaning the injustice of it all and calling for the arrest of Lieutenant Glitsky rather than of their poor boy.

Both Curtlee parents were in the front row in the courtroom, and seeing them so close, Durbin's bile rose again. "Those smug fuckers," he whispered to Novio. "I wonder if they actually believe Ro didn't do any of this or if they just don't care. I mean, how do you go on supporting your son if you know he's a killer, a literal killer?"

Novio, enjoying the buzz in the room, straining for a glimpse of them, said, "Maybe the person he killed, she's so far down the evolutionary or economic scale you don't think she counts as a human being. Either that, or he had a good reason. Good enough, anyway."

Durbin shook his head. "Good enough. Right."

Now, several of the players had begun to appear in the courtroom through the back doorway that led to some holding cells and the judges' chambers. Two bailiffs led the way, followed by an elderly woman who took the court reporter's seat in front of the judge's bench and another younger woman, the court clerk, who sat at a table next to the court reporter.

When he saw the next people come through the door—a man and a woman, both in full police uniform—Durbin leaned over to Novio. "That's Glitsky, the guy with the hawk nose and the scar. And Vi Lapeer, the new police chief."

Next came Farrell, his eyes still bloodshot but wearing a well-fitted and expensive-looking dark suit with a white shirt and red power tie.

Just behind him was another woman whom Durbin recognized. "What's she doing here?" he asked Chuck.

"Who?"

"The one with the legs. Amanda Jenkins."

"How do you know her?"

"She was the prosecutor in Ro's trial. I didn't know she was involved in this."

"I'm starting to think everybody but the dogcatcher's involved in this."

By now, Glitsky and Lapeer had passed through the low railing that separated the gallery area from the courtroom's bull pen. They took seats in the reserved section of the first row next to a pair of young uniformed police officers—one white and one black—while Farrell and Jenkins got themselves settled at the prosecutor's table, just in front of them. Even from his relatively distant seat, Durbin fancied he could almost feel the chill between the two prosecutors.

At the defense table, a well-dressed, elderly white-maned man sat. At some perhaps prearranged signal from one of the bailiffs, the man got up and, turning, said something to the Curtlees where they sat in the front row. Finally, nodding, he walked through the courtroom to the back door by the judge's podium, and on out.

"Showtime," Novio said.

Durbin swallowed against a rising nervousness. "Getting close."

Behind them, an energy shift rumbled through the gallery and Durbin turned in time to see the mayor himself, Leland Crawford, come through the back door chatting in a serious vein with Sheila Marrenas. He went up and, after getting the attention of everyone in the courtroom, sat in an empty, obviously previously reserved, seat next to Cliff Curtlee. At this move, Amanda Jenkins whispered something to Farrell and the district attorney, apparently startled, half turned in his chair to see for himself. The message couldn't have been clearer.

With absolutely no fanfare, the Curtlees' lawyer reentered through the back door with his client.

The last time Durbin had seen Ro Curtlee, on the day of the original verdict against him nearly ten years before, he'd been a clean-shaven, good-looking young man with short-cropped hair, wearing a three-piece business suit and tie. Now, shackled hand and foot in his orange prisoner's jumpsuit, jail slippers, and with a large cast on his slinged left arm, Ro was the picture of middle-aged dejection and defeat. His uncombed over-the-ears hair and general unshaven, disheveled appearance added to the impression, as did a still-swollen mouth, a bandage over the bridge of his nose, and a black eye. As he shuffled through the courtroom with his lawyer on his way to the defense table, the gallery first and briefly went silent, and then broke into a low roar of indignant reaction.

Novio, smiling next to his brother-in-law, leaned over and, his hand covering his mouth, whispered, "Good move. Going for the sympathy vote."

Durbin started to pick up some antipolice slurs—Nazis, thugs, bastards—from the other side of the gallery, but before they got out of hand, Ro got himself seated next to his lawyer at the defense table, and the bailiff came into the courtroom by the judge's podium and bellowed, "All rise. Department Eleven of the Superior Court of the State of California is now in session, Judge Erin Donahoe presiding."

· 11

At first glance, Donahoe's diminutive size seemed of a piece with a low-key, even shy personality. When she was thoughtful or amused, her features were not unattractive—a bobbed little nose, light blue eyes, fashionable rimless eyeglasses, and shoulder-length light hair shining enough for a shampoo commercial. When challenged or confronted by turbulent forces, however, the look changed quickly and dramatically—the eyes squinted down, the laugh lines around them vanishing into exaggerated crow's feet, the small mouth pursed into a disapproving button, a flush tending to rise into her cheeks. Now, as she ascended the podium, it was clear that something had already compromised her composure. She wore an air of defensiveness around her as obvious as her formless black robes.

As the gallery sat with her, she cast a dark eye on Ro Curtlee—Durbin couldn't tell if it was in reaction to his injuries and general appearance or because she knew he was a rapist and killer. But the look didn't soften as she brought her gaze to the prosecution table, and then up to the gallery, which hung quietly—now even more quietly—in anticipation.

"Let me state for the record," she began in a low voice that barely carried to the bar rail, much less the back of the courtroom, "that I've got eighty-five lines and thirteen preliminary hearings to get through today, and I mean to get through them all." Cases in superior court are called "lines"—each defendant taking up one line on the computer printout prepared for the calendar courtroom.

96

"At the request of Mr. Farrell, I'm going to call Line Twelve first. I expect to get this circus out of my courtroom so I can get down to business. Would counsel announce their appearances, please?"

After they'd done so, Donahoe announced that she wanted to make it clear that this was an arraignment and bail hearing, not a preliminary hearing. "We're not spending all morning on this. Mr. Farrell, understood?"

"Yes, Your Honor."

"Mr. Denardi?"

"Clear, Your Honor."

"All right. Would the clerk call the line, please?"

From her desk, the clerk didn't even look up: "Line Twelve, *The People of the State of California versus Roland Curtlee.*"

"Mr. Denardi, does your client waive instruction and arraignment?"

Denardi, on his feet. "Yes, Your Honor."

"Plea?"

Prompted by his lawyer, Ro Curtlee stood up and said, "Not guilty."

Donahoe stayed with the logistics. "Before discussing a time waiver, counsel, I take it you want to argue bail."

All sense of decorum and procedure immediately dissolved. Denardi, still on his feet, came out swinging. "If it please the court. In the course of a bogus no-warrant arrest by Lieutenant Glitsky and two other officers, my client was severely beaten on Saturday night, some of the results of which you can see here today . . ."

"Your Honor." Amanda Jenkins jumped up at her table. "I object to counsel's description of a 'bogus' arrest. Defendant had gone to Lieutenant Glitsky's home and threatened him and his family, which under Penal Code Section Four twenty-two . . ."

"Your Honor, if I may." Denardi didn't wait for permission to speak, and Donahoe made no attempt to stop him. "Counsel's characterization of Mr. Curtlee's personal visit to Lieutenant Glitsky's home as a threat that rises to the level of four twenty-two is absurd and completely unsupported by any facts or evidence."

Counsel are usually expected to direct all their remarks to the judge, but they were already long past that and Donahoe didn't seem inclined or even able to stop them. Jenkins turned and spoke directly to Denardi. "You're denying he went to Glitsky's home?"

The elderly defense attorney shook his head as though something amused him. "No, he went to the lieutenant's home, all right, but more or less to lodge a personal protest about the fact that the lieutenant had come to Mr. Curtlee's home just the previous night, and for just as little reason."

"Just as little reason? You can't be serious. Lieutenant Glitsky was investigating the murder of a witness in Mr. Curtlee's previous case. That's a compelling reason."

"If you believe that's really what it was, and not pure harassment."

"Well, gosh, maybe I won't just accept your bought-and-paid-for opinion, Counselor. But that's what the evidence shows." Jenkins swung back to the judge. "Your Honor, these allegations of harassment and police brutality are ridiculous on their face. The witnesses in Mr. Curtlee's previous case are being murdered one by one. Any sane person has to know that Mr. Curtlee is in this up to his neck."

"Ridiculous!" Denardi exploded, giving full voice to his rage. "Just look at the man! What's ridiculous has been his treatment at the hands of the police. He's been battered half to death. You call this . . . ?"

Suddenly Donahoe seemed to realize that the give-and-take in the courtroom had gotten completely out of her control, and she cleared her throat and lightly tapped her gavel. "Ms. Jenkins, Mr. Denardi. Let's not get into a personal squabble here, all right? I'm sure we'll get to the bottom of this and resolve it to everyone's satisfaction. Would you both mind sitting down, please? Thank you. Now, moving along, Mr. Farrell, do the people have information for bail purposes?"

After the near brawl that had been developing, the silence that suddenly reigned in the courtroom was unsettling. It took Farrell a few seconds to get to his feet. "Your Honor," he began, "the defendant is currently awaiting trial for murder and has been out on bail since his release from state prison. Within days of his release, one of the witnesses in his murder trial has been killed. After Lieutenant Glitsky went to question him about his whereabouts at the time of that murder, the next day Mr. Curtlee went to the lieutenant's home and threatened him and his family."

Denardi wasn't going to let this pass and again rose to his feet. "Your Honor, we've heard this before and it's simply not true."

Farrell, again ignoring protocol because Donahoe didn't seem to care about it, turned to his opponent. "It's absolutely true, Tristan, and you know it."

"I know nothing of the sort, Wes. You tell me one word of actual threat that Mr. Curtlee said. Or even that Glitsky alleges he said."

"He pointed at Glitsky's daughter and made a point of saying she was a nice-looking child."

Raising his hands theatrically Denardi let out a laugh and turned to the judge. "I rest my case, Your Honor. Calling a child nice-looking is hardly a threat."

Now Farrell raised his own voice, losing his temper. "*Going to the house, by itself, is a threat.* Mr. Curtlee's a convicted rapist and murderer out on bail. He's a suspect in the murder of the chief witness and he went to the house of the police inspector assigned to the case. You'd have to be crazy not to see what's going on here."

Again, finally, Donahoe lowered her gavel. "Gentlemen," she said. "Please." Then, "Mr. Farrell, I believe you were talking about bail. What was the original bail, by the way?"

"On the murder, ten million dollars, Your Honor. When officers tried to arrest Mr. Curtlee in this case, he took a gun and tried to kill one of them. Attempted murder of a police officer is a no-bail offense."

Nodding sagely, she asked, "Who set the bail on the murder?"

"Judge Baretto."

"And what are the people requesting this time around?"

"We want the scheduled bail, Your Honor. No bail in light of the current offenses and the defendant's history."

"Ridiculous!" Denardi said. "That's insane."

Donahoe simply nodded, acknowledging the interruption, but tacitly condoning it.

"And what are the charges, exactly, this time?" she asked.

Farrell looked down at his notes, impassive in the face of what he knew to be more problems. He and Glitsky and Jenkins were at least on relatively firm ground charging Ro with the one count of threatening an executive officer that Glitsky had gone down to arrest him for. But the fracas during the arrest had overshadowed that original charge and now Farrell was stuck with Glitsky's and Jenkins' egregious overcharging. But there was nothing for it. He had to brazen it through. "One count of threatening an executive officer (four twenty-two), one count of attempted murder on a police officer (six sixty-four/one eighty-seven). Three counts assault on a police officer with a deadly weapon (two forty-five[d][one]), both of these latter two with firearm enhancement. Three counts," Farrell went on, "battery on a police officer (two forty-three[b]). All charges with a twelve-oh-two-two point one enhancement, since the defendant incurred these charges while he was out on bail."

"Your Honor!" Denardi again, on his feet. "There was no attempted murder. One of the officer's duty weapons fell out of its holster and Mr. Curtlee picked it up."

"And pulled the trigger," Jenkins said.

"I don't think so, Amanda. And beyond that, Your Honor, the alleged assault was pure self-defense. The police arrived at his house without a warrant and then attacked Mr. Curtlee when he went outside to find out what was going on with more police presence out in his street. This was a bogus arrest, as I've said before. Anyone would have resisted it, would have been justified resisting it, even with force."

This speech got a little rise out of the gallery, and yet again, Donahoe made no effort to control it, but rather let it run its course.

"Your Honor," Farrell said over the slowly subsiding hum. "All three police officers involved in the arrest are in the courtroom and are willing to testify about—"

But here, finally, Donahoe seemed to disapprove. Her mouth went tight and the flush came up in her face. "We're not turning this into a preliminary hearing, Mr. Farrell. I believe I made that clear during my opening comments. The question is about bail. And, to be honest, I'm tempted to send it back over to Judge Baretto and see what he thinks we ought to do."

"Your Honor." Jenkins stood up next to Farrell and tried with only minimal success to keep her voice neutral. "With respect, as Mr. Farrell has already said, the people seek no bail at all. Not even at the ten-million-dollar level. That the defendant has been allowed back on the street at all is a mockery of the judicial process."

"Now, now," Donahoe said. "I don't know if that's a little too strong . . ."

"It's a mockery, all right," Denardi said, again rising and getting into the act. "But it's these charges that are a mockery. Not only fabricated and vindictive, they're—"

"All right, all right, Mr. Denardi, that's enough. I take your point. Now just give me a minute here, would you all?" The judge looked down and ruffled through some pages in front of her. Picking up her pen, she made a few notes while the courtroom hung in suspense. Finally she looked up and offered a confident smile first to the prosecution table, then over to the defense. Mixed signals everywhere it was possible to send them. "I think Judge Baretto's set a bit of a precedent here. Due to the questions about the legality of the arrest itself and so forth, I believe a reasonable bail would be five hundred thousand dollars."

At these words, the courtroom exploded into applause that got interrupted by Jenkins, who could no longer restrain herself. "Your Honor!" she exploded.

"Oh, counsel," Donahoe said. "There's no jury here. You don't have to make a speech to impress anybody. You know as well as I do that defendants have rights. We'll get to the bottom of all this"— apparently one of Donahoe's pet phrases—"the charges and so on, after the preliminary hearing. And at that time, I'm making a note to revisit the bail question in light of the facts that come out during that hearing."

Another wave of what was clearly approbation made itself felt in the gallery, and Donahoe smiled, acknowledging that she'd made a crowd-pleasing decision. "Now, Mr. Denardi," Donahoe went on, "I assume that you'd have no objection to waiving time."

She was asking the defense counsel if he'd agree to postpone the preliminary hearing of his client beyond the ten days that the law provided. And of course it was to Ro's great advantage that Denardi did this. And then he'd waive time after the preliminary hearing so the trial wouldn't start within the sixty days the law provided, either. In fact, this was the beginning of the defense's orchestrated delaying tactics that could postpone a trial for a year or more.

"Your Honor!" Again Jenkins stood, although by now she was running out of steam. "The people object to waiving time."

Donahoe looked not unkindly down at her. "Thank you, counsel, but of course counsel is entitled to time to prepare. Mr. Denardi?"

"Defense will waive time, Your Honor. We're going to need considerable time to do a background check on these arresting officers. Two months from today to set?"

"Granted."

"Thank you."

"You're welcome." Donahoe looked down for one last time at Farrell and Jenkins and gave them a slight shrug of her shoulders, as if telling them she didn't have much of a choice in the matter of her rulings. Then, moving along, she nodded to her clerk. "Call the next line," she said.

Everybody was standing up, clearing room for the next case.

Durbin watched Ro Curtlee break into a smile and rise at the defense table with his attorney. Turning around, Ro reached over the bar rail, nodded at the mayor, shook his father's hand, and put an arm around his mother, drawing her in with a hug.

No sign of pain now, Durbin noted. No hint of hangdog.

"What a travesty," he whispered to his brother-in-law. "I'm trying to believe this, and I don't know if I can."

"It's a great country," Novio said. "You gotta love it."

Durbin found that he couldn't keep his eyes off the man he'd helped send to prison so many years ago. Ro broke from his mother's embrace and looked out over the gallery. When his eyes got to Durbin, he stopped for a long beat.

Could it be that he recognized him?

Durbin quickly looked down and away, avoiding eye contact, his heart suddenly a pumping jackhammer in his ears. When he felt it was safe, that Ro had moved on to someone else, he again looked up. Sure enough, Ro's gaze had now brought him back around to the front, where Glitsky and Lapeer and the two younger officers had come up to the bar rail by Farrell and Jenkins, all of them clearly dejected and angry.

Durbin might have been afraid to have any eye contact with Ro

Curtlee, but that didn't seem to be Glitsky's problem. When Ro's line of sight got to the lieutenant, the two of them stared at each other for a long moment. Ro put his smile back on, shook his head as though they'd all just enjoyed a good prank together, and pointed a finger at Glitsky. Then, to Durbin's shock, he cocked his thumb and "shot" him.

Glitsky didn't react in any way. His face a solemn mask, the scar white through his lips, he kept up his stare until, at last, Ro looked away.

"Jesus," Durbin said.

"What?"

"You see that?"

"Yeah, I did. Your Ro's a pretty ballsy guy."

"He scares the shit out of me. I think he might have just recognized me."

"And what would that mean?"

"I don't know." Durbin threw a quick glance back up to the front, where Ro was still talking to the mayor and his parents and his attorney and one of the bailiffs, trying to get them moving, get him out of the jail clothes, and get his new bail processed. "Maybe nothing," Durbin said. "But if it is anything, it's trouble."

"After all these years, I don't think so."

Durbin shrugged. "I hope you're right." He breathed out heavily. "Maybe I shouldn't have come down here to see this. If he's going after people from his last trial and he sees me . . ."

Novio put a hand on Durbin's arm. "Easy, Michael. If he went after this woman from his last trial, it was because she was going to be part of his next one. You, not the same at all."

"Okay. I guess you're right."

Why, Durbin wondered, had he come down here after all? Probably, he thought, because he had wanted to see his work finished at last, this criminal back in jail where he forever belonged. And now that had not happened and he suddenly realized that he was very frightened—he didn't want any part of Ro or any of the Curtlees even marginally aware of his own life.

By now the rows behind them had cleared and they started filing out with the crowd. In a couple of minutes, they were outside in the hallway, Durbin now anxious to be gone, to be no part of this anymore.

But the hallway was a crush of humanity, only a small percentage of it moving toward the stairway. Everybody else milling, talking, caught up in the drama, maybe waiting for the opportunity to rub an actual elbow with the mayor.

Durbin made a half turn into an opening before him in the throng and found himself shoulder-to-shoulder with Sheila Marrenas. She had her microphone out and was interviewing some of the random people who'd been inside the courtroom. Durbin had no sooner recognized her than she turned and stuck the microphone up into his face. "Hello, Sheila Marrenas of the *Courier*. Quick comment, sir. In light of what we heard in there about the arrest of Ro Curtlee, do you think that we've got a serious problem with police brutality here in San Francisco?"

Before he'd even thought about it, he found himself answering. "Not really, no. Nowhere near as serious as the problem with judges continuing to give rapists and murderers a get-out-of-jail-free card."

Obviously surprised at his answer—most of the "regular citizens" she'd quote in tomorrow's article were ringers, supplied by the Curtlees—she stepped back and looked up at him, studying his face while her own took on a questioning look. "Don't I know you?" she asked.

"I don't think so," he said. "I'm sure I'd remember."

She kept looking at him.

"If you'll excuse me," he said, "I'm trying to get to the stairs."

OUR TOWN

By Sheila Marrenas

Tyranny advances by small increments.

Just last week, as recounted in this column, Roland Curtlee, the son of the publishers of this newspaper, was released on bail while he awaits a retrial for a crime that he may or may not have committed over a decade ago. Though convicted in the homicide of a woman with whom he admittedly had an intimate relationship, Mr. Curtlee was recently ordered released from prison, citing prejudice against him in the courtroom during his trial, by the Ninth Circuit Court of Appeal. While his lawyers prepare for his new trial, Mr. Curtlee was released on bail. And there matters should have remained, and no doubt would have remained if not for the extra legal efforts of San Francisco's police department, and in particular its head of homicide, Lieutenant Abraham Glitsky.

Glitsky had been the chief investigator in the original case against Mr. Curtlee and a prosecution witness during the trial. Within days of Mr. Curtlee's release from jail, another witness in Mr. Curtlee's trial, Felicia Nuñez, died in a fire in her apartment. Although this death has not been ruled a murder, Glitsky took it upon himself to call upon Mr. Curtlee at his home, ostensibly to verify his alibi for the time of the woman's death, but in fact Glitsky did not conduct a formal interrogation at all. The visit, then, served no purpose other than to harass Mr. Curtlee.

Wishing to discuss this issue further with Glitsky, Mr. Curtlee called on the lieutenant at his home the next day, an act that Glitsky quickly and spuriously labeled a threat to him and his family. With this "threat" as his pretext, Glitsky again appeared with other policemen at Mr.

Curtlee's home. Showing no warrant and in complete disregard for Mr. Curtlee's rights, Glitsky tried to place him under arrest. When Mr. Curtlee demanded an explanation, officers attacked and badly beat him.

In the ensuing melee, the police battered Mr. Curtlee about the head and shoulders, causing multiple lacerations on his scalp and face, and breaking his arm, before they manhandled him into their waiting police car for the trip downtown.

Yesterday, charged with several absurd criminal counts, including attempted murder, this farcical (were it not tragic) travesty of justice came to an end when Judge Erin Donahoe once again released Mr. Curtlee on bail, and this in spite of the show of force orchestrated by police, with the new chief of police, Vi Lapeer, in attendance along with District Attorney Wes Farrell, Assistant Chief DA Amanda Jenkins, and Glitsky himself along with the two other arresting officers.

Rarely have the police in our town so clearly demonstrated their utter disregard for privacy, civil rights, and due process as it has in this case. The fact that Lieutenant Glitsky remains in a position of authority argues strongly that this unconstitutional behavior, and police brutality in general, is condoned by law enforcement and prosecutors at the highest levels. And when the rule of law goes out the window, as it so clearly has in this case, we may be sure that tyranny has taken another step forward, and a true police state is that much closer to becoming reality.

12

On the following Friday morning, Glitsky came out of his bedroom at a few minutes after seven and stopped a minute at the kitchen door to watch his daughter work on her pancakes. Intent as a sculptor, Rachel was wiping a loaded forkful around her plate, catching every possible drop of syrup, humming quietly to herself. Finally, quick as a mouse, she brought the bite to her mouth and popped it in, only now looking up and seeing her father. Having her mouth full didn't stop her from breaking into a grin and talking. "Daddy's up."

"That he is. How's my sweetie pie this morning?"

"Good."

He came over and kissed the top of her head. "We'll continue after you've swallowed, okay?" Walking over to the stove, only a couple of steps in their small kitchen, he poured water from the simmering teakettle into the cup that Treya had waiting for him on the counter. When he turned around, he saw that Rachel had scrunched her face into a question mark. "Is today Saturday?" she asked.

"Nope."

A pause. "Are you wearing your bathrobe to work?"

"Sure."

"Really?"

"Really. I thought it would be fun. What do you think?"

"I didn't think they'd let you."

"Who?"

"Everybody."

"You think somebody would try to stop me? What if I gave them my look?"

"What look?"

"This one." With his scar, his hawklike nose, and jutting brow, Glitsky had a fearsome visage when he frowned, and now he leaned in close and gave his daughter his best shot, accompanied by a threatening growl.

She broke into laughter.

"Hey," Glitsky said, "that's supposed to scare you. What kind of a cop would I be if I couldn't scare people?"

"Maybe you scare other people, but not me. I know when you're teasing."

"I wasn't teasing. I was practicing."

"You better practice more, then."

Glitsky sat down, sipped at his tea. "You're right. Maybe I'd better. Where's your mom?"

"Back with Zack. I think he wet again." She went back to her pancakes for a minute, and when her mouth was completely full, she said, "You're not really wearing your bathrobe to work, are you?"

"Really? No. I'm just a little slow getting dressed this morning."

"Mom was, too, you know."

"I didn't know that."

"She had on her bathrobe, too."

"She did? Maybe we'll start a club."

———

Glitsky rarely took a day off. When he'd had his heart attack and then, not so long after that, had been shot, he'd drawn down significantly on his sick leave. His recovery from the shooting featured medical complications too numerous to mention and he'd gone on long-term disability for the better part of two years. In short, during his career the city of San Francisco had already paid him for five hundred and thirty-two days—he'd counted and kept track—when he hadn't gone in to work. This bothered him. He figured that was more than enough and he generally felt that it wouldn't be right to take any more, especially when he wasn't sick.

Likewise, except for the births of Rachel and Zachary, Treya hadn't taken a day off for the whole time she'd worked for Wes Farrell's predecessor, Clarence Jackman. Now she was only a few weeks into Farrell's administration, and she didn't want to make an unfavorable impression on her new boss by missing work before he clearly understood that she wasn't the kind of person who took days off when it suited her.

Now Treya came into the kitchen and stopped when she saw her husband, sitting drinking tea in his bathrobe. She only had time to give him a quick questioning look before Zachary barged his way in around her and over to the table. Their son had been hit by a car the year before and now wore a helmet against further brain trauma whenever he was awake and ambulatory. He got into his chair and looked in disbelief at his plate. "Rachel ate my pancakes!"

"You weren't here."

"I was, too!"

"But you left."

"Hey, hey, hey." Treya came over to the table. "Stop bickering. I'll make some more pancakes for both of you two. Abe? How about you? The batter's all ready."

"I could probably force myself. Thanks."

"More pancakes, coming up," Treya said.

"Hey!" Zachary asked. "How come you aren't dressed yet?"

"Hay is for horses," Glitsky said. "And I'm taking a day off."

At the stove, Treya stopped ladling batter into the frying pan. "Really?"

Glitsky nodded. "Really."

"What are you going to do?"

"Nothing. Maybe go to lunch. Maybe see my dad. Think about things."

Treya leaned against the stove, her arms crossed over her chest. "How'd you like some company?"

"I wasn't going to ask," he said, "but if you're offering, I'd like it a lot."

———

Durbin got into work, letting himself in through the back door, about a half hour late. He received an arched eyebrow from Liza Sato, his assistant manager, as she turned around and spotted him, but he simply evaded the unspoken question with a wave and a stop at the coffee machine.

Twenty-eight years old, personable, super-competent, single, and very easy on the eyes, Liza was in Durbin's opinion one of the main reasons that the business was so successful. She'd opened the place on time this morning, as she had on the previous Monday when he'd gone down for Ro Curtlee's arraignment. The franchise handled UPS, FedEx, and Parcel Dispatch, and was a registered Postal Service office as well, and this morning, by the time Durbin got there, customers stood in lines at every one of the seven workstations.

About a half hour later, the morning rush just about abated, Durbin's private telephone line rang in his office. He walked back inside the half-enclosed glass cubicle and picked it up on the second ring.

He had barely finished saying hello when he recognized the voice of his neighbor from across the street. "Mike. Thank God you're there. You've got to get back home right away. Your house is on fire."

———

On the way out, blowing through streetlights and stop signs, almost praying he'd be pulled over, Durbin tried Janice's numbers on his cell phone and got nothing but her outgoing messages.

He caught his first glimpse of the smoke—lots of smoke—as soon as he'd cleared the escarpment that ran from Union up to Broadway. He was still two or three miles away and the dark plume had already risen in the still, clear air to the height of the Sutro Tower. This was no small grease fire in a kitchen. Tires squealing, he finally turned onto his street, Rivera, and immediately saw that he wasn't going to get within a couple hundred yards of his house, which in spite of the presence of six fire trucks spraying water from at least four hoses still looked to be completely engulfed in flames.

———

Janice's sister, Kathy Novio, stood next to Durbin by the incident commander's station near one of the trucks. Her arms folded over her heavy jacket, she made no effort to conceal the tears that coursed down her cheeks. "I can't stand this," she said.

"I know. Me, neither."

"I keep thinking she might be in there."

Durbin put his arm around her. "We don't have any reason to think that."

"Michael, she wasn't at work." After she'd gotten Durbin's call, immediately before she'd come up here to the fire scene, Kathy had driven by Janice's office over by the Stonestown shopping center, which was relatively near her own home, and even though the lights weren't on, she wanted to be certain and so she banged on the door for almost a full minute to no avail.

"I know. You said that. That doesn't mean she's in there. She might be on some errand she didn't tell me about."

"With her phone off?"

Durbin shrugged. "Sometimes she forgets to turn it on. Sometimes she forgets it entirely. Why would she be in there anyway?"

"I don't know." Her eyes went back to the now-gutted house. The flames were mostly contained by now, although men still worked a couple of the hoses and a pillar of thick, black smoke continued to rise into the sky. Her voice broke. "I'm just so afraid that she is."

Durbin reached over, put his arm around her shoulders, drew her in next to him.

———

Chuck came jogging up from where he'd parked a couple of blocks away. Kathy threw her arms around her husband and he embraced her, patting her back consolingly and whispering words of comfort. Then, over her shoulder, he said to Durbin, "I'm sorry it took so long to get here. I didn't check my messages until after my morning class." His eyes went to the house. "God, Michael, Jesus." Then he paused in a kind of double take. "Where's Janice?"

Kathy, blotched and tearful, made a mewling little noise and just shook her head against him.

"We don't know," Durbin replied. "Not at work. Not answering her phone."

Chuck threw a glance at the smoldering ruins, came back to Durbin, gesturing now toward the firemen. "Do these guys know anything?"

"Not yet. The arson inspector couldn't get inside until, like, five minutes ago."

But even as Durbin spoke, the arson inspector—Arnie Becker—emerged from the front door. He'd stuck his hands deeply into the pockets of his coat and walked, leaning slightly forward as though into a stiff wind, with a slow deliberation. His shoulders sagged. Looking up, his eyes glanced over where Durbin stood—the incident commander had introduced them to each other soon after Durbin's arrival—and then quickly he looked away. In a few more steps, he'd come up to the IC's table.

Durbin, who'd moved away from the immediate area when his brother-in-law had come up, now broke out of their little knot of neighbors and other onlookers and got back over to the table in time to hear Becker say the word *police*.

"What do you need the police for?" Durbin asked.

The two men turned to look at him. The expressions on both of their faces were so obvious that neither of them really had to say anything, but Becker reached out a hand and placed it gently on Durbin's arm. "I'm sorry," he said, "but there's a woman's body in there in one of the upstairs rooms."

Kathy and Chuck had come up directly behind him, and now she split the air with a keening scream. "Janice! Oh God, no! Janice!" As Chuck turned and held her, she covered her face with both of her hands and broke down.

———

After they left messages at their jobs saying they wouldn't be in, both leaving their excuses suitably vague, Abe and Treya dropped the kids off together at their respective school and preschool, then had come home and gone back to bed. Closing in on noon, they had finally gotten dressed and now sat in a booth at Gaspare's.

"This is the best pizza in the city, you know that?" Treya said. "I don't care about any of those newfangled places, or even the other old ones."

"Tommaso's?" Glitsky said.

"Very good, no question. Just not this good."

"A-sixteen."

Treya shook her head. "Again, delicious, but too long a wait. So let me ask you a question."

"General category of pizza?"

"No."

"Okay, hold it." Glitsky put down his pizza slice. "No, wait, it's coming to me. The Battle of Thermopylae."

"Wrong. The what?"

"The Battle of Thermopylae. And how can you say it's wrong when you don't know what it is?"

"I know what it is, or was. It was a battle between the Greeks and somebody, maybe the Persians, I think."

"Correct. Very good. What year?"

"What year? I'm sure. Sometime around ancient Greece. Close enough?"

"How about four-eighty BC."

"I'd say definitely yes. What a relief to have that nailed down. That sounds just perfectly right."

"It is completely right. And yet you said it was wrong."

"It was wrong because it definitely wasn't the answer to my question, which was going to be, if I remember correctly, if you felt as guilty as I did."

"What's it going to be now?"

"What's what going to be?"

"Your question."

She shook her head, smiling. "That silver tongue of yours got to wagging so much I don't even remember."

"Something about if I felt guilty." He reached over the table and put his hand over hers. "You really feel guilty?"

She cocked her head sideways. "A little bit." Now sighing. "I feel like I'm letting Wes down. He's clueless enough about his appointments and his schedule as it is anyway. If I'm not there to spoonfeed him . . ."

"He's a big boy."

"Not so much, really. And pretty much out of his depth."

"I've noticed."

"You're not the only one. I know you don't read the *Courier*, but he's taking some pretty serious abuse there."

"That paper's a rag. Nobody reads it."

"Well, that's half right. The 'rag' part. But don't kid yourself, Abe. People read it. It swings a lot of votes."

Glitsky shrugged. Votes were not part of his universe. And his respect for those people to whom votes were the issue was minuscule. "I don't know. You want my opinion, Wes deserves to swing in the wind a little."

"I don't know how you can say that, Abe. He came down on the right side with you last week."

"Only under great duress. And let's not forget that the reason Ro Curtlee's out in the first place, and the reason we got threatened, is because Wes didn't step up and do the right thing the first chance he got. He could have demanded no bail, and got it."

Now she covered his hand with hers. "I know that. He was naive, hoping to keep the Curtlees happy. He knows that, too, now. And I know you did the right thing. But I don't think Ro would dare do anything to us now."

Glitsky made a face. "Well, that's the hope. I'd be a lot happier if Wes pushed a little on getting his new trial date set. But as to whether I feel guilty taking a day off . . . I don't plan to make a habit of it, but after Monday, and now he's out again, and I still don't have enough inspectors or the budget to hire more." He let out a breath. "I don't know, Trey. I feel I'm a toxic presence at the Hall, and I've got to let some of this anger leach out before I poison my own troops. If I'm going to do that, I might as well quit altogether."

"Are you really thinking about that?"

"Sometimes. Frequently, in fact. I don't know what the point is anymore."

"Same as it's always been, babe. Putting killers in jail."

"Yeah," Glitsky said. "But then they let 'em out."

"Not always. Not even often."

"I know, I know. You're right. But that's why I need a day off here. Get some perspective back. Speaking of which . . ."

He reached down and pulled his cell phone off his belt.

"If it's the office, don't . . . ," Treya said.

But Glitsky was shaking his head. "It's not downtown," he said. "It's Arnie Becker. I ought to get this." And he pushed the connect button. "Arnie, it's Abe. What's up?"

13

"Of course," Becker was saying, "we won't know for sure until—"

"Arnie." Glitsky held up a hand and cut him off. "You got any doubt at all?"

Becker drew in a large breath through his mouth. The stench of the burn was strong, but a whiff of the pervasive scent of cooked meat could bring even a strong man's stomach up. "Very little," he said.

They were standing, hands in their pockets, on the second floor in the bright sunlight that shone through the collapsed roof of Michael Durbin's home. The temperature was in the midforties, abnormally cold for San Francisco in February. The body was still in place in the burned-out shell of the upstairs bedroom, itself pretty thoroughly destroyed. The coroner's van had just arrived out front, but the crime scene unit, with their surgical masks in place, had been photographing and collecting what little evidence they could since before Glitsky's arrival about twenty minutes ago.

Though the face was unrecognizable, this body was in somewhat better condition than Felicia Nuñez's had been. Neither of this woman's shoes, in this case low-heeled black pumps, had been burned away completely. One had come off, possibly from the power of the hoses during the active phase of fighting the fire, and had wound up under the bed, about eight inches from the woman's right foot. But the other shoe still appeared to be a snug fit on her left foot. There were no unburned scraps of clothing under the body, no sign of a bra or other underwear, and Becker's conjecture from those facts was that the woman had been naked either at or shortly after the time she died and was set ablaze. Due to the relatively light amount of charring where the woman's body was in contact with the floor, Becker told Glitsky that if she'd been wearing any clothes, they would not all have burned away.

"What about DNA?" Glitsky asked. "I mean, if the burning wasn't really so bad."

"Well," Becker said, "it's all relative. You can see for yourself that not *so* bad doesn't mean not bad. And it's also pretty clear where the fire got started, same as with Nuñez. So all in all, I'd say DNA's not a good bet, although of course we're going to try." Becker glanced again over at the body. "So the similarities. That's why I called you directly, of course."

"I appreciate it." Glitsky sucked carefully through his teeth, turned away so the body was out of his line of vision. "Although I can't say it makes much sense."

"What has to make sense?"

"I mean, if this was Ro Curtlee. First, the sheer balls of it. After last week."

"He's telling you to go fuck yourself."

Glitsky's mouth twitched at the profanity. "So he just picks some random woman?"

Becker shrugged. "Maybe he knew her."

"Yeah, but everybody else he's done has been a domestic. How'd he meet somebody out here? A normal civilian, I'm guessing, right? Any word about whether this was the cleaning lady or somebody like that?"

"I don't think so, Abe. The husband and some other family are down there." He pointed out to the street. "They're all wrecked, and they all think it's the wife. She's the only female who would have been in the house. The daughter's still at school. He called and checked."

Glitsky looked up through the gaping hole in the roof above them. "Dear God," he said. "How old is she? The daughter?"

Another shrug. "I don't know. School age."

"You're right," Glitsky said. "What difference does it make?" He took a last look at the body, closed his eyes against the horror of it, and shook his head. "So who is she?"

"If it's the wife, her name's Janice Durbin. Her husband's . . ."

Glitsky put his hand on Becker's arm and gripped it. "Michael."

"Yeah. How'd you . . . ?"

Nodding, verifying to himself the sudden and unmistakable clarity, Glitsky pulled in a last, quick breath. "He was the jury foreman at Ro's trial."

———

"I don't know why I agonize about taking days off," Glitsky said. "Nobody else even seems to notice when I do."

"Maybe," Amanda Jenkins said, "that's because you're actually physically here in the building talking about a case, so to someone who isn't paying close attention it seems like you're on the job somehow. And just for the record, can you explain to me how it would be different if you weren't taking a day off?"

"Not too, I guess. You put it that way."

"Well, there you go." She pushed her chair back from her desk, leaned back, and put her feet up on its surface, displaying a good 80 percent of her extraordinary legs in the process. "You want to get the door? Certain people see us talking, they're liable to think we're colluding to obstruct justice, like we did last time."

Glitsky turned and closed it.

Jenkins crossed her arms, gave him a flat look. "So what are you going to do?"

"I don't know. That's why I'm here talking to you. You might have an idea."

"Not any that I'm proud of. Well, that's not true. I've got one."

"Hit me."

"Before anything else, I'd rule out arresting Ro again."

Glitsky allowed himself a small, grim smile. "That was my thought, too. Which, of course, leaves him free to go around killing other people whenever the mood strikes him. But hey, that's not my decision."

"Don't be bitter."

"No. Why would I be bitter?"

"Good. For a minute there, I thought I detected a trace."

"Nope. Bitter-free, that's me." A wooden chair sat along the wall next to the cabinets, and Glitsky pulled it around and straddled it backward. "But in actual fact, I've pretty much decided that I'm going to pretend Ro isn't any part of this Durbin murder, lower my own profile."

"That's probably smart. You show up around Ro again, it's a circus before it even starts."

"That doesn't mean I'm not going to be all over it."

"No. I didn't think it did. So what's the plan?"

"The plan is I don't make the connection to Ro. Not in public, anyway."

"And what's that get you?"

"Time, if nothing else. Maybe the Curtlees back off. Meanwhile, I go out and talk to people like any homicide inspector would. Develop a theory of the case, maybe even a list of suspects. I don't get near Ro until something, some solid evidence, leads back to him, which is what we're going to need anyway if the good Mr. Farrell is ever going to charge him with anything again in our lifetimes."

"Except you've already got that up front. Something leading back to Ro."

"What's that?"

"The shoe, the MO, the jury foreman's wife. Take your pick. The guy all but drew you a picture."

"Well, that's the other thing."

"What?"

"Arnie Becker's theory is that this is Ro flipping me off. Actually, flipping both of us off, you and me."

"I'm flattered."

Glitsky shrugged. "So how's he going to feel if he's gone to all the trouble of killing somebody else and leaving all these clues to rub what he can get away with in our faces, and I don't put it together? Instead, I go barking up another tree and don't give him the satisfaction."

It took her a moment, but then she nodded. "He's going to want to tell us what he did. And dare us to try and prove it."

"*Need* is more like it. It's going to flush him. Or, it might. At least it's a shot."

Glitsky was thinking that Treya was right about her boss. Without her organizational presence and staff sergeant demeanor, he'd be lost as an administrator. So much so, apparently, that in her absence this afternoon he'd simply closed up shop and disappeared. The lights in the outer office—Treya's domain—were dark when Glitsky showed up, no visitors waited for their appointments with the DA himself, and the door to Farrell's office was closed. Crossing the room and putting an ear to the door, he heard no sound. Not expecting to get an answer, nevertheless, he rapped sharply on the door three times.

Nothing.

And then, just as he was turning to go, the sound of footsteps came from within. Glitsky stopped and was all but at attention, facing the door when Farrell opened it. The district attorney was in his shirtsleeves and the lights in his own office were turned off, the blinds pulled against the bright sunshine outside. Glitsky thought he might have just interrupted a nap. "If this isn't a good time . . . ," he began.

"No. It's fine. I was just meditating for a minute. You ever do that, Abe?"

"Not so much. I don't get much free time."

"Twenty minutes a day, that's all it takes. Everybody ought to be able to find twenty minutes."

"I keep looking for them," Glitsky said. "I think the kids must steal 'em."

"Oh, that's right. Your kids are still at home, aren't they?"

"Only for another eighteen or twenty years. But who's counting?"

"You're right. I don't think I would, either, under those conditions. Probably wouldn't meditate, either." Suddenly Farrell seemed to remember not just where he was, but who he was. His face went slack for a moment, then reanimated itself. "But here you are. What can I do for you? You want to come in and sit down for a minute? Is everything all right with Treya? How's she feeling?"

"Better," Glitsky said.

"She'll be back in on Monday, I hope."

"That's the plan."

"Good. Good. Well, come on in." Farrell hesitated, then moved back a step. When Glitsky had gotten past the door, Farrell closed it behind them. He turned on the room's overhead lights, then walked over to one of his couches and sat on it, motioning for Glitsky to do the same. But Glitsky remained standing.

"What do you got?" Farrell asked.

"Ro's done it again."

Farrell dropped his head, then slowly brought it back up. "You've got to be shitting me."

"No, sir. Janice Durbin. Wife of the foreman of his jury. Set her on fire either before or after he killed her, burned the house down around her. Naked, with shoes on her feet. Might as well have left a business card."

"Sounds like he did." Farrell brought a hand up and rubbed the side of his face. "Jesus Christ, Abe, what are we going to do?"

"I thought you might go back to Baretto."

Farrell's shoulders heaved, a spasm of bitter laughter. "He wouldn't touch this thing, not after Donahoe. Now two judges have ruled Ro's no danger to the community. No way does Baretto pull him back in."

"So at what point do the shoes and the MO count as evidence?"

"Honestly, probably no point."

"Maybe I should go talk to him, make the case."

Farrell shook his head. "Your credibility around Ro is in the shitter, Abe. This is all coming across as a personal vendetta." He hesitated. "Maybe I shouldn't mention this, but I had Vi Lapeer stop by here this morning. Unexpectedly."

"What'd she know?"

"It's not what she knew. It's what she wanted. She wanted advice."

"About what?"

"About the fact that Leland told her he wants you out. Not just out of this investigation, but completely out. The political heat's just too much for him. According to him, half the city thinks you guys are the Gestapo. And you're the poster child."

"That's Marrenas. The woman's toxic." Glitsky finally took a seat across from Farrell. Coming forward, he let out a breath. "So what was your advice?"

"I told her she should stick by her guns and support you. The mayor wouldn't dare fire her so soon after bringing her on. Of course, I may be wrong. I haven't been right in so long I forget what it looks like. But I told her he'd look like a complete fool for making her his choice for chief in the first place."

"He threatened to fire her?"

"I think it was more understood than stated. But the message was clear enough."

"So I should quit?"

"I won't lie to you, Abe. That's an option, though not a good one. Better would be to get something real on Ro."

"I thought I did that last time."

"Yeah. Well, we saw how that played."

Glitsky took that in silence for a beat. Then, "Well, in any event, I've got my case file and notes from the original investigation, which I'm reviewing for the retrial. With Nuñez gone, we've still got her testimony from the first trial, but reading it to a jury is not going to be anywhere near as strong as hearing her would have been. Which leaves the one other witness, Gloria Gonzalvez."

"But she's disappeared, too, hasn't she?"

"I haven't really started looking. She may turn up. Plus, I want to go see the other rape victims again, the ones who got bought off, if they'll talk to me."

"Why would they do that now, after all this time?"

Glitsky shrugged. "I don't know. Maybe they won't. But maybe it's bothering one of them they didn't do the right thing." He held up a hand. "I know. Long shot. But worth a try."

"It's your time."

"Speaking of which, we're still looking at August for the retrial?"

"Minimum. Unless you get something sooner on Nuñez, or this latest woman."

"If I do," Glitsky said as he stood up, "you'll be the first to know."

14

From the early years of their social and business prominence, the Curtlees had staffed their homes and some of their businesses with Guatemalan or El Salvadoran help. Rather than gamble with undocumented aliens, they could hire on site down in Central America and provide work visas, medical insurance, and an almost unbelievable standard of living for those lucky enough to be chosen. In return, they found their employees from these countries to be honest, hardworking, loyal, grateful, and—perhaps most important—fearful of being returned back to their homelands.

Just at about the end of Ro's trial, one of their talent scouts in El Salvador had been approached by Eztli. In Nahuatl, the language of the Mexica (meh-SHEE-ka), the people who white men call Aztec, *eztli* means "blood." As is also the common custom among his people, Eztli had only one name. It fit him well.

Thirty-five at the time, he already spoke excellent, unaccented, and idiomatic English, courtesy of an American father who'd disappeared when the boy had been twelve. He had been in the regular El Salvadoran army for a decade beginning when he was sixteen. Connections he'd made in the service paved the way for civilian work as a majordomo for Enrique Mololo, one of the country's drug lords. Mololo, unfortunately for himself, had decided that he did not want to share his profits or contacts with Mara Salvatrucha, one of the most powerful criminal organizations in the world. This decision had proved fatal for Mololo. If Eztli had not been on an errand to pick up one of Mololo's new cars when the military-style raid on his boss's compound took place, he almost undoubtedly would have died that day, too.

But as it was, he had missed that party. Instead of going back home to Mololo's place, he had called on the Curtlees' procurer, for whom he'd supplied the names of several young women over the years.

He needed to get out of the country. He had skills. He was willing to work.

And the Curtlees were only too glad to have him.

Now, on an overcast Sunday afternoon, Ro sat in the passenger seat of the 4Runner while Eztli drove south along the ocean on Highway 1. Ro's left arm was still in its cast, but other than that, he bore little resemblance to the man he'd seemed in Judge Donahoe's courtroom only six days before. He was clean-shaven, well-dressed in khakis and a black silk Tommy Bahama shirt. He wore expensive Italian loafers with no socks. He'd lost the bandage he'd been sporting over the bridge of his nose. The swelling around his mouth had gone down, and only a slight yellowing remained where the black eye had been.

Ro's idea when he woke up that morning was that he'd go down to the O'Farrell Theatre, get his ashes hauled by one of the girls in the booths—couldn't get too much of that after being inside nine years. After that, he didn't know. The afternoons tended to drag as a general rule. Maybe he'd go back to bed.

But then, coming back home from the O'Farrell, he found Eztli waiting for him. The butler reiterated how he'd been feeling terrible about not being there when the cops had come to get Ro. Okay, he had an excuse—he'd been out with the parents, doing bodyguard work. But protecting the family—all of the family—that was his job. He should have been part of it when Glitsky and the other cops came by. Now Eztli wanted to make it up to Ro somehow, show him a good time at least.

Sunday was his day off and some gamecocks were fighting at a place he knew down near Pescadero. Maybe Ro would like to go? It was a hell of a show. Girls watching it, getting into it, it made them hot.

Given his prejudices and predilections, Ro normally wouldn't have gone out of his way to accommodate or hang out with one of the household help, whom he generally viewed as stratospherically beneath him.

But Eztli was different.

First, of course, he was a guy—strong and experienced. He could handle himself, and this was always a plus.

Second, and much more important, was the fact that while Ro had been in prison, Eztli had suggested to Cliff and Theresa—worried sick about their son's safety behind bars—that he network amidst the greater Hispanic community and put out the word among the prison population, particularly the violent Mexican gang EME, that Ro wasn't to be molested; that, in fact, protection for him would be rewarded.

The two men—butler and convict—had met in the prison's visitors room several times before Ro's release to negotiate rewards and payouts and in the course of these meetings had developed an easy bond if not yet a true friendship. But in any event, Ro was inclined to relax his usual standards—for a day at least—and see what kind of fun the butler could provide for him.

So here they were, sharing a doob, just passing Half Moon Bay, the golf courses, the Ritz-Carlton there on the right.

"No," Ro was saying, "I'm not going back in. They'll have to kill me first."

Eztli took a hit and passed the joint across. "Your mom and dad believe it won't come to that."

"That's what they keep saying, anyway. But I don't know. They told me starting out they had that prick Farrell on board with them. That didn't work out so well."

"Yeah, but look what happened."

"What do you mean?"

"I mean, you're out."

"No thanks to Farrell."

"No?" Eztli shrugged. "Okay."

Ro held some smoke in his lungs while he looked over at his driver. Suddenly now he got the strongest sense that he'd intuited several times in the prison's visiting room that there was more going on inside the man's brain than might immediately be apparent behind the stony, expressionless exterior. His parents had kept Eztli on for the better part of ten years, and they were very smart and shrewd people who did not much let sentimental attachments get in their ways. If Eztli were just muscle, he would have made some mistake and been long gone by now. But not only was he very much still a presence, he actually lived in the big house with the family. Clearly he had an agile brain and contributed on other levels as well.

To say nothing of the fact that he'd probably saved Ro's literal ass in prison, and maybe his life as well.

The young man blew out the smoke he'd been holding. "You don't agree with me?" he asked. "About Farrell?"

Eztli kept his eyes on the road, took a minute before he answered. "I believe what your mother and father believe."

"What's that?"

"That if Farrell wants you in jail, you're in jail."

"But he . . ."

Eztli was shaking his head. "He's playing a game."

"Why would he do that?"

"Because he's a politician. He's playing both sides. That's what they do." Eztli held out his right hand and Ro handed him the joint, which he sucked down to its last half inch. Letting the hit out, he went on, "Look. Don't kid yourself. Farrell makes the call. He goes to a judge—any judge—and says you don't get bail, period, then you don't get bail. But he didn't do that. Not either time it's come up. Meanwhile, he gives your lawyer half a year to get up to speed. Which won't happen in any six months, either. That'll go a year, maybe two, maybe forever. And this makes Farrell the best friend you got. He's giving you time, and time's the main thing."

"For what?"

"Hey, come on, for everything." Eztli flashed him a look. "For doing what you have to do."

———

Gloria Serrano, née Gonzalvez, loved doing her own family's laundry. She sometimes felt she could do it forever in perfect happiness, so long as it was in her own house, for her own sons and daughter and husband. She loved the smell of it—the musky tang as she pulled the clothes from the hamper as well as the sweet detergent scent when it came out of the dryer almost too hot to touch. She liked to separate the whites from the colors, to take the shirts out as soon as they'd dried so that she could fold them so they wouldn't wrinkle.

She even loved the challenge of finding the lost sock that seemed to go along with nearly every load.

Now, Sunday afternoon, her one day off, she had her piles of clothes stacked and folded on the wooden workbench next to the washer and dryer in the garage of the two-bedroom house that she and Roberto had finally managed to buy in Sunnyvale.

Today one of her husband's red socks had made itself disappear. Gloria went down to one knee and put her head almost inside the dryer, then pulled back and reached in with her hand to turn the drum. No sock.

She hoped it would not be among the clothes she'd already folded. The only other place it could be was the washer itself, but she was usually very careful about making sure the washer was empty before she started the dryer because this was when she often found the coins and also, very occasionally, the bills, that she hid to use for presents for Roberto and the children.

Since she'd bought the last present for Ramon's seventh birthday in November—a Lego battleship that he'd loved and rebuilt so far about twenty times—she'd amassed a new total of nearly twenty dollars, including today's unusually large haul of two dollar bills and a quarter.

She never considered that she was stealing from her husband by keeping the money she found. The money always went back to one of them. She looked on it more as though it were a fine that fate imposed on her husband when he didn't check to empty his pockets before he threw clothes in the hamper.

But that sock was missing, and she didn't really want to unfold all of her already folded clothes and check again. Maybe in the excitement of finding so much money earlier, she hadn't been as careful as she usually was. So she opened the washer and reached around where a sock might have stuck in the spinning process. And today—a good luck sign—she found it clinging to the top of the drum.

She wasn't about to run a whole load of drying for one sock, so she took the wet sock and its dry partner and threw them both into the dryer, where they would wait until the next load went in. Then she gathered the other clothes in her arms, opened the garage door to the kitchen, and went to distribute them through the house.

She was making enchiladas for Sunday dinner and their wonderful smell stopped her in her tracks in the kitchen. Caught in a rogue wave of emotion, she put the clothes down on the table and pulled out a chair to sit on. Roberto had taken the children—all the children, bless him—to Costco for their biweekly run there, and this had left Gloria free to clean and do the laundry in an empty house, get it ready for the next week.

After a minute, she got up to pour herself some of her delicious Guatemalan coffee. Sitting back at the table, she wrapped her hands around her mug and stared out at the overcast sky through her kitchen window.

The color of the sky didn't matter. Sitting with her clean washing in her own house on a Sunday afternoon, drinking the wonderful coffee, smelling the good food that they'd have for dinner, she felt kissed by God, in complete contentment.

And who could ever have imagined she would have gotten to here? Especially after those first few months when she'd just arrived to work with the Curtlees. And after their horrible son, who'd started in on her within the first few days, finally got his way again and again over the months she'd stayed.

What else was she going to do? Whom could she turn to? The family chose to turn at best a blind eye to Ro's advances. And, at worst, they were complicit. That she'd eventually gotten out and placed with another family had been miracle number two.

And that would never have happened if the new girl, Dolores—the one Ro had finally killed—hadn't been on her way in the pipeline from Guatemala. The poor thing.

Gloria had no doubt that, but for the grace of God, that might have been her.

And then the scary months before and after she'd actually gone in and testified and Ro had gone to jail, when Cliff and Theresa Curtlee had first tried to buy her silence, and then had threatened her, through their lawyers, with extradition. But even with all of their connections, they had not been able to call on as many as Gloria herself had among her extended family. So they could not track her as she disappeared first to live with friends of some cousins in Gilroy, nor after she met and married Roberto and reestablished herself as a housekeeper in Sunnyvale.

Now she had a good business cleaning twenty-five homes in Palo Alto and Menlo Park every week—steady, legal work, and two employees besides herself. She had a dependable babysitter, her own home, a family, and a documented, hardworking husband who loved her.

And—she thanked God every day—no Ro or any other Curtlee in her life.

Not now.

Not ever again.

———

The Novios had a semi-enclosed redwood gazebo in their back-yard, hexagonal in shape, about ten feet in diameter. When Chuck came out to get firewood as dusk closed in on this cold and cloudy Sunday evening, he noticed his brother-in-law sitting on the bench that encircled the inside of the gazebo. He was faced away from the house, canted forward, his elbows on his knees, hands clasped in front of him.

Chuck walked over and knocked on one of the posts and Michael's shoulders rose and fell as he looked over. "Hey."

"You all right?"

"Just taking a break."

Kathy had insisted that the whole Durbin family stay with them at least until the memorial next Thursday. Individual pockets of grief were piled up inside the house like snowdrifts. Kathy. Chuck's twins. And Michael and Janice's own Allie and their boys—angry Jon and devastated Peter. All of them were flopped, wasted on the furniture in front of the television, tuned to sports round the clock.

"Not really so all right, though," Durbin added.

"No. Of course not. I hear you." Novio sat down across from him.

Durbin raised his head. "I keep wondering what I'm supposed to do now. Next. You know?"

"I can imagine. If Kathy died . . ." He shook his head. "I can't think about it."

"No," Durbin said. "No reason to." A beat. "I'm just trying to get my arms around what happened. I can't put together any kind of a plausible scenario. I mean, why was she home? What was she doing there that time of morning? She was supposedly going out the door right behind me, and next thing we know, somebody else is in the house and she's dead up in the bedroom. How does that happen, Chuck? What's that about?"

"What do the cops say? They got any theories?"

Durbin's face went dark. "Fucking cops. Don't get me started. They got nothing. No lab reports. The autopsy won't be done until maybe next month. They're not even ready to say somebody killed her yet, not on purpose, anyway. She might have just happened to be home when whoever it was started the fire. Maybe she ran upstairs and tried to put it out and died of smoke inhalation."

"So at least they're saying it was arson?"

"Apparently. But that's the other thing. I told you not to get me started."

"Too late now. What's the other thing?"

"This guy Glitsky, the inspector? When he was here, it was like I was part of his investigation. Like I could have had something to do with it."

Chuck nodded in understanding. "Yeah. He had some questions for me, too, while we were waiting for you to come downstairs."

This information straightened Durbin right up. "He talked to you? He *questioned* you? What about?"

"My cell phone. Or rather, Janice's cell phone, which didn't burn up because it was hanging from a peg behind the kitchen door. Evidently, he said, I got twelve calls to or from her in the past two weeks. I told him that evidently I did. So what? We were planning a surprise party for Kathy's fortieth next month. Was there something sinister about that?"

"What'd he say?"

A shrug. "He just let it go, as he should have. But Jesus, talk about shaking every tree. I know it's his job, but can you say ridiculous?"

"Yeah, well, I hear you. And the funny thing is, before yesterday, I would have told you Glitsky and I got along all right."

"Before yesterday? You knew Glitsky personally?"

"Not saying we were friends exactly, but after Ro's trial we went out together a couple of times, just comparing notes on how the Curtlees were fucking around with both of us. So I figure he knows who I am, basically. But yesterday, I get the strong impression that he doesn't really think it's out of the question that I killed her, either."

"He's just turning over rocks."

Durbin shook his head. "Maybe, but stupid and a waste of his time. I told him Janice and me, we were having a few problems, same as every other married couple with teenagers on the planet, but nothing we couldn't work out . . ."

"You guys were having problems?"

A shrug. "Nothing we couldn't fix, Chuck. Nothing to kill her over, trust me."

"No, I didn't mean . . ."

Durbin waved him off. "It doesn't matter. The point is Glitsky's ears go up and he's all 'How long have you been having these difficulties?' and 'Were you seeing anybody, a marriage counselor, like that?' I tell him maybe he hasn't heard, but Janice was a psychiatrist. We weren't anywhere near therapy. Anyway, bottom line, I shouldn't have mentioned anything. Next thing I know, he tells me he's talked to some of my people down at the shop. He wants to know where was I that I got in late Friday morning? I told him I didn't even realize I had been late. And he goes, 'Yeah, like a half hour.' And then waits, like I've got something to tell him. Then he starts asking about Liza."

"Who's Liza?"

"My assistant manager at work. Smart and cute. She's sticking up for me when Glitsky's down at the store asking questions about how late I was, how was I acting . . ."

"He actually went to your store?"

"First thing. Before he came to see us here. I told you. I'm on his list."

"But that's just so ludicrous."

"It's beyond that, but then he's going on about my relationship with Liza. Like maybe it's because of her I decided to kill Janice? I want to strangle the guy." His temper flared again suddenly. "Thinking it could be me, for Christ's sake!"

Chuck came forward on his bench. "He couldn't really think that. He's just getting started. Let the evidence come in, get the autopsy done. It'll all work itself out."

Durbin leaned back against the wall of the gazebo. "You're right. You're right." He brought a hand up to his forehead, his eyes dull, shot with red. "I'm just so done in." Suddenly Durbin cocked his head, life coming into his eyes.

"What?" Chuck asked. "It's not too often you actually see the lightbulb go on."

Durbin stared out over Novio's shoulder.

"Mike? What is it?"

Durbin let out the breath he'd been holding. "You know the troubles I told you we'd been having, Janice and me? I think she was having an affair."

Novio went still before he finally shook his head. "No way, Mike. I don't think so. Not Janice." Then, "Really? You know this? With who?"

"One of her patients, if I had to guess." The idea growing on him, he straightened up. "I was just wondering who could have had a reason to have done this. No way it was just random, someone picking our house and deciding to burn it down. But if she was involved with somebody and wanted to break it off, and he came over and went into a rage . . . I mean, that's somebody who would have a motive, some kind of personal connection to tell Glitsky about, get him looking at somebody besides me."

Nodding, going along with it, Chuck said, "At least it's someplace he can start. Or he can go with my other theory."

"What's that?"

Chuck hesitated. "That this might not have been about Janice at all. That she was just a way to get at you."

"Me? Who'd want to get at me? What for?" But then the obvious occurred to him. "Ro Curtlee."

Novio shrugged. "The first witness who got killed after he got let out, didn't he burn her place down around her? And you said you thought he recognized you in court last week. So I start thinking maybe . . ."

Durbin held out a hand, stopping him. "God in heaven," he said.

15

"I really think we ought to move to New York," Theresa Curtlee said on Monday morning. She was at breakfast downstairs with her husband. She would alternately sip from a porcelain coffee cup, a leaded-crystal Riedel wineglass filled with Pellegrino water garnished with a slice of lime, and a small glass of grapefruit juice. On her plate she'd sliced off two small bites of pineapple. The table between her and Cliff groaned with food, most of it destined for the disposal: several bowls and platters of French toast, scrambled eggs, sausages, bacon, smoked salmon, bagels, English muffins, bran and blueberry muffins, a composed fruit salad. "There really is no reason we have to live with the constant aggravation here."

Cliff moved his copy of the *Courier* off to the side. "It would be difficult to run the businesses from New York," he said. "And we don't want to uproot now at our ages. Although it is tempting, I must admit. All this madness with Ro. I just pray now that they let it drop."

"You don't think that Glitsky is really going to let it drop, do you? Sometimes I'm afraid he might actually be lying in wait somewhere when Ro goes out."

"I don't think he'd do that himself. But he might in fact hire someone else. No, not even hire. It would be some kind of a favor."

She put down her cup. "That's what I mean, Clifford. Why do we have to live with that fear every day? I don't understand why we can't have him removed somehow."

"We tried that before, if you remember. He's resilient. I was sure he'd quit when they moved him to payroll. But no, here he is again, and again apparently with the support of his chief. These cops and their stupid loyalty. And there's just no getting rid of our brand-new chief. Not for a while, anyway."

"So here we are again." Theresa dabbed at her lifeless lips. "I don't really understand what's the point of acquiring influence if we can't keep ourselves a little bit insulated from this riffraff element? Isn't this what we work for? Instead, with all the money we hand out to that same element and all the good we try to do, it just doesn't seem right."

"It isn't right, Theresa. But it's the way this town is. Basically insane."

She cut another small slice of pineapple and chewed it primly and completely. "And I don't suppose," she said, "that our good Mr. Farrell would let us take Ro with us if we went East, would he? Maybe just for an extended vacation?"

"I think not."

"So why again did we donate all that money to his campaign?"

"He was the lesser of two evils, Theresa. And in his defense, I have to say that he could probably have made a stronger stance against bail and kept Ro in jail, which he did not do. So I think, all in all, the campaign money was well spent. So far, at least. If he doesn't try to get too cute and fancy pleasing everybody."

Theresa's eyes went to the platter of bacon in front of her. She moved it forward a couple of inches before thinking better of it and pushing it back. Reaching for her grapefruit juice, she asked, "Why are they so out to get him?"

"Ro?" He picked up a bite of his own bacon, chewed, swallowed, and sighed.

"I mean," she asked, "what did he do that was so terrible? Sowed a few wild oats? Show me a young man who hasn't done that." Suddenly Theresa's eyes glistened with the threat of tears. "When

I think of the time he's already lost and now finally they let us have him again . . . but for how long? I don't know if I can bear it if they take him away again. I just don't understand the witch hunt, Clifford. I really don't. What did he really do? I just don't understand it."

"What he did," Cliff Curtlee began, "was he committed the grave sin of not apologizing for the class he comes from, our class. And in this city, as you know, there is no greater crime. Because we're all exactly equal, don't you see?"

"But that's so patently absurd."

"Nevertheless, that is precisely what—and I take my share of responsibility for this—that's precisely what we didn't take seriously enough at the trial. I mean, yes, he might have gotten a little out of control with some of these girls, and of course that was wrong, but he was young and really, who were they? Did they count in any meaningful way? Would they ever?"

Just at this moment, Linda Salcedo, one of their young and attractive staff, came through the door from the kitchen holding a pitcher filled with freshly made coffee. "Ah," Cliff said, "here is my savior. Perfect timing. A little more, please, just half a cup. There, that's good, thanks. You're a dream, Linda, what would we do without you?"

Linda gave him a thin smile and curtsied politely. "*Gracias*." And turned toward Theresa. "*Señora?*"

"No thanks, dear, I'm fine."

Another little bow and the young woman disappeared back into the kitchen.

"Darling girl," Theresa said.

"Wonderful," Cliff agreed, then continued on his earlier topic. "Not saying that if Ro in fact hurt one of these girls, there shouldn't be some punishment, but clearly his sentence was out of all proportion to the damage he did. And our failure—mine as well as his lawyers—was that we didn't understand how deep the prejudice of those jurors went, that class divide. The jury wasn't going to forgive him. They were going to make him an example. In retrospect, and I've agonized over this a thousand times, we should have played him down market, the way we did last week. That worked pretty well. That judge couldn't help but see him not as a boy with a little money and maybe a leadership attitude, but as a beaten-down victim."

"I hated seeing him like that. That's not who he is."

"No. But that's who he may have to be if he wants a lighter sentence next time. Or even no sentence at all."

"But best would be if there is no next time."

Cliff nodded. "Of course. I agree. And I know that Tristan and Ro are working on that now. So we'll just have to wait and see how that turns out. And here again, we still may be able to prevail on Mr. Farrell to hold off scheduling the new trial for quite some time, or even canceling it altogether, especially if none of the earlier witnesses can be found to testify again, which looks like it may in fact be the case."

"Let's hope so. But if they do reschedule"—she lowered her voice—"I really think we might want to send Ro someplace safe if we can, where they don't extradite."

Cliff sucked in a breath. "Well," he said, "of course that's a possibility. But it's a ten-and-a-half-million-dollar decision, Theresa. We could do it, but let's exhaust all our other options first."

———

Without making a conscious decision to do so, Farrell stopped by his former law offices on Sutter Street. He was still one of the name partners at the firm Freeman, Farrell, Hardy & Roake, even though his private practice had dried up on the not-unreasonable assumption that it was a hard sell to clients seeking a defense attorney if you happened to be the person also charging them with their crimes. Still, he supposed that his name had a certain advertising value to the firm; and in terms of the other shareholders in the firm, the plain fact remained that out of the four name partners, three were essentially uninvolved in the practice: David Freeman was dead, Farrell himself was the DA, and Gina Roake was spending most of her time writing her second novel after the modest success of her first one.

This left as the only practicing name partner Dismas Hardy.

Farrell came up the main staircase into the lobby and strode across to the circular reception area. Behind the low wall, Phyllis sat at her keyboard, multitasking away in her multiple roles as secretary, chief receptionist, and gatekeeper to Hardy's office. Catching Farrell on approach, her fingers stopped moving as her mouth first pursed in faint distaste, then rearranged itself into an arctic smile.

"Mr. Farrell," she enthused. "Welcome back."

"Thank you, Phyllis. Is Diz in?"

Clearly the question she was hoping he wasn't going to ask. Her lips reassumed their pained expression and she lifted her arm so that she could consult her wristwatch. "He's got a *scheduled* appointment in twenty minutes," she said, emphasizing the vast difference between that appropriate business moment and Farrell's unexpected appearance. "Is he expecting you?"

"No. I just thought I'd drop by for a minute. Maybe you could buzz him for me? Or I could just . . ." He made as if to go around her station and straight to Hardy's door.

"No! No!" She held up a restraining hand. "Let me just tell him you're here." And she lifted her telephone and pushed a number.

One minute later, Dismas Hardy closed his office door behind them both. "She's armed, you know?" he said.

"Are you kidding?"

Hardy shook his head. "Not kidding. As of a couple of months ago. She pointed out, and rightly so, I might add, that if somebody really wanted to get by her and into my office to see me, there was no way she could physically stop them. There would be nothing she could do. So I went down with her and we bought her a big ol' gun. Three-fifty-seven Magnum. Hollow point slugs."

"All to stop people from seeing you?"

"Without an appointment," Hardy said. "That's the crucial distinction."

Farrell sat on one of Hardy's Queen Anne chairs. "Like the appointment I didn't have this morning? And to think I actually made a move in the direction of your door."

"You're lucky she recognized you and held her fire."

"You don't think that's carrying the whole thing a little far?"

"I would," Hardy said, "if it were true."

Farrell sat back in his chair. "I'm slowing down. You really had me. Ah, but to discuss the possibility gives it a sort of truth. I have a T-shirt that says so."

"You have a T-shirt for everything," Hardy said. "You want some coffee?"

"Sure. Two sugars, please."

Hardy stirred, carried the cup and saucer over. "People still not joking around too much down at the Hall?"

"Not as much as you might think," Farrell said.

"So you haven't heard about the two Canadians playing twenty questions?"

"No, but . . ."

Hardy couldn't wait. He started right in. "So the guy who's 'it' thinks up the word *moosecock*. And the other guy's first question is, 'Can you eat it?' and the first guy goes, 'Well, yeah, I guess you could.' So the other guy thinks a minute and says, 'Would it be moosecock?' "

Farrell had a mouthful of hot coffee when Hardy got to the punch line. His reaction was immediate, trying to hold the coffee in for a half second or so, during which time Hardy thought he might be choking. But then Farrell lost the fight altogether and exploded into laughter as a fine spray of coffee filled the air in front of him. "Oh God, Diz, I'm sorry. Your rug . . ." Farrell had his handkerchief in his hand; coffee was coming out his nose.

Another bout of hysteria shook him. And another.

Hardy whirled on the spot, quickly peeled off a couple of paper towels from the wet bar's roll, went to a knee, and began dabbing at the rug.

Farrell came down with his handkerchief and joined him. But the residue of the laughter still hung there between them. The rug hadn't sustained any major damage. Farrell got back up and sat again on his chair.

Hardy's own grin creased his face. "I should have waited till you swallowed. Don't worry about the rug. It's my fault."

Farrell sat back, sagging in the chair. "Wow," he said. He took a few more breaths, retaining his equilibrium. When he'd gotten himself together, he got down to it. "I was just hoping to hear an objective voice around all this Ro Curtlee stuff, that's all. I'm getting it from both sides in the newspapers, Sam's barely talking to me, Amanda Jenkins still might quit over it. And we're not even talking about Glitsky."

"What about Abe?"

"He thinks Ro's killed somebody else. A woman named Janice Durbin."

"And she is?"

"The wife of the jury foreman at his trial. But Abe can't arrest Ro again now, not after the fiasco last week. Crawford wants him shitcanned just on general principles anyway. And Vi Lapeer's had to go to bat for him, which makes her own job security a little tenuous, to say the least. The whole thing's just a complete clusterfuck, and Sam might be right thinking it's all my fault. But I don't really know what else I could have done, or could do now, for that matter."

Hardy stalled for a moment, sipping his coffee. "What do you want to do?"

"Go back to Baretto. Just rewind the clock."

"Unring the bell," Hardy said. "If only we could. What would you do different?"

"I'd recommend in the strongest terms that bail would be inappropriate, that Ro was a killer and a danger to the community."

"Forgive my ignorance, but what did you tell him last time?"

"Last time, I didn't say anything. I sent Amanda to court and let her do her thing." At Hardy's look, Farrell went on, "I know what you're thinking. You're thinking I buckled under to the Curtlees."

"I don't know anything about you and the Curtlees, Wes, so I promise you, that's not what I was thinking. What happened, they lobby you?"

"They probably thought it was subtle, but it was more or less a full-court press."

"And after that, you didn't go chat with Baretto?"

Wes shook his head no. "But I wasn't going to before that either."

"Why not?"

"Besides the fact that it would have been totally unethical? I actually thought it was his decision. And, you know, ten million bail isn't exactly chump change."

Hardy sipped his coffee.

Farrell's shoulders settled. He shook his head. "I fucked up, didn't I?"

Hardy shrugged. "How long had you been in office when you made the call? Three days?"

"Something like that. But I had another chance last week with Donahoe and I blew that one, too. And now we've got another dead person and I wouldn't be surprised if we're going to see more of them."

Hardy took a minute. "How about the grand jury?"

"I've got no evidence, Diz. And I don't mean a little. I got nothing."

"Then how do you know it's Ro?"

"He leaves the shoes on his victims. Both women have a connection to his trial. He's a psycho and he's loving this."

"That's evidence. It might be enough for the grand jury. Then they indict him for both killings and there's no bail."

"So he gets arrested twice in a week? How's that look?"

"Who cares? It's happened before. And the grand jury's going to take longer than a week anyway to get your indictment. Then send a SWAT team down and bring him in. Maybe you'll get lucky and he'll resist arrest again and you can shoot him dead."

"Your mouth to God's ear," Farrell said.

Hardy shrugged again. "Look, Wes, you're the DA now, not a private citizen, and certainly not a defense lawyer. Get used to it. Whatever you do, you're going to make enemies. So, given that, the only thing you can do is what you think is right. You think this guy needs to be in jail, find a way."

Farrell took this advice in silence. After some seconds, he reached out and sipped at his coffee. After he swallowed, he met Hardy's eyes. "Shit."

"I know."

"I asked for this, didn't I?"

"That's the rumor."

Farrell dragged himself to his feet. "Well, Diz, I appreciate the straight talk. And sorry again about the rug."

"Don't mention the rug. I'll tell Phyllis the machine malfunctioned and spit coffee all over. She'll want to buy a new one, and then I'll say I really like this old one, in spite of the malfunctioning aspect. We ought to go around on whether or not to get a new one for a couple of weeks at least. It'll be really fun."

Farrell smiled in spite of himself. "Why again did I quit working here?"

"Destiny came calling. And you're welcome back anytime. But Wes . . . ?"

"Yeah?"

"While you're still in public service, do yourself and everybody else a favor and put this fucker away."

16

He picked up the phone in his office on the first ring. "Glitsky."

"Lieutenant, this is Michael Durbin."

Glitsky took a beat. "How are you holding up?"

"To be honest, it's a challenge these last couple of days."

"I'm sure it is." Glitsky, surprised by this call, scratched at a spot on his desk.

"Lieutenant?"

"I'm here."

"We didn't talk about it much when you came by on Saturday, but over the weekend I realized maybe I should have . . . What I'm trying to say is that I felt in the aftermath of Ro's trial that we had developed something of a personal relationship."

Glitsky considered his words before he spoke. "We had a couple of cups of coffee together afterward. I remember that."

"As I recall, Lieutenant, you drank tea."

"That's right. Still do."

"Well, I felt then that we had a certain simpatico between us, both being hassled by the Curtlees as we were. I thought maybe we could kind of have a little off-the-record talk now like we did then."

"About your wife's case?" Glitsky pulled his yellow pad up in front of him.

"In a way, yes. I got the impression—I should have mentioned it at the time, I know—that you thought I was some kind of suspect."

The thought that Michael Durbin was any kind of a real suspect had never really entered Glitsky's mind, and for an instant he felt a degree of satisfaction that he'd sold his objectivity so convincingly. But he didn't want to confide that, or anything else, to the man he was talking to. "Mr. Durbin," he said, "I've just begun my investigation. I've got any number of people who could conceivably be suspects and probably . . ."

"But wait. No, no, no. You can't have me as one of those people, because I'm not in it. I can't be a suspect, Lieutenant. You know that."

"How do I know that?"

"Because you knew who I was back after Ro's trial, and I haven't changed. You know that I'm no killer. I couldn't kill a fly. I didn't kill my wife or light the fire."

"We don't even know if the fire killed her yet, sir, or if somebody else killed her and then set the fire. We're hoping to get some lab and autopsy reports soon, and then we'll have more of an idea of what we're even looking at."

"Okay, fine, but whatever that is, my wife's dead, and the investigation into her death can't include the possibility that I had anything at all to do with it. Which is what I keep feeling you must be considering. And especially when I think you and me must already know for a fact who did this anyway."

"We do?"

"Oh, come on, Lieutenant. Think about it."

"I've been doing little else."

"And Ro Curtlee hasn't occurred to you?"

Glitsky said nothing.

Until at last Durbin pressed on. "All right. Maybe it's not the most obvious thing in the world. I admit it didn't occur to me until yesterday. Which was probably because you had me so rattled with your questions . . ."

"Why would Ro want to kill your wife?"

"To get back at me. Just like he burned up that other woman, the witness."

"Yes. But she could testify against him. She was a threat in the here and now. Your wife had no connection to him and wouldn't have any influence on his future. It's not the same thing at all."

"It's him. I know it was him. Listen, I was at his bail hearing last week and of course now I realize that was probably a mistake, but he turned around and looked right at me. I'm sure he recognized me. And that gave him the idea. Now he's paying back old debts."

Glitsky suddenly realized that this was almost precisely the type of lead that he hoped he would uncover in the course of his investigation. Durbin's information came from an independent source and led to Ro without any reference to Glitsky or the police department. It was a legitimate lead in the case that he would have to follow up, even if he'd never heard of Ro Curtlee. "That's a provocative theory," Glitsky said.

"It's a damn sight more than that. I'll bet you anything it's what happened."

"Well, then, hopefully we'll be able to prove it."

"Not if any part of you is still thinking it could be me. You've got to concentrate on Ro, for God's sake. Before the trail goes too cold."

At the vehemence of Durbin's comments, a small part of Glitsky's brain nudged him with the idea that Durbin was protesting too much. But he cast that niggling quibble aside—Ro was certainly Janice's murderer and Glitsky could understand Durbin's desperation to see him apprehended and charged. He had just lost his wife, after all. And Ro was very much a person to suspect and to fear. Glitsky, his voice matter-of-fact, came back at him. "I'm going to go where the trail takes me, sir. And from your information here today, it sounds like it might be heading toward Ro."

"There's no *might* about it."

"Maybe not," Glitsky said, "but it's my job to make sure."

Arson inspector Arnie Becker showed up unannounced at Glitsky's office that Monday morning and now he was sitting across from the lieutenant listening to his wrap-up, where the bottom line had been that no one had seen anything suspicious near the Durbins' house on Friday morning. "This guy's luck is just phenomenal," Glitsky was saying. "Somebody should have seen something, everybody going to work or school about the time the fire started? And nobody saw anything like a purple Z-Four."

"How many cars do you think the Curtlees own, Abe? Six? Eight? Fifteen? They got a whole fleet, I'm sure."

"You're right, you're right." Glitsky ran his hand back over his scalp. "I just want something, almost anything, so badly I can taste it."

"Well, I might be able to help you there. I've got some news."

"Talk."

"I just came from Strout downstairs." Downstairs meant the coroner's office outside the back door of the Hall of Justice. Strout was the octogenarian medical examiner who seemed immune to the city's policies on retirement, probably because he was so good and so fair that no one wanted to rock that particular boat. "First things first. Even without a tox yet, now there's no doubt it's a murder. Hyoid bone's broken, which, by the way, same with Nuñez. So Janice was strangled and dead before the fire started, assuming of course that she didn't strangle herself after she set it."

"No," Glitsky said, "let's rule that out."

"And it was definitely set, although—a bit of a surprise here— the accelerant was downstairs in the kitchen and dining room, both, and spread up from there. Newspaper and gas, if you're keeping score. He brought the gas in one of those big plastic Diet Coke containers, pretty much melted away, but identifiable, the twenty-ounce one."

Glitsky received that information with a brusque nod. "What kind of accelerant did he use with Nuñez?"

"Gas, again, with some of her clothes."

"Any container in that one?"

"Not obvious. Nothing I found. And I looked."

"So," Glitsky asked, "he didn't light Janice on fire."

"Well, she was upstairs in a house. Nuñez had just the small apartment. So he didn't have other options with Nuñez. But he made the best of what he had to work with. And actually, lightly balled-up newspaper is pretty much the best accelerant you can use. So maybe he's refining his technique."

"But Janice didn't burn as much as Nuñez, did she?"

"No. Not really close, actually. And that leads to the other thing."

Glitsky perked up. "Tell me you got DNA."

"Did not, but, maybe something we can work with, we did get chlamydia."

"You're saying that Janice had it?"

Becker nodded. "Strout wasn't even looking for it, and one of his assistants caught it on the slide. So he rechecked. No doubt about it."

Glitsky sat back and crossed a leg. "When I talked to the husband, Michael, he said they were having some problems. Serious, but nothing to kill her over. Now I know what kind of trouble it was, and maybe it was more serious than he let on."

"So we know she was having an affair," Becker said.

"Or he was," Glitsky countered. "She finds out he's given her chlamydia and they get in a fight and he kills her. Or she's given it to him. Same result."

"Yeah," Becker said, "except he didn't kill her. Ro did. Married people have problems all the time and they don't necessarily kill their spouses over them."

Glitsky theatrically used his finger to clean out his ear. "I'm sorry, Arnie. I thought I just heard you say spouses don't kill each other. In which case, this department might have enough inspectors after all."

"Are you getting squishy on Ro?" Becker asked.

"No," Abe replied without hesitation. "I'm just trying to fit this chlamydia thing into the picture."

"Well, the good news," Becker said, "is that Ro's going to test positive for chlamydia, too, when you get him locked up again."

"Not necessarily, not if he used a condom," Glitsky said. "Not if he didn't rape her at all, and there's no forensic evidence that he did, am I right?"

"No, not yet," Becker said, then added, "Do rapists use condoms?"

"Your higher class of rapists, you bet. All the time." Glitsky sat back in his chair, his right hand stretched out before him, drumming his fingers on his desk. When he spoke, it sounded like he was working it out for himself. "Ro might not have raped Janice, if in fact he didn't, because she wasn't like his other victims. She wasn't anything personal to him. Just a way to get to Durbin. How's that sound?"

"Anything that includes Ro sounds good to me, Abe. I examined the Nuñez scene and the Durbin scene, so you're talking to a true believer."

"That's two of us," Glitsky said.

———

In his personal parking space behind his store, Durbin sat in his car and waited for some inner voice to give him the secret password that would get him moving. The solid cloud cover had finally broken up and splotches of sunlight had been coming and going for the past ten minutes, pushed along by a strong freshening breeze.

He didn't really know what he was doing here. But then he hadn't really known what he was doing earlier that morning back at Chuck and Kathy's either, except rattling around in the big house after the kids had all gone off to school. So he'd gotten into his car and told Kathy he was going to go check on things at his place of business.

At last, he opened the car door and let himself into the back of the shop. The little bell rang over the door and a couple of his employees turned at their windows, registering surprise and worry, but he simply waved a hand in acknowledgment, turned into his office, and sat down behind his desk.

It didn't take Liza Sato ten seconds to appear in the doorway. Wearing jeans and a cowled fisherman's sweater, with her hands on her hips, she wore an expression of equal parts frustration and concern. "What in the world are you doing here, Michael?"

He tried a smile that died halfway. "I'm not all that sure, to tell you the truth. It seemed like a good idea at the time." A vague gesture. "How's everything out there?"

"Everything out there is fine. Except you shouldn't be here."

"Where else should I be?"

"How about back home?"

"That's kind of the problem, Liz. Home's gone."

Her eyes widened and her hand went to her mouth. "Oh, I didn't mean . . ."

"It's all right. I know what you meant. You want to come in?"

"Sure." She closed the door behind her, then leaned back against it with her arms crossed. "Michael, I don't know what to say. I am just so, so sorry."

His shoulders rose and fell. He spread his hands on the surface of his desk, then simply shook his head and shrugged again.

Liza pushed herself off the wall and came around the desk, where she draped an arm around his shoulders, leaned down, and kissed the top of his head. She felt his body heave in a sigh, then she let go and boosted herself onto the desk. "Really," she said, "you don't need to be here."

"I know. But I don't know where else I should be." He let out a breath. "I stopped by the house, where the house was, this morning. You know how weird that was? I mean, I leave there Friday and it's my home, where my kids live, where all of our stuff is, where most of everyday life happens. And then this morning I go by and all that's gone. And Janice with it." He looked up at her. "I just don't have any idea what I'm supposed to do now."

"You don't have to do anything."

"No. I've at least got to somehow be there for my kids. Although thank God for school, which is where they are now. I don't know how they're . . . hell, who am I kidding? I don't know anything." He paused. "I'm sorry. I didn't come down here to cry on anybody's shoulder."

"That's all right," she said. "You can cry all you want, Michael. Crying's okay."

"Well, it's not. Not really." He quickly patted her knee, right there next to him. "But thanks for the offer." Pushing himself back a little farther away from her, he said, "I heard you met Inspector Glitsky on Saturday morning."

She nodded. "He came by, yes."

"And evidently I was late getting to work on Friday?"

"Were you?"

"That's what he said. Or rather, somebody who works here said I was. He seemed to think it was important."

"In what way?"

"In the way that I might have stayed around to make sure the fire was well advanced before I started driving to work."

Liza's face went dark. "That's just nuts! He can't really think that."

"I was late, though, wasn't I?"

She thought a moment. "Well, I remember I opened up, but beyond that . . ." She shrugged. "But really, though, so what?"

"Well, I finally remembered, wracking my brain all weekend, just a couple of other little things on my mind. I stopped for gas coming in, got stuck behind an RV who needed like a hundred gallons, then got caught in a line inside after the pump told me I had to go to the cashier to get my receipt, which I never wound up getting anyway because the guy two people in front of me started screaming something about getting the wrong Lotto ticket. Anyway, in case anybody asks again, which they probably won't."

"I don't think it was a big deal anyway, Michael."

"Well, Glitsky kind of made it seem like one. And you'd think I would have remembered all that insanity at the gas station. But I swear to God, it all just went away."

"Maybe something to do with your house burning down and your wife dying. You think that could do it?"

"Yeah. Maybe that. But I just wanted to tell you."

"I never thought anything about it, Michael. Really."

"Well, good. But I think the question is going to be moot anyway."

"Why's that?"

"Because I'm pretty sure I know who did it."

17

Ro Curtlee and his lawyer, Tristan Denardi, sat at the bar at Tadich Grill, both of them eating cioppino.

"I know you're not supposed to ask," Ro was saying. "I know you don't want to know. But I'm telling you anyway. I wasn't anywhere near the place. I did not kill Nuñez, though it doesn't break my heart to see her out of the picture."

"Well, she's not quite out of the picture, Ro." Denardi, for all of his theatrics in the courtroom, cut a more or less paternal, patrician, low-key figure. A full head of silver hair, an unlined face that suggested time spent in a tanning salon, a beautifully cut Italian suit with a gold silk tie. "They're still going to use her testimony from last time."

"Sure. But it won't be her on the stand giving it again. You said they're just going to read what she said last time, right?"

"Right. There's no other option."

"So how convincing is that going to be?

"Not very. And I know and agree, it's a definite plus for us. Although I admit I would have liked it better if she were still alive and we could persuade her not to testify at all. Or even to change her testimony. Plus, then there wouldn't be any question at all of your possible involvement in her death."

Ro rolled his eyes. "How many times do I have to tell you . . . ?"

Denardi raised his hand, palm out. "I understand that. I'm not accusing you of anything, Ro. It's just that the timing, her dying in the week after you're released. You have to admit it's unfortunate."

"Not my problem, Counselor. And not yours." With his good hand, Ro stabbed a scallop. "Seems to me our one problem remaining is that other witness, Gonzalvez. We've got to find her and make her change her mind either about what she's going to say or whether she really wants to say it at all. We don't want her showing up as a surprise if this thing ever goes back to trial."

"No. I understand that. But as I've explained to you, she disappeared right after your trial. She's likely to stay disappeared. I think that if your parents haven't been able to locate her, it might prove to be a little difficult for anybody else."

Ro shook his head. "I don't buy it."

"Why not?"

"Because they weren't really looking for her. They were going to hassle her, maybe, put her out of work if they could, but once she was gone they let it go. What was the point? But now, for us, it's a different story. Now, she alone could swing a jury. You see that?"

"I acknowledge the possibility, yes."

"Well, then, I say we find her first."

"How do you propose we do that?"

"You got private eyes who work for you, don't you?"

"Sure. Several."

"Well, put one of them on it."

"You know, Ro, the rumor is she's in Guatemala. She's really not coming back."

"I'm just saying, why not be sure?"

———

In spite of how he'd left it with Arnie Becker, Glitsky had his tape recorder out on Michael Durbin's desk in the back of the shop. The door was closed behind them, rendering into a muted white noise

157

the normal business dealings taking place out front among the customers. Glitsky had recognized Liza Sato among the employees right away from his Saturday morning interview, and twice now, in his peripheral vision, he'd noticed her at the window, coming back to check on how things were going between her boss and the cop.

He'd already covered Durbin's belated and labored explanation of his tardiness coming into work last Friday morning. Durbin had then mentioned his suspicions about Ro Curtlee, and Glitsky had dutifully listened and asked the appropriate questions. Now, though, with that line pretty much played out, he thought he'd bring things a little closer to home. "But having been at the arraignment, you knew about the recent history between me and Ro? The arrest and so forth?"

"Sure."

"I'm just curious why you didn't come by and say hello to me then."

"Well, you were obviously busy and in the middle of things. And I was way back in the gallery. I would have had to wait and then walk back through a lot of people. And then of course I didn't have anything specific to talk to you about, either."

"So what happened this morning, with the phone call to me?"

"Well, I put it together about Ro and me yesterday and I thought you'd understand. I mean, knowing all the background with Ro and me and all."

"It would be easier to sell the idea to me, is that it?"

"I didn't really think of it in those terms. I figured I'd pass along whatever I knew to you. I thought I was doing the right thing."

"Well," Glitsky said, "as far as that goes, you did fine."

"That's a relief. I didn't mean to cause any trouble. I just thought . . . well, you know. Ro. He's a dangerous man."

"Yes, he is."

"Listen." Durbin cleared his throat. "Could we take a short

break, maybe get us something to drink? I'm dying of thirst. Could I offer you some water? Coffee? Coke? Only diet, I'm afraid."

"Thanks. I'm good, but you go ahead."

Durbin got out of his chair and walked around Glitsky and out into the hallway. Glitsky turned off his tape recorder and looked around at the small, well-ordered office. At a glance, it reinforced his view that Durbin was an organized, well-ordered guy.

After a minute or so, he returned with a clear plastic cup full of ice cubes and an oversize plastic bottle of Diet Coke. He poured a splash into the glass, let the foam settle, and poured a little more, then placed the bottle on the desk between them.

Glitsky turned his tape recorder back on. "When we talked Saturday," he began, "you mentioned that you and your wife were having some troubles."

Durbin stopped mid-drink and set his glass down. "I don't understand," he said. "Why does that possibly matter now?"

"Why would it matter any less than two days ago?"

"Because two days ago we didn't know that Ro had killed Janice. Now we do, so what difference does it make if things had been a little difficult lately?"

Glitsky framed his answer carefully. "Just because Ro had a reason to kill Janice doesn't mean that he did, or someone else did not. We don't know that Ro did."

Durbin's voice got loud. "The hell we don't. What the hell more do you need?"

Keeping his calm, Glitsky replied. "We need evidence, sir. Fingerprints, DNA, somebody seeing him at your house. Something a jury will need to convict."

"So go look around him to find your evidence. You're not going to find it sniffing around whatever problems my wife and I might have been having."

Glitsky, somewhat taken aback, slowed himself down before he replied. "I get to ask the questions here, sir. If you don't want to answer them, that's fine. But we'll have the answers sooner or later."

"Are you seriously telling me I'm a suspect here?"

"I don't have a suspect yet. I'm looking for one."

Durbin slammed his fist on the desk. "You got one, for Christ's sake. You need a map? Can I draw you a picture? It's Ro Curtlee."

Glitsky took a beat. "Was it you who was having an affair?"

Durbin shook his head. "Jesus Christ! I don't believe this." He paused. "Should I be getting myself a lawyer?"

"That's your absolute right, if you feel you need one."

"This is bullshit."

"No, sir. It's a murder investigation." Glitsky sat back, his mouth set in a thin line. "And for the record, you should know that I'm not a fan of that kind of language. So we can either be civil with each other or not. Again, it's your choice. I'm trying to find out everything I can about your wife so I'll have a better idea of where to look if I'm going to locate her killer. Do you want to help me or not?"

"Of course. In fact, I've given him to you."

"And I'll be looking into that, I promise. In the meantime, you're here and I need to know who your wife might have been seeing. Or who you were."

Slumping back, Durbin sucked in a lungful of air. Brooding for another moment, at last he said, "I wasn't having an affair. With her, I'd bet one of her patients."

"Do you have any idea how long this might have been going on?"

"I don't know anything about it, except just the bare fact, and maybe not even that. We hadn't been . . . intimate . . . for a couple of months. At least a couple of months, though I wasn't keeping track. A long time, I'll say that. But I don't want you thinking I didn't love her anymore, because I did. I do. I was sure we'd come out of it."

"So you never called her on it? Confronted her directly?"

"No."

"Not on last Friday, either?"

"No. Not then. Not ever." He suddenly reached for the glass in front of him and drank deeply from it. "You ever go through a bad time with your wife, Lieutenant? Sometimes you just wait it out, you hope something gives."

"Of course." Glitsky had no intention of discussing anything about his marriage with Michael Durbin, or anyone else for that matter. "Would you happen to have a list of her patients?" he asked.

"No. They'd be at her office, over by Stonestown." Durbin gave him the exact address and suite number. "If you can get at 'em. She was super-protective about her records. Patient/doctor privilege, you know."

"I've heard of it. Is there anything else you can think of that you might want to tell me about?"

18

The way it worked with Eztli was that nearly every day he got most of the day off. He had no regular duties down at the Castro Street offices of the *Courier*, where Cliff and Theresa spent most of their time during daylight hours. Back home, Eztli was in charge of the general upkeep of the house, though, supervising the cleaning, kitchen, and gardening staff, coordinating visits from repairmen and deliveries. He was a very efficient manager, and these duties, even at their most onerous, would rarely keep him occupied until noon, after which his afternoon time was his own. When he wasn't out on special projects, the Curtlees expected him to be home and dressed in his business suit to greet visitors and to serve as a generally unobtrusive bodyguard and butler.

He had a license to carry a firearm, courtesy of a sheriff from a small county in the Central Valley, so when he was dressed up in the house, he packed an ugly black semiautomatic under his arm in a shoulder holster. Sometimes he also wore it when he was outside. He had not shot anyone since a few months before he'd come to the United States.

Today, since Eztli was out with Ro and had already learned that anything might happen—he really liked the vibe around this kid—his gun rested snug up under the arm of his black Oakland Raiders jacket. Eztli had both dropped and then picked up Ro at Tadich Grill and now he pulled the 4Runner out into traffic with his passenger back aboard and said, "Somebody joined in with us. Waited with me in the garage the whole time." When Ro turned around, Eztli said, "The white Honda, looks like an Accord. White guy, tie, no coat, half bald . . ."

"Got him," Ro said, and came back around facing front. "You know him?"

"Never seen him before."

"So. One of Glitsky's plainclothes guys."

"Got to be."

"All right."

They drove a few blocks farther west until just short of Polk, Ro told Eztli to pull over into the next parking spot he saw and keep the car running. When he did, the white Honda, which had been following about three cars behind them, cruised on by, the driver apparently whistling to the radio, eyes straight ahead.

"Guy's going for the Academy Award," Eztli said. "Now what?"

"Now he's going to turn to go around the block and catch us again, so let's get on his ass instead."

Eztli pulled out in a squeal of rubber, then at the corner and against the light cut in front of a bus coming up Polk Street and fell in behind the white Honda just in time to see it turn right again at the next corner. Eztli didn't need any instructions—accelerating up the block, he almost went onto two wheels as he turned steeply uphill and had gained half his ground by the time the Honda turned right again at the next corner.

This time, as Eztli got within sight, they saw that the Honda had done their old trick of pulling off to the side and coming to a halt.

"Block him off," Ro said, and Eztli pulled a hard right into the driveway just in front of the Honda. Before their 4Runner had even come to a complete stop, Ro was out onto the street, the middle finger of his uncasted hand extended. "Hey!" he yelled, all the while flipping off the man who'd been tailing him. "Hey!" Coming right up to the window, now. "You want to get off my ass? What the hell are you doing?"

The window came down and the man, not at all impressed with Ro's outburst, held his wallet up with his left hand, flashing his badge. In his right, he held a gun that was pointed directly at Ro's face.

"And who the fuck are you?" Ro asked. "I've about had it with you guys, you know that?"

Seeing Eztli coming up, too, hands in the pockets of his Raiders jacket, the man held the badge up farther so that Eztli could see it, too. So there would be no misunderstanding. "I'm an inspector with the DA's office, and I'm here to make sure you two boys don't get yourselves into any more trouble."

"Well, I'm here to tell you to stay the fuck out of my life. I've got my rights here. I can go where I want and do what I want. You hear me?"

Eztli put a restraining hand on Ro's arm and leaned down. "Did Wes Farrell put you on this?" he asked quietly.

"We have other DAs," Matt Lewis said. "I take assignments from many of them. Now get back in your car and move along."

"Fucking Jenkins," Ro said to no one, then to Eztli, "Got to be Jenkins."

"She's an extraordinarily determined woman, isn't she?"

"Yeah, and those legs go all the way up, I bet. I'd like to get myself some of that, wouldn't you, Ez?"

"I would not turn it down."

"I'm telling you exactly once more, move along."

"Ooh," Ro said, leaning in toward the car. "I'm thinking maybe we hit a nerve here, Ez. Maybe the man here's already had some of that."

Matt Lewis raised his gun hand a little higher.

Ro, eyes on the gun, began to step back, but Eztli was right behind him, solid as a wall. "So Farrell didn't assign you," Eztli said. He did not retreat one single step. "Nice wheels, by the way. Is that the Accord?"

By way of answer, Lewis pointed the gun at him and said, "One."

Eztli kept his calm. "The officer wants us to back up, Ro," he said.

"I hear him."

"Then by all means let us comply." He backed up and pulled Ro along with him, talking easily as they walked back to the 4Runner, "The city doesn't use Hondas as city vehicles, so how does he stay in touch without a radio?"

"His cell?" Ro replied.

"Not when he's driving," Eztli said. "That would be against the law." He went around the bumper of the 4Runner, opened his driver door, got in, and started the engine.

Matt Lewis, shaking from adrenaline, put his Glock back into its holster. He turned on the ignition and waited for the 4Runner to back out and drive away.

———

As they turned back west onto California Street, Ro asked, "What was all that about his car? The Honda?"

Eztli glanced at the rearview mirror. "What's he doing now?"

Ro turned around to look. Lewis was right behind them. "Just driving."

"No phone?"

"No. Unless he's on speaker."

"Does he appear to be talking?"

"No."

"I'm thinking not. No Bluetooth on that model. It's too old."

"So?"

"So it's his own car. He doesn't have a radio. He's not using the phone."

"Right."

"So no one knows where he is or what he's doing."

"Somebody knows he's assigned to tail us."

"How do they know we didn't shake him?"

"Okay, but again, so what?"

"So you'll see."

They rolled across Van Ness, Franklin, Gough, Eztli's eyes flitting back and forth between his rearview mirror and the road ahead. As they approached Fillmore, he suddenly flicked on his signal and pulled over into the left-turn lane.

"Where're we goin'?" Ro asked.

"Just taking a little detour. Too much traffic up here."

Heading south now, they stayed on Fillmore as it morphed in only a few blocks from a well-traveled, high-end shopping street to a nearly empty thoroughfare through one of the city's ghettos. Eztli, already driving slowly, slowed further at each corner while he checked the traffic on the cross streets. Turk Street was deserted in both directions, and he suddenly turned right, continued about halfway down the block, then pulled over and came to a stop.

"What now?" Ro asked.

"I'm tired of this guy. You tired of this guy?"

"I'm tired of all of 'em."

"Okay, then. You see anybody?"

"Where?"

"Anywhere."

Ro spun around, checked the sidewalks, the street itself. "No."

Eztli nodded. "Me, neither."

Behind them, Matt Lewis had pulled over as well and put the car into park, but he hadn't quite decided what he was going to do. There was no point in following these clowns all over the city so long as they knew he was following them. Amanda's original idea, sprung on her own initiative, had been to see if they would lead him back to any of their suspected crime scenes or to her missing witness, Gonzalvez. Or, failing that, to someplace where they simply did something else illegal, and then he could call in the troops and arrest them again. They both had figured, given who these guys were, it wouldn't take too long.

But now when Matt Lewis looked up, he saw Eztli coming again around the back of his car. Impatient now with the absurdity of this situation, he'd just about decided to drive around them and come back another day. But now here came the Aztec in his Raiders jacket, looking like he had something to say. So Lewis lowered his window and leaned his head outside. "What now?"

Eztli was almost up to him, his face placid, even apologetic. "Oh," he said. "Nothing much. I just forgot . . ." With no further warning, he brought his gun around from where he'd been holding it out of sight, and in one fluid movement pressed it up close to Matt Lewis's head and pulled the trigger.

19

Dismas Hardy's suggestion to have the grand jury indict Ro Curtlee on a no-bail multiple-murder charge had grown on Farrell all day as he prowled the offices on the third floor of the Hall of Justice, taking the pulse of his staff.

When he'd started on his rounds, he still didn't quite trust that he was contemplating the right decision. Indeed, when he'd first heard about the Nuñez killing, he'd considered and rejected the grand jury solution for what he thought had been sound reasons: that he'd only have sixty days to bring Ro to a trial that would probably not convict him; that his acquittal on that charge would make it much more difficult to bring him back to a retrial in his initial case; that in any case, he'd be out on bail again in another couple of months. He could have asked the court to join the cases for trial, but he couldn't count on having that motion granted. And if the cases had been kept separate, it would have been a train wreck.

But that was before Janice Durbin.

With that murder, Farrell's personal priorities had evolved. He'd finally come to believe that keeping Ro behind bars was a valid end in itself, for no matter how long a time. If he could get the grand jury to indict, he'd take sixty days as a good start and work on getting more jail time from there—try to move up the retrial date, work on Baretto and Donahoe to revisit their bail decisions, whatever it took.

The lawyers on his staff were generally a bunch of hard-core prosecutors, and the events of the past few days, particularly Ro's bail hearing, had cut into the team's morale in a big way. Now Farrell's suggestion that he circumvent the judges' rulings met only with untainted enthusiasm. Finally he was the boss and acting like it.

Taking charge.

Not one of Farrell's assistant district attorneys had any doubt about Ro's guilt, both originally on the rape and murder charges at his trial, and then with the two latest victims—Felicia Nuñez and Janice Durbin—and all of them seemed to believe that the grand jury idea was legal and liable to conclude with Ro sitting in a jail cell where he belonged.

Now, closing in on five o'clock, having made his decision, Farrell called his own task force together. If he was going to go to the grand jury, he needed to know everything relevant that anyone could give him on Ro Curtlee. His office continued to be logistically challenged, however, and so he had his invitees seated willy-nilly, Medical Examiner John Strout and Police Chief Vi Lapeer on the couch, Arson Inspector Arnie Becker on an ottoman, Glitsky and Amanda Jenkins on a couple of folding chairs brought in from Treya's office.

Farrell himself sat on the sturdy oak library table. After he asked them to turn off their cell phones and then thanked everyone for coming at his summons, he got down to it. "I think it's pretty clear with this Durbin homicide that Ro's taking this time out of jail as an opportunity to pay back some of the people who helped put him away in the first place.

"Abe and Amanda, I know you've both argued that same thing right from the start, and I want to apologize to both of you for not making a stronger case against bail in the first place. You were both right. I was wrong.

"And for the record, Abe, your instincts were also right about trying to arrest him for the threat against you. Even if you'd waited and gotten a warrant, I believe Her Honor Erin Donahoe would have done what she did, bail-wise. So now the situation really couldn't be clearer—if we're going to override these bail decisions, and we must—we've got to get him indicted, and I mean yesterday, for no-bail murder.

"So"—he spread his palms, supplicating—"I need you all to help me. I know we've got the shoes on both victims, we've got the connections and motivations related to his trial, the fire in both cases. None of which, I'm sorry to say, rises to the level of convincing evidence. It might work for the grand jury if I tap-dance enough around the related motives, but it would be nice to have something else in the line of evidence since we're going to get huge media on this, and I'm predicting they're not going to give us a pass just 'cause we're the good guys."

For a moment, no one spoke.

Glitsky looked at Becker, over to Amanda, back to Farrell. "That's all we've got, Wes. Except they were all strangled and naked except for the shoes. But that's not enough evidence, either."

All of the people in the room knew the extent to which the grand jury was a prosecutor's tool. There was no judge at the proceedings and no defense attorneys allowed to refute or even argue against any of the DA's assertions. Still, although the standard of proof was low, it was in theory nevertheless based on evidence. And so far they didn't have much.

"How about witnesses?" Farrell asked. "Arnie?"

"On Nuñez, we have two people over on Baker who saw a car like Ro's around the corner. Probably the same car. And no, they didn't catch or notice the license number, and nobody saw him get in or out of it. Otherwise, pretty much zero."

"How about the same car at the Durbin site?"

Becker shook his head. "Not yet. Still canvassing, but I'm not holding my breath."

Farrell let out a disappointed sigh. "John?" he asked.

The ancient doctor scratched at his white hair. "I know y'all been talking about rape an' hopin' to pick up some DNA, but the Nuñez woman was too burnt for any analysis whatever. Wasn't anything like fluid left to test. And Durbin, best I can tell, there wasn't any rape at all. Although I did, I told Arnie here this morning, I did find that she had a dose of chlamydia. The bottom line is that there's nothin' I can point out proves either one of 'em was raped at all. So I wouldn't be comfortable putting that in your MO."

"What about the chlamydia?" Farrell asked. "Would she have been contagious?"

"Yeah, but even if it got passed on to Curtlee, there's no provin' it came from her. So what's that get you?"

Amanda Jenkins cleared her throat. "If I may?" she said. "How about if we think about the one trial that Ro's had? I mean, there was no question about evidence in that case. We had the two witnesses solid, and his DNA with his victim."

"Yeah," Farrell said, "but he's already been tried, convicted, and appealed out on that one. You can't punish somebody for winning an appeal by recharging him with something more serious."

"Of course. But how about if you take it from a completely different angle? Tell the grand jury that you're joining that first case, *Sandoval*, with these later two. So you're not upping the charge in *Sandoval*, which is the legal objection. And why are you joining the cases, then? Because the first one is the motive for the others. So now you've got multiple murder, and that's a special circumstance, and that's no bail. And that way—I really like this, Wes— you also make a neat end-run around the sixty-day issue. If his attorneys press for trial, they're shooting themselves in the foot because we've got him again cold on the first one."

Farrell, swinging his feet as he contemplated, sat with the idea for a long moment. "It's good, Amanda, but I still think we're on some pretty shaky legal grounds."

"Not really. If we tried charging the Sandoval rape again, definitely. But we're not. So the specials this time out aren't murder/rape, but multiple murder. And if we've got the evidence to convict him on one, and we do, that's all we need."

Farrell, clearly warming to the general idea, still wanted more specifics. "So how exactly do I sell it to the grand jury?"

"That these are all connected? Aside from the fact that it's pretty self-evident on its face, you just tell them, 'Ladies and gentlemen, Janice Durbin was a suburban housewife. She wasn't robbed, she didn't have any known connection to gangs or to drugs. Who else in the world would want her dead except Ro Curtlee, and what was his motive? Revenge on her husband, pure and simple.' "

Really into it now, Amanda looked around the room and found herself selling it to everyone. "You remind the jury that their standard of proof isn't reasonable doubt, but merely probable cause. Could any one of them really believe that Mrs. Durbin getting killed right now was just a coincidence? Did they want to live with that? No, even though there's ten years between them, these murders are obviously all connected, so obviously that it can't be ignored. And more murders are going to keep happening, with who knows how many other victims, until Ro is back in jail."

Farrell, nodding easily now, finally said, "I think so. I think that might work." He looked around. "Anybody else have anything to add?"

Vi Lapeer spoke up for the first time. "It would be better if this didn't leak."

"I hope," Farrell said, "that goes without saying."

"Sorry." Lapeer's smile was tight and unyielding. "In Philadelphia, sometimes that wasn't always so clear." Now she turned to Glitsky. "I'd try to get your investigations on these two new cases assigned to an event number"—this meant that the investigations would have an unlimited budget from the city's General Fund—"but I'd have to get His Honor to sign off on that, and we can't go there. So given that that's not going to happen, do you have enough personnel, Abe?"

"I could move people around, maybe assign out overtime," he said, "but who's going to pay for it?"

"How about if you go over budget, you don't get dinged? On my guarantee."

"Thank you," Glitsky said. "I'll find some troops and put them on it." He turned to Farrell. "So what's our time frame on this?"

Farrell shrugged, looked over to Jenkins. "Amanda?"

"If I drop everything else, I can present most of it next week, that is a week from tomorrow. Or you could, Wes, if I brought you up to speed."

"It's your case," Farrell said.

"All right." Jenkins, clearly pleased, let out a breath of relief. "I'll need every witness I can get, both from Ro's trial and from the ongoing investigations. If all goes perfectly, maybe we can hope for an indictment two weeks from tomorrow."

"Jesus Christ," Arnie Becker said. "That long? He could wipe out half the city in that time."

Jenkins threw him a look. "Maybe, but that long would basically be a world record for speed, Inspector," she said.

"In the meantime," Lapeer said, "I can keep it out of the homicide budget and authorize putting someone on him twenty-four/seven."

"I've already done that," Jenkins said.

This was news to Farrell. "You did?"

"Well, he volunteered, actually. Matt Lewis. One of our inspectors," she explained to Lapeer. "Matt thought I might be a next possible target and wanted to keep an eye out. And it wasn't twenty-four/seven. Just his shift and then maybe a few hours at night."

"He'll want some backup, then," Lapeer said.

"That would help," Jenkins said.

Farrell surveyed the room briefly. "All right," he said, "it looks like we've got a workable plan with a reasonable timeline. Longer than I'd like in a perfect world, but probably the best we can do. Amanda, since you're going to be presenting to the grand jury, why don't you take point coordinating all these efforts with what you're going to need. Couple of weeks, with any luck, we'll get this animal back where he belongs before he can do any more damage. I want to thank you all again for . . ."

A knock on the door interrupted him, followed immediately by Treya from the outer office. "I'm sorry to interrupt," she said, "but Abe, somebody hunted you down and there's an urgent call for you out at my desk."

20

In the decade or so that it had been since he'd last shot anybody, Eztli had almost forgotten the pure adrenaline rush and pleasure of violent action, of simple pure killing. He didn't realize how much he'd missed it, having to make do over the years with the vicarious thrills of gamecock or dog fighting. Now, the taste of blood still fresh in his mouth, it was as though he'd been sensation deprived, weaned slowly, methodically, and successfully off his drug and then reintroduced to its power and its beauty.

In ways he didn't try to understand, he knew that Ro was somehow the source of this drug. Before Ro had gotten out of jail, Eztli had been marking time, comfortable and secure, with the Curtlees. And then, suddenly Ro appeared at the home with his energy and fearlessness, and Eztli, riding around with him, catching the high-tension vibe of the younger man, had in the past days woken up from what felt like a long sleep. Ending in the climax of the gunshot to the man's head this afternoon. Ro, perhaps even unwittingly, had been the catalyst, the gateway to the drug.

And Eztli was going to protect that source.

Now at around nine o'clock, he was sitting in his car alone, parked across the street from Buena Vista Park in the Upper Haight. Wes Farrell lived in a medium-size Victorian home just down the block that Eztli and Ro had checked out—the address compliments of one of Denardi's private investigators—as one of Ro's first excursions after he'd gotten home. Farrell, Eztli knew, was going to be the key to whatever happened with Ro—and Farrell was weak and indecisive.

He could be controlled, and much more effectively than with Cliff and Theresa's carrot-and-stick, relatively subtle approach.

The trick, Eztli felt, was to see the man in his natural environment and determine where, when, and what kind of pressure to bring to bear on him to control his decision-making. What Eztli had said to Ro was true—Farrell was his best friend. It really wasn't in Ro's, or Eztli's, best interests to eliminate Farrell, to take him entirely out of the picture. No, Farrell needed to be part of any equation that could keep Ro permanently out of prison. He would be crucial to that.

Eztli simply had to make him understand the seriousness of the situation. So far, Farrell had mostly stood aside and let things happen, and the Curtlees' influence had carried the day. But eventually he was going to have to make a decision—to prosecute Ro or to let the matter drop. Eztli did not want him confused as to the proper choice.

So he had to get to know him a little more. See where the pressure points were.

———

When Farrell dragged himself back into his home at nine thirty that Monday night, he could not ever remember being so tired. Somewhat to his surprise, the house was completely dark. Well, he wouldn't blame Sam if she had decided to go out to have dinner somewhere by herself or even with one of her friends. He'd been terrible company lately.

Tonight he hadn't called her to tell her he'd be late, hadn't even thought about it in the hurricane of emotion and upheaval that had swept through his office at the news that Matt Lewis had been found shot to death in his car out in the Fillmore district. Amanda Jenkins breaking down, inconsolably wedged between grief and guilt, John Strout, Treya, and Farrell himself administering to her while Glitsky and Becker headed out to the crime scene. Lapeer herself, the chief of police, had gone down to the magistrate on duty to try to get whoever it was to sign off on a search warrant for the Curtlee home, since no one had the tiniest doubt as to who was responsible for Lewis's death.

Farrell flicked on the light by the front door and in a second he heard the familiar *click, click, click* of Gert's nails on the hardwood floor as she came padding out of the kitchen to meet him. She'd probably been sleeping in her bed in there, and now he reached down and petted her. "Where's your mom?" he asked, putting down his briefcase, turning on more lights, heading for the refrigerator.

The answer came in the form of a note she left him on the kitchen counter:

"Wes—Sorry if this seems abrupt, but we both know I've been thinking about taking a little time off from us for a while now. You not calling or making it home tonight, after all of our discussions about just keeping on communicating with one another . . .

"Anyway, it was a wake-up call telling me that I should actually do something, rather than just taking things as they come and building up resentment against you. If I was choosing to stay around here and just keep taking it, whose fault is that? So I'm going to be staying over at Marianne's house for at least the next few days and I'd appreciate it if you'd leave me my space so I can think about what comes next for us. I don't know, maybe you won't want me back once you get used to me being gone, either. You've got to admit we haven't been having much fun lately. I'm not really much of a politician's wife, or even girlfriend, I'm afraid. I just don't seem to have much of a stomach for it. The compromises, the deals, Ro Curtlee, all of it.

"I do still love you—I do—and I'm fine. But I don't know if I can live anymore, or want to, the way we've been lately. Sam

"P.S. Gert has had dinner, but probably needs a walk before bed.

If you want, you can leave her at the Center during the days, and I'll drop her back here at night, if you're going to be around. Just let me know."

Farrell let himself down on one of the kitchen chairs, laid the note on the table in front of him. Gert had put her head on his leg and he scratched the top of it absently.

After some time had gone by—he had no sense of how much— Gert started nudging his leg and whining. Moving like a zombie, Farrell put her leash on her and retraced his steps back to the front door, and then out into the night.

The street that his house was on mostly encircled the park, and he and Gert had a regular route they walked in the morning and before bed where she took care of her business. The park itself, now in the dark, was its usual open expanse of nothingness, and suddenly tonight, as he walked around its periphery, Farrell in his numbness gradually became aware of an ominous something that he couldn't quite put his finger on.

Stopping, he looked out into the park's center. Several of the lights in the street all around were out, and he couldn't for the life of him remember if they'd been working over the past few days. Ahead of him, there were no lights at all, either in the park or on the street. At the end of the leash, Gert started in with a high-pitched whining. Farrell walked on a few more steps, then stopped again.

He stood completely still for a minute or so. There was no sound at all in the street, not any movement that he could see. Finally he whispered down to his dog, "Come on, girl. Back we go."

But Gert, with hair standing up now down the center of her back, strained at her leash, growling low and harsh, and now barked at something out in the invisible distance.

Keeping a tight rein on her, Farrell moved up next to her head and petted it. "Come on now, come on." Pulling her around, heeling, back toward his house.

When they got back inside, he closed and locked the front door behind him. He took off Gert's leash and started to go back again into the kitchen. As a matter of course, whenever he did this, Gert would tag along next to him. But this time, she turned back to the front door and another low rumbling came out of her.

"Hey, easy now," he said. "It's okay. Everything's okay." But holding her by the collar, he opened the door again and took a quick look outside at his benign street upon which nothing moved.

After he finally got Gert calmed down, doing her business out the back stairs in their tiny backyard and then lying back down on her cushion in the kitchen, Farrell went over to the liquor cabinet and pulled down a bottle of Knob Creek bourbon. He free-poured himself most of a juice glass full, threw in enough ice cubes to take the liquid to the rim of the glass, then drank it all off in a gulp.

This—losing his woman and imagining threats on empty streets—was not by any stretch what he had bargained for when he'd run for DA. In his heart, he didn't really think that he was that serious a person. He had some verbal skills and he got along reasonably well with people from most walks of society, but he'd never considered himself to be a leader of men. He had originally been talked into running for DA with the thought that he'd bring a measure of enlightenment to the law enforcement community within the city. From his perspective as a lifetime defense attorney, he had believed that there was in fact often a problem with cops using more force than was justified. He thought that police often overstepped their mandates with immigrants as well as many of the other assorted minority populations in town. And by the same token, he'd represented a host of people who had made mistakes and, no question, were not angels—but through a mixture of glib humor and just the right amount of backbone, he had never felt in danger from most of these miscreants.

Well, there had been one. Mark Dooher had been Farrell's best friend for years. A fellow attorney, but inhabiting an entirely different stratosphere from Farrell's, Dooher had been counsel to the Archdiocese of San Francisco, among a host of other high-end clients. When Dooher's wife was killed in a home invasion, the overweening, overreacting police—Abe Glitsky, in point of fact—had launched what Wes took to be a vendetta against his friend, eventually bringing him to trial charged with his wife's murder. Farrell had taken on his defense, and in a brutal and grueling trial against Amanda Jenkins, had won an acquittal. That trial, moreover, marked the beginning of Farrell's rise to prominence in the city's legal community.

The only problem was that Mark Dooher—pillar of the community, wonderful father and husband, legal face of the Archdiocese—had, in fact, been guilty of killing his wife. And also guilty of raping a woman while he'd been in college. And killing another man with whom he'd been selling drugs in Vietnam. And gutting with a bayonet another young attorney with whom he'd been in litigation.

And then he had tried to kill Farrell, too.

Now, with Ro Curtlee, Wes felt that he was once again up against a true sociopath who might have given Mark Dooher a run for his money. He'd been out of prison for less than a month and he'd almost undoubtedly already killed three people, including Farrell's own investigator. And no one, apparently, seemed to be able to stop him. Vi Lapeer had volunteered to put a watch on him around the clock until the grand jury could issue an indictment against him, but she wouldn't have had time to do that yet today. Ro could be out there on Farrell's street right now, sitting in a car, lying in wait. He might break in here and light the place on fire.

One thing seemed certain—Ro was committed to staying out of jail. It seemed obvious to Farrell that he'd prefer to die resisting arrest—look how he'd fought with Glitsky and his two men—than go back to prison. So he wasn't afraid of anything. He would attack any and every person whom he wanted to punish or who threatened his freedom. Felicia Nuñez, Janice Durbin, Matt Lewis. Gloria Gonzalvez, wherever she was. And to that list Farrell felt he could confidently add Amanda Jenkins, Glitsky, and his family.

And himself.

————

Glitsky turned the keys—first the dead bolt, then the regular lock—in his front door as quietly as he could. It was sometime after midnight. Inside, he untied his shoes and slipped out of them, then picked them up and went around the corner to his small living room, where Treya stood up from where she was sitting on the couch and said, "Thank God you're home. If you could spare one, I could use a hug."

She stepped forward into his arms. Held him as tightly as she could. He dropped his shoes onto the floor and she felt something give in him and she reached up behind him and pulled his head down to the crook of her neck. He let his head rest where it was, heavy, and she could feel the thick, strong muscles in his neck letting go of the tension in them. After another moment, his arms came up around her, too, pressing her against him, so hard she almost, for a second, couldn't breathe.

She didn't care. This was all she wanted. If she couldn't catch a breath, she would do without it.

He exhaled completely, nuzzled his head into her neck and kissed it two, three times. Then straightened up. "You've been up all this time?"

"Apparently."

"How's Amanda?"

"As bad as you'd think. Maybe worse. She thinks it's her fault."

"It's not."

"No. I know that. It's going to take her a while, though. You want to sit?"

"I believe I could."

Treya sat back down where she'd been waiting on the couch and pulled the blanket she'd brought out of their bedroom up around her. Glitsky eased himself down sideways at the other end of the couch.

"You get anything?" she asked.

"Do you want to count getting rejected on the search warrant?"

"Even with the chief herself requesting it?'

"Even then. Same rules for the chief. You need probable cause."

"How about Matt Lewis was following him and Ro shot him?"

"How do we know Lewis was following him?"

"That was his assignment."

"How do we know he ever caught up with him?"

"Because we do. Didn't he call Amanda?"

"At lunchtime. This, the shooting, was at least an hour later, maybe more. Maybe in that time he lost them and went on to something else, and whatever that was got him killed."

"Does anybody really believe that?"

"No."

"And who's 'them' now?"

"Another guy was driving, not Ro. Matt Lewis didn't know him but told Amanda he looked more or less American Indian. They came out of the Curtlees' house together. I'm thinking it's the bodyguard I met the first time I went out there."

"So Matt Lewis followed them for an hour. Isn't that probable cause right there? They must know the chief isn't making this up."

"They might know it, but they're not signing the little piece of paper." Glitsky drew a hand down the side of his face as though he were wiping dirt off it. "A law enforcement officer, Matt Lewis, is shot execution-style in his car on a deserted street in a very bad part of town. Crawling with the drug trade. Fifty people within the sound of the shot could plausibly have done it. Why pick on Ro Curtlee?"

"Because we know he did it?"

"Well, one little bit of proof, and the judge signs off. But . . ." He shrugged.

"So who was the judge?"

"Chomorro."

Treya clucked disapproval. "So now there's three of them?"

"What do you mean?"

"Baretto, Donahoe, Chomorro. Doesn't anybody on the bench want to put this guy in jail?"

"Not more than they want to protect his civil rights." Glitsky went on, "Do you know what it takes to win a contested judicial race, Trey? A hundred and fifty grand walking away, two fifty if you want a landslide, and there's no limit on contributions to a judicial race. Slick, huh. Bottom line, the whole bench is terrified of the Curtlees."

"So who did his initial trial, again?"

"Thomasino."

"How about taking him your warrant to sign?"

Glitsky was shaking his head. "No. You want a warrant signed, you've got to go to the sitting magistrate, and this week it's Chomorro. Randomly. This, I need hardly tell you, ensures the impartiality of the law."

"I don't want impartial. Not in this case."

"Well," Glitsky said, "in fact, you do. But it wouldn't break my heart if we got lucky now and again."

Treya tightened the blanket around her shoulders. Sitting with her thoughts for a minute, she said in a small voice, "Do you think we need to be worried? Us, I mean."

Glitsky heaved a sigh and moved down the couch next to her. "I'd say I'm worried enough for all of us, but that's probably not what you want to hear." He took her hand in both of his. "I like to think he's made his point with us just to rattle my chain. Hurting you or the kids doesn't get him anything, and he knows I'd hunt him down and kill him. Coming after me or us doesn't help him with his retrial, either. So, logically I think he's probably done with us. I hope. Beyond which, the chief's putting on a few teams to follow him around the clock."

"You don't think he'll be able to shake them?"

"I don't know. I wouldn't rule it out."

Treya closed her eyes, took in a breath. "Well, be that as it may, after tonight . . . I mean, I've been thinking. I don't know if I can feel right leaving the kids with Rita anymore. Or at school. Even if you say there's no risk . . ."

"I'm not saying that."

"I know." She took another shaky breath. "This isn't like anything else, Abe. This is a truly crazy person."

After a moment, Glitsky nodded. "I can't argue with you. You're right. What do you want to do?"

"I think I want to go away for a while. All of us. Until this blows over somehow."

Glitsky's nostrils flared and his mouth went tight, the scar going white through his lips. "I can't do that, Trey. Not in the middle of this."

"Why not?"

"Well, if for no other reason, that's telling Ro he wins."

"So what if he wins?" Treya's voice took on an edge. "It's not you against him."

"I'm not so sure about that."

"Well, then, all the more reason." She brought her hands together over his. "If it's that personal, then you really are in danger. Don't you see that?"

"I do, okay. But I can't run just because some psychopath is out to get me. There are protections in place and there's no reason to think they're not going to work."

"There isn't? Tell that to Mr. Lewis."

But Glitsky shook his head. "I don't really think he can touch me or you or the kids. Or that he has any reason to."

"And you're willing to bet all of our lives, or any of our lives, on that?"

"Trey," he said. "That might be a little dramatic, don't you think?"

She let go of his hands, and now very suddenly Glitsky realized that she'd quickly worked herself into a cold and unaccustomed fury. "I'm willing to take grief for being dramatic when our children's lives have been threatened, Abe. And in fact I'm kind of outraged you're not taking it a lot more seriously."

"I am."

"No, you're not. You're thinking of all this in terms of your *job*, of you versus Ro Curtlee, and who's going to win, and you're willing to risk losing all of this, our home"—she gestured at the room around them—"losing Rachel or Zack or you and me . . ."

"We're not going to . . ."

Now, tears of anger and frustration in her eyes, Treya slammed both fists into her lap. "*We will if one of us is dead, Abe! Don't you see that? How close does it have to get? Just like poor Matt Lewis, all the sudden, poof, gone forever. And never even saw it coming.*"

"Hey." Reaching out, he touched her shoulder. "Treya . . ."

Brushing his hand off, she turned on him. "Don't touch me! I'm not being hysterical or dramatic. I don't need to get calmed down. You're talking logic, but don't you see that that man can take all this away, *on a whim*, everything we've ever built together and care about? And you're willing to risk that? Why? Because of your job? Your career in law enforcement? I can't even believe we're having this discussion."

"I told you I don't think the likelihood . . ."

"*Fuck likelihood, Abe! Fuck that!*"

The profanity hit Glitsky with a titanic force, snapping his head back. She knew that he had a visceral intolerance for that kind of language, and in all the time they'd been together, she'd never said anything like that around him. He ran his hand over his forehead—his blood was rushing to his head, his stomach roiling—and he stood up and walked over to the front windows, trying to grab a breath.

"I didn't mean—" he finally got out. "Whatever I said, I didn't mean it. Of course you can go. Of course, no risk is tolerable. I'm so sorry. I didn't mean to criticize you. You are completely right. If you need to go, you need to go. The children need to go."

"And what about you?"

He turned back to face her, met her eyes, waited, shook his head no.

"How is this possible?" she asked. "How can we have come this far and I don't even know you?"

"Trey," he began, "you know me. You know who I am. I've been a cop ever since . . ."

She held up a hand, stopping him. "Oh, spare me," she said. "Spare me, please." And standing up, she gathered the blanket around her and spun on her heel around the corner and back to their bedroom, closing the door hard behind her.

21

At seven forty-five the next morning, a homicide sergeant inspector named Darrel Bracco knocked at the door to Glitsky's office, which was open, although the lights inside were off. The lieutenant slumped in his chair, nearly reclined in fact, his outstretched arm around a cup of something on the desk. "You wanted to see me, Abe?"

"I did. Come on in."

"Lights?"

"No. Leave 'em, please. Take a chair."

Obeying orders, Bracco entered the office and sat. Glitsky made no effort to sit up straighter. Even in the dim light, Bracco could see a grayish pallor under the lieutenant's light brown skin. His body language screamed exhaustion, although when he spoke, the words came out with a clipped precision. "You heard about Matt Lewis."

It wasn't really a question. Even if word of the shooting hadn't permeated as if by osmosis into every inch of the Hall of Justice building itself, the shooting of the DA inspector had been the lead story on all the local network news programs last night, and had made headlines in both the *Chronicle* and the *Courier* this morning.

Bracco knew that the whiteboard on the wall behind his head already had his name down as the lead investigator on three active homicides: a no-humans-involved gang-banger shooting in the Lower Mission, a tragic shaken baby case out in the Sunset, and a fiftysomething unmarried insurance broker who'd gotten himself stabbed to death the week before in the alley outside Alfred's Steak House. These, Bracco felt, put him at about the limit of his capabilities, particularly since he was working solo lately.

But now Glitsky was asking if he'd heard about Matt Lewis, and Bracco said, "Sure. Terrible thing. And I'll take it if there's no choice, but if somebody else wants it, my plate's pretty full."

"I'm not asking you to take it, Darrel."

"Sorry. I just thought . . ." He shrugged. "Go ahead."

"So what have you heard about it?"

"Lewis? Not much. Out there in the 'Mo' "—this was department slang for the lower Fillmore—"it could have been anything. Who's got the case?"

"Nobody. Not yet. I might wind up taking it myself." Glitsky turned his cup. "So you haven't heard anything?"

"No."

"What if I told you he was following Ro Curtlee around?"

Bracco kept his reaction low-key. "That's not come out."

"No."

"Is it true?"

"True enough."

In all of the news reports, Glitsky had carefully declined to state whether they had a suspect, or even a person of interest, in the shooting. It appeared to be a random, perhaps drug- or gang-related, homicide, but no one yet knew for sure. The investigation was continuing. That was all he could divulge.

"So . . ." Bracco waited.

"So I need a volunteer to call Curtlee's lawyer to ask him for an interview, and for obvious reasons that can't be me. No way is Denardi going to let that happen, but we have to ask. I don't want the accusation that we never gave him a chance to tell his side of the story."

"But supposing he says yes, do you want me to talk to him about this Lewis thing?"

"Actually that and one other case. Janice Durbin."

"Don't know her."

"Friday, her house burned down around her. Just like with Felicia Nuñez, who happened to be a witness in Ro's trial. Also, like Felicia, strangled. And this latest victim, Janice Durbin, was married to the jury foreman in Ro's trial."

"I'm seeing a pattern," Bracco said.

"No flies on you. But the good news is that because of Lewis, and the fact that we know he was following Ro around, you've got a reasonable, even plausible excuse to talk to Ro, see what he says he was doing yesterday. And while you're at it, get his alibi for Janice Durbin, if he's got one."

"You think he'll talk to me?"

"Not a chance in the world. But we've got to do the drill."

Bracco said, "Lewis was really tailing him?"

"What, Darrel, you think I'm making this up?" But then, hearing how brusque he sounded, he held up a hand in apology. "Sorry," he said. "I didn't sleep last night. But yeah, Lewis was tailing Ro, at least until an hour or so before he got shot. That was his last check-in with Amanda Jenkins, outside Tadich's, where Ro met his lawyer."

"Then what?"

"Then Ro came out and hopped in his car with his driver."

"And Lewis took off after them?"

"Said he was going to, anyway. After that we don't know."

Bracco considered, then gave a brusque nod. "Close enough for me."

———

It was nursery-school day at the DA's office. Treya came in late, getting on toward nine o'clock, trailing her two children. About fifteen minutes later, Farrell showed up with his dog in tow. Luckily Gert was well-behaved and liked children, so it wasn't the chaos it could have been. But neither was it exactly a finely tuned, professional office environment.

Now Rachel and Zachary were coloring together on the library table in Farrell's inner office, while Gert had stretched out under them. Treya and Wes had some important issues to discuss and they had migrated out to the reception area, Treya's domain, and closed the doors both into Farrell's office and leading out into the hallway so they could have some privacy.

Farrell was perched on the front of Treya's desk. "For how long?" he asked her.

"I don't know. As long as it takes." Treya stood leaning up against the wall of law books in the outer office. "I'm not leaving the kids with this kind of risk."

"Do you know where you're going?"

"I've got a brother in LA. We'll start out down there. And then Abe's father has a place here in town where we'd be welcome, although that may be too close. I don't want to be find-able."

"And what's Abe going to do?"

Treya's mouth went a little loose before it tightened up again. "He's staying on. He says it's only going to be a couple of weeks, now. Hopefully. I mean, until Ro's in jail again."

"If we can get an indictment. And now, with Amanda . . ." Farrell ran his hand back through his hair. "She was going to be presenting the case, but I don't know if she'll be able to pull it together quick enough after this Matt thing."

"You could do it yourself."

"I know. I might. But meanwhile"—he spread his hands out in front of him—"what am I supposed to do around here with you gone?"

"I'm sorry about that, sir, I really am. I wish there was some other way, but I don't see what that would be. I'm sure there's somebody good here in the building who could cover for me."

"You are? You got a name for me?"

She crossed her arms and shook her head. "No."

A silence built up between them.

"This is a real problem, Treya. You realize that? The more I get used to the idea, the more it's a real problem."

"Yes, sir, I understand. It's a real problem at home, too. But what am I supposed to do? I've got the vacation time accrued."

"That's not the issue."

"I'm sorry, but it's my issue. I can't keep the kids here. I'm afraid of what Ro might do to them. And you know he's capable of it, whatever it is."

Farrell digested her answer for a moment, then shook his head in disgust. "Fuck," he said. "Pardon me."

"The least of my worries," Treya said. "Anyway, I just wanted to tell you in person, see if I can help you find a replacement."

"In one day?"

Treya tried to put on a brave face, but it didn't take. She shrugged. "That's all I can try for. I'm sorry."

Wes boosted himself off the desk and looked straight across at her. "You know, Treya," he said, "if you do this, I don't know if I can guarantee that I'll be able to take you back in the same job. That's not a threat. It's just reality. I need somebody who's in here every day."

"I realize that," she said. "I couldn't ask that you take me back."

"Just so you know."

"Yes," she said. "I think that's clear enough."

———

Bracco found out why Denardi had agreed to the interview when he showed up at his downtown office and found Cliff and Theresa Curtlee there, too, along with Ro. Tristan Denardi introduced them both to Bracco, explaining that they were here not only in support of their son, but as representatives of their newspaper. Bracco understood that clearly, no matter what happened, their presence meant that the *Courier* was going to spin this interview as a further example of police overreaching.

Denardi crossed an ankle over his knee, revealing a flash of argyle sock over his highly polished black brogues. The impeccably dressed elderly attorney took his cup of hot coffee on its saucer and placed it on the low table in front of him in the conference room.

"I'm not sure my client has anything to say to you," he said to Bracco when they settled down to business. "In fact, I'm fairly certain that he doesn't. It's clear that you people have a vested interest in harassing Mr. Curtlee, and I hope we've made it equally clear that we're not about to let such harassment go uncontested. Now you're here asking about my client's whereabouts on last Friday morning, and we're not inclined to provide that information without some sort of explanation as to why anyone should care where he was or what he was doing."

Bracco sipped at his own coffee to give himself some time. The silent presence of the Curtlees unnerved him. He looked from the solid, unyielding parents over to Ro Curtlee in his pressed blue jeans and form-hugging black T-shirt and his eight-hundred-dollar cowboy boots. He still wore the cast on his arm from his altercation with Glitsky and his patrolmen; his face, though, had all but cleared up. He'd shaved this morning and his hair was neatly combed.

When he noticed Bracco's eyes on him, Ro smiled dismissively.

Bracco chose his words carefully. "I'm investigating another case and would like to clear your client from suspicion."

"You mean he's under suspicion in another case?"

"Only in the sense that we don't have a suspect yet in this other matter. I am in the process of trying to eliminate possibilities."

"And Mr. Curtlee is among those possibilities?"

"Yes."

A bark of a laugh from Ro, and then he sat back in his uphol-stered chair. "Unbelievable," he said.

Theresa Curtlee finally got on the boards. "Truly," she said.

Denardi held out a warning palm toward both her and his cli-ent. "Ro. Theresa. Please." And then, back to Bracco. "This other case? A homicide, I presume."

"Arson murder, actually."

This brought a tight little turn-up of Denardi's lips. "Of course. And how would Mr. Curtlee be even remotely connected to this hypothetical arson murder?"

"The victim was the wife of the foreman of his jury. Janice Durbin."

Another prim smile from Denardi. "I see. And maybe you could draw me a road map, as it were, of how this poor woman's unfor-tunate death leads in any way, even remotely, to Mr. Curtlee?"

Bracco kept it simple. "She was strangled, and somebody lit a fire. The same thing happened to Felicia Nuñez. And of course Ms. Sandoval was also strangled. There would appear to be some-thing of a coincidence. So if your client will cooperate and we can eliminate him as a suspect, I'd like to do so. I just don't see what your objection could be."

Cliff Curtlee ostentatiously cleared his throat but said nothing.

Denardi took his cue. "Well, on general grounds, Inspector, my objection is that we American citizens have the right to our pri-vacy. Mr. Curtlee doesn't have to tell you or anybody else what he was doing on Friday morning or any other time."

"No. Of course not."

"On the other hand." Denardi turned toward Ro again and some signal must have passed between them. "If you'd give my client and me a couple of minutes alone, Inspector, we might be able to come to some accommodation. If you don't mind." With that, lawyer, client, and his parents all stood and left the conference room.

Bracco sat back, crossed his legs, and leaned back to take in the large canvases of modern art and the leather-bound shelves of books, and photographs of the famous and powerful. He cast his glance out over the city—the chop on the bay far below, the scudding clouds, the Ferry Building and Bay Bridge elegantly sweeping out to Treasure Island.

Then, as though it had been choreographed, and maybe it had been, Denardi, Ro, and the Curtlees came back into the conference room.

"Inspector," Denardi began before they'd even sat down, "it would be wonderful if you could pass a message back to your colleagues in the police department that we are always ready to cooperate with its investigations when the proper procedures are followed. Mr. Curtlee is ready to make a statement about his actions last Friday morning. Do you have a tape recorder to get it down for the record?"

"Sure."

They sat down in their previous seats. "If you don't mind, Ms. Curtlee will be taking notes as well."

"Fine." Bracco pulled out his pocket recorder and placed it on the table. After his standard introduction, he asked Ro Curtlee what he'd done on the previous Friday morning.

"I woke up late, about nine fifteen, in the house here," he said. "I went down and said hello to my parents, who were just finishing breakfast, and then had some breakfast of my own—served by our lovely Linda."

"We'll corroborate that," Cliff Curtlee said, gesturing toward his wife. "Both of us. Would you like to know what we ate, too?"

Bracco kept his composure. "That won't be necessary," he said. Turning back to Ro, he asked, "And after breakfast?"

"I showered and put on some clothes and at about eleven I was at my doctor's where he checked the cast on my arm. How's that? Want to go later?"

"Yes, please." They ran down Curtlee's actions through the whole day until he joined his parents again later for dinner. "That's good," Bracco said when they finished. "Let me ask you a couple more questions about the morning. Is there anybody here who might have seen you in bed before nine fifteen?"

He thought for a moment. "Linda knocked at nine. That's what woke me up. It kind of pissed me off if you want to know."

"So nine, then? And before that?"

Denardi had had enough. "Before that, Inspector," he said, "he was asleep in his bed at his home. Is there anything difficult to understand about that?"

"No."

"Well, then." Denardi clapped his hands. "I believe that's what you came here for. You've got your statement, willingly delivered. Full cooperation. Now if you'll excuse us . . ."

Bracco made no move to reach for his recorder. Instead, he nodded amicably. "Hey, though," he said, as though he'd just thought of it, "now that we're talking, how's the food at Tadich's lately? Good as ever?"

The furtive look between lawyer and client disappeared almost as quickly as it came, but not so quickly that Bracco didn't see it. And they both knew that he'd seen it.

"The hell with this," Ro Curtlee said to Denardi. "This is never gonna end unless we do something about it. I'll tell you what, Inspector, I'll take a fucking lie detector test. We got to put an end to this. How'd you like that?"

Denardi extended his arm to its full length. "Ro!"

But the young man went on, "No, Tristan, this is just bullshit! The same shit they been laying on us since all this began. I didn't shoot anybody yesterday or any other day. I finished lunch and me and Ez went to the planetarium . . ."

Denardi actually came out of his seat. "Ro! Shut up! That's enough!"

But Ro couldn't seem to get himself under control. He stood up, too, now pointing at his attorney, his face flushed with anger. "What? I'm supposed to just take this? He just accused me again . . ."

"Don't talk, damn it!" Denardi nearly bellowed. "Don't say another word!" Then he turned to stare down at Bracco. "This interview is over," he said. "Right now."

Bracco got his hands on his recorder first thing. Leaving it on, he stood and backed away a couple of steps. "What are you going to take a lie detector about, Ro? I never mentioned anybody getting shot."

"Don't answer that," Denardi said.

"He already did," Bracco said.

"This is absurd." Cliff Curtlee got to his feet.

Denardi reiterated, "He didn't admit a goddamn thing."

"Oh. Okay, then. He's got nothing to worry about."

Ro took a step toward him. "I got nothing to worry about anyway, dickhead."

"Ro. Enough." Denardi moved his bulk around in front of his client. "Get out of here, Inspector."

"Sure," Bracco said, backing away. "I'm gone," he said. "Nice chatting with you all."

22

The only *Courier* reporter who worked in an office instead of in one of the cubicles on the main floor city room was Sheila Marrenas. She had earned this eminence not only because she was an excellent stylist as a writer, with a distinctive voice, but because her column, "Our Town," was the most widely read and popular recurring feature in the newspaper. She had a great eye for news and especially for conflict disguised as news. It didn't hurt, either, that Marrenas had early on been inculcated with a belief system that coincided with the politics of the newspaper's owners, and that she could and did express these views with the passionate conviction of the true believer.

Now she came into her office, fresh from her lunch with the mayor's press secretary, a bit of a coup in itself, her brain considering the slant to take on Leland Crawford's first weeks in office, to cast him in the best possible light. She wasn't overly concerned with her objectivity, which so many other news outlets had long ago proven to be a spurious virtue when it came to reporting. Besides, she was a columnist now—not just a reporter. She was all about opinion, nuance, point of view.

Marrenas knew that newspapers were about wielding influence and molding public opinion, and the point was that Leland Crawford had accepted a great deal of the Curtlees' campaign money and now, even at the very beginning of his administration, was showing signs that he knew which side his bread was buttered on. He could be a crucial ally in the political wars that were always on the horizon in San Francisco. A flattering column by her on his first weeks could go a long way toward setting his inclinations toward them into concrete. Maybe she could contrast Crawford's own bold agenda and no-nonsense activism with Wes Farrell's fairly abysmal continuing performance to date.

That might really shake things up.

Her phone was ringing as she came through the door and she reached over her cluttered desk to pick it up, chirping her name in her trademark response.

"Sheila. Cliff . . . Something's come up. You got a minute? . . . Good. I'll be right down."

She went behind her desk, opened her drawer, and took out her hand mirror, checking to make sure that every little thing about her face and hair was as it should be. She needn't have worried. At forty-three years old, she possibly looked better than she had at thirty. Certainly she'd grown into her style, which was professional and cultured. She'd tamed the wild mane of frizzy black hair she'd had ten years ago with soft curls now, settling about her shoulders. And her face had never been a problem. Her olive-tinted skin was not simply clear, but luminous, small pored, and glowing. Her smile, under the sultry coals that were her eyes, was genuine and generous after the braces had come off at last about six years ago.

She was more than comfortable with her looks, and now as she put the mirror back in her drawer, she allowed herself a small smile, thinking that it was almost a shame that she wasn't inclined to consolidate her position here at the paper by seducing Cliff, who clearly had always found her attractive. Her taste, though, truth be told, ran much more to Theresa, but—she asked herself— what would be the point of seducing the second in command?

"Ahh, here you are. Looking even more lovely than usual, I might add."

"Oh, stop, you flatterer." But she was smiling as she stood and came around the desk, offering first one cheek to Cliff, then the other one, kissing the air on either side. By long custom, when Cliff came down to her office to visit, they sat on either end of the leather couch that ran along under the window with the view down onto Castro Street.

"So how'd the lunch with the mayor go?" Cliff asked by way of warm-up.

"His press secretary," she corrected him, "but it went very well. She's very quotable. I got some good stuff. You'll see." She shifted, facing him on the couch, tucking one leg up under her. "But you've got something hotter."

"Not so much hot as in sexy," he said, "as hot as in urgent. It's Ro and the police again."

A small bubble of laughter shook her. "You've got to be kidding me. You'd think after last week they would have learned."

"I don't know if they're capable of learning."

"I don't, either. Was this Glitsky again?"

"No, although with Glitsky running homicide, it's obvious where the orders came from. This is an inspector named Bracco."

Marrenas nodded. "Darrel. I know who he is. What did he do?"

"Well, maybe we should thank him, actually, since he's giving us this story. But he came up to Tristan Denardi's office today to ask Ro some questions. Tristan didn't want to let that happen under any circumstances, but on reflection I thought since you weren't available, it might be a good idea if Tristan and Ro went ahead so long as Theresa and I came along to represent our interests."

Her eyebrows went up in surprise. "Go on."

Cliff, sitting sideways on the couch, leaned in toward her. "Anyway, Glitsky, it turns out, is working on another murder, just some random murder across the city out in the Sunset. Although Glitsky naturally thinks maybe it isn't really random. He thinks Ro's got something to do with this one, too, and he had Bracco ask for the meet today to get Ro's alibi for the time of the murder."

"This other murder, you mean?"

"Yes, and I know. It's bizarre."

"So what's the possible connection to Ro?"

"You'll love this. You remember that difficult jury foreman at Ro's trial?"

"Michael Durbin." Suddenly she snapped her fingers. "That's who it was!" she said, her eyes flashing.

"Who?"

"This guy outside the courtroom last week who wouldn't give me the time of day. It was Durbin. I *knew* I'd seen him before."

"At Ro's arraignment? Why was *he* there?"

"I have no idea." She shook her head. "So, what are you saying? Somebody killed him?"

"No. Somebody killed his wife. And then burned down the house around her."

Marrenas took in a quick breath and let it out in a rush. "That's not very nice."

"No. But the point is that the police apparently somehow think, by some tortuous logic, that Ro had something to do with it. In fact, it's so obscure that I can't believe anyone really thinks it, but it seems like it's going to be the next point of attack on Ro. And this in spite of the fact, as Ro told Bracco this morning, and Theresa and I backed him up because it was true, that he was sleeping at home at the time that this murder occurred." Lowering his voice, Cliff went on, "And here's the thing, Sheila. He *was* sleeping in his room. This was last Friday. I remember distinctly and so does Theresa. He came down and had breakfast with us at around nine or nine thirty and I promise you on my word of honor that he hadn't been out killing some woman in the Sunset an hour before, and then setting her house on fire. That just didn't happen."

Sheila picked up his thread. "But the cops still came to question him?"

"Right. And you want to hear another one? That DA investigator who got shot yesterday out in the Fillmore?"

"Yes?"

"Evidently that was Ro, too. If you ask Bracco or Glitsky."

Marrenas nodded admiringly. "Wow. Ro's been busy."

"Hasn't he? Isn't this just totally outrageous? In fact, he had lunch yesterday with Tristan Denardi at Tadich's, the two of them talking about their legal strategy, then he and Ez went to the planetarium together. They did not stop and kill a DA investigator on the way." He let out a deep sigh. "This is long past amusing, I must tell you."

Marrenas got up, stretched her back, showing off the merchandise, and walked across her office. When she turned around, she asked, "So what do you want to do?"

Cliff came forward to the last few inches of the couch's seat. "Well, the story itself, the cops suspecting Ro for every murder committed since he's gotten out of jail, that's got to get out. But more particularly, there's got to be another story around this Durbin murder, and one that doesn't have squat all to do with Ro, since it's absolutely definite that he didn't kill her. Or anybody else.

"Now we've got public opinion largely on our side, I think, especially after your last couple of brilliant articles on police brutality. It would be interesting to illustrate how badly the police can get off course when they've got a preconceived idea and they're out to get an innocent man. Do you think you could do some looking around and write that story?"

"With my eyes closed, sir. With my eyes closed."

———

"Are you and Mommy mad at each other?" Rachel asked.

They had parked at the airport in the hourly lot, and now they were walking out to the terminal. Treya had wanted Abe to just

JOHN LESCROART

drop them off at the curb by the departures lane, but he had over-ruled her and said he wanted to be with them all for as long as he could. To which Treya's response had been silence.

And which, in turn, led to Rachel's question.

The two of them, father and daughter, were about fifteen feet behind Treya and Zachary, lagging on purpose. Glitsky's daughter was holding his hand with one of hers, pulling her small pink rolling suitcase with the other one. Her monkey doll, Alice, rode on Rachel's back, its hands Velcro'd together under her chin.

Glitsky said, "No. We're having a disagreement, that's all."

"But you're not mad at her."

"I said no."

"I know, but I think she's mad at you."

"She might be at that."

"Why?"

"Because I'm not going with you."

"Why aren't you? Isn't this a vacation? Mommy said it was like a vacation."

"I know. But 'like' a vacation isn't the same as a vacation. If it was a real vacation, I'd be going."

"But why can't you go on this one?"

"See if you can guess."

She looked up and over at him. "You'll get mad."

"I won't. I promise."

"Okay, then. Work."

"Correct."

"It's always work."

"Now you do sound like your mother."

"But do you have to work this time?"

"If I didn't think I did, don't you think I'd be going with you?"

"I don't know. Probably."

"No. Definitely. And you know why? Because I love you. I love all of you."

202

"Even Mommy?"

"Especially Mommy."

At this moment, Treya and Zachary got to the escalator leading up to the security checkpoint, and Treya turned around, yelling back to them. "C'mon, you two, can't you try a little harder to keep up?"

Rachel again looked up at her father. "I don't care what she says, she's mad."

"I think you're right," Glitsky whispered.

———

Then they were where the line for security began. In Glitsky's arms, Zachary wore the modified bicycle helmet he'd been living with for over a year now. The four of them had already done the "sandwich hug" with Rachel holding on to both Abe's and Treya's legs. Now Glitsky lowered Zachary down next to Rachel and told them to hold hands and stay together and guard the luggage for just one minute while he and their mother said a little private good-bye.

Glitsky took Treya's hand, and after only a slight hesitation, she moved off with him a few steps away. He put his arm over her shoulder and drew her around into him. For a moment, she simply stood there, arms at her side, but then he felt and heard her sigh, and she came full around in front of him and brought her arms up against his back.

Pulling her head away, she stretched up and kissed him. "I love you," she said.

"I love you, too. I'm sorry about . . ."

She brought a hand around and put it up against his lips. "Shut up, okay. I'm sorry, too. This is just what I've got to do."

"I get it."

"And you do what you've got to do."

"Right. Those are the rules. For the record, I'm going to be fine. And careful."

She put some work into a smile. "Okay. Sure you will."

"You take care of our guys."

"I will."

"And we talk every day. Deal?"

"Deal."

"And you're all coming back."

"There's no question of that. Really. None." She stretched up and kissed him again. "I've got to go. I love you."

"Me, too."

After another fleeting half smile, she turned toward the children and Glitsky waved good-bye to them. He heard them say good-bye and tried to get out a word or some facsimile of a smile, but it was no use, so he waved good-bye one last time, then turned and started walking back toward the parking lot.

23

When Glitsky got in from the airport, Bracco had been sitting out in the detail waiting for him. After Glitsky had listened to the tape, the two men had discussed it for a while, and then had decided to bring it to Wes Farrell and let him make whatever decision he wanted about it.

Now Farrell's and Glitsky's footfalls bounced off the walls as they walked side by side down the internal corridor that ran behind the courtrooms on the second floor. They were both exhausted and neither had the will nor the strength to try to make conversation. It was near to the end of the business day, and most of the courtrooms to their right were empty. On the left were the doors to various judges' chambers. The corridor itself echoed with the desultory conversation of a couple of shackled groups of defendants in orange jumpsuits and bailiffs who were waiting at the other end of the hall for the elevators that would take them up and then across to the jail behind the building.

Farrell and Glitsky stopped in front of a closed door with an etched panel on the wall next to it that read: THE HONORABLE LEO CHOMORRO.

Farrell gave Glitsky a hopeful shrug and hesitated one more second. They heard some continued, muted conversation behind the door, and then Farrell reached out and knocked. He had of course called to make the appointment, and so they were expected.

Behind the door, a chair scraped on a hardwood floor and then they were both shaking hands with Judge Chomorro, still in his robes, whose strong Hispanic presence filled most of the doorway. Standing a few steps behind him, in a business suit, hands clasped easily in front of him, was Judge Sam Baretto, there in Chomorro's chambers for God knew what reason, and who stepped forward to greet Farrell and Glitsky, and then excused himself and walked out into the hallway, closing the door behind him.

After these somewhat stilted salutations, Chomorro invited Farrell and Glitsky to sit around the cherry table that he apparently used as his working desk. The table had a computer on one end and took up a good portion of the middle of the room, which was about as plain a judge's chambers as Glitsky had ever seen. Aside from Chomorro's diplomas and awards and four or five photographs with politicians, two of the four walls were bare. Another wall contained law books. A set of golf clubs resided in one corner. Otherwise, the room was basically empty except for the table, the chairs, and a love seat.

After they were all seated, Chomorro cleared his throat. "Well, here we are, Mr. Farrell, at your request. What can I do for you?"

"Your Honor, I realize that this is something about which you've already ruled yesterday, but we've got new evidence, so I'll try to keep it short and sweet. This morning, Inspector Bracco of homicide conducted an interview with Ro Curtlee, with whom I know you're familiar . . ."

Chomorro's visage had gone dark, but he said, "All right, go ahead."

"Lieutenant Glitsky and I have listened to the tape of this interview and we both believe that it is incriminating on its face, and now we'd like to play it for you."

"To what end?" Chomorro asked.

"To once again ask you to sign off on a search warrant at the Curtlee home."

Chomorro's mouth went tight. No one here kidded themselves

that this was a small or casual request. The Ro Curtlee story was already as high profile as they came. Chomorro knew that if he reversed his decision about letting a search proceed at Ro's house, it would be headline news. To say nothing of what the Curtlees themselves might try to do to scuttle his career. Of course justice was blind and all that, but in fact it was simple prudence not to needlessly antagonize powerful people. Yesterday, Chomorro had turned down the chief of police not so much because she did not have probable cause, which was the standard, albeit a flexible and subjective one, but because given the Curtlees, the actual standard in the real world was *very* probable cause. And he would forget that only at his own peril.

Chomorro dragged in a lungful of air and let it out. "All right, let's hear what you've got," he said.

Farrell turned his head, said, "Abe," and Glitsky placed the recorder on the table between them. "The voices," Glitsky explained, "are Inspector Bracco, Ro Curtlee, and his lawyer, Mr. Denardi. You'll also hear the Curtlees, Cliff and Theresa, a time or two, but don't worry about them." He pressed the play button, and Bracco's introduction came out of the speaker, then Ro Curtlee's voice:

"I woke up late, about nine fifteen, in the house here. I went down and said hello to my parents, who were just finishing breakfast, and then had some breakfast of my own—served by our lovely Linda."

"We'll corroborate that. Both of us. Would you like to know what we ate, too?"

"That's Cliff Curtlee," Glitsky explained.

"I can follow it," Chomorro said impatiently.

Nevertheless, Glitsky said, "Now Bracco."

"That won't be necessary. And after breakfast?"

Glitsky. "Ro."

"I showered and put on some clothes and at about eleven I was at

my doctor's, where he checked the cast on my arm. How's that? Want to go later?"

They fast-forwarded to the critical part of the conversation.

"Hey, though, now that we're talking, how's the food at Tadich's lately? Good as ever?"

"The hell with this. This is never gonna end unless we do something about it. I'll tell you what, Inspector, I'll take a fucking lie detector test. We got to put an end to this. How'd you like that?"

"Ro!"

"No, Tristan, this is just bullshit! The same shit they been laying on us since all this began. I didn't shoot anybody yesterday or any other day. I finished lunch and me and Ez went to the planetarium . . ."

"Ro! Shut up! That's enough!"

"What? I'm supposed to just take this? He just accused me again . . ."

"Don't talk, damn it! Don't say another word! This interview is over. Right now."

"What are you going to take a lie detector about, Ro? I never mentioned anybody getting shot."

"Don't answer that."

"He already did."

"This is absurd."

"He didn't admit a goddamn thing."

"Oh. Okay, then. He's got nothing to worry about."

"I got nothing to worry about anyway, dickhead."

"Ro. Enough. Get out of here, Inspector."

"Sure. I'm gone. Nice chatting with you all."

Glitsky reached out and switched off the recorder.

Chomorro cocked his head to one side, curiosity writ large on his features. "That's it?" he asked. "Falls a little short of a confession, don't you think?"

Glitsky spoke in measured tones. He didn't want to appear to be hard-selling it if it was supposed to be self-explanatory. "Bracco never mentioned what he was talking about, Your Honor," he said, "and Ro went right to the killing yesterday of Matt Lewis. It couldn't have been more obvious."

"Actually, it could have been a lot more obvious, Lieutenant. This man, Ro Curtlee, knows that you both are pulling out all the stops to get him back in jail. In spite of the rulings of two of my colleagues. So your inspector alludes to his whereabouts yesterday afternoon and Ro assumes, correctly I might add, that he is now a suspect in another murder that happened at that time. Do you really think it's that odd that he could predict which murder that was? It's been all over the news. It would have been more surprising if he hadn't known."

"Your Honor," Farrell said. "This man shot one of my investigators . . ."

"'Allegedly' shot, Mr. Farrell. As I tried to explain to Chief Lapeer yesterday. The 'allegedly' goes away after you get a conviction."

"Your Honor"—Farrell didn't give in—"with respect, it's a fact. My guy was following him. Look at what's happened since Ro got out of jail. He's . . ."

But Chomorro, heating up a bit himself, held up a finger. "While we're on that, I got the impression from the first part of that tape we just listened to that Ro was under suspicion for yet another homicide and giving his alibi for that. Isn't that true? Lieutenant?"

"Yes."

"On what evidence in that case?"

"The connection, Your Honor. She was the wife of his jury foreman. Her murder and the burning of her body was the same MO, not only as the killing Ro got convicted on, but as his first victim after he got out, Felicia Nuñez."

"Another 'alleged' victim, I'm afraid. Is she not?"

Glitsky couldn't keep the reproach out of his voice. "She's a real enough victim, Your Honor. She's just as dead as can be. As is Janice Durbin."

"And yet," Chomorro said, "on the tape, Ro gives a completely plausible alibi for the time of the Durbin murder, does he not? And his father backs him up. What do you say to that? So is he no longer a suspect there?"

"'Plausible' doesn't mean true, Your Honor," Glitsky replied.

"It does if it gets enough corroboration."

"His parents and their employees. What do you expect they're going to say? He's lying. They're all lying."

"Maybe, maybe not." Chomorro all but collapsed back into his seat. He took a slow breath, then came back to Glitsky, then over to Farrell. "Gentlemen," he said in a conciliatory tone, "I understand your predicament. I even empathize with you. I know you believe that this man is a danger to the community, and quite possibly, even probably, you are right. If he had said to your inspector, 'Yeah, I killed that inspector. What are you going to do about it?' you'd have your warrant signed by me before you turned off the tape. But what you have isn't enough, not nearly enough."

"Your Honor—" Farrell began.

But Chomorro cut him off, again with a raised finger. "Please. So, the bottom line is we've got to do it by the book. That's the only way it works, and both of you know that. We start arresting people and searching houses without probable cause, we all might as well close up shop, because we're no longer working under the rule of law. And the rule of law is what we do here, do we not? So my answer, and I'm afraid it's a final answer, is no."

"Well," Farrell said. "Thanks anyway for your time, Your Honor."

"If you get anything truly substantial," Chomorro replied, "anything that rises to the level of probable cause, I'll be happy to revisit this anytime. I'm just saying what you've got now isn't enough."

"I thought it was worth a try," Glitsky said.

"It couldn't hurt." Chomorro stood up, announcing that the meeting was over. He shepherded them over to the door, making small talk, and just as they were about to go out, he said, "You know, this kind of thing is more or less what a grand jury is all about. Make your case to them and they might indict."

"Yes, Your Honor," Farrell said. "Thank you. That was and remains our Plan B."

"You still might need more than you've shown me," the judge said.

"We're working on that," Glitsky said.

"But we're also thinking," Farrell went on, "about attaching the first murder, the one he got convicted on, with these latest, which makes it multiple murder, which makes it a special circumstances case. But as I say, it's going to take a couple of weeks to put the thing together. Maybe longer than that."

Chomorro hung by the door, holding it open, perhaps not completely willing to be sending them away with so little result or even encouragement. "I know this seems to have gotten personal to both of you, but if this guy did any or all of this, he's got to have slipped up somewhere and if he did, I'm sure you'll find out where."

"That's what we keep hoping," Farrell said.

"But it's already not soon enough," Glitsky added.

———

Though his office entitled him to, Farrell found that he didn't want to use a driver all the time. For the daytime events that made up such a disproportionately large segment of the job—when he was going out and speaking before civic groups or doing lunch fundraisers—he was happy for the company and sometimes protection afforded by the rotating police inspectors who ferried him around in one of the city's few Lincoln Town Cars. Most days, though, he found that he preferred to drive in on his own, park in his designated spot behind the Hall of Justice, and drive home.

This morning, though, between the sleepless night he'd experienced along with the actual fears for his physical safety, he called in and had the car come pick him up at home. Now, coming out of the Hall in the dark at quarter to six, he was extremely grateful for the perk. Dragging with fatigue, Gert on her leash alongside him, he let her pull him by the coroner's office on the right and then the jail on the left and over to where the car sat waiting.

His most regular driver, with whom he got along very well, was Sergeant Ritz Naygrow. Tonight, Ritz was still on duty behind the wheel, undoubtedly working it for the overtime, and by the time Farrell got to the car, he had come around and opened the door for them. Gert immediately jumped into the backseat and settled down, and Wes climbed in behind her. Ritz closed their door and then went around and got himself arranged behind the wheel.

But though he put the car into gear, he didn't take off driving right away. "So where are we off to on the people's business tonight, sir?" he asked.

Farrell had already closed his eyes and slumped back in his seat. Now, with what felt like Herculean effort, he opened them. "I hope the Chinese Merchants, if my calendar isn't wrong, which it might be. Treya's gone on vacation with no warning and she keeps my book. And I thought my back, too. Or did."

Ritz looked back at him. "You didn't know she had a vacation coming? How'd that happen?"

"She didn't know it, either. She's Glitsky wife, you know that?"

"Sure." It took him a second, then he half turned in his seat. "Oh, the threat. Ro Curtlee."

"She took it pretty seriously."

"I would, too."

"Well, we've got people on him around the clock now. Hope that slows him down some. He is one bad motherfucker. Still, I wish Treya hadn't gone off. I don't know what I'm going to do without her."

"You want," Ritz said, "I'll swing by Ro's place while you're talking to the Chinese Merchants tonight and shoot him dead. Then you can say I was with you the whole time, and we're good. And then you can call Treya and tell her she can come back, the coast is clear."

"Okay," Farrell said. "Let's do that. That's a good idea."

"Long as we got a plan," Ritz said. "So where are we going?"

"The Mandarin Oriental. I think."

"At least it'll be good food."

"Don't kid yourself, Ritz. It might start out good, but by the time it gets to my plate . . . Let's just say they don't call it the rubber chicken circuit for nothing. Now I'm going to close my eyes."

"The Mandarin's like five minutes away, sir. That's a short nap."

"It's five minutes more sleep than I've had since yesterday." After another few seconds, Farrell opened his eyes and said, "Are we going?"

"One other thing, if you don't mind."

"Sure. What?"

"If you could let dispatch know if you're going to be bringing your dog along to work when you want the car? The thing is, I'm pretty allergic."

"To Gert?"

"To pretty much all dogs, sir. Cats, too. Pollen. You name it."

"I'm sorry about that, Ritz. I didn't know. So, what, you wouldn't take the gig on those days?"

Ritz shrugged. "Other guys could cover. Just to let you know."

"Okay," Farrell said. "I'll try to call and let somebody know. If I can remember. When I'm bringing Gert down."

"Is that likely to be often, you think? Just so I can plan?"

"I don't know, Ritz. Sometimes, I guess. I don't really know." He paused, slumped down farther with his hand over his eyes. "My girlfriend left me, too," he said. "Last night."

Ritz spun his head to look at him. "Are you shittin' me? Sam?"

"Sam."

"Man, first Treya, then Sam."

"Actually the other order. Sam, then Treya, but yeah. Then you, if you want to count people leaving me for one reason or another."

"It's not like I wouldn't stay if you really wanted me."

"It's all right. You do what you have to do."

Ritz took a beat. "Man, you are having some bad week here."

"I know," Farrell said. "I feel like a Haitian with a Prius."

———

Abe Glitsky's father, Nat, was rinsing what few dishes they'd used tonight in the kitchen of the small duplex he shared with Sadie Silverman on Third Avenue just off Clement Street. The kitchen was in the back of the flat, and although its dimensions were only about ten-by-eight feet, they used it for a dining room as well, sitting while they ate on their spindly wooden chairs and eating off one of Sadie's dainty occasional tables from her old house.

Nat wasn't exactly robust anymore, but then again, at eighty-three, he wasn't in the ground, either, so there really wasn't much to complain about. His weight was down from his lifetime high of 180 to about 155 pounds, and most disturbing, he'd lost an inch and a half of his original five foot ten—where had that gone?—but he still had all of his hair, now wispy and white, but still there, thank you very much.

At the table sipping at the thimbleful of port she'd poured herself, Sadie turned the page of her book, sighed, and closed it. "I don't get all these vampires," she said. "This is my third try on one of these books and I just can't get myself to believe them."

"Maybe that's because there are no vampires in real life."

"But there are no Star Wars in real life and I love those. Or hobbits. Or time travel, either."

Nat turned around at the sink. "When did there stop being time travel?"

"Stop."

Nat turned back to the dishes, ran a sponge over a plate. "If I didn't believe the first two books I read," he said, "I wouldn't have gone to the third."

"That's because you're so impatient. I like to give things a chance."

"Good. Now I know what I'll get you for Valentine's Day. Number four. And I am not impatient. My patience is legendary."

Sadie sighed again. "But everybody's reading these."

"Not me."

"That's because all you read is the Torah."

"That's all I need. You might even like it more than vampires. Besides, you read it enough and you know all the good parts by heart and then you can carry it around inside you."

"And David begat Solomon, and Solomon begat . . ."

"Hey! You don't have to believe in that stuff, but I do."

"I believe David begat Solomon, maybe. But that whole Moses and the parting of the Red Sea thing . . ."

Nat turned around, drying his hands. "Miracles, Sadie. They happen every day. You and me, for example."

She couldn't help but smile, pointing a finger up at him. "That's cheating and you know it. Bringing it around to us. We just got lucky."

"Luck schmuck. We're a miracle and you know it."

"All right. I'm not going to fight you about it."

"You'd better not. You might be smitten for ingratitude."

"Smitten, there's a word."

He stepped over and kissed the top of her head. "I'm going to cut a piece of honey cake. You want a bite?"

"Small," she said.

And the doorbell rang.

"Your father's right, Abraham. You don't look too good. Are you eating?"

"Sure," Abe admitted.

"Like when?"

"When what?"

"When did you last eat?"

"I'm eating now. This fine homemade honey cake."

"Or sleep?" his father asked.

In the tiny kitchen, on his dainty chair, next to the two older people, Abe could have been a giant. "How 'bout we leave off with the third degree?" He swallowed his bite of cake, sipped from his cup of tea. "Are you following this Ro Curtlee thing at all?"

"Some trouble when you arrested him," his father said. "I read the paper."

"I arrested him for threatening the kids. They gave him bail and let him out again, and Treya decided she couldn't . . . she had to get the kids out of here."

"To where?" Sadie asked.

"LA. Her brother's place."

Nat's bite of cake stopped halfway to his mouth. "You're saying she's gone?"

Abe nodded. "This afternoon."

"Why'd they let him out?" Sadie asked.

"They're insane. They don't live in the real world."

"Vampires," Nat said.

"Not exactly, Pops, but close enough. Anyway, as you can see, I stayed."

"Is she mad at you?" Sadie asked.

The corner of Abe's mouth went up a quarter inch. "I want to say she understands, but I'm not sure."

"What's not to understand?" Nat asked.

"Me, staying. Why my job is more important than my kids, or maybe even—she thinks—my life." He twirled his eggshell-thin china cup of tea in its saucer. "The thing is, she left her job. She thinks I should have left mine."

"She quit her job?" Sadie asked.

"She's taking vacation days, but it's going to amount to the same thing."

"So what are you going to do?"

"I don't know," Abe said. "Not to complain, but the job's just one frustration after another, I don't have enough manpower to do it, if I go down to LA with Treya, somebody else will just step in and muddle through or, more likely, muck it all up, which is what it feels like I'm doing anyway. But I feel like I've got to stay, there's no other way to explain it. I took it on. I can't hand it off to somebody else. It sounds stupid and outdated, but I feel like it's kind of my duty."

Nat took a moment, then said, "I don't hear any question there."

"No, I know," Abe said. "There really isn't one."

24

Tristan Denardi's first meeting this morning was with his private investigator Mike Moylan, who got himself settled into one of Denardi's wing chairs and said, "I can't find her."

Denardi, signing papers at his desk, stopped and looked up in surprise. "What do you mean? You always find everybody. And usually within five minutes."

"I know. But not this time. She just dropped off the radar."

"But you've told me that was impossible."

"Very hard, but not impossible. First, you've got to use cash only, no credit cards ever. Second, you get a false set of identity papers, and third, you cut all ties with your previous life. You do all that, and remember that most people can't, and you're disappeared."

Denardi sat back. "Gloria Gonzalvez was that sophisticated?"

"Evidently, although it doesn't take so much sophistication as it does pure will. Anybody wants, they can go cash only. And fifty bucks, maybe a hundred, buys you all the ID you'll ever need. But most people, somebody dies in the family or gets married or has a kid, either somebody contacts you or you hear about it and need to get back in touch. And Gloria hasn't done that, not that I could find anyway."

Pensive, Denardi put his pen down and sat back in his chair. "Could she still be in witness protection?"

"I don't think so. They usually only keep them until they testify. Then they're on their own."

"So what did she do after she testified? You get any kind of a trail at all?"

"No. She just vanished. Somebody must have coached her."

"This will not please my client."

"I'm sorry, sir. I can keep working on it if you want, but if she hasn't turned up on any of my databases, I don't know where I'd start."

"Did you try that—what do you call it?—the pizza list?" Moylan had fascinated Denardi with the so-called pizza list soon after he'd found out about it himself. As everyone who's ever ordered a pizza by phone knows, the first thing they ask for is your phone number. Second is your name. This database—most if not all of the pizza stores in the nation—is then sold to various marketing organizations or otherwise interested persons, such as private investigators. It is a very potent tool for locating people.

But Moylan was shaking his head. "No."

"Why not?"

"Expense, mostly. You gave me four hours, besides which I don't think she's Gloria Gonzalvez anymore."

"How about just Gloria?"

"How about it? Probably."

"So. You look for Glorias."

"Tris, there's probably forty, fifty pages of Glorias. Single spaced. Once I can even find them. You want me to call each one individually?"

"Maybe if you just start with California?"

Moylan chuckled. "Yeah, that'll narrow it right down to maybe two thousand names. If I call 'em all, we're talking maybe a full week, maybe two, eighty hours, and then maybe no results at all. Which, don't get me wrong, I'd be delighted to do, but you'd want to know what you're signing off on."

Denardi sucked at his teeth for a moment. "My clients really want to talk to her, Mike. She's the last witness standing and they think they can persuade her that she doesn't want to testify again."

"And I wish them luck. But you know," Moylan went on, "if she's this invisible, I doubt if the DA's going to be able to find her, either."

"That's a good point. But if they do find her first, they'll slap her back into protection and then we're screwed. I'd rather we get there before they do."

"So you want me to keep on?"

Denardi nodded. "Give it a week, see what you come up with."

Sheila Marrenas walked into the front door of Michael Durbin's store and stood in line, to all appearances patiently waiting her turn. When she got to the counter, she took off her dark glasses, smiled at Michael, flashed her press card, and asked if she could have a few minutes of his time.

His face went pale at the sight of her. "I don't think so, no."

"You don't want to get your side of the story out there?"

"My side of what story?"

"Your wife's death. I understand you've been talking to Inspector Glitsky . . ."

"How did you know that?"

She shrugged. "It doesn't really matter how I know, Michael. I talk to people. They talk to me. I'm giving you an opportunity here that you're going to need, and I really do think it's in your own best interest at least to address some of the issues I'm hearing about."

"Why? So you can treat me as fairly as you did last time?"

"I gave you every chance back then to defend yourself and you made the same mistake then that you're trying to make again now."

"And what's that? Defending myself against accusations that have not one grain of truth in them?"

"You're telling me you never stole anything from that job? Paper, supplies, anything like that? You never filed a false timesheet?"

"I'm still not going to talk about that. God knows that whatever I did, and it wasn't much, was part of the culture of the firm. Everybody there was doing what they accused me of."

"And everybody would include you, wouldn't it?"

"Whether or not it does, I've already paid enough for it, whatever it was. You know, everything you ask is of the when-did-you-stop-beating-your-wife variety. Every answer's the wrong one."

"All right, then," she said, "getting down to it. When did you?"

Durbin lowered his voice and leaned in toward her. "You get the hell out of here right now."

From somewhere down the counter, suddenly Liza Sato appeared at Durbin's sleeve. "Is there a problem?" she asked. "Michael, is everything all right?"

"Not even close," he said. "As of this minute, we're refusing to give service to this woman. I want her out of here."

But Sheila Marrenas, spotting the name tag on Liza's chest, wasn't going without a fight. Now she shifted her attention to the assistant manager. "Ms. Sato," she said, "is it true that Mr. Durbin arrived late to work last Friday morning?"

"Don't answer that, Liza! Whatever you say, she'll twist it."

Sato shook her head at Marrenas. "I've got no comment," she said. "Except that my boss wants you out of here." She turned to Michael. "Should I call nine-one-one?"

The four other customers and five other clerks had been trying to ignore the ongoing exchange, but suddenly the place had gone quiet. Durbin looked back and forth along the counter, then nodded to his assistant. "Give her ten seconds," he said.

"All right," Marrenas said, backing away. "But don't blame me if your side of things doesn't get in my column. I'm trying here."

"You're trying to sandbag me, is what you're doing. You've got about two more seconds and then Liza calls the police."

"It's your funeral," Marrenas said. "You brought it on yourself." And turning, she walked out of the shop.

————

"No." Bracco sat with his feet up on his desk in the homicide detail. "That isn't quite true. I said the investigation is continuing. Beyond that I have no comment."

"But," Marrenas countered, "you interviewed Ro yesterday at his lawyer's in connection with these murders?"

"All right."

"And you contend that this isn't part of the pattern of harassment we've seen against Ro Curtlee over the past weeks."

"Absolutely not. There's been no harassment of Ro Curtlee or anybody else."

"So you've been looking at someone else, besides Ro, as a suspect?"

"We're looking at the whole world, ma'am."

"Including Michael Durbin?"

Bracco paused. "We have found no evidence linking Mr. Durbin with the crime."

"But you have no evidence on Ro, either."

"I've already said everything I have to say on that issue."

"Why did you feel the need to interview him, then?"

"To give him the chance to eliminate himself as a suspect."

"And did he do that?"

"Well, as you know, he provided an alibi for the time of Janice Durbin's death."

"So that eliminates him, right?"

"Unless the alibi doesn't hold up." Bracco brought his feet down off the desk. "Listen, Sheila, I'm sorry but I'm going to have to cut this short. The investigations are continuing. That's about as much as I can give you."

"The Matt Lewis investigation, too?"

"I'm not the investigating officer on that case," Bracco replied.

"But you also asked where Ro was when that crime was committed?"

"A cop gets killed, we throw a wide net."

"And again, with no evidence against Ro?"

"Both investigations are continuing," Bracco said. "We have not eliminated anyone as a suspect."

———

No sooner had he hung up with Marrenas, though, than Bracco realized that what he'd told her was true—Glitsky hadn't eliminated any suspects in the Janice Durbin murder. Glitsky and Becker might be 100 percent certain that Ro Curtlee was guilty of killing her—and Ro sure as hell looked guilty to Bracco of the Matt Lewis murder—but the plain fact remained that Ro had given Bracco an alibi for Durbin's time of death and four people who could corroborate it. Granted, by no stretch could this corroboration—his parents, Eztli, and the maid or morning cook, Linda—be deemed unimpeachable. But what if they were all telling the truth? And if Ro, in fact, had not been at the Durbin home—and no physical or other evidence placed him there—that meant that someone else had killed Janice.

"Earth to Bracco. Come in, Darrel."

He looked up, startled to see Glitsky hovering over his desk. "Abe! Hey." In his chair, he straightened to attention.

"I've got to learn that trick," Glitsky said. "Sleeping with my eyes open."

"I wasn't sleeping. I was thinking."

"Good. Thinking is one of the approved activities. What about?"

"Well, Sheila Marrenas called me. I just now got off the phone with her."

"I hope you didn't tell her too much."

"I said that our two investigations are continuing. Durbin and Lewis. We didn't have suspects for either."

"She believe you?"

"She didn't care. She's going to write what she writes anyway, whatever that spin might turn out to be."

"So what were you thinking about?"

"Well, since that's what I went out there to find out, it looks like Ro's got an alibi for Durbin."

"If you believe it."

"He's got four people he says will back it up."

Glitsky said, "The parents and two servants."

"True. I'm not arguing with you, Abe. I'm just saying . . ."

"No. It's a good point," Glitsky conceded. He had lowered his haunch onto the corner of Bracco's desk. His eyes had gone to a half squint. His mouth was tightly closed and a muscle worked in his jaw. "I'll keep it in mind."

"And," Bracco hesitated, "while we're talking, one other thing."

"What's that?"

"Ro's arm."

"What about it?"

"It's in a cast. Still. Righteously broken in the fight with you, was it not?"

"All right."

"All right, so you told me that Janice Durbin was strangled, didn't you? Manual strangulation, not a ligature." Ligature was a strangulation device, such as a rope or a belt.

Bracco stopped and leveled his gaze at his boss, waiting for the impact of his words to kick in. He didn't have to draw the picture any more clearly. Every homicide cop knows how extraordinarily difficult it is to strangle someone to death, even under the best of conditions, using both of one's hands. The struggle tends to be violent and protracted. The idea that someone could do it one-handed, while probably physically possible for a very strong and committed person, was close to far-fetched. When he was sure from his lieutenant's change of expression that Glitsky had understood his point, Bracco went on, pressing it. "Did Strout find any signs she'd been knocked out before she got strangled? Lacerations or abrasions or bruises to the head?"

"I'd have to check to be sure, and I intend to, but my memory says no."

Bracco leaned back in his chair. "So Ro is holding her down with his knees," he said, "and she's bucking and kicking under him and he never hits her to knock her out—I mean, he's got a heavy cast on, right? And instead he's got her by the neck and strangles her with one hand? This, when we know he's in possession of a gun because that's what he killed Lewis with, and he doesn't use that?"

25

Shaken more deeply by Bracco's objections to Ro as Janice's killer than he cared to show, Glitsky walked down to the third floor, where he would sometimes drop in on Treya in the middle of the workday just to say hello, share a few bons mots, touch base. Today he made it as far as the hallway that led to the DA's office and nearly stopped at the outer door to Farrell's lair—Treya's office—noticing that her desk was still unoccupied—no replacement, yet, anyway. Standing in the outer doorway, he heard Farrell's voice emanating from inside. In a few steps, he passed Treya's workstation and stood in the open doorway where he saw Farrell sitting on one of the couches, a telephone to his ear. "No, I have no comment," he was saying. "No, sorry, no comment. I'm afraid I'm not going to talk about that."

Glitsky knocked once on the doorjamb. Farrell looked up and, indicating the telephone, shook his head in disgust, and then waved Glitsky in and motioned him to one of the chairs while he continued listening and then said, "I'm sure, but we'll just have to see how that turns out . . . well, no . . . I mean, yes, of course, you're going to do what you have to do. But the same is true of me . . . I know, and I'm sorry about that, but I've got an appointment that's just showed up here and I can't really say any more at this time . . . All right . . . All right, thank you."

Farrell hung up, flipped the bird at the telephone, then looked at Glitsky, who had not yet sat down, and said, "Some son of a bitch leaked the grand jury. That, if you didn't guess," he added, gesturing at the phone, "was Marrenas."

"She's getting around today," Glitsky said. "Twenty minutes ago, she was talking to Darrel Bracco, but not about the grand jury."

"Well, then, she must have talked to somebody in between, because what you heard just now was all grand jury all the time. She even had the strategy of combining the cases so we'd get to specials and beat the bail problem."

Glitsky walked over to Farrell's library table, knocked the wood on the top of it a couple of times, thinking, then turned around. "It couldn't be Chomorro. I wouldn't pick him as capable of doing that. He couldn't give us our warrant, but I got the impression he was on our side."

Farrell, nodding in agreement, said, "But remember who was in his office when we got there, just having a nice little chat?"

"Baretto."

"That's the magic word. You win a hundred dollars."

"You think he called her? Marrenas?"

"Yes, but it doesn't matter who called who. There's a lot of candidates. Someone in the clerk's office, a bailiff, a court reporter. The point is she's got it and she's going to print it, which means Ro and Denardi will know, if they don't already by now."

"Well, so they know. So what? It wasn't the original plan, but it shouldn't make any real difference."

"No?"

"Not really. I don't see how it could, anyway."

"How about if Ro gets to one of the grand jurors first or to Amanda or even to me?"

Glitsky leaned back against the table. Pensive, frowning, he scanned the room, settled back on Farrell. "You could call Marrenas back and tell her she got it wrong. Whoever told her, they got it wrong. You've thought about it since you hung up and she really needs to know you're not going to the grand jury. Period. The strategy of combining all the cases is flawed. There's not enough evidence. It just couldn't work. You're waiting until Ro's retrial."

"And then what?"

"Then you go to the grand jury anyway."

"You're saying I lie?"

"No. God forbid. You just changed your mind again after you hang up with her. Oops, sorry. You forgot to tell her that part."

Farrell settled back into the couch, put a hand to his temple, rubbed at it. "Just to spin it out," he said. "So I go to the grand jury and get my indictment and arrest Ro, whereupon Marrenas then tells the whole world that I flat-out knowingly lied to her. What's that do to my credibility with the fourth estate?"

"Who cares by then? You've got your indictment. Ro's in jail. He doesn't kill anybody else in the meantime. Sounds like a winner to me."

Farrell shook his head. "I can't lie, Abe. I've got to leave it at 'no comment.' It's a secret proceeding, for Christ's sake. I can't talk about what I'm doing with it. That's the whole point of the damn thing. And why? So grand jury witnesses don't get threatened or worse by the lowlifes they're testifying against. So I can put on my cases without fear of reprisal, which let me tell you, I've got a shit-load of right now. I mean true, actual fear. If I didn't know they had a twenty-four-hour tail on Ro, I think I might be completely paralyzed."

"Well, on that," Glitsky said. "The first shift already lost him."

———

Ro and Eztli were a little high, laughing at how easily they had eluded the more-than-obvious city vehicle that had been parked on the street since early morning. Ro had simply lain down on the floor in the backseat while Eztli pulled out of the driveway, waved to the cops, and drove off in the 4Runner on his mid-afternoon errands. Three blocks out, he had pulled over and Ro had gotten back into the passenger seat. If it wasn't so funny, they agreed, it would be pathetic.

Now they were in a warehouse in the industrial area just north of San Bruno, another Peninsula suburb. Later that night, the warehouse was going to be the venue for about six rounds of pit bull fighting that would begin around eight and go on until past midnight, but Ro had gotten a call from Tristan Denardi earlier in the day reporting on his private investigator's lack of progress locating Gloria Gonzalvez, and Ro was quickly losing his patience. This woman had to be found and neutralized, or he was going to go back to prison. And if Denardi wasn't going to be able to find her, Ro had to make it his own business.

So he'd discussed the problem with Ez, and as usual, the man had a sound, workable idea of how to get some results. Eztli had long ago developed a relationship with Lupe García, who not only ran the dogfights, but was the go-to guy in the Bay Area Guatemalan community if you wanted to borrow money or bet on almost anything or buy a weapon or drugs or get a woman to be your maid or your sex slave or both.

When Ro and Eztli caught up with him, escorted by two of his bodyguards, Lupe was in the inner shell of the warehouse, a huge, prefabricated sheet-metal space very much like the inside of a circus tent, complete with bleachers surrounding the ring, fourteen feet in diameter, where the fighting took place. Lupe was hosing down the carpeting that the dogs needed for traction, cleaning it from the previous night's fights. He could have farmed out this work—certainly it was far beneath his station—but he liked to get down on the floor with the smells and the damp and the blood.

Ez and Ro and the bodyguards waited while he finished up, turning off the hose, drying his hands on a towel and coming over to them, a warm smile of greeting on his face. Lupe wasn't a big man. Perhaps five foot eight and wiry, he wore long hair pulled back and blue jeans and cowboy boots and a canvas jacket over a plaid shirt. A heavy-looking silver cross hung off his left earlobe. Tattoos covered the backs of his hands and disappeared into his shirtsleeves. He and Eztli greeted each other with clasped hands and one-armed hugs.

They spoke in Spanish, of course. Lupe reminded Ro of any number of La Eme gang members from prison. They hadn't been particularly interactive with the Caucasian population, but none of that seemed to be in play here. As Eztli explained both Ro's presence and the nature of their business, Lupe glanced over from time to time with an expression that indicated acceptance. From his attitude alone, Ro had obviously been in prison, and he was putting up not only the up-front thousand dollars to Lupe for his trouble—beaming as Eztli gave him the envelope—but the other five thousand to the person or persons who gave him the where-abouts of the woman who, ten years before, had been Gloria Gon-zalvez, one of the two key witnesses in Ro's trial.

Back in their car, on the surface streets back toward the freeway, Eztli drew deeply on the joint and said, "I like Lupe, but I've got to believe we were smart not to be carrying the other five thousand with us. You saw his reaction to that kind of reward."

"I get the feeling if we had given it to him," Ro said, "he would have thought about keeping it."

"Not just thought about it." Eztli's shoulders heaved a bit with his low, rumbling laughter. "He's probably trying to figure out how to get his hands on it right now. But that's not our worry. He'll have an army of guys working the problem by tomorrow."

"How long did he think it would be?"

"He'd be surprised if it was more than a week, word gets out. That's a lot of money for these guys."

"It's a day or two of Denardi," Ro said. "Nothing."

"Well, there you go." Eztli took another, long hit, and let out the smoke. "Different worlds."

———

When he'd been in private practice, Farrell had availed himself of the superb gatekeeping services of his firm's indomitable Phyllis.

For the past half dozen years, he'd never picked up a phone in his office without a very clear understanding of who was on the other end. Since he'd come on as DA, Treya had performed the same function.

In the short time she'd been gone, the phones had become one of Farrell's more constant problems. He really had to get another person sitting out there at the reception desk, but in spite of his warning to Treya that he couldn't guarantee her job when she got back, what he wanted was to have her out there again as soon as she felt it was safe.

And he *really* didn't want to promote someone on a temporary basis to cover his phones and, to some extent, share his secrets, mostly because once they were in, they might make a stink and try to fight to stay and piss around with the union when Treya reappeared; but also because he was starting to get some appreciation of the value of trust. And he trusted Treya. The person he chose to sit in for Treya might very well turn out to be a spy of some kind for his political enemies. Or at least able to be turned.

Farrell didn't want to risk it.

But now the phone was ringing on the table in his office and he didn't know who it was and he really couldn't justify not picking it up. And so, sighing, that is what he did. "DA's office," he said. "This is Wes Farrell."

"Mr. Farrell"—an unmistakable voice—"I've heard some very disturbing news. This is Cliff Curtlee."

"Mr. Curtlee. How are you?"

"Well, not too goddamned well, if you want to know the truth. I thought we had some kind of an understanding, you and I."

"In what way?"

"In the way that you were going to cut out all this bullshit surrounding my boy. I thought it got all worked out pretty well at that charade of a hearing last week, Ro's back out on bail, when I know goddamn well you could have gone in and told the judge no way.

So, given that bail got granted, I thought we—you and me—we were still working within the bounds of our understanding. That you had to do what you had to do politically, but that basically Ro stays out of jail until the retrial. Wasn't that it? I know it was."

"Well, not exactly . . ."

"Yeah, but close enough. Now it's unconscionable what that madman Glitsky put my boy through when he arrested him, but even then, okay, he'd had his shot and it didn't work and I thought with you riding just a little bit of herd on him, that would be the end of it until we got back to the retrial, whenever that turned out to be. And then next thing I know, my lawyer and Theresa and I are sitting with Ro through another interrogation."

"That was a police decision, sir. Not mine."

"All right, all right. I'm not going to split hairs with you on that. But what I am concerned about, and the reason I called you directly, is one of my reporters here told me that you're planning on using some kind of fancy legal strategy to go to the grand jury and get my boy behind bars again."

"I can't comment on that, sir. Grand jury proceedings are confidential."

"So you're not going to confirm to me that you're planning on taking a case to the grand jury and yanking Ro back into jail?"

"I'm neither going to confirm or deny it. I'm not going to comment."

"Well, you'll understand if that makes me feel just a little bit as if you're going to go ahead and do it."

"It's no comment, sir. Either way. I can't undermine the foundation of how the grand jury works."

"My reporter had it on very good authority," Curtlee said.

"Well, whoever told her has a big mouth. You want to tell me who that was?"

"Even if I did know, and I don't, I couldn't reveal my reporter's source. You know that."

"Well, then," Farrell said, "I guess we've both got our secrets."

A silence hung on the line. Then: "I want to make something very clear to you, Farrell. You and I had a deal about my son not going back to jail . . ."

"Not saying we did, sir, but if we did, that was before he started killing people."

"Oh, make some sense, Farrell. You believe that?"

"The evidence inclines that way."

"Fuck. There's no evidence or Glitsky would have his ass in chains already. So don't give me evidence. So here's what I'm saying to you. I don't want this grand jury thing to move forward. It would be a bad thing for you personally if it did."

"Are you threatening me, Cliff? 'Cause we've done some very recent research into the legal penalties for making threats to officers of the court."

"Now you're threatening me. All I'm saying is you'll be happier if this grand jury thing stops right now. Assuming it's going on, of course. And if it's not, then there's nothing either of us has to worry about."

———

Eztli and Ro were stationed at the bar at MoMo's, a popular eatery where they'd just had lunch across the street from where the Giants played ball. Eztli didn't drink much, but here in the early afternoon Ro had already put away four shots of Jack Daniel's and a couple of draft beers along with sharing two joints of Eztli's very good marijuana. Still, the younger man seemed little the worse for wear.

Ro was chatting up one of the cocktail waitresses named Tiffany, a fresh-faced, young, tawny-haired woman with a terrific smile and an aggressive bosom. "No, it's absolutely true," he was saying. "I was away for nine years."

"No way." She looked past him at Eztli. "Is this the truth?"

"Yes, ma'am," he said. "And finally released on appeal."

"Oh my God," she said. "I mean, it's cool and all that they finally let you out, but nine years! How could you have stood that?"

"I just kept telling everybody who'd listen that I was innocent," Ro said. "I guess I just never lost faith that this is maybe the one country in the world where if you're truly not guilty, you can finally get to some kind of justice. Sometimes it takes a while, but I've got to believe that the system really does work."

Tiffany touched the back of his hand, resting there on the bar, with a well-lacquered perfect fingernail. "Well, you are way more together around it than I think I could ever be. If it were me, all I'd think about was how much of my life I'd lost. I'd be just so incredibly bitter, I think."

"That's one way I could be, I suppose, but really, think about what a waste that would be. I mean, look at me now, sitting in a terrific restaurant in the world's greatest city, young and healthy, having a conversation with a beautiful woman . . ."

"Oh, now . . ."

Ro held up his good hand. "It ain't braggin' if it's the truth, dear. I hope I'm not being too forward, just stating an obvious fact. And my real point is I don't want to spend one day of my life looking back in regret. All that other stuff is behind me. I'd rather be looking forward with hope. And life is so good right now, my goal is to work like the devil to keep it that way forever. Are you allowed to drink if you're still on your shift? Can I buy you one?"

She tossed her hair and favored him with a megawatt smile. "I'm sorry, I can't." Again, she brushed the back of his hand with her fingers. "Back in a second," she said, "I've got to run, check my tables."

After she'd moved off, Ro turned to Eztli. "You were right. I thought if I mentioned prison, she'd run like the wind."

He shrugged. "Some do. Most don't. Depends on how you play it."

"If things work out from here," Ro said, "I'll just get a cab home from her place. Or stay there and catch up with you tomorrow."

"Cool. Whatever." The cell phone chirped at his belt and Eztli picked it up, read the screen, and said, "Your dad."

———

"He's living with a woman named Sam Duncan," Cliff said. "She runs the Rape Crisis Counseling Center out on Haight Street."

"You've got to be kidding me," Eztli said. "Given everything, that is just too perfect."

"I know it is. You couldn't have made it up any better. But it doesn't really matter what she does. The point is that Sheila has talked to some of her sources at the Hall of Justice and she tells me that Farrell's going ahead with some more legal shenanigans, now with the grand jury, that he thinks will wind up getting Ro back in jail and without any possibility of bail."

"How many times can they keep putting us through this?"

"Evidently as often as they want."

"So how would you like me to handle it?"

"Well, the idea is that we want to get the message to Farrell, but we don't want anything that he can point to as even a remote personal threat, the way Glitsky did. The way they're all charged up down there at the Hall, Sheila says, one of them stubs their toe, they're going to try to connect it to Ro and get him back downtown. I think what we've got to do is make Farrell see that it's in his best interest to just back the fuck off, give up on the grand jury nonsense, use his brain."

"And you think this woman is how we get to him?"

"I don't think we want to have her be hurt, Ez. I don't think that would accomplish anything, other than get 'em all more rabid down there. But I'm thinking, maybe some damage at the place she works, nothing serious, but so that Farrell can't help but get the message. I'll leave it to your discretion."

"And what's the time frame?"

"Whatever's comfortable for you. Do what you do, get your plan together. Next couple or three days, maybe, but it's flexible."

———

Glitsky was talking to Bob Grassilli in Missing Persons. Outside Bob's window, the day had grown blustery again, and inside the small office the whistle of the wind reverberated with an insistent regularity. Grassilli was a career desk cop in his midforties, balding, and a good forty pounds over his ideal fighting trim. He smiled easily under his reddish brush of a mustache.

"I don't even know if this is where I'd look, Abe. Eight or nine years is a pretty cold trail. You've tried all the usual databases, I'm assuming."

Glitsky nodded. "Driver's license, Social, immigration, you name it. I've been on it for a couple of hours already. So now I'm thinking what if she got married and changed her name?"

"She'd still have her same driver's license number. And passport, I'm assuming. You say she's legal?"

"She came up from Guatemala on a work visa. That was still in effect when she went into witness protection. Afterward, I don't know."

"Did she become a citizen?"

"Again. Don't know."

"Well, if she did, there'll be a record of that someplace. Which of course is worthless if she later changed her name. But did you ever think maybe she just went back home? She's a crime victim here, right? Maybe she just doesn't want to be here anymore."

"I think that's likely, tell you the truth, Bob. But how do I find one particular Gonzalvez in Guatemala? It's like locating a Smith here."

"Well, welcome to Missing Persons," Grassilli said with his trademark smile. "If anybody really wants to disappear and stay disappeared, it's not rocket science. Unless, hey, you might consider hiring a private eye. They've got databases they can buy or download that we're not allowed to use. 'Course, they're not allowed to use them, either, but out in the private sector, no one's checking."

"That's really swell news, Bob. Heartening, in fact."

Grassilli shrugged, showing some teeth under the mustache. "I'm just the messenger, Abe. That's the way it is."

"Yeah, well, I don't have enough budget for my own men. How am I going to even try to justify hiring a PI?"

"I'd say you're probably not."

"I'd say you're probably right."

26

OUR TOWN

By Sheila Marrenas

The tendency of the San Francisco Police Department to over-react, harass, and brutalize the citizens of our town has been well-documented over the years in this column. Mayor Leland Crawford's appointment of Vi Lapeer, an African American woman, as chief of police raised hopes that these practices would not be tolerated any longer under his administration. These hopes were for the most part dashed over the past couple of weeks, most notably in the police treatment of Ro Curtlee, the son of this newspaper's publishers.

As readers of this column already know, Mr. Curtlee was recently released from prison by the Ninth Circuit Court of Appeal. Then, here in the city, Judge Sam Baretto ordered Mr. Curtlee freed on bail while awaiting his retrial, a decision that did not sit well either with District Attorney Wes Farrell, or with the head of homicide, Lieutenant Abe Glitsky. Within days of Mr. Curtlee's release, Glitsky presented a new set of spurious charges against him and, in a widely publicized incident, arrested him after first beating him seriously enough that he required hospitalization.

And again, a superior court judge—Erin Donahoe—ruled that Mr. Curtlee posed no danger to the community. She again released him on bail.

But in our town, it doesn't seem as though the regular workings and procedures of the criminal justice system apply once prosecutors and police, even contrary to judges' rulings, have preconceived notions about a person's guilt. And this is why, yesterday morning, Mr. Curtlee again found himself facing yet another bit of gratuitous harassment from the police, an interrogation—fortunately this one did not turn violent—for the murder last Friday of a woman named Janice Durbin. This interrogation, in which Mr. Curtlee voluntarily and cooperatively participated, unearthed a solid alibi for Mr. Curtlee for the time of the murder. Beyond that, the inspector who conducted the interview, Darrel Bracco, told this reporter that there was *no evidence* implicating Mr. Curtlee in the crime. Hearing this, one might be tempted to ask, as this reporter was: "Well, then, if there is no evidence, upon what criteria did you decide to interrogate Mr. Curtlee? How could this be viewed as anything but harassment?"

In reply, Inspector Bracco had no comment.

However, police have determined that Mrs. Durbin was in fact a murder victim. Since someone did kill her, and Mr. Curtlee has demonstrated that it could not have been him, why are the police still fixated on his possible involvement? Might not the solution to this mystery, as it most always does, lie closer to home, among Mrs. Durbin's intimates? A cursory investigation by this reporter has already determined that Mrs. Durbin's husband, Michael Durbin, for example, cannot account for his whereabouts at the time of his wife's death. Moreover, sources at his place of business told this reporter that Mr. Durbin may be romantically involved with another of his employees.

This is specifically not to accuse Mr. Durbin of any wrongdoing, but merely to indicate possibilities in the murder investigation that, to date, the police seem to be willfully ignoring as Glitsky and Farrell continue their personal and extralegal vendetta against Ro Curtlee.

———

"You've got to sue her," Chuck Novio said. "Her and her newspaper and the Curtlees personally. This is the most appalling libel I've ever read."

It was a few minutes after seven A.M. and they were all sitting around the dining room table, Michael and Chuck and the three Durbin children. Kathy and the twins were in the adjoining kitchen making eggs and bacon and toast. They would be cremating Janice today at eleven o'clock and so the kids and Chuck were all taking the day off from school. Durbin's second son, Peter, had been the first one up and hence the first to read the article, and he'd barely gotten through it before he went running up the stairs to wake his father and show it to him.

"But she says she's specifically not accusing me of anything," Durbin said.

"That's BS, pure BS," Peter said. "She's saying you did it, Dad. That you killed Mom."

"You're not going to let her get away with that, are you, Dad?" Jon asked. "You don't go after her hard, you're basically admitting that she's right." The elder son slumped back in his chair with his arms crossed, staring out into nothing with a sullen eighteen-year-old malevolence.

"I agree with Jon, Mike," Chuck said. "You've got to go after her."

Allie, the thirteen-year-old down the table, barely holding back her tears until now, had been silent all morning, and she finally spoke in a tremulous voice. "You didn't though, did you?"

Durbin reached out a hand across the table and covered his daughter's with his own. "No, sweetie. Of course not. I loved your mother and I miss her so much."

"Me, too. I already miss her so much." And Allie's tears broke.

Kathy—her own eyes bloodshot and teary with grief and lack of sleep—swooped in from the kitchen and put her arms around her niece. "Nobody thinks your father did anything wrong at all," she said. "You just don't even have to think about that."

"Marrenas thinks it," Jon said. "And now maybe half the city. And now Dad's got to deny it, plain and simple."

"I don't have to dignify what she wrote by responding to it. That's lowering myself to her level and I'm not going to do it."

"You gotta do it, Dad. You've got to say loud and clear you didn't do it, if you didn't . . ."

Michael slapped his palm flat against the table, cutting Jon off. "Of course I didn't do it, goddamn it! I hope we haven't gotten to that."

"No," Chuck put in, "don't be ridiculous."

"Then just deny it," Jon said. "Come right out with it."

Michael was shaking his head, his fury building, when one of the twin's voices came from the kitchen. "Hey! There's somebody in a TV van pulling into the driveway."

"Damn." Chuck stood up, craning to see out the dining room windows. "How'd anybody know you were staying here?"

"Somehow I just bet Marrenas knows," Michael said. He was getting up, too. "And if she knows, the word is out. Maybe I'd better go see what they want."

"You know what they want," Peter said. "You're right, Dad. I wouldn't tell them anything."

"Wrong, Peter," Jon said. "What have we been talking about here? He's got to deny it or it sounds like he did it. That's why Allie's crying. It sounds like it to her, too. It would to anybody."

His voice notching up in volume, Durbin whirled on his older son. "What are you saying? Don't talk like that."

"I'm just saying . . ."

And the telephone rang.

"Christ, what a circus," Chuck said. "You want to get that, Les?"

Leslie, one of the twins, picked it up in the kitchen. "Just a minute," she said. "Uncle Mike, it's for you. He says it's Jeff Elliot from the *Chronicle*."

"Jesus," Peter said.

"I'll get these clowns out front," Chuck said.

"I'm not talking to anybody from the *Chronicle*."

"They might get it right, Dad," Jon said.

"There's nothing to get. I keep telling you."

"So tell him that if that's what it is," Jon said.

"I wouldn't," Peter said. "Don't tell 'em nothing."

"Jon, wait a minute. Look at me," Durbin said. "What do you mean, 'if that's what it is'? I don't like your tone or the implication. I didn't have anything to do with your mother's death."

"That's what you keep saying. So what's that thing Marrenas said about you getting it on with somebody at work, too? Why'd she say that if there's nothing there?"

"Jon!" Kathy snapped. "Stop talking like that. Right now. That's ridiculous!"

"Yeah, sure, right." The lanky kid suddenly pushed his chair back with an obscenity and stomped out of the room and up the stairs.

"Jon!" Durbin called after him. "Son!"

But the sound of steps continued until a door slammed upstairs.

"What's his problem?" Peter asked.

And Durbin just shook his head, his hands outstretched in a supplicating gesture.

"Uncle Mike!" Leslie's voice, calling from the kitchen again. "He's still waiting."

"Let him wait. No, tell him I can't talk to him. No, wait, I'll tell him."

"Don't get roped in, Dad," Peter said.

"Don't worry, I won't. Christ."

Allie, her face wet and blotched, turned away from her aunt's embrace. "I don't want this to be happening anymore," she sobbed. "I just want my mommy back. I want my mommy."

———

Eztli was up early that Thursday morning, too.

Ro had kept up the press on Tiffany from MoMo's, and by the time Eztli had left on his own at around three thirty, Tiffany had finished her shift and Ro had stood her to a couple of Cuervo shots with—it looked like—a whole lot more to come.

Which was all good as far as Eztli was concerned. The more-than-obvious plainclothes cops parked on the street by the Curtlees, even though they'd lost the trail yesterday, looked like they were going to stick around. So the longer that Ro stayed away from home, the more mobility he'd have, at least until they caught up with him again.

Fortunately, and Eztli didn't really understand why this should be, they weren't following him. Maybe it was because yesterday he'd driven off, apparently alone, and then returned all by himself as well. Did they think Ro was still in the house, holed up? Well, whatever, it wasn't his problem. They weren't on his tail, and that was the main thing.

By a little before eight, the day clear and chilly, he'd driven the Z4—he loved that car!—down to Haight Street and found a parking space diagonally across from the glass storefront that announced the location of the Rape Crisis Counseling Center. Getting out of the car, he crossed the street and walked by the front of it. A heavy-looking wood-and-metal park bench was chained and padlocked along the front of the building. The Center didn't officially open for about another half hour, but there was a light on and some movement inside.

The glass front, he thought, presented some promising possibilities. He could come back later tonight, when it was dark, and shoot out the window, but he wasn't convinced that this would be the kind of unambiguous message that he was trying to deliver to Farrell through his girlfriend, Sam. Anyone could have a grudge with the policies or personnel of the Center and it wouldn't be as clear a signal as Cliff Curtlee would want to send.

Eztli walked down to the end of the block, then crossed the street and came back the other way, familiarizing himself with the lay of the land. It was typical Haight Street—almost exclusively small business storefronts. When he got back to his car, Eztli checked his watch and saw that the Center would be opening in another twenty minutes. While he was here, he might as well wait. Then he could go in and ask for Sam Duncan, telling her that it was important that Wes Farrell abandon his plan to bring Ro to the grand jury. As it had many times before, he knew that his simple presence could work magic.

But then suddenly a black Town Car turned into the street, pulled up, and stopped directly in front of the Center. After a second or two, the back door opened and Wes Farrell himself stepped out, followed by the yellow Labrador that he'd been walking with the other night out in front of his home. As Eztli watched, the two of them went up to the front door of the Center. Farrell knocked and a dark, attractive woman opened the door, then took the leash. After only a few seconds of conversation—obviously they'd already discussed leaving the dog, and therefore she must be Sam—Farrell walked back to the limo and it drove off.

Eztli sat thinking in the driver's seat of the Beemer, ideas dancing around in his mind, until after a couple more minutes, the door to the Center opened again and the woman came out onto the sidewalk with the dog on its leash, which she then attached to one of the legs of the park bench. When she patted the slats of the seat, the dog obediently hopped up and settled itself on the bench.

Eztli waited and watched for a few more minutes. The street was slowly waking up. The woman in the Center turned the CLOSED sign over to OPEN, then came out and put two large red dishes— food and water—on the sidewalk under the bench. The dog hopped down, ate, and drank some water. Then, as dogs do, it sniffed around and anointed the leg of the park bench before it went back to its place up on the bench and stretched out to sleep in the morning sunshine.

———

If Glitsky's three-bedroom flat had a characteristic feature, it was that the thirteen hundred square feet of it always felt crowded. When he'd first moved in here with Flo thirty-some years before, they'd already had two boys, Isaac and Jacob, and within the next year added Orel. After Flo had died of ovarian cancer, the three boys filled up the two bedrooms off behind the kitchen, and a housekeeper, Rita, had taken up nearly full-time residence behind a screen in the barely serviceable living room. By the time Treya and her daughter, Raney, moved in with Abe and Orel, the household reverberated with the noise of the two teenagers, and now they, too, had gone only to be replaced by Rachel and Zachary, who were themselves not exactly monklike in their habits.

Now there was no trace of any of the children, nor of Treya for that matter, and Glitsky sat drinking his morning tea at the table in his tiny kitchen, experiencing the unaccustomed silence as a palpable and ominous presence.

When the telephone rang, he had just picked up his cup and the *brrring* was loud and jarring and unexpected enough that he twitched and spilled some tea over the cup's edge and into his lap. Jumping up, furious at himself, brushing his pants to get the liquid off, he finally made it over to where the phone hung on the wall and picked up the receiver, growling his name into it.

"Abe. It's Vi. Sorry to call you at home, but you weren't at the office yet and I thought I'd take a chance."

The implied rebuke did nothing to elevate Glitsky's mood. "No problem," he said. "What's up?"

"I wondered if you happened to see the 'Our Town' column today."

"Not yet, no."

"Well, then it's lucky I reached you so I could give you a heads-up. She's pretty much all over you about your handling, or mishandling, I should say, of this Janice Durbin thing. I got a call from Hizzoner first thing this morning—and yes, if you're wondering, at home—and he read me the riot act about what's going on and I must say this wasn't the way I envisioned spending my first month or so on this job, defending myself and my chief of homicide every time I turn around."

"She's an irresponsible lunatic," Glitsky said.

"That may be true, but she's got Leland's attention in a big way, and he's all but screaming for your head."

Glitsky let out a deep sigh. "You know, Vi, at this point, I'm almost tempted to say give it to him. Who needs the aggravation? If you ask me to, I'll resign right now."

"Don't tempt me, will you? I don't want you to resign, especially over this, which strikes me as you just trying to do your job. Not to mention, imagine my future if I cave to this kind of idiocy the first time it rears its ugly head. But I've got to have some answers for Leland and for the public before this gets any further out of hand."

Again, Glitsky blew out heavily. "What's she say? Marrenas."

"Basically it's the same old. In your zeal to get Ro Curtlee back behind bars, you're ignoring a far better suspect who's right under your nose."

"And who's that?"

"The Durbin husband, who doesn't have an alibi and is also evidently having an affair with one of his employees."

"She printed that?"

"To that effect. And of course then the question is, why aren't you concentrating on him instead of picking on Ro?"

"Maybe because Ro did it. Although, for the record, you should know that I've interviewed the husband at least twice already and plan to do it again because it's such a good time. Meanwhile, you'll notice I haven't arrested anybody yet—Ro or Michael Durbin or anybody else—and that's usually a clue that I don't have a viable suspect."

"Well, if that's the case, it might be in your best interest to prepare some kind of statement to that effect, and I'll do the same."

"It should go without saying."

"Yes, well, that's not how it seems to be playing this time."

"How about just saying we can't comment because the investigation is continuing?"

"How'd that fly last time you tried it? I think we've got to be a little more forthcoming. I'm serious here, Abe. I don't know how long I'm going to be able to keep my own job if this keeps up. I'm on thin enough ice as it is. Let's try a little proactive appeasement, how's that sound? Put on a little show for the home team."

27

Fifty-eight people were in attendance at the crematorium service. Glitsky sat in the back row listening and taking notes as the relatives and acquaintances of Janice Durbin stood up to give their eulogies. A borderline tearful but controlled Michael Durbin got up and extolled his wife as a partner, provider, helpmate, and mother. Kathy Novio, breaking down several times, invited everyone over to her house for the reception afterward, then talked about her sister's childhood, her passion for her family and patients and career, and her belief that the world was a good place, a safe place, and how in spite of what had happened to her, Kathy was sure that Janice would not want anyone to come away from this ceremony with negative feelings or despair. Two other girlfriends, one from college and one from medical school, talked about how much fun she'd been, how dedicated a friend. Her pastor, who appeared to have known her fairly well, talked in a resounding baritone about her volunteer activities with the mentally handicapped, her generosity, and her faith.

It was, Glitsky thought, pretty much the usual stuff. But amid the tributes to Janice Durbin's life, he found himself unable to stop wondering which of the guests here, and he thought it must have been one of them, had given her chlamydia. Or if Janice had spread the disease to someone in this room.

While the last of the talks was winding down, he went out and stood by the back door and let the crowd flow out past him. He didn't know if anyone recognized him, and he certainly didn't pick up any sense of hostility from any of the guests for the way he was screwing up the investigation into Janice's murder.

Glitsky had met all the kids and the Novios the previous Saturday, and now when the families came out, straggling behind the rest of the crowd, he saw that the trauma of the past few days had taken a heavy toll.

Kathy, in stark contrast to her talk inside, was nearly ashen with anger and grief. She held hands with both of her daughters, glistening eyes straight ahead. A couple of steps behind her, her husband walked in a kind of stiff-legged attention. The elder Durbin boy, Jon, his face a cloud of fury, cleared the door and immediately walked away from the general direction of the crowd. Michael Durbin, following, walking next to the middle son, Peter, on one side of him, and his daughter, Allie, holding his hand on the other, called out to him, but Jon half turned and waved a dismissive hand and kept walking away.

Glitsky had come to the service as part of his chief's appeasement strategy, thinking that some reporter from the *Courier* or the *Chronicle* or one of the TV stations might be among the audience, and would interpret his presence there as having something to do with his investigation, and not to do with Ro Curtlee. In fact, he had arrived at the ceremony with every intention of pulling Michael Durbin aside and trying to get some clearer information either on his alibi for the time of the murder or on the situation, if any, between him and Liza Sato. He even considered that he might reveal the chlamydia angle and see where that led them.

But seeing the family now so rawly exposed, and with the children around, he simply met Durbin's eye and nodded in apparent sympathy as he walked past and let them all go to their waiting cars.

———

"I think you should call Jeff Elliot back." Chuck was drinking a beer, sitting on the counter in his kitchen, talking to Michael

Durbin while the reception continued in full swing in the living room. "Give the guy an interview in the *Chronicle*, go on the offensive."

"What's the offensive going to get me?" Michael asked. He held a glassful of bourbon and took a drink of it. "It's what Peter said this morning, the more I deny it, the more it sounds like I'm hiding something."

"Mike." Chuck put a hand on his brother-in-law's shoulder. "Listen to me. We know who did this, right? So, you notice anything missing from the Marrenas column? Like all the reasons we know it was Ro. Did she mention that you were the foreman of Ro's jury? No. Or the murder of that other woman, the witness? No. Or any other very good reason Glitsky might have been concentrating on Ro instead of you? That's a lot you could tell Elliot right there that somehow isn't making its way into the conversation, don't you think?"

"I don't know. I don't think anything anymore. I mean, even Jon's starting to have the idea that . . ."

But Chuck cut him off. "No, he's not. He's just devastated by his mom dying, and who can blame him? He doesn't really believe you had anything to do with it, I promise. Hell, he's eighteen. He's trying to find someplace to put all this emotion he'd rather deny he's feeling, so Marrenas gives him the idea and he takes it out on you."

"He's smarter than that."

"Maybe, but he's all fucked up right now. Just let him work it out."

"What other choice do I have, anyway? I don't know where he's got to."

"He'll be back, don't worry about that. Meanwhile, you call the *Chronicle*. You know they'll talk to you. Get Ro out there in front of the story where he belongs."

"That son of a bitch. But then what if he comes after me, or the kids?"

And at this, Chuck drew a breath, drank off a slug of beer. "I hadn't thought of that," he said.

"I haven't thought of too much else." He lifted his glass to his mouth and half emptied it. "I know what I should do, I'm not kidding." Lowering his voice, he said, "I ought to go kill the guy myself."

Chuck shook his head. "No. That's a bad idea."

"I've got a fucking shotgun out in my garage. I've had it forever, from back when I used to hunt. They can't trace a shotgun. I go over there to Ro's house some night, knock on the door, start shooting. Then I throw the gun in the bay. And tell Glitsky I was, say, with you the whole time, drinking away my sorrow."

"I've already said that's a bad idea. Now I'll say it again. That's a really bad idea."

"I don't have any other ideas."

"Well, lose that one. It totally sucks. You're not a killer, Michael, you couldn't do that. It would ruin your life."

Durbin tipped up his glass, finishing the drink. "As opposed to what it is now, you mean?"

———

Sheila Marrenas was waiting just outside the door of the outer lobby of the chief's office when Vi Lapeer got back from her lunch meeting. She was talking to one of her chief detectives and didn't notice the reporter until Marrenas stood up and blocked her way. "Excuse me, Chief. I've just got a quick question for you."

"And I'll be glad to answer it," Lapeer said. She looked at her watch. "In forty-five minutes at my press conference. That's why we have press conferences. So I can talk to the press. Now if you'll . . ."

She started forward, but Marrenas moved to the side, blocking her. *"This can't wait!"*

"Well, I'm afraid it has to, because . . ."

Marrenas stepped directly in front of her. "Isn't it true that you've assigned round-the-clock surveillance to follow Ro Curtlee wherever he goes? And that you've authorized budget and even overtime for this surveillance? And in spite of all this time and overkill, no one seems to know where Ro is right now? Isn't that true? Is that your idea of efficient use of an already overextended police budget? How can you possibly justify such an expensive, useless waste of money and personnel?"

Lapeer's mouth hung half open in shock, although she quickly recovered. "I have no comment," she said. "No comment. Now if you'll excuse me . . ."

And with that, the similarly astonished assistant chief next to her took her arm and, without touching Marrenas while moving her gently to the side, got her inside the lobby to her office and closed the door behind them.

———

Hector Murillo was not aware of the concept of six degrees of separation. He was a twenty-seven-year-old day laborer who'd come up from Mexico in 2004 and who remained undocumented. For the past eight months, Hector had been a regular in the four-man landscaping crew of Roberto Serrano. He was still pretty much low man both because he'd worked for Roberto for the shortest time and because he was Mexican and not Guatemalan.

But that was basically okay.

The difference between low man and high man wasn't so great anyway, not when his boss Roberto himself did whatever had to be done—grunt work like cleaning out gutters or spreading decomposed granite by the cubic yard—as well as the mowing and blowing and trimming. All in all, Hector was grateful to have a regular job, where he got paid in cash every week.

Hector lived in a trailer park just east of the 101 Freeway in Mountain View, and many nights he would hang out drinking beer with other men, mostly from Mexico, who found themselves in situations very much like his own. This was what he'd been doing last night when Jorge Cristobal, one of the guys from the park, had mentioned the five-thousand-dollar reward that Lupe García was offering to find a woman whose name used to be Gloria Gonzalvez. Evidently her mother had died in Guatemala and she had come into some money, and her lawyers had contacted the well-connected Lupe in the hope that, for a portion of the inheritance, he could help locate her so they could all get paid.

That was the story, anyway.

At first, Hector didn't think much about this, other than to try to fantasize how much five thousand dollars really was. He made sixty-two dollars a day, six days a week, about fifteen hundred dollars a month, and that covered food and rent and clothes and beer, but not much else. He didn't own even a share of a car; he had no insurance. And even so, he had amassed a savings of exactly zero after two-thirds of a year of steady work.

It wasn't until he'd been lying in bed, trying to sleep with that huge number floating around in his brain, that he realized that Roberto's wife's name was Gloria. She was also Guatemalan—or at least he assumed she was, since that was Roberto's nationality. It would certainly be odd if she wasn't.

He woke up with the possibility still fresh in his mind, thought about it through their first six houses in the morning. He did not want to give away what he knew to anyone. He knew Roberto and if he told him about the reward, and if his wife had been Gloria Gonzalvez, Roberto himself would go to Lupe and claim the reward and Hector would be lucky if he even got any small part of it. The same went for his three coworkers. If they had any idea what it was about, in exchange for any information they gave him, they would undoubtedly want to share part of the reward themselves. Jorge Cristobal from the trailer park was going to be bad enough if he was going to be the intermediary between Hector and Lupe. It looked like whoever claimed the reward was going to be stuck with someone like Jorge. But at least if Hector came to Jorge with the truth—if it was the truth—about Roberto's wife, then he would still have some leverage and might be able to keep Jorge's cut of the five thousand to a minimum.

Five thousand dollars! It was unfathomable.

They didn't take much time for lunch, no more than twenty minutes, but Hector arranged it so that he sat near to Roberto, who tended to sit somewhat apart from the crew normally, and halfway through their food, he struck up a conversation with his boss, under the pretext that he had a girlfriend himself and was thinking about marriage.

"How long," he asked in Spanish, "have you been married?"

Roberto shrugged. "Eight years."

"And how is it?"

"Good. I got lucky. Gloria works hard and she's a good mother. Don't marry a girl who doesn't like children."

"That isn't the problem," Hector said.

"If you already have a problem, maybe you should think about this decision some more. You shouldn't have problems before you get married."

"Well, maybe it isn't one. I don't know. It's why I wanted to ask you."

"You don't know if you have a problem?"

"I know what I have. I don't know if it's a problem."

Roberto waited.

"She's . . ."

"What's her name?"

"Maria."

"All right."

"Maria has lived here already for seven years."

"Is she a citizen? Because then, yes, marry her."

"No. Not yet. She is like me. But she has gotten ideas from some of the women she knows. She says it's not right that I should force her, if we become married, to change her name."

This seemed to confuse Roberto for a moment. "What would she change her name to? There is no better name than Maria."

"Her last name," Hector said. "To mine. Murillo."

"Murillo is a fine name. Why would she not want to have it?"

"It's not about the name. It's about being a modern American woman."

"But she's not American."

"No. But she speaks good English. She wants to fit in here. It's the new culture, she says."

Roberto frowned. "She will never fit in to the culture here. Doesn't she know that? Her children, maybe, or their children, but maybe not. I don't want to tell you what to do with this woman, but I'll be honest. This doesn't sound good to me." He took a bite of his burrito, chewing as though he was considering the issue from all angles.

Hector took the opportunity to go on. "So your wife, there was no problem, she changed her name?"

Roberto nodded. "Of course. It was never discussed. I would not have discussed it. She is my wife, she has my name."

"That is what I've been thinking," Hector said. "Except then I wonder if it is just that she doesn't like the sound of it, Maria Murillo."

"Nonsense. The sound of a name. What does that matter? What is her name now?"

"Gonzalvez," Hector said. "Maria Gonzalvez."

Roberto said "Ha!" and threw his hands in the air in a gesture of triumph. "You know this was my wife's name, Gonzalvez? Once she changed, she has never missed it. You tell your woman that. And if she still won't do it, I don't advise that you go ahead with this marriage. A woman who doesn't want to take your name, she sounds like she could be a lot of trouble."

———

Eztli bought two piroshki—meat-filled pastries—from one of the little Russian shops in the nearby neighborhood. He started eating one of them while walking back toward Haight Street, and when he'd finished that, he unwrapped the other one and pressed four of the little tablets he'd bought at the hardware store into the bottom of it. He threw the wax-paper wrapper and the package that the tablets had come in into a trash receptacle sitting on the sidewalk two streets down from the piroshki stand.

Coming around the corner a block away from the Rape Crisis Counseling Center, he turned right and strolled casually along, taking in the storefront windows as he aimlessly window-shopped. Stopping two doors down from the Center, checking out the vacation specials in the travel agency's window, he waited while a couple of elderly women stopped to interact with the cute yellow Lab on the bench, now very much awake and receptive, licking their hands as they petted it.

28

Farrell stood in a brown study in the mid-afternoon, aimlessly flicking the handles at his foosball table, keeping the ball in play.

Someone knocked on his door. He looked up, stopped defending, and the ball went into the right-hand goal as he said, "Come on in."

"Where's Treya?"

"Don't ask. Get the door, please."

Amanda Jenkins wasn't showing off her legs today. She was wearing stone-washed jeans and a simple black T-shirt. She hadn't combed her hair since she had gotten up and didn't look like she'd had too much sleep before then, either. For the first split second when he saw her, Farrell almost cracked wise about her appearance here on the job, but one look into her red-rimmed eyes told him that wouldn't be sensitive or wise, and so instead he said, "I don't expect you to be in here, Amanda. Maybe you want to take a couple of days off, give things a chance to settle."

"Are you kidding me?" she asked. "That's why I'm in here. I don't want anything to settle. I want to string that bastard up by his balls."

"You want the grand jury?"

"Absolutely. I want it sooner than you do."

"I doubt that." He came around and leaned back against the foosball table. "Could you get the case prepared sooner?"

"If I don't sleep, and that's what seems to be happening."

"Well, don't sacrifice your prep. You don't want to go in and not get him."

"I'll get him. I swear to Christ I'll get him."

"You think—really?—by next Tuesday?"

"Well, I've got all the evidence from *Sandoval*, I've got testimony about Matt's assignment, I've got Nuñez and Janice Durbin and revenge, and then I'll have to see what else I can gather from Abe, but . . ."

"Speaking of which, did you see Marrenas's column this morning?"

"Fuck her."

"Well, sure, but you didn't read the column?"

"No. Why?"

"She's turned up the heat on Abe in a big way."

"On Abe? How can that be?"

"He's not investigating Michael Durbin. He's fixated on Ro. It's a vendetta. Blah, blah, blah. And meanwhile, just in case things are getting too dull around here, guess who called me yesterday about this grand jury thing?"

Jenkins ran her hands through her hair. "What is this bullshit, Wes? This is *Alice in Wonderland*."

"Yes, it is. Welcome to San Francisco."

"So who called you about the grand jury? Marrenas?"

"Well, yes, of course, first. But the real fun part was Cliff the-man-himself Curtlee, who seemed to think that the personal threat is an effective negotiating tool."

"Runs in the family."

"Apparently. Anyway, there's no goddamn instruction booklet on this DA thing I seem to have gotten myself elected to. He's threatening me and I'm holed up here in the office without any clear plan on how to fight him. Not exactly kicking ass doing the people's work. I'm starting to think that this is something that try as I might, I just don't have the chops to do."

"We'll get him, Wes. We really will."

"Well, somebody's going to get somebody. That's for sure." Wes finally crossed the room and half collapsed on the couch. "And don't think I don't realize how much of this is me, is my fault." He looked up at his chief assistant. "I am so, so sorry, Amanda, about Matt, and about you. To say nothing of the other victims. I ought to be impeached."

"Well, hold on that," Amanda said, striving to lighten it up. "Not now when you're just starting to get it."

"Don't kid yourself," Farrell said. "I don't get it at all." Wes's cell phone went off at his belt and he pulled it out, looked at the screen, and told Amanda, "This is Sam. I've got to take it. It'll just be a minute." He pushed the answer button. "Hey . . . No, I'm just . . . Easy, easy. What? . . . She's what? . . . Well, call the police, get somebody down there right away. I'm on my way, too."

Closing the phone, Farrell's face was a study in confusion and panic.

"What?" Amanda asked. "What now?"

"Somebody fucking killed my dog," Farrell said, his voice breaking. "They killed my fucking beautiful dog."

Glitsky drove back from the crematorium service to Polk Street where he parked and got in the line for the Swan Oyster Depot. An hour and a half later, he reemerged from the very far end of the bar, his stomach uncomfortably stuffed, into the sunlight, having broken about every dietary law he knew of either for a sometimes–kosher Jew or a recovering heart attack victim. He'd had two dozen raw oysters, half a dozen clams, a half loaf of sourdough bread with an uncounted number of pats of real butter, half a Dungeness crab with mayonnaise and more melted butter, and his first two beers—in fact, his first sip of any kind of alcohol—in over three years.

Back out in his car, he called Treya down in Los Angeles and they had a short conversation that resolved nothing. She still wasn't coming home, the kids were fine. He told her about the Marrenas article and she had said, "Well, what would you expect?" And then, after five more minutes, he told her he loved her as he said good-bye, and she'd said, "Okay."

Actually getting some rubber from his tires as he pulled out of his parking place, he drove in a cold fury out to the Curtlees' house. There was no sign of any twenty-four-hour watch on the place, but then Glitsky realized that the surveillance team might be out following Ro around. On the chance that Ro might show up, although God knew what he planned to do if that happened, Glitsky sat in the street across from the house for about twenty minutes until his head became too heavy to hold up.

Waking up from the following forty-minute doze, disoriented and cotton mouthed, he started the car back up, hung a U-turn, and headed back downtown, never exceeding the speed limit by less than fifteen miles an hour, the dark side of his nature almost hoping that some patrolman would try to pull him over or write him up or fuck with him in any way.

Bearded and burly, Jeff Elliot was in his wheelchair in his glass-enclosed office downstairs at the Chronicle Building, and of course when he'd heard that Glitsky was at the front desk, he'd had them send him right on down. He might have done this in any case, since the two men had known each other, mostly as tacit allies, for more than twenty years. But today Glitsky was big news, and if he wanted to make time for Jeff, Jeff would find time for him.

And now here he was, looming in the doorway, breathing through his nose, his mouth under tight control, the scar through his lips burning white. Glitsky's menacing face wore a brand-new, terrifying expression that Elliot couldn't read. And in fact, so threatening was the visage that Elliot unconsciously backed himself away before he recovered and put on a welcoming smile, perhaps meant to disarm.

"Doctor Glitsky," he said. "To what do I owe the pleasure?"

"Off the record until I say so."

"Okay, sure."

"I want to kill somebody, Jeff. I mean literally. And I figured if I didn't get myself off the street, I actually might do it."

"Ro Curtlee?"

"He'd be a start."

"Sheila."

"Yep. Her, too. I thought maybe you could talk me out of it."

"Why would I want to?" Finally letting out the breath he'd been all but holding, Jeff indicated the chair just to the left of his door. "You want to sit?"

Now Glitsky eased a breath out, and nodded as though convincing himself. "I could sit," he said. And he did, ramrod straight.

Jeff regarded him for another brief moment. "Bad day at Black Rock, huh?"

Glitsky shook his head. "If you only knew."

"You want to tell me your side, I'll get it into print."

"Just so you're perfectly clear on it," Glitsky said, "I haven't ruled out anybody yet in the Durbin murder, including her husband, including Ro Curtlee. But to pretend, as Marrenas did, that Ro doesn't have a bona fide motive, is just insane. He saw Michael Durbin at his arraignment last week and recognized him. It's a matter of public record that Michael was the jury foreman in his trial and that he persuaded a few of the hanging jurors to come around to convict. So there's a revenge motive and anybody who doesn't believe it's there is deluding themselves."

Elliot picked up a transcribing tape recorder from his desk and held it up.

"Knowledgeable sources?" Glitsky asked.

"How about high-ranking sources within the police department?"

"Sources with knowledge of the investigation."

"Sold," said Elliot, and he turned on the tape recorder.

———

Back in the 4Runner, Eztli picked Ro back up at around four o'clock at MoMo's, where he'd had another lunch and sat in the same seat in the bar that he'd anchored yesterday. Tiffany was on duty, working the late shift today, and Ro wasn't going to wait around until two o'clock or whenever the hell it was that she got off, so he had called Eztli and asked for the pickup. "So what'd I miss?" Ro asked him as they drove down the Embarcadero. "I feel like I've been gone a week. That girl is one enthusiastic piece of ass. Once more and I think, I swear to God, she might have broke it."

Eztli looked across at him with something very like affection. He loved this kid's attitude. "You're breaking my heart," he said. "And there have been a couple of developments, mostly that they've pulled off the tail."

"Must have been going around. I pulled off a little tail myself." Ro chuckled at his cleverness. "You wouldn't have a jay on you, would you?"

"Sure." Eztli pulled a joint from his inside pocket and passed it across. "The tail being the cops who were supposed to be following you," he said.

"Well, they didn't do shit anyway." Ro lighting up, sucking in a lungful of smoke. Then, blowing out, he asked, "But I don't get why'd they pull 'em off. Not that it matters."

"Sheila's been busy. She told Lapeer she was going to write up all about the tail tomorrow, how it was more harassment, and Lapeer just can't take any more heat."

"I would love to fuck that woman."

"Lapeer?"

"No. Well, maybe. But I'm talking Sheila. Hit?" He passed the joint across. "So. Just like that we're free again?"

Eztli had a toke. "Looks like."

"You got any plans?"

"Nothing definite."

"Well, I was thinking," Ro said. "I got an idea."

———

Glitsky talked to Jeff Elliot for more than an hour, then stopped back at the Hall to show his face. Farrell had gone off somewhere, and most of Glitsky's own troops were running on autopilot, writing up their cases in the detail. In the detail, he'd received a nice, informal show of support from all the homicide inspectors, and taking any little bit of goodwill where he could get it, had stayed just to shoot the breeze for a while.

Now he was driving around and around, trying to find a parking spot someplace within five or six blocks of his duplex and running out of hope.

Not helping matters, out to the west, a fog bank presaged the end of the cold and clear weather they'd been tolerating. Next up, Glitsky thought, ought to be cold and wet. There it was, black and foreboding, bearing down on him from thirty blocks away.

When his cell phone rang, he was tempted to simply turn it off without even looking at it. He'd already worked a full and grueling day, he felt a little sick from his stupid lunch, and he was exhausted. But on second thought, he thought it might be Treya, and he looked down to check.

Michael Durbin.

"Lieutenant," Durbin said. "You've got to get over here. You're not going to believe what he's done now."

29

By the time Glitsky got out to Rivera Street, the bank of bad weather had completely engulfed the neighborhood. Wipers slashing back and forth against the thick mist, his lights on in the fog and darkness, Glitsky pulled up at Durbin's address and could barely discern the outlines of the house from the curb.

A figure sat behind the wheel of the car Glitsky pulled up behind, and no sooner had he pulled over when the driver's door of that car opened and his headlights revealed Michael Durbin stepping out into the street. Glitsky killed his lights and ignition and was out of the car before Durbin got back to him.

"Thanks for coming out. I really think this is something."

Glitsky crossed his arms against the chill. "Well, let's go take a look."

In silence, Durbin led the way up the driveway and back behind the house to where an unattached garage filled up half the backyard space. Because it wasn't part of the house, it had escaped any fire damage, and now with bits of broken glass and cinders crunching under their feet, they proceeded around to a side door. A bare lightbulb burned over the door.

Durbin reached into his pocket for a set of keys and fitted one into the dead-bolt slot. "I probably should have thought about touching the doorknob," he said, "but it never occurred to me there'd be anything to see in here."

Glitsky glanced down at the standard plain brass doorknob,

something that would take and hold a fingerprint beautifully. "Hold on. So you've already gone in this way?"

"Just the once."

Backing Durbin away, Glitsky stepped closer, pulling on the pair of latex gloves that he always carried with him. "I'll open it this time. I don't want you to touch anything else out here or inside. Nothing at all. Is that clear?"

"Sure."

Glitsky turned the dead-bolt key and gripped the doorknob with his gloved hand, turning it and pushing. The door came right open, and he stepped into the doorway and felt to the right of the door for the indoor light switch, which he turned on, bathing the room in brightness from three lines of track lighting up in the ceiling.

Somewhat warned of what to expect, Glitsky still wasn't completely prepared for the sight that greeted him. Durbin had obviously used this place as a painting studio. Somewhere between a dozen and twenty very large, colorful, and—to Glitsky's eye— professional-looking portraits of very real people stared back at him from canvases that were stacked and leaning all along the back and side walls. In the center of the wide-open space, three others of what looked to be works in progress sat on the ground, leaning up against the wooden tripods or easels that held them.

Someone had come in here, though, and slashed every one. Sometimes only once, sometimes five or six times, the canvas simply shredded, but there was no painting Glitsky could see that hadn't been cut into. And what made the vandalism all the more disturbing were the pictures themselves. Glitsky did not consider himself any kind of connoisseur of art, but these paintings—none of them less than three-by-four feet, and a few as large as six or even eight feet on a side—were clearly the work of, at the very least, a talented artist. Whatever else his misgivings about Durbin, the man's work had an undeniable power and quality.

Glitsky was standing as though hypnotized just one or two steps inside the door when Durbin came up next to him. Glancing over at him, he was not unduly surprised to see what might be incipient tears in his eyes.

"You're thinking Ro did this?" Glitsky asked.

"Absolutely."

"How would he have known these were even here?"

"Marrenas. She wrote about my derivative, amateur, ludicrous stuff back in the day while she was libeling both of us. This place has been my studio forever. I never made any attempt to hide it. Why would I? Who cared?"

Glitsky found himself focusing on one of the unfinished paintings sitting on the floor. It was a woman's face, filling the frame with almost no background showing. Durbin had caught her turning around, her beautiful dark eyes a mystery, her skin touchable. Even with the one slash through her right eye and down across her nose and lips, she was arresting, especially caught in that pose. And, of course, even so, the portrait wasn't yet completed. "Is that Liza Sato?" he asked.

"Yeah. Or was."

"Did she come over here and pose for you?"

"No. No, of course not. People don't have the time to pose. I don't have the time to work with them that way, anyway. Mostly I just start with a picture, a photograph." He was staring at the piece. "She's beautiful, isn't she?"

Glitsky nodded. "Yes, she is. Did your wife ever see this?"

Durbin shook his head. "I keep telling you, Lieutenant, I didn't kill Janice. I didn't do this, either, slash my paintings. This is my life's work for the past ten years."

This might be true, but Glitsky was aware that he hadn't answered the question. "Did your wife ever see this?" he asked again.

Defeated, Durbin's shoulders sagged. "I just don't know. She wasn't my art's biggest supporter, Lieutenant, and I couldn't blame her. I couldn't sell these things back when we really needed me to."

"They look pretty saleable to me."

"Well, thank you, but you don't know the market. Or how to play it. It's brutal out there for realistic fine art, which is unfortunately what I do, what I've always wanted to do. But it doesn't pay the bills. And that's the bottom line when you've got a wife and kids. Sad but true. So I haven't even tried to sell in years." He ran his eyes over his ruined work. "But that doesn't mean this doesn't break my heart. That this doesn't feel more wrong than almost anything I can conceive of."

Glitsky could not help but understand; this was a soul-shattering display of pure inhumanity. Glitsky's own stomach had gone hollow at the waste and destruction. But he was also aware that Michael Durbin might still have performed this vandalism on his own works in an effort to keep Ro Curtlee in the picture as a viable candidate for Janice's murder. The timing—coming so soon after Ro had provided an alibi for the time of the crime—was suspicious, as was the fact that Michael Durbin had been the one who had discovered these slashed paintings.

Which led to Glitsky's next question: "So when did you come upon all this?"

"Just before I called you."

"You just remembered these were back here?"

"No, Lieutenant. Obviously I knew they were here all along. And I knew the fire hadn't touched the garage, so there was no urgency to see how they'd made it."

"So were you coming back in here today to paint?"

"Why does it matter why I was coming back here? My wife's dead. My kids are falling apart. My life as I've known it is over. After what Marrenas wrote this morning—and you should know this as well as me—the vibes even at my real job got too weird to handle. Plus, it seems one of my people there is leaking to her . . ."

"Why do you say that?"

"Somebody told her about me getting in late last Friday."

"Do you know who it is? Or why?"

"Liza Sato thinks it's a guy named Peter Bassey, who's jealous because she likes me." A nonplussed look. "Hey, what can I say? We like each other. We get along. Not a crime last time I checked. So Peter's poisoning the well at work, and I had the whole afternoon off and yawning before me. So I came to hang out here." He raised a hand at the destruction. "And found this. And then called you. If Ro's been here, maybe he left some sign of it. What do you think?"

Glitsky didn't answer. He was punching numbers on his cell phone. Bringing it up to his ear, he said, "This is Abe Glitsky with homicide. I need a crime scene unit as soon as I can get one."

———

Her cheeks wet with tears, Sam Duncan sat disconsolately on one of the sagging sofas in the raggedy reception area where she worked. Wes Farrell, all cried out, sat beside her, holding her hand. Gert's body lay on the other side of him, her head in his lap, his other hand gently stroking her head. Animal control was on its way and Sam was still trying to get a grip on what exactly had happened. Although to Wes, this was not a mystery.

"I mean," Sam said, "she'd been out there on the bench all morning, just lying in the sun like she does."

"Did you see anybody stop?"

"Wes, everybody stopped. Little kids, old ladies, every homeless person that passed by. This was Gert, remember. Everybody's favorite dog, you know?"

"I do know. But then somebody stopped and poisoned her."

"We don't know that. Not for sure."

"I do."

"How?"

"I just do. She was—what?—five years old, in perfect health, and now suddenly she's foaming at the mouth and she's dead. That doesn't just happen."

"Sometimes it does. Why would somebody want to kill a sweet dog like her?"

"It's got nothing to do with her. You remember the horse's head in the bed in *The Godfather*? This was the same thing. This was Cliff Curtlee."

"But I've met him, Wes. He's a charming man. He gives money to the Center, for God's sake. He wouldn't do something like this."

"Not himself, no. And he's charming all right, but he'd order this in a heartbeat, and I'll bet you a million dollars that he did."

"But why?"

"To warn me that he's serious. He's not kidding around. And to give me a good idea what he'd do next. Except next time, to someone closer to me, like you. Maybe even to me myself."

"He'd do next if what?"

"If I continued to pursue this grand jury thing on his little boy."

She ran her free hand over her head, through her hair. "God, I can't believe this. How can this be happening?"

"We both know the answer to that, Sam. I didn't push hard enough denying Ro bail. Now he's had a taste of freedom again and he's not giving it up without a fight. Or a whole lot of fights." His eyes went down to his dog. "Goddamn it!"

Sam reached over and touched Gert's head gently, left her hand on Farrell's thigh. "So what are you going to do now?"

"I don't know. I don't really have any idea. Take Ro out right now. Convene the grand jury for an emergency session, like, tomorrow, and just march in with Amanda's basic case."

"But you were saying this was Cliff Curtlee, not Ro."

"I know. It probably was. I don't know if it even matters. It's all so fucked up. Which is why another part of me wants to just call Cliff and tell him I've gotten his message and he wins. We're calling everybody off anything that has to do with Ro except the retrial, which isn't calendared until next August anyway. Maybe that would slow down the carnage."

"You believe that?"

Farrell shook his head. "No. Ro's still going to want to find the other main witness, a woman named Gloria Gonzalvez. She's still going to be in danger. No, she still *is* in danger, which is pretty much why I can't just give up, either, besides the fact that it's the last thing I want to do. Giving up is not happening. I've got to keep the pressure on these pricks. Let them know that they picked the exact wrong guy if they think they can pull this shit and get away with it."

"But what if they come back at you with something worse?"

"One of us, you mean?" He shook his head. "I'm not going to give them any time. Although I know that if they're capable of this"—he gave Gert's body a pet—"there's nothing they wouldn't do. I could get you moved to someplace safe until this is over."

"I don't want to do that."

"No, but it might be smart."

Sam let go of Wes's hand, stood up, and crossed over to the door. Standing there, arms crossed, looking out into the darkness and fog, she might have been a statue but for the slight rise and fall of her shoulders. Finally she took in a big breath and turned around. "Fuck that. If they're not driving you off, they're not pushing me out, either."

"Yeah, but you didn't sign up for this, and I did. It's not the same thing."

"Close enough."

"No, it's not. Aren't you the one who moved out a couple of days ago because of how badly I was doing the job? And you know, you were right. I couldn't have proven it any better these last couple of weeks if I'd tried."

She had moved now back to the couch, going down to one knee in front of him. "That wasn't about your job, Wes. It was about you and me communicating about what you were doing, what was in your life. The way we are right now, for example. And you can't let these people get away with stuff like . . . like this. And worse."

He looked at her imploringly. "I have to be honest. I don't know exactly how I'm going to stop them, Sam, what I'm precisely going to do, but I'm sure as shit going to try. There are just no other options. Even if it's probably true that I'm not the best man for the job."

"But you are, Wes. You might be the only man left standing who can actually do it."

"You got any ideas on how?"

"Not just at the moment, but we'll get one. I promise."

"We?"

"Yes, we. Of course, we. What did you think?"

30

Durbin stayed at the garage behind his burned-out house with Glitsky and the CSI unit for about two hours. The team worked quickly and efficiently, lifting fingerprints from likely surfaces and taking photographs, gathering dust devils and sweeping up fibers and hairs and whatever else they might have been looking for. They found nothing that might have been immediately incriminating to Ro Curtlee or anybody else—no probable slashing instrument, for example—and since the next steps of the investigation would take place at the police lab, they declared themselves finished and left. The whole time, Glitsky was a desultory and vaguely threatening presence, keeping Michael away from the other officers and offering little in the way of information or even conversation.

Now, at around eight o'clock, Durbin let himself in the kitchen door at the Novios' home. The house was dark and mostly quiet, although it sounded as if someone was watching television somewhere. Michael was a bit surprised to see Kathy all alone perched on a stool at their granite counter, with a drink of some kind in front of her.

She'd been crying recently and looked up as he came in. "Hey," she said at the low range of audible.

"Hey." He got to the counter and stopped. "You all right?"

She lifted her shoulders an inch.

"What are you drinking?" he asked.

"I don't know. Bourbon, I think."

"You feel like company? I know you've had nothing but company all day, so if you don't . . ."

"No. If you want. It's fine. The bottle's on the counter over there. You can hit me again, too, if you don't mind."

Michael got himself a glass and ice and filled it with bourbon, then crossed over and refilled Kathy's. Sitting down on the stool next to her, he took a sip. "Has Jon come back?" he asked.

"Not yet. He texted me and said he was staying out."

"Till when?"

She gave him a glance. "Till he gets back, I'd imagine. He's all right, Michael. He'll be okay."

"He thinks it's possible I killed Janice."

She shook her head. "I doubt it. He's just upset. Everybody's upset and everybody shows it differently."

He took another pull at his bourbon. "So where's everybody else?"

"The girls are watching TV. Peter's already asleep upstairs, I think. Chuck's at school."

"At school?"

"Papers he's got to grade." She sipped her drink. "It never ends."

"I don't know where he gets the energy."

She gave him a sideways look that he couldn't read. "He conserves it in other places."

Not knowing what to make of that response, Michael said, "I guess so."

They both drank again.

"I shouldn't have said that," Kathy said. "I think I'm probably drunk."

"That's all right. You've earned it."

"No, but I shouldn't criticize Chuck. But sometimes it's just so difficult, a day like today, for example, with a million people in and out and so much going on emotionally and sometimes you just think wouldn't it be nice if your husband didn't have to go out and work and instead could stay and be with you and maybe be . . . I don't know. Be like we were." She wasn't sobbing, but tears were again suddenly rolling down her cheeks. "I mean," she said, "I just think of poor Janice dying with no warning, one minute alive and then gone forever and it makes you question what's important and why you're doing the things you do and why you're not spending more time with the person you supposedly love when she really, really needs you instead of correcting your goddamn papers for your stupid students."

She wiped her cheeks with her hands, picked up her drink, took another sip and put it down. "I'm sorry, Michael. I'm so sorry. I don't even know what I'm saying. I'm just still all so upset. It's just I feel so alone. So completely alone. I know you know."

"I do."

"I shouldn't be mad at Chuck. It's not him. I'm just mad at the whole world."

"That's a good thing to be mad at," Michael said. "I'm pretty much at the same place." He picked up his drink and drained the glass.

———

Dismas Hardy, the managing partner in Wes Farrell's firm, was Abe Glitsky's best friend. He lived with his wife, Frannie, out on Thirty-fourth Avenue near Clement Street. And though this was not directly on the way home from Durbin's house, it wasn't far out of the way, either. When Glitsky drove by, lights shone in the living room and smoke emanating from the chimney was faintly visible for a few seconds before it disappeared into the fog. A parking space on the opposite curb clinched the deal and Glitsky hung a U-turn and pulled into it.

Hardy opened the door to his stand-alone Victorian home, wearing an old worn pair of jeans, destroyed Top-Siders, and a faded blue pullover sweater that had seen better days. "Sorry," he said, "no solicitors. Maybe you didn't see the sign by the gate."

And he closed the door on him.

Glitsky could have simply knocked on the door, or rung the bell again, but this of course in some obscure but important way would have been losing, so he put his hands into his jacket pockets and settled in for the long haul. Hardy held out for nearly a minute and it might have gone longer if Frannie hadn't somehow gotten in the act and finally opened the door, to all appearances surprised to see him.

"Abe. Jesus, you guys. How long were you going to stand out there?"

"As long as it took. Diz would have opened the door eventually."

"Would not," Hardy said. Then added, "All he had to do was knock."

"In your dreams," Glitsky said.

"So would you like to come in now?" Frannie asked. "Rather than stand out here freezing all night."

"That'd be nice."

"Ask him to say please," Hardy said. "That ought to be good for another fifteen minutes while he decides."

She turned on her husband. "There's something truly wrong with you, you know that?"

"Not so much wrong," Hardy answered, "as elusive, fleeting, ethereal, hard to define. In the best possible way."

"I'm with you, Fran," Glitsky said. "I define it as wrong. I've been telling him the same thing for years."

"Okay, that does it. Now he's really going to have to say please."

"Oh, for crying out loud." Frannie grabbed Glitsky by the arm, pulling him inside and closing the door after him.

"This is why I love her," Hardy said. "She makes the tough decisions look easy."

Five minutes later, Hardy and Glitsky were sitting in armchairs in front of the fire, Hardy with a neat Scotch and Glitsky with a cup of green tea that Frannie had made for him. "And okay," Glitsky was saying, "I know what you read about this morning, how I'm all over Ro Curtlee about these murders . . ."

"I don't read the *Courier* except under grave duress."

"Well, that's good to hear. But the plain fact is Ro's got an apparent alibi for this Janice Durbin thing, and her husband really doesn't."

"You're thinking it's him?"

"I'm thinking more it *could* be him. But I really don't see it. I mean, the guy's a legitimately talented artist. I can't see him slashing his own paintings, trying to frame Ro, and then not leaving anything around that ties it to Ro. Does that make sense?"

"Not much."

"So yeah, I'm thinking it's still probably Ro, but if I'm wrong and Wes takes my case to the grand jury . . . You see the problem?"

"Of course. He gets off on one charge and the whole thing falls apart. So don't use Janice."

"But without her, we don't have the motive connection to Ro."

"Sure you do. The witness—what's her name?—the first woman he killed when he got out."

Glitsky nodded. "Felicia Nuñez. And that's one connection with his trial, but without Janice Durbin, that's all we've got, the one. That's not a pattern."

Hardy looked at the fire, sipped at his drink. "How about Matt Lewis?"

Glitsky held his palm out and rotated it. "Tenuous at best. And again, Ro and his butler, they both have an alibi. Evidently the two astronomy buffs decided to take in the planetarium show."

"Well, at least it's credible," Hardy replied, tongue well in cheek. Then, more seriously, "I don't trust too many perfect alibis," he said. "It smacks of premeditation."

"Doesn't it, though?"

"So what are you going to do?"

"I don't know. It looks like it's all going to come down to Janice Durbin, but we don't have anything solid on Ro there. At least I'd like to resolve my doubts about the husband before Wes goes ahead with the grand jury."

"Well, something will either break there or it won't."

"Yeah, but I don't want the next break to come in connection with another murder."

"Like who?"

"I don't know. Anybody. Wes, Amanda, me. I'm not kidding you. The other and now last witness from his trial, if he can find her."

"Who is she?"

"Gloria Gonzalvez. One of his rape victims."

"You got her in protection?"

"No." Glitsky's face showed his frustration. "I can't find her, either."

A frown creased Hardy's brow. "So as it stands now, she's not testifying in the retrial?"

"Not unless we can locate her."

"So even that retrial . . . you've got testimony but no actual witnesses?"

"Right."

Hardy made a noise in his throat that Glitsky read very clearly—without witnesses, even the retrial was in very serious jeopardy. Ro might never actually get back into prison. Hardy had another sip of Scotch. Frannie appeared from the back of the house and asked Abe if he'd like a refill on his tea.

"I think I'm good, thanks."

Frannie nodded, hesitating, and then said, "I know it's short notice, but we just found out our little darlings are both going to be home this weekend. Maybe you and Treya and the kids could come over on Saturday for dinner, just simple."

Glitsky took another moment before he said, "They've all gone down to her brother's in LA. More of this Ro Curtlee stuff. Treya's afraid Ro's going to come after one of the kids."

"Treya's not afraid of anything," Frannie said.

"Well, not much," Glitsky admitted. "But Ro Curtlee got her attention. She's definitely afraid of him."

"So when's she coming back?" Frannie asked.

"That," Glitsky said, "is a good question. Hopefully someday."

Hardy reacted immediately, coming forward in his chair, leaning in toward his friend. "Oh, come on, Abe. Of course she's coming back."

Glitsky nodded thoughtfully, as though he were considering the question. At last, he let out a short breath. "That's the hope," he said, "but I'm not sure I'd bet on it."

———

When she heard the voice on the intercom say that it was Michael Durbin at her door, Liza didn't know what to make of it at first.

He had never before been to her place, a nice one-bedroom apartment at Chestnut and Laguna, not far from the store. Liza had been more than a little bit in love with him now for well over a year. The feeling had developed from an original natural simpatico—she'd had another boyfriend at the beginning—that had turned to friendship in the years that they'd worked together.

And then finally at the Christmas party two Decembers ago, they had been shooting pool together at one of the North Beach bars they'd all repaired to after the dinner, and as she leaned over to take her shot—she was wearing a low but not particularly plunging neckline—she noticed him noticing her. Janice had already gone home and Liza had definitely had too much to drink. Michael had smiled and shrugged as if to say, "You caught me." Her eyes had locked into his and she straightened up, walked around the table right up to him, and told him flat out that she loved him.

He told her he loved her, too, and then leaned down and kissed her with a deep, passionate, open-mouthed hungry kiss that had weakened her knees.

But then, almost immediately afterward, while they were still holding each other, he realized what he'd done, and he pulled away, saying he was sorry, he shouldn't have done that, it had been a mistake.

The next Monday, back at work, he'd taken her out to lunch and apologized again. It wasn't that he didn't find her attractive, he told her, and didn't love the person she was, but he was married to Janice and committed to her and to their family. He'd had a moment of infatuation with Liza that in his weakness he'd given in to, but that was all there could ever be between them.

If she was uncomfortable continuing to work with him, he'd understand and help her find another job with at least equal pay and benefits if he could. Or, of course, if she'd like to stay on, he would be happy to keep her, but there could be no repetition of what had happened the other night.

And there had not been.

Without hesitation, she pushed the button that opened the downstairs door and let him in. And now she opened the door to her apartment, and he came out of the elevator and turned to see her standing there. When he got to her, she stepped into his arms and they stood embracing, holding on to each other as though for their lives.

31

Ro's idea from earlier in the day was more or less in the line of a game.

He had been talking to Tiffany about some of the things that had changed in the years that he'd been in prison, not just iPods and phones and all the technology, but the other changes that made the world feel so different in the day-to-day.

The giant malls and the enormous discount stores, with everything you could ever want to buy all in one place. Or, on the opposite scale, all the closed-up independent bookstores. Now, you wanted to buy a book, Tiffany said, you had your basic one or two choices, Borders and Barnes & Noble, and they were pretty much the same. Or coffee shops, Starbucks on every corner. Who could have predicted that? And for coffee?

But that example had led Tiffany to tell him about another one of the latest things going around in the city, which she had at first found hard to believe, but which, according to some friends of hers who'd actually seen it, wasn't even uncommon—people were carrying guns openly around in public. This was mostly facilitated, evidently—according to Tiffany—by Twitter and Facebook and other stuff on the Web about which Ro was ignorant, but these people would somehow all get in touch with one another and meet at some predetermined Starbucks location, where they were making some Second Amendment point by showing up wearing their guns out in holsters like in the Wild West.

This was happening every day, she said, and why at Starbucks stores she didn't know. But it wasn't only the coffee shops. Over just the past weekend, a posse of more than seventy people had showed up at Baker Beach, all of them carrying. Wild, huh?

Ro thought so.

The catch was that the guns could not be loaded. That would be illegal, as there were city, county, and state laws forbidding carrying loaded weapons around. But astoundingly to Ro, carrying the unloaded guns themselves, as long as they were not concealed, was not only not illegal, it was specifically protected by the Second Amendment.

Which made no sense, because you could carry your piece unloaded with a clip or four in your pockets and basically load up the gun in about the time it took to rack a round into the chamber. But the point, to him, wasn't whether it made any sense but that it happened at all. People walking around with perfectly usable guns on their hips? He told Eztli that the two of them really ought to go around the city and see if they could find one of the hot spots, and that's what they'd done.

They got lucky just about the time they were going to quit, getting on toward five o'clock, at a Starbucks pretty close to where they'd begun at MoMo's, out at Fisherman's Wharf. As they drove by, from the street they saw not only that the place seemed to be unusually crowded, but three black-and-white patrol cars were pulled up out front. Neither Eztli nor Ro had any fear of the police in general, and beyond that they knew that the policemen here at Starbucks were beat cops. If anything, their presence added to the spice. So Eztli pulled into a parking garage a block away, removed the bullets from his own weapon, and tucked the gun into his belt. He also removed the jacket from his suit, leaving it on the car seat, so there would be no misunderstanding about whether the gun was concealed or not.

And the two of them had strolled down to check it out.

Sure enough, there must have been thirty-five or forty people waiting for or drinking their super-tall macchiato or whatever it was, and packing heat. The uniformed cops—now eight of them—were politely but carefully checking to see that none of the guns were loaded. All of the demonstrators were reasonably well dressed and well behaved. Many seemed to be professionals. Most were men, although there were more women than Ro would have guessed, six or eight of them.

By the time Ro entered the store, he was probably the only person left inside besides the employees who were not armed.

They stayed long enough to have their own coffees, still flying on their reefer, and until the crowd had started to disperse. Of course, as they'd expected, the cops did not recognize them. Back at the garage, they waited out on the sidewalk until they saw one of the demonstrators—a paunchy, middle-aged, balding man in casual business attire with what looked like a big semiautomatic with custom-made grips in a holster on his hip—pass them and turn into the entrance.

Eztli had come up quickly and silently behind him and put him down and out with one rabbit punch, and less than five minutes later, Ro was wearing the gun and had the guy's bullets in his pocket and the two of them roared out of the garage, howling with the good, clean, sheer fun of it all.

Now, at eleven thirty or so, Ro turned off the TV in his room. He wasn't so much tired as he was bored, and when he was bored, invariably he got horny. And he sure didn't want to wait around until two o'clock or whenever Tiffany got off. Besides, he didn't want to start up anything regular with any one chick. Not when there was so much opportunity a lot closer at hand.

Ro's room was on the third floor, at the other end of the house and one floor up from his parents' bedroom. Eztli, the cook, and the two cleaning girls had their rooms two floors below his parents, on the basement level. To facilitate communication in the seven-thousand-square-foot home, the Curtlees had installed a sophisticated intercom system between the various floors and rooms.

Starting to get excited by the idea he was developing, Ro got up off his bed and crossed over to his dresser, opening one of the drawers and taking out the gun that he'd scored that afternoon. He hefted it in one hand and then the other, appreciating its weight and appearance. It was a beauty, he thought. Brand-new, or as good as. A big mother with an oversize magazine with a seventeen-round capacity, about a foot long, with a bright satin stainless finish and custom wooden grips. The kind of gun that could get your attention from across the room.

———

Twenty-year-old Linda Salcedo heard the faint buzz of the intercom through her blankets and for an instant couldn't place where the sound was coming from. Then, coming fully awake, she waited in the dark of her room to see if she'd imagined it, or if one of the Curtlees in fact needed her for something, even at this time of night. That would be unusual, since her duties keeping the rooms spotless kept her busy throughout the day. By the time she'd helped clean up after dinner, she normally had her nights to herself. But of course, if anyone needed her at any time—to restock toilet paper, get some hair out of a sink, change a lightbulb, anything—she would have to go and take care of it.

And yes, here it was again, the intercom buzzing.

Sighing, throwing the covers off, she padded barefoot over to her door and pushed the reply button. *"Sí?"*

"Linda. Hi. This is Ro upstairs. Sorry to bother you so late."

"Is no bother." *No, I was just sitting up here at midnight waiting for something to do, hoping one of you would call.*

"Good. Listen, I was getting out of the shower and I knocked over the shampoo bottle and got it all over the floor. I wondered if you could come up and get it cleaned up. I wouldn't want to get up and slip on it in the middle of the night."

"Okay," she said, letting out a frustrated and weary breath. *You spilled some shampoo? You wouldn't want to try cleaning it up yourself, would you? Heaven forbid.* "In two minutes, *sí?*"

"*Sí,*" he said. "Two minutes is fine. Even three. Take your time."

"*Gracias.*"

"*De nada.*"

She had been sleeping in her nightgown, and now she considered taking it off and getting dressed again in her regular uniform, but that seemed a lot of effort to simply go upstairs and clean up a little spill, which would probably take her all of one minute. So she decided she would just put on her bathrobe and her Crocs. She'd be done and be back down here in five minutes and then she could just go back to sleep.

No one else seemed to be awake in the house, but the halls were lit with tiny night lights in the wall sockets, and in the light of these she walked up the three flights to the top floor, then turned left at the top of the stairs and went to Ro's door, closed, at the far end of the hall. Gently she rapped on it.

"Come on in."

When she opened the door, she was briefly surprised to see that Ro had turned the lights out in here already. Probably just going to sleep, he had no reason to talk to her again—he'd already told her what she needed to do.

"Would you mind closing the door behind you?" she heard him say from where she knew the bed was.

She did as she was told, and now there was nothing but darkness. She stood stock-still inside the room, waiting for her eyes to adjust so she could go to the bathroom where he'd spilled the shampoo.

"You can turn on the light," he said.

Again, she did as he requested, half turning away to the switch by the door. When she came back around and looked at him, she did a little half jump backward, accompanied by a frightened little yelp, her hand to her mouth, her eyes wide with terror.

Ro was naked on top of the covers, with a full erection. He was holding a gun on her, centered at her heart. With his other hand, the arm in a cast above it, he patted the bed next to him and broke a big smile. "Nobody has to get hurt here if you act smart," he said. "Just come on over and take that robe off you. And you and me, we'll lay down and get ourselves comfortable."

———

Driving back from Liza's to Chuck and Kathy's place, all Michael Durbin knew for sure was that he was a mess.

There was guilt but also, no question, elation over the time he'd just spent with Liza. He told himself that he hadn't gone over there to go to bed with her, but simply because he felt like he needed someone to talk to whom he could trust and who believed him. But did he know even as he was driving over to Liza's that they would probably wind up having sex? And even if he did, so what? So soon after Janice's death, that's so what, he told himself. And yet, Janice was truly dead, now cremated. He had been faithful, as he'd sworn he would, until death did they part. And he didn't owe her anything after that.

He didn't understand so much of what he was going through and he thought that Liza was sensitive and smart enough to help talk him through it all. Janice gone. His paintings now gone. His eldest son thinking he was capable of murder. The beginnings of full-scale mutiny at work. And while he was at it, why not add the facts that he'd slept with a new woman for the first time in twenty years? That, also, he was driving around with his shotgun in the trunk of his car.

He hadn't seen any need to tell Glitsky the real reason why he'd gone out to his garage earlier in the evening after the memorial had worn down. He had only inadvertently stumbled onto his slashed paintings; he had not come to the garage to do anything with his paintings. He had come to get his shotgun. He wasn't quite clear on whether he wanted it more for protection or for aggression, but once the idea of having the thing near to hand had taken hold, he found himself powerless to resist it.

Parking in the Novios' driveway, he checked the time on the dash before he turned off the engine: 1:21. He got out of the car and went back and opened the trunk. There was the shotgun, still, and the box of twelve-gauge ammunition that went with it, so he picked them both up and carried them around to the kitchen door. No point having a weapon, he thought, if you couldn't get to it in an emergency.

In the living room, one light burned. Michael came through the kitchen, and Chuck looked up from where he sat in his reading chair, one stack of papers lying on his lap, another on the floor next to him.

"You're still up?" Michael said.

"Couldn't sleep." He pointed vaguely. "What are you doing with that thing?"

"Keeping it handy."

"Is it loaded? I don't think I'm comfortable with a loaded gun in the house."

For an answer, Michael broke open the barrel and looked down through it. "Both barrels empty." Then he held up the small cardboard box. "Ammunition over here."

"Where are you going to keep it?"

"Near me. Did Kathy tell you the latest?"

"I didn't see her. She was asleep when I got in. What's the latest?"

Michael sat down, the shotgun on the coffee table between them, and told him about the slashed paintings.

"All of them?" Chuck now sat all the way forward in his chair.

"Every one."

"Son of a bitch," Chuck said. "Why did he do that?"

"Why did he kill Janice? Same reason. To get at me."

Chuck sat back as though exhausted. He glanced down at the shotgun, up at his brother-in-law. "Don't get me wrong," he said. "I can see where you'd be tempted."

"I'm a lot more than tempted, Chuck. If it wasn't for the kids . . ." He broke off, his train of thought derailed. "Speaking of which, have you seen Jon tonight?"

"No, but I didn't look in on any of them. Why?"

"He wasn't home by the time I left tonight. He texted Kathy and told her he'd be late. I'd better go look." And with that, he was up and out of the room.

Chuck came forward in his chair again, reached out and picked up the shotgun, broke it open over his knee, and checked the barrels again. Then closed it up.

Michael appeared back in the doorway. "He's still not here. Shit."

"He's a big boy, Mike. He'll be all right."

"I hate this. I hate all of it." He took a step into the room. "What are you doing with the gun?"

"Making sure it isn't loaded. You shouldn't be walking around with a loaded gun, Mike. Jon comes home late, you might shoot him by mistake."

"I doubt that. Where is he?"

"Staying with friends, I'm sure. Text him, tell him you're worried."

Durbin, back at the sofa, sat down heavily. "You're right. You're right."

"And you might think about getting some sleep."

"You, too." He paused. "I think Kathy's been missing you."

Chuck looked up sharply, a frown etched in place. "Why do you say that?"

"She mentioned a little something about it."

"That's none of anybody else's business."

"I didn't say it was. I'm just passing along the information for what it's worth. From a guy who's just lost his wife to a guy who's still got one."

Chuck stared at Michael with what seemed like true malevolence for a long few seconds, then finally let out a heavy breath. Looking down at the pile of papers on the floor, the smaller stack on his lap, he managed a weak smile. "Sorry, Mike. I think we're probably both done in. Maybe we ought to call it a day."

32

CityTalk

By Jeffrey Elliot

Sources close to the investigation yesterday sat down with this reporter to explain the events of the past few weeks related to Ro Curtlee and the murder of Janice Durbin. San Francisco's beleaguered head of homicide, Lieutenant Abe Glitsky, has been under fire from both Mayor Leland Crawford and from printed accusations of harassment and police brutality in a rival newspaper.

It is public record that Glitsky and Curtlee have a long history as antagonists, beginning with the former's arrest of the latter for rape and murder back in 1998, charges for which Mr. Curtlee was convicted and sentenced to twenty-five years to life in prison. Early this year, the Ninth Circuit Court of Appeal overturned that conviction and ordered a retrial, and since that time, Mr. Curtlee has been free on bail. Also, since the time of Mr. Curtlee's release, three people with connections to his earlier trial have been murdered. These are Felicia Nuñez, a prime witness against Mr. Curtlee; Matt Lewis, an investigator for the district attorney's office; and Janice Durbin, the wife of the foreman of the jury in the Curtlee trial, Michael Durbin.

And only last week, in a highly publicized sequence of events, Lieutenant Glitsky arrested Mr. Curtlee again on

JOHN LESCROART

charges ranging from death threats and resisting arrest to attempted murder. During his arrest, Mr. Curtlee fought with police, including Glitsky, and sustained several injuries, including a broken arm. Two of the arresting officers were also injured. And again Ro Curtlee was released on bail.

The common denominator in all of these crimes is Ro Curtlee. Officers sought and obtained an interview with Mr. Curtlee, in the presence of his lawyer, to determine his whereabouts and activities at the time of these latest two murders in an effort to eliminate him as a suspect in either of them. He provided them with alibis for both, and that is where the matter stands at this time.

Despite the hysteria generated by the *Courier*, a Curtlee-owned newspaper and no friend of the police, there seems no evidence suggesting that these have been other than straightforward murder investigations. Police have named no suspects in the Matt Lewis or Janice Durbin murders.

What has been widely publicized as police harassment in some circles may well instead be seen as a simple attempt by the rich and powerful to use their political and media influence to insulate themselves from investigation for a series of brutal crimes.

———

Glitsky, at his kitchen table, nodded in a kind of grateful relief as he read these last words. As usual, Jeff Elliot had gotten it right, his tone reasonable. Maybe this, he thought, sipping his tea, would help to lower the temperature a little around all this madness and he could get back to just doing his job.

He folded up the *Chronicle* and was rinsing out his mug, getting ready to leave the duplex and go to work early, when the telephone rang. It was just after six o'clock, which gave the trained investigator in him a clue as to who it possibly was, he hoped. He took the

290

two steps across the kitchen and picked up before the second ring.

"Hello."

"Hey."

"Hey. Everybody okay?"

"Everybody's fine, except I miss you."

"You do?"

"I do. Of course I do."

"I thought you were furious at me."

"Mad, not furious. Frustrated. Now I'm over it and just miss you."

"I miss you, too. I can fly down this weekend if you're going to stay."

"If I'm going to stay."

"Are you?"

"I don't know. I haven't decided. It seems so stupid and melodramatic to be down here, but up there it felt real and scary. I just don't know what he'll do, Abe."

"Nobody does. That's what makes him so scary."

"I mean, what are the odds he'd really try anything with any of us?"

"If there're any odds, they're too great."

"Now you sound like me."

"Good. You're obviously the smart one." He paused. "You know, on second thought, maybe you ought to think about staying down there a few more days. I can fly down, make it a vacation for the weekend. How's Sixto holding up with the kids?"

"My brother? Are you kidding? He wants to keep them forever."

"Maybe we could do a little negotiation. Get a night away."

"I could do that."

Glitsky took a breath. "I wasn't sure we were okay. We're okay?"

"We're different, but okay. I don't do the risk thing so well."

"You shouldn't have to."

"You shouldn't, either."

"Well, then I should change jobs."

"Which you don't want to do."

"No. I don't. Somebody's got to hang in there and do it, and I'm temperamentally suited. It's a curse but it's who I am."

"I know. And I don't want you to change. I love who you are."

A sudden surge of emotion made his head go light. He put his hand up to steady himself against the wall. "I'll call when I know what time I'll get in at Burbank," he said.

———

Lou the Greek's opened for business at six o'clock in the morning every day but Sunday. The bar/restaurant occupied a semi-hygienic, semi-subterranean space directly across the street from the Hall of Justice, and this location made it a favorite for cops and jurors and lawyers. At lunchtime, it tended to be packed with humanity, the tiny tables and six-person booths equally hard or impossible to come by, and this in spite of the fact that the only item on the menu was the special, a mostly edible, sometimes not, sometimes delicious combination of flavors and textures drawn from the rather disparate culinary cultures of both Greece and China. Only Greece and China. Lou's wife, Chiu, upon whom the *Chronicle* had a few years before bestowed the sobriquet "Most Creative Chef in the City," had an undeniable knack, no doubt about it—souvlaki char siu bao, barbecue red pork moussaka, hot and sour and lemon curd dolma stew, crispy duck pita pockets, and the ever-popular and mysterious yeanling clay bowl.

But before lunchtime, and especially in the early morning, Lou's was a haven for serious drinkers, not so much the indigent or homeless alcoholics as one might suspect, but in general a well-dressed and bleary-eyed clientele of men and a few women who often were in line down the steps to the front door by the time Lou opened up at the crack of dawn. The stools at the bar, which had closed four hours earlier, were usually filled up before Lou could ring up the first sale.

On this Friday morning, though, the main action wasn't at the bar, but in the booth farthest from it along the right-hand wall. And nobody was drinking anything alcoholic. A galvanized Farrell, positively dapper in Armani, had made some important decisions and in fact had already sprung into action during the night, and finally he'd contacted the principals who would need to be involved in his plan and told them that he needed them at Lou's by seven A.M.

So he was sitting against the wall next to Amanda Jenkins and looking across the table at Glitsky and an uncomfortable Vi Lapeer. Everybody had already expressed their condolences and outrage about Wes's dog, Gert, then said nice things to Abe about the morning's "CityTalk" column, and after that vein had played itself out, Farrell drank some of his coffee, cleared his throat, and spoke in a voice that though firm was so quiet that it could have been a stage whisper.

"This is the most off-the-record conversation any of you will ever have with me. I would vastly prefer it if not one word of it got out to anyone beyond the four of us. Is that acceptable to all of you?"

Eyebrows went up in surprise all around the table, but no one objected, and within a few seconds all nodded their assent.

"All right, then," Farrell went on, "I've asked you all here this morning because after all he and his family have put us all through the last couple of weeks, I've decided that enough is enough. It's my intention to get Ro Curtlee back behind bars by tonight."

"Fuckin' A," Jenkins said, pumping her fist. "*Yes!*"

Although he nodded again in apparent agreement, Glitsky's brows came together in his default frown while Chief Lapeer, sitting across from Farrell against the wall, squinted in consternation, threw a quick glance at Glitsky, then came back to Wes. "How are you planning to do that?"

"The short answer is that I'm going to indict him." He spent a few moments bringing everyone up to speed on the grand jury, explaining the relatively newly hatched strategy of tying via motive Ro's earlier conviction to the current crimes he was suspected of committing, thus creating the special circumstances Farrell would need to outright deny him bail.

When he finished, Amanda had a perplexed look on her face. "I understand the strategy, Wes, but the grand jury doesn't meet until Tuesday, and even then . . ."

But Farrell was shaking his head. "I've called them into emergency session this morning at eight o'clock."

"This morning? But how did you . . . ?" Amanda began.

"I called them at home last night. I got fourteen of them to commit to be there and left messages for the other six, and I only need twelve. So we're good to go."

"Except that I'm not nearly prepared."

"That's not going to be your problem. You know the basic argument. That's what you're going to give them."

"But without any new evidence, it's not going to be enough."

"We've got solid gold evidence from the original trial. For *Sandoval*, I already have the good Dr. Strout coming in to say she was raped. I've got the evidence tech to say that the sperm in her was Ro's. And since Nuñez is dead, we can read her transcript into the record. That's all we should need for her.

"Then Strout can talk about how Nuñez is dead, the crime scene guys say that the body was naked except for she was wearing shoes, and Arnie Becker says it was arson. We get a detective to say that Ro was out on bail facing a trial during which Nuñez was expected to testify. That gives us multiple murder specials and the specials of murdering a witness to prevent testimony."

Jenkins, obviously excited by these possibilities, still had her doubts. "What about Janice Durbin? We have a *Johnson* problem." She was referring to the case that requires the district attorney to tell the grand jury about possible exculpatory evidence. "If we try to subpoena Curtlee's alibi for Durbin, which is his parents, they'll know what we're doing. Denardi will at least delay the whole thing, maybe block it indefinitely."

"Right," Farrell said. "So here's what we do. We get the indictments for Sandoval and Nuñez first. We start the grand jury on Durbin, maybe even present a couple of witnesses, then we subpoena Ro's alibi—his parents and employees—but by then he's already in custody for the first two, and they can screw around as much as they want. When we get the indictment for Durbin, we join it up to the other two. We don't, we still have him in jail on multiple murder, no bail." He looked around at a quorum of clear skeptics. "Listen, I've spent thirty years hearing that as far as the grand jury is concerned, any DA worth his salt could indict a ham sandwich. Well, I guess we're going to find out if I'm worth my salt and prove it once and for all if we can."

"But doesn't that mean you'll have to try him on those charges?" Lapeer asked.

"Eventually, maybe."

"I thought it was within sixty days," Glitsky said.

Farrell allowed himself a self-satisfied smile. "Yes, and if Ro's lawyers want to argue that they're ready to go to trial in sixty days, guess what? Then they're obviously ready to defend him on the remand trial, aren't they, since it's the exact same case? They can't have it both ways."

Glitsky held up a finger. "Don't get me wrong, I'd love to see him in jail yesterday. But I've still got concerns about Janice Durbin."

"What about her?"

"Well, Ro's got the alibi witnesses. Even if they're all lying, that's a lot of firepower for a jury to ignore, even a grand jury . . ."

"By the time they hear from those alibi witnesses, he's already in custody for our two best cases," Farrell said. "I think they'll indict in spite of the alibi, but if they don't, no harm, no foul."

"Okay," Glitsky persisted, "but for the real trial . . ."

"Then we're back to what I just said a minute ago. They can't have it both ways. If they're ready for one trial, then they're ready for both, or either. And meanwhile Ro's out of circulation, which is a consummation devoutly to be wished, I think we all agree."

"Amen to that," Glitsky said.

"Hear, hear," Jenkins added.

Lapeer finally spoke up. "So what do you need me for, Wes?"

Farrell drew a breath, twirled his coffee cup around for a moment with both hands. "I know you've been taking a beating on this since the minute you took office, Chief. I also understand why you were persuaded to withdraw your surveillance people you had attached to Ro."

Lapeer's brow clouded. "How did you even hear about that?"

"Word gets out, Chief. That's the way it is. But even so, I thought you might have given me the courtesy."

"We've all got jobs we're trying to hold on to here, Mr. Farrell," she said. "If His Honor gets one more excuse to let me go, and this surveillance was going to be one . . ."

Farrell held up his hand. "I said I understood your problem. So now I'm asking you to do what I'm doing."

"And what's that?"

"Pretend that none of this—what we're talking about privately here this morning—none of this is happening. Pretend that we're not going ahead with the grand jury. We're beaten and cowed into submission. Pretend that we're not keeping Ro under surveillance."

"But, in fact, we're not."

"Well. We will be." Here Farrell took a beat, letting out a breath he seemed to have been holding with an almost audible sigh. "What I propose we do this morning is send out a couple of unmarked vehicles to the Curtlees' home, starting as soon as this breaks up here. They've got five automobiles up there—three in the garage, and a matched set of white SUVs usually driven by their butler and the household staff. Any one of those vehicles leaves the premises, we trail them. First stop they make, somebody sticks a GPS under the bumper."

Lapeer had her hands clasped tightly in front of her on the table. "And why are we doing this right now?" she asked.

"Two reasons. First, from everything he's done so far, Ro is almost undoubtedly on the lookout for the other witness in his trial, a woman named Gloria Gonzalvez, and if he finds her, it probably won't be pretty. To say nothing of the fact that we're looking for her as well so she'll testify again at the retrial. There's a reasonable chance he might lead us to her, and if he does, we want to get her into protection."

"So you're saying you want to try to follow him again?" Lapeer asked.

"No," Farrell admitted. "I don't think we can do that. Too much manpower, not to mention it's too expensive, and too much visibility."

"Okay, so if we're not following him, how do we know if he gets near her? And PS, he might not stay in the car anyway. He leaves it at the BART station, then what?"

Glitsky cleared his throat. "Well, plus, Wes, I've got a problem, too."

"What is it?"

"If we have to follow every car that leaves the house, sooner or later they're going to notice and talk about it. Odds are decent somebody among them thinks about a GPS."

"I don't even want to think about the press reaction if that comes out," Lapeer said. "We think we're on the hot plate now . . ."

Amanda all but snapped. "We can certainly justify wanting to keep some kind of tabs on a convicted rapist and murderer, which let's not forget is what Ro is. Whatever spin Sheila Marrenas puts on it, this is a reasonable and defensible strategy."

Lapeer shot back at her. "So is everything else we've done, and it doesn't seem to have made any difference. Especially to the mayor."

"Fuck the mayor," Amanda said. "He's just casting for votes, as always."

"Well, you'll pardon me if I don't want to challenge him any more than I already have. If we don't play by the book . . ."

"This is by the book," Glitsky, the voice of reason, put in. "There's nothing illegal about either tailing him or planting a GPS, provided the car is in a public place and we attach it to some exterior part of the vehicle. No Fourth Amendment problem. It's legal. Period. Even the Ninth Circuit thinks so, and they don't like much that we do."

Farrell did a little drumroll on the table. "Here's the deal, people, quite simply, we can't lose him again. Especially if we get this indictment today, which I am determined to do. We'll want to serve it immediately. And to do that, we've got to know where he is." He scanned around the table. "Can we all be on board with that?"

Amanda and Glitsky were both nodding, and Farrell zeroed in on Lapeer. "Vi?"

Finally she came to her decision. "Let's just be extra goddamn careful planting these goddamn devices, can we?"

33

At ten o'clock sharp, Eztli walked up the stairs and found Ro alone, sitting at the dining room table having a breakfast of coffee, fruit, and bacon. Barefoot, and dressed in gray sweats he might have slept in, he hadn't yet shaved or combed his hair.

"I just got a call on my cell from Lupe García," Eztli said. "Somebody says they found Gloria Gonzalvez."

Ro put down his forkful of cantaloupe. "You've got to be kidding me."

"No. I don't think so."

"In two days?"

"I told you, money talks."

"Awesome," Ro said. "Where is she?"

"The guy won't say till he sees the money. Which is only smart."

"So what do we do?"

"Well, he's down at Lupe's now."

Ro took a bite of bacon and chewed ruminatively for a moment, then pushed his chair back and grabbed a last sip of coffee. "Time is money," he said with a victory smile. "Let me throw on some clothes, I'll be right back down."

"I'll be waiting," Eztli said. "And Ro?"

"Yeah."

"You're not going to like this, but don't bring the gun."

Ro stopped in the doorway. "Don't bring the gun? What are you talking about? I love that thing."

"I know you do, but you don't want it anywhere near you if we get pulled over for any reason. Which, as we've seen, can happen. Your parents would kill me if I let you get arrested for something that stupid."

"They're not going to arrest me again. Or even try."

"If you're carrying, they won't have a choice."

"What about you?"

"What about me?"

"You're packing, am I right?"

"I have a license to carry. And of course it's not the same piece after the other day. That one's in my safe in my room until I have a chance to get rid of it."

"But I just got mine. You got any idea how long I've been without a piece? A guy feels naked, and not in a good way."

Eztli sighed with a hint of impatience. "I realize that. I know it's a disappointment. But getting our hands on that piece was the exercise yesterday, fun and instructive. And in a pinch, you'll know where it is. But today we won't need it. Good?"

"I don't like it, but yeah. All right."

———

Because they had to make a stop at the bank for cash, they didn't get down to Lupe's until about noon. Once there, they drove around the back of the by-now-familiar warehouse to where a double-wide trailer sat incongruously up against a hill that looked as though it had been strip-mined at the back of the large parking lot. A brisk breeze blew under a pewter gray sky as they got out of the SUV and up the steps to the front door. They rang the bell and a short, heavy-set Latina answered. With a mere nod for an introduction, she directed them past the kitchen and eating area and along a short hallway to what was obviously the man's business side of the trailer.

Lupe and three other Hispanic men sat, each with a bottle of Negra Modelo beer, in a large living room that would have been spacious but for the clutter. Besides the enormous flat-screen television set, a low black-glass coffee table, a metal bench, two couches, and three leather Barcaloungers, Lupe or whoever had a penchant for storing things out in the open, and all around the periphery of the room on the floor were both opened and still-closed cases of beer and tequila, used pizza boxes, piles of girlie and dog-fight and hot-rod magazines. The three windows—two on one wall and one on the other—had no curtains, and even with the overcast day, the room had a certain brightness.

When Eztli and Ro entered, Lupe stood up and he and Eztli greeted each other with an arm around the neck and a chest bump. Lupe then nodded in a businesslike way to Ro and said something in Spanish that Eztli answered, then translated for Ro. "He says this is a good way to find people. Put out a reward."

Ro shrugged. "Whatever works," he said.

"Here is your man. Hector." Lupe reverted to English for Ro's benefit. Turning around, he pointed at one of the men who'd come forward in one of the Barcaloungers, and who upon hearing his name stood up, his face with a hopeful, helpful expression and his hands clasped in front of him.

Ro looked at him and laughed. "Guy looks like he's going to piss himself." He gave what sounded like a dog bark and at the same time made a quick lurch in Hector's direction, and the diminutive worker jumped as though a current had passed through him. Everybody except Hector got a chuckle out of that. Ro straightened up and laughed again, then turned back to Lupe. "Tell him I don't bite." Then, directly to him, "Easy, José, I don't bite."

"Hector," the man said in a quavering voice.

"Hector, José, whatever. The point is, where's Gloria?"

Hector threw a plaintive look at Lupe, who interpreted it and said, "First the money."

"First the money. Naturally." Sighing dramatically, nodding, Ro reached into his jeans' front pocket and extracted a thick stack of folded-over hundred-dollar bills. Handing them over to Lupe, he said, "You want me to count 'em out?"

"No," Lupe said. "If it's wrong, he will tell us." He looked back over to Hector, whose eyes were glued to the bills. "All right, Hector, they've come all the way down here to talk to you. Time to tell them what you know."

Hector pulled out his cell phone. "This is the woman you're looking for, sí?" He showed Ro the picture.

He recognized her immediately. "That's her, all right. Where is she?"

But Hector, perhaps understanding that he only had leverage until he gave up his information, put on an apologetic face. "I am sorry, but before, I will need the money," he said in English.

"There's the money," Ro said, gesturing to it. Then, to Lupe, "Give him the goddamn money."

Lupe turned back to Ro. "What is he going to do with all of this money? Where is he going to put it? Does he even have a bank account? I'm trying to save him a lot of trouble."

"Ask me if I give a shit," Ro said.

With a final small show of reluctance, Lupe held out the wad of cash, then reverted back to Spanish, saying something to Hector, who simply took the bills and nodded in satisfaction, stuffing them into his pants pocket.

Ro turned to Hector. "Okay, you got the money. Talk to me."

Out of his other pants pocket, Hector extracted a folded piece of paper, opened it, and passed it across to Ro. In pencil, written in block letters, he saw the name GLORIA SERRANO and a street address with the word Sunnyvale under it. He pointed at the name and asked Hector, "So, Gloria Serrano."

"Sí."

"You know for a fact she lives at this address?" Then a thought occurred to him. "What if it turns out it's not the right one?"

DAMAGE

Hector made a face. "I know it's the right address. I know her husband."

Ro said to Lupe. "You know where this fucker lives if he got it wrong?"

Lupe turned and spoke in Spanish to one of the other two men. "Near Jorge," he said. "He can find him."

"He'd better be able to."

"Really," Lupe said. "No problem." He pointed at the piece of paper. "That is your woman."

Hector said a few more sentences in Spanish, after which all the other men looked around at one another and laughed.

"What's funny?" Ro turned to Eztli and asked.

"Hector suggested a way that Lupe could get some money out of this was that maybe after the woman gets her inheritance, Lupe could go by and see if she'd like to give him some of it for helping to find her so she could claim it."

After a minute to let it sink in, Ro threw a baleful look at Hector and said, "Good idea, José." Then, "Let's go, Ez. We're done here."

———

Lupe, his crew, and Hector were still standing around while Lupe went to one of the windows to watch Eztli and Ro get into their car and drive out of the lot.

When they had gone around the corner of the warehouse, Lupe turned around and walked over to where Hector stood waiting for something else to happen with Jorge Cristobal and Lupe's companion, a wiry rail of steel named Daniel.

"Hey, man," Lupe said to Hector in Spanish. "You still look like you got to pee. You got to take a leak, is that it?" Murillo was in fact shifting his weight from foot to foot, hands in his pockets as though he were cold. Lupe's face, set in a half smile, didn't signal a warning of any kind as he brought his fisted right hand up in a vicious punch to Hector's cheek.

The backs of the young man's knees hit the glass coffee table and he fell heavily over it and down on his back to the floor. Before he had any time to even begin to recover, Daniel was on him, his knees on his arms, holding them useless, pummeling his face and head with a flurry of punches. After he'd knocked any chance of a fight out of him, he jumped back up to his feet and, with the fury still on him, kicked at his head two, three, four times.

Until at last Lupe reached out and grabbed him. *"Daniel! Bastantes!"*

Seemingly unable to stop himself, Daniel struck out another time with his boot, then finally, reluctantly stepped back, breathing hard. He continued to back away while Lupe went around the table and leaned down over Hector's now nearly motionless body. He reached into the boy's jeans pocket and pulled out the folded wad of bills, then straightened up and kicked Murillo in the side once more for good measure. *"Idiota!"*

Then he turned to face Jorge and Daniel, peeling hundred-dollar bills off and counting them out: ". . . *dos, tres, quatro, cinco* . . ." He handed the first five hundred to Jorge, then counted out another equal share to Daniel. Finally he looked down at Hector, still unconscious. "I offer this little prick two thousand dollars and he tells me no, the money is all his?" He walked back over a couple of steps, hawked and spit on him, then looked over at Daniel. "Go dump this trash someplace," he said. "Jorge, get us both a couple of beers, would you?"

———

Farrell only needed twelve to issue an indictment, but as it turned out, he persuaded fourteen of the grand jurors to come in on their Friday off for the emergency session. Now and for the past hour and a half they were seated in front of Amanda Jenkins and listening attentively, many taking notes, as she finished outlining her case against Ro Curtlee.

Jenkins knew that in spite of the earlier Sandoval conviction, this

DAMAGE

was going to be close. She needed twelve votes to indict, and she was all but certain that she had ten, but all four of her skeptical jurors had independently peppered each of the witnesses so far with questions about the lack of physical evidence in the Nuñez case.

And one of them, a retired schoolteacher named Julian Ross, had in the course of his questions gone from the specific to the general, which Amanda feared in this case might sway the others: What had taken so long to bring this ten-year-old case to the grand jury? Jenkins had assured them that while she could not discuss specifics, it was for delays that had nothing to do with the strength of the evidence and that they should not consider it. Didn't Inspector Glitsky find it unusual that police had uncovered no physical evidence implicating Mr. Curtlee in the Nuñez murder? Glitsky had emphasized the motive, the way the body was found, and other similarities between the killings.

Amanda was nearly to the end.

Farrell had told her to let them take a short recess before they received instructions and began to deliberate. He had something more he wanted to bring before the grand jury.

———

And now here Farrell was, sitting at the witness stand. He'd come up during the break after Amanda had called him on her cell phone. A couple of clerks from the DA's office had accompanied him, one of them pushing a dolly that held a good-size cardboard box, which they'd picked up and deposited on the evidence table in front of him.

Farrell's presence here was extremely problematic, to say the least. He knew that, if not political suicide, the legal fallout of having the district attorney be a witness in his own case would be enormous. Certainly the courts would say that, with the chief prosecutor as a witness, the office would never be permitted to continue handling the matter. They might even toss out any indictment as a product of prosecutorial misconduct. He could see the words like *unethical* and *indefensible* appearing in the ultimate decision.

Farrell knew that what he was supposed to do was call the attorney general's conflict staff and turn the case over to it. And if he hadn't known it, Jenkins had told him that three times in the five minutes before he took the stand.

He flat didn't care. *At least if I get run out of office*, he thought grimly, *I can wear any goddamn T-shirt I want.*

So they had cleared everyone from the room except Amanda, Farrell, and the grand jurors. What was happening here would remain secret until a transcript was prepared and turned over to the defense. And in the meantime, hopefully Ro Curtlee would be behind bars while they regrouped and formed a plan to keep him there. Even if it was the AG who ended up with the case, Farrell and his office would have done what they could.

And then it began.

Under questioning by Jenkins, Farrell told the grand jury why he was before them. "Yesterday afternoon, I received a telephone call from Cliff Curtlee, the father of Ro. He had come into the information that I was planning on convening this grand jury at its regular time next Tuesday, when I would present the evidence that you've heard today and seek a no-bail indictment against Ro."

"Tell the grand jury what he told you," Jenkins said.

"He said to me, and I remember the quote exactly. 'I don't want this grand jury thing to move forward. It would be a bad thing for you personally if it did.' "

Suddenly Farrell had to grip the front rail of the witness box, almost as though he were going to faint. Swallowing, blinking back his emotions, he struggled to regain his composure. "Excuse me," he said. "This is difficult."

Jenkins had the box he'd brought earlier into the courtroom marked as an exhibit and put it in front of him. "Tell us, please, do you recognize the contents of this box?"

"I do."

"Will you please show the contents to the grand jury."

Opening the top of the carton, Farrell reached in with both hands, lifted Gert's body out, and laid it gently on the table. Giving her a last loving pet, he looked up at the members of the jury, several of whom appeared stricken.

"This was my dog, Gert. She was on the street in front of my girlfriend's place of business yesterday."

Jenkins then asked. "Mr. Farrell, what if anything did you do with Gert's body?"

"I had it taken to the police laboratory early last night for testing."

Amanda turned to the panel and explained. "Mr. Farrell can't testify about the results of the test because he didn't do them himself, but what he was told by the lab techs explains what he did next, which is why I'm going to ask him, 'Mr. Farrell, what did you learn from the lab?'"

Farrell couldn't keep the emotion out of his voice. "Somebody poisoned my dog."

"Mr. Farrell, you talked about your partner's place of business. What is that place of business?"

"She runs a rape crisis center on Haight Street."

"Does it have surveillance equipment?"

"It does."

"Based on what the lab told you, did you go and download some photographs from that surveillance equipment?"

"I did."

Jenkins produced an eight-by-ten black-and-white photo of the BMW Z4 and had it marked as an exhibit. "According to the surveillance equipment, when was this photo taken?"

"Right about the time the dog was poisoned," he said.

"Can you see the license number on that vehicle?" Jenkins produced a certified DMV record, had it marked as an exhibit, and handed it to Farrell. "Tell the grand jurors, Mr. Farrell, based on the photo and those records, whose car was parked near the rape crisis center just before your dog was poisoned."

"The records indicate," Farrell said, "that the car belonged to Ro Curtlee."

Jenkins let a long minute pass before she concluded. "Questions from the grand jury? Mr. Farrell, you're excused."

After being admonished, like every other witness, by the foreperson not to discuss his testimony, Farrell got up and, nodding soberly as he passed Jenkins, walked out of the room.

———

Down in his office, Wes closed and locked his door behind him. His whole body was shaking with the cynical enormity of what he'd just done. Crossing over to the foosball table, he grabbed two of the near handles and put all of his weight on them. Closing his eyes, he sucked in a deep breath, swallowing against the urge to throw up.

He'd been through difficult times before in his trials, his failed marriage, with his children, in his life, but never before had he completely abandoned his essential view of himself as a good man, an honest man, a man of good character. And he had just—willingly, knowingly, with aforethought—done exactly that.

He didn't kid himself. He knew that what he'd said and shown the grand jury might have been marginally relevant—even there he was on thin ice. But he also knew that the way he did it, appearing as a witness in his own prosecution, was at very best unprofessional if not flat-out unethical. He had done something he knew he wasn't supposed to do.

In the grand jury room, there was no check on his power. It was virtually absolute, and it had corrupted him absolutely. He remembered what Treya Glitsky had told him in his first days in office: that his predecessor Clarence Jackman had stayed on because he'd become addicted to the power. And now Farrell had a clear understanding of what she had meant.

This was his Rubicon—he was cheating, he knew he was cheating, he would cheat again under similar conditions.

And then suddenly the shaking within him stilled into a calm acceptance. He let go his death grip on the handles, got his weight back onto his feet. Surveying the shattered remnants of his conscience as though from a great height, he felt neither guilt nor pain, only a mild regret at its former gentle insistence upon the right and the fair, the last vestige of his idealistic youth.

What mattered most to him was that, in the sacred secrecy of the grand jury room, Jenkins would get her twelve votes.

34

"I'm sorry, Abe," Amanda Jenkins said. "I just can't seem to stop crying."

"Crying is okay. It's not like baseball. We allow crying in law enforcement, even encourage it. There are classes." Trying to keep it light.

It didn't work. "I don't know whether it was the dog, the stupid beautiful dog. Or relief. Or even Matt. I mean, Matt . . . I still can't believe . . ." She couldn't go on, dabbed at her eyes with her handkerchief.

Glitsky put an arm around her. She had come down to his office to share with him what she hoped would be the upcoming good news about the indictment, except that as she started telling him it had blindsided her. In the end, she couldn't stand being cooped up inside the Hall of Justice any longer and she'd borrowed Glitsky's spare raincoat and they'd snuck out the back stairs down to Bryant, and now were walking east in the misty, cold, gray, windy early afternoon.

"You know what else I can't stop. I can't stop thinking I want them to kill him," she said. "I want this indictment so bad, and then I want him to just think about resisting arrest and have them kill him."

"Maybe they will."

They walked another half block in silence. Glitsky tightened his arm briefly around her shoulders, and then let it drop as they continued side by side.

"Assuming we get the vote, you think we'll really get him?" she asked.

"I don't see why not. We got him last time. Not without a little difficulty, but we got him. We'll get him again."

"Who's going out?"

"Lapeer's picking a couple of special teams. Assuming the grand jury decides soon enough, they'll be waiting for him when he gets home."

"Not you?"

Glitsky's mouth went up a quarter inch. "Wiser heads prevailed."

"I'd have thought you wanted to be there."

"I did. She took my interest into consideration."

Another half block. A restaurant with happy early TGIF revelers. A body repair shop. A tattoo parlor. Four homeless people.

"Gets home from where?" Jenkins asked.

"Wherever they wind up going."

"They?"

"Him and the butler. They left at around ten thirty. We got him tagged with the GPS when he stopped at his bank about ten minutes later."

"So where'd they go after that?"

"San Bruno for a half hour or so, and finally Sunnyvale now for a while. I checked just before you came in. He was still there."

"What's down there?"

"I don't know. Some lunch place, maybe. A whorehouse. I . . ."

Glitsky came to a standstill, put his hand on Jenkins' arm.

"What? Abe?"

"I just had a horrible thought," he said. "I could be wrong. I'm probably wrong."

"What?"

Glitsky was already turned around, starting back toward the hall. "We've got to get back and find out for sure," he said.

JOHN LESCROART

"Abe? What?" she asked again.

"Not what, who," he said. "Gloria Gonzalvez."

——

Gloria built her work schedule so she would get the maximum time with her children. There was no avoiding leaving her baby, three-year-old Bettina, every day with Angela, who was a find, at eighteen really more like an older sister than a babysitter. But with the boys, Ramón and her six-year-old, Geraldo, both of them finally spending their full days in school, she could leave home just after they caught the bus at eight, clean her five or six houses—only four on Friday!—and still be home by the time they got there at three thirty or thereabouts.

Today she'd finished a little bit earlier than usual, dropped off her two helpers at their apartments, then did a little grocery shopping for dinner and the weekend before stopping by Angela's to pick up Bettina. Now she had an hour or so before the boys got home as she turned into her block, enough time to get dinner started and play with her baby alone, which was such a rare and special treat that they both loved. Her street, down in the flats just to the west of the freeway, was wearing its shabby winter coat today, the trees bare, the small, stand-alone houses in dull and faded pastels, what lawns there were as gray as the leaden sky above.

This was a neighborhood of working people, and the line of cars that sometimes made parking at the curb so challenging at night and on the weekends was missing, making the street feel all the more deserted. Gloria thought it was a little odd to notice a brand-new white SUV parked a couple of houses down from hers. People on this block didn't buy showroom-quality Toyotas or Lexuses or whatever the car was. It was out of place enough that she glanced over as she drove by and was reassured by the Latino driver—well dressed but clearly one of them, someone who belonged here. Maybe someone's cousin, she thought. Or new boyfriend.

She pulled her own rust-stained green midnineties Honda into

312

her driveway and pulled all the way in so that she could enter by the back door directly into the kitchen. She had Bettina buckled behind her in her backward-facing baby seat, and she went around to the car's back door, opened it, leaned over, and gave her a quick kiss on the cheek—"*Momento, chica.*" Then she opened the car's front passenger door to get out her two grocery bags and closed that door when she had them both.

With a bag in each hand, she turned and went up the three steps on her back stoop. Putting the bags down, she fished for a second in her purse for her keys, then found them, and opened the back door. Picking up the bags again, she brought them inside the house, put them on the counter, and then remembered that she'd bought some Häagen-Dazs Dulce de Leche ice cream, Roberto's favorite. She didn't want to let that get warm and start to melt, so she dug down in the bag for it and crossed the kitchen to put the carton in the freezer.

All the while, she'd been softly humming to herself, as she did when she was happy, and suddenly she thought she heard something. Closing up the freezer, she stopped and listened intently, her head cocked to one side.

What had that sounded like?

The answer came to her in a flash—a car door opening!—just as she turned and bolted for the back door and out onto the stoop.

And there was a man already halfway out of her car on Bettina's side, the close side to her, straightening up and turning around, holding her baby in his arms.

She stopped, her eyes wide with terror, frozen.

Ro Curtlee was holding her baby.

"Hey, Gloria," he said with his terrible smile. "All these years and you're still a damn fine-looking woman."

———

Glitsky placed a cell phone call to the Sunnyvale Police Department while he was jogging back to the Hall of Justice. Since he hadn't placed it as a 911 call, the dispatcher down there put him on hold before he could get a chance to state his business. Two blocks later, as he was getting to the steps of the Hall, he gave up, hung up, and tried 911, which was busy.

Inside the building, he lost his signal altogether.

He ran down the internal hallway that led him to Southern Station, the police precinct located on the ground floor within the Hall of Justice where a sergeant named Mildred Bornhorst was monitoring the GPS results. Here Glitsky learned that Ro's car was still parked down in Sunnyvale, where it had been for more than an hour. Glitsky got the relevant information, such as it was, to give to the emergency operator, but again he couldn't get past the busy signal.

It was not until he was in his office again—the clogged river of humanity in the lobby, the long ride up in the world's slowest elevator—that he could punch up the emergency numbers again on a landline. This time through a disturbance in the Force he got through and in another two minutes was talking to a Sergeant Bransen at the Sunnyvale Police Department.

"The suspect is Ro Curtlee," Glitsky was explaining. He spelled out the name. "He's out on bail on a rape/murder charge . . ."

"There's no bail on a rape/murder charge," the sergeant said.

"Don't ask," Glitsky snapped. "In any event, he's armed and dangerous. He's due to get indicted on multiple murder within the next couple of hours, so if you can get in his face any way you can, we'd appreciate it more than I can tell you."

"Get in his face? What's that mean? Is he indicted or isn't he?"

"He should be by the time you find him."

"What if he isn't?"

"Then you can at least slow him down."

Another hesitation, then Glitsky heard, "And what's he doing again?"

"I think he's threatening or harming one of the witnesses who's going to testify against him."

"Who's that?"

"Gloria Gonzalvez, although that might not be her name any-more. She might have gotten married or just changed it."

"All right. So Gloria somebody."

"Right."

"And where does the GPS put him?"

Glitsky had written down this information, and now he consulted his notepad and said, "It looks like the nine hundred block of Dennis Drive, between Burnham and Agnes."

"Okay. What's the address they're in front of?"

"I don't know exactly."

"License number of the car?"

Glitsky gave it to him.

"Okay. And where the woman lives? Her address?"

"I don't know that, either."

A slight hesitation on the other end, perhaps a sigh of impatience.

Glitsky's blood pounded from his temples to the center of his forehead. "Look, the guy is serious as a heart attack and he's down there now. He's probably stalking this Gloria woman. You need to just send some units down and check it out. Be a presence. You see a guy who looks like he doesn't belong, get his ID. If it's Curtlee, hold him or if the indictment's come down, take him in."

"You suggest we go door to door?"

"Yeah. Absolutely. If you have to."

"Can I get the spelling of your name again?"

"Sure." Glitsky blew out heavily to release some of his own frustration, then spelled it out for him. "I'm head of San Francisco homicide."

"All right. I hear you. I'll send a unit over."

"More than one would be better."

Another hesitation. "I'll see what I can do."

On the way down to Sunnyvale, and although it was illegal even for a cop like Glitsky to use his cell phone while he was driving, he checked in again with Sergeant Bransen. He had sent a couple of squad cars over to Dennis Drive, but there had been nothing suspicious going on there. His officers had not seen fit to go door to door.

Glitsky placed another call back to Southern Station at the Hall and talked to SFPD's own Sergeant Bornhorst again, manning the GPS feed since the morning. From Bornhorst he learned that Ro's car had moved on from its Sunnyvale location and was now on the 280 Freeway going north, back up toward the city. There were no units, Highway Patrol or local, in any kind of pursuit, but Bornhorst assured Glitsky that as soon as word of the indictment came down, if it did, police could pull the car over and pick up Ro—it would take some coordination with mobile units, but they could get it done.

Glitsky was sure she was right. But because of his own history with Ro, as well as the new chief of police's need to avoid the appearance of anything personal sullying the arrest, Lapeer had rather pointedly taken Glitsky out of the decision-making process on her strategy to serve Ro with the indictment and get him back into custody. The chief was assembling a special team for the takedown, and from what Glitsky had heard, it was going to be near or at Ro's house, where he could be expected—eventually—to turn up.

Assuming, of course, that the grand jury could make up its mind on indictment for the first two murders before the end of the day.

By this time, Glitsky was two-thirds of the way down to Sunnyvale. He could still be useful. He had his own reasons for finding Gloria Gonzalvez.

During his drive down the peninsula, the clouds had bunched up and condensed and now a stiff cold rain pelted his windshield as he turned into Dennis Drive. Cruising the length of the street, fortunately only one block long, there was still just barely enough light to assure himself that, sure enough, neither of Ro's two probable vehicles were parked at the curb.

Finding a space more or less at random, he parallel parked into it and sat for a moment hoping for a break in the rain, since he realized to his chagrin that he only had his regular Mountain Hardwear jacket—he'd loaned his raincoat to Amanda Jenkins for their walk up in the city and she no doubt still had it. Finally giving up as the rain kept falling, he got out and jogged from his car to the nearest house that showed a light, got under the front door overhang, and rang the doorbell.

After a moment, the inside door behind the screen opened a crack and a female voice said, "Yes?"

Glitsky, a large black man with a fierce countenance and a long scar up and down across his mouth, almost never encountered less than a severely reserved welcome from his unexpected appearance at someone's door, if not one of actual fear. And this woman was proving to be about typical. So he had his badge out and introduced himself, then continued: "I'm looking for a woman whose first name is Gloria who lives on this street. Her last name used to be and maybe still is Gonzalvez. I believe she may be in danger and I'd like to talk to her."

The woman didn't open the door any farther, simply said, "Sorry," and closed it.

Glitsky didn't waste any time hoping to alter her worldview about how to act if policemen came to her door requesting information. Instead, reasoning that she would probably at least know the name of her next-door neighbors, he skipped the next house, and the one after that, jogging through the rain, and a few houses down another house had lights showing and he turned in and tried again. This time the resident was a middle-aged African American man and he opened his door and actually gave Glitsky a smile. "Wet enough for you out there?" he said.

"Just about." Glitsky held up his badge and gave him his pitch.

The man didn't have to think about it. "That'd be Gloria Serrano." He actually came out and stood next to Glitsky on the small porch, pointing to be helpful. "She's four houses down on the other side, the blue shutters. Is she all right?"

"I hope so," Glitsky said. "Thank you."

"You need any help?"

"No. You've been one. Thanks."

Half a minute later, Glitsky rang her doorbell. It was apparent that several people were inside. There was a bit of commotion— children's exclamations and then an authoritative man's voice. When the door opened, Glitsky was holding his badge out again and looking at an obviously angry, worried Hispanic male of about thirty-five. He was holding a fireplace poker in his right hand and looked ready to use it at the slightest provocation.

"*Sí?*"

"Abe Glitsky, San Francisco homicide," he said. "*Homocidio. Comprendo?*"

Behind the man, the small living room was well lit. Two young boys stole glances at Glitsky around their father's legs. Glitsky caught a glimpse of a woman sitting on the couch who appeared to be holding a toddler on her lap, and now hearing Glitsky's name, she stood up and came into the light. "Roberto. It's all right," she said. "I know him. Let him in."

———

She offered Glitsky a small bath towel to dry his head and his face and hung his soaking-wet jacket on the back of a chair over a heating duct. The house was pin neat, bare bones, and warm, the windows cloudy with condensation. Glitsky sat down across from her, sideways to Roberto, at the Formica table just off the living room. She had the toddler back on her lap, while the father ordered the young boys to sit quietly on the couch, which they did without a word of resistance. To Glitsky, there seemed to be enough tension in the room to spontaneously combust.

"I'm so glad I found you," Glitsky began.

She forced a polite smile. "It's good to see you, too. Is there a problem?"

"Well." Glitsky's relief at seeing her alive and unharmed was substantial. "There may be. I don't know if you've heard, but Ro Curtlee has been released from prison."

She glanced—a warning?—at her husband, then pulled the toddler in closer to her, her arms encircling her, bouncing her on her knee. She shook her head no. "How did that happen?"

"He appealed the guilty verdict and they're going to give him a retrial. In the meanwhile, they let him out on bail."

"Why did they do that?"

"There's no good answer to that. The point is, they did. So you haven't heard from him?"

"No. Why would I have heard from him?"

"He might want to talk you out of testifying against him again. Because if he has a new trial, we're going to need you to give your testimony again."

"But I have already done that, last time."

"Yes, I know."

"Doesn't that count anymore? What I said?"

"Yes. But it will be more persuasive if you tell it to a jury again."

"I am sorry," she said. "But I do not think I can do that another time."

Glitsky, of course, never thought this was going to be easy. "I can understand how you feel that way," he said. "But it's come to the point now where you are the most important witness from the last trial if we are going to hope to put him back in prison."

Gloria looked again at her husband, whose eyes had never left

Glitsky, and who hadn't moved a muscle since he'd sat down. "How has it come to that point? What about the other witnesses? What about Felicia?"

Glitsky took in a quick breath and came out with it. "Felicia is dead."

Gloria crossed herself, her lip quivering.

"She was in a fire," Glitsky said.

"Since Ro got out of prison?"

A hesitation, then a nod. "Yes."

"He killed her."

"Maybe. That's not impossible."

Suddenly Roberto spoke up. "She cannot do this again," he said. "That is all."

"Well, I'm afraid that's not all, sir. I've been trying to locate Gloria for almost a month. Now that I've found her, all of you, I'd like to put her—and now your family—into a witness protection program until the trial."

"No. We cannot do that," Gloria said. "I did that last time when I was alone, but now we have jobs, a life, as you see. I can't just disappear again."

"It would only be until you testified, like last time."

"And when would that be?"

"August, at least. Maybe later."

She almost broke a smile at the absurdity of the request. "No," she said. "I am no threat to him, and he is no danger to me if I don't testify. So I will not. It is simple."

Glitsky all at once felt a chill settle on him, and he shivered against it. He did not want to bring undue pressure to bear on this woman, but she had to realize the danger of her situation. "Do you know how I found you here?" he asked her, and when she shook her head no, he went on, "We put a tracking device—a GPS unit— on Ro's car. He drove down to this street today and stayed here nearly two hours."

Roberto and she shared another blink of a look. "I was not here," she said.

"You didn't see him? He didn't talk to you?"

This time Gloria's glance at her husband conveyed a true message: Don't say a word. "No," she said. "I will simply call his parents and tell them I won't testify. He will not come back."

Glitsky held his hands clasped tightly on the table in front of him. He became aware of the tension in them and consciously willed them to relax. He didn't want to snap or become argumentative, positions from which there'd be no extrication. He met Gloria's eyes, tried to soften what he knew was the harsh set of his features. "He came by here this afternoon and threatened your children, didn't he?" he said in an even tone. "Isn't that what really happened?"

She was not even remotely skilled as a liar. After her eyes went wide, she looked over to her husband for help, who couldn't manage much more than a what-can-you-do shrug. Finally she shook her head several times, much too quickly. "I just told you."

"Yes, you did. You told me he didn't do anything like that." Glitsky leaned in toward her. "Was that the truth?"

Again, she silently begged her husband to step in, but either he couldn't read the signal or he didn't know what to do with it. Her eyes went across the room to the two boys sitting on the sofa. She wrapped her arms more protectively about the toddler on her lap. At last, she shook her head again. "I did not see him," she said. "I don't know why he was parked here."

Glitsky lowered his voice to an all-but-inaudible whisper. "I don't want to alarm your children, Gloria, but I think he came down here to kill you just like he killed Felicia Nuñez. And then when he saw you had children, he had a better idea."

She just stared at him.

"He needs to be back in prison," Glitsky said, "so that he won't be able to hurt anyone else."

"He will not hurt my children if I don't testify," she said. "There would be no reason."

"How do you know that?" Glitsky asked. "How can you be sure of that?"

"Please. It is no use." She lifted her chin and met his eyes. "I just know."

35

Driving back up to the city on the Bayshore Freeway, the car's heater blasting away and his windshield wipers swishing at top speed, Glitsky tried to console himself with the fact that at least now he had a name and address for Gloria Serrano and that other, more persuasive souls in the DA's office might convince her that she needed to testify again against Ro. That might still happen, he thought, especially once they got him back into jail and he was no longer a direct threat to her children.

His mind kept returning to the question of how Ro had located Gloria so quickly, and again it returned to the old familiar theme of the city's stupid police budget. He was sure that Ro's success was a function of his ability to hire private investigators who could use private and in some case downright illegal methods to locate missing persons, or persons who wanted to be missing. He was working himself up into a fine lather about it as his cell phone chirped on the seat next to him.

Seeing the name Wes Farrell on the screen, he dispensed with the preliminaries. "Tell me we got the indictment."

"Better late than never. We got the indictment. Fifteen minutes ago."

"Hallelujah!"

"That's what I said, too. Sorry I didn't call you sooner, but I thought Vi needed to know first."

"True enough. She got her teams in place?"

"Not yet. I only just called her. Last she heard from her GPS people, he was already back in town from somewhere down the Peninsula."

"Sunnyvale," Glitsky said. "He found Gloria Gonzalvez."

"God, shit, no." Farrell's voice went hollow. "You're not telling me . . ."

"No. He just threatened her kids because it was so much more fun. Now she's saying she won't testify against him. It might be a hard sell getting her back on board."

"Well, maybe when she finds out he's back in jail . . ."

"That's what I was hoping, too. So did the chief say how long it would be before they could move?"

"She said she had to gather the troops. Some of 'em evidently have already gone home, though they're all on call. Then she first wanted to make sure where Ro was going. Next place he stops, which her guess is his house."

"Her guess?"

"He's in the city on Nineteenth Avenue heading that way. You got a better idea?"

"No. I suppose not."

"But?"

"Nothing." Glitsky wasn't going to criticize the chief who'd mostly stood up for him under serious and unrelenting pressure. But inwardly his guts churned that she had not chosen to put someone on Ro's car's tail from the minute he'd come into town, and maybe even before. But like Glitsky and maybe more so, Lapeer was probably dealing with budget issues. "I just want to see him off the street."

"Probably won't be more than a couple of hours," Farrell said.

"Less would be better."

"You want to call Vi and tell her that?"

"No," Glitsky said. "I don't think that would be productive."

———

Jon Durbin had just been getting home late last night when he saw his father pulling out of his uncle and aunt's driveway. Not really having any idea of where his father could be going late on a Thursday night, he had followed him up through Golden Gate Park, then right on Geary down to Laguna, and finally north to Chestnut, where he parked at the curb.

Pulling over a half block away, Jon had watched his father get out of the car and walk to the entrance of the large apartment building that anchored the southwest corner. After ringing outside and then opening the lobby door, he had disappeared inside.

Jon followed a minute later and stood looking at the bank of inhabitants' names on the mailboxes. When he saw the name Sato, he almost couldn't believe it, and then he totally believed it, and his hand went to his stomach as it turned over on him.

His father and Liza.

How sickening, how gross, how fucking *obvious*.

Did his dad really think he could get away with this? Did he think they were all complete gullible morons?

After that, he hadn't been able to face going home at all. He stayed with his best friend, Rich, and had gone on to school in yesterday's clothes with almost no sleep.

Today he had seethed all day, a blackness growing within him minute by minute, and after school ended he had first gone back to Rich's, and then decided that he had to deal with this somehow, bring it out in the open. So he had come back to the Novios' at around quarter to five, about when the rain had unleashed.

He still wasn't sure what he was going to do. But something.

He had made it back to the house without having to explain much to Aunt Kathy, who was still wrecked—as they all were except his goddamn father—by the plain fact of his mother's murder. He went upstairs to the bedroom he was sharing with Peter, took a shower, and changed into some other clothes, then lay down on the bed, closing his eyes.

When Peter came in a half hour later, he opened them. "Hey."

"Where have you been?"

"Rich's. Just hanging out. Except earlier last night. You know what I did last night?"

"Who cares?"

"You will. I followed Dad."

"When?"

"When he went out. You didn't know he went out?"

Peter shook his head. "I crashed early. You followed him? Why? Where to?"

"Because I wanted to see where he was going. And guess where that was. Liza Sato's."

This information stopped Peter short until he could finally form the question, "Why did he go there?"

"Why do you think?"

"I think probably because she's his friend and he needed somebody to talk to."

"Yeah, either that or he's fucking her."

"Bullshit! You don't know that. You don't know anything." Then, the fully realized thought of his brother's meaning dawning on him, Peter stepped up close to where Jon sat up on the bed and said, "Are you saying you think Dad killed Mom? Is that what you're getting at, 'cause if it is, that is just such bullshit."

"You think it's bullshit that he's having an affair and nobody's talking about it? I think that sounds to me like the reason he had to kill Mom."

"He didn't have a reason to kill Mom. He didn't kill Mom. He loved Mom." Peter broke into tears. *"He loved her, goddamn it. He loved her!"* In a sudden fury, he struck out with both hands, slamming his brother's shoulders, knocking him back on the bed. "Fuck you!"

Jon's feet came up off the floor and he kicked out, hitting his younger brother in the chest, knocking him backward as he came scrambling up off the bed, screaming more obscenities, throwing punches wildly. Peter charged back, head down, catching Jon around the waist, slamming him back against the room's wall, knocking over one of the bed lamps in the process.

Jon came back up, swinging and connecting, hitting Peter in the face, at which the younger brother let out an animal scream and, his nose now spewing blood, came at Jon with everything he had. They both went over the bed and fell off the other side and into one of the mahogany end tables, splintering it, knocking down another light, which came crashing down around them.

———

Michael Durbin surveyed the wreckage of the boys' room, at a complete loss at how to deal with this latest disaster. He turned back to Chuck, who stood at his shoulder. "I don't know what to say except I'm so sorry. Of course I'll pay for any damages."

"Payment's not the issue."

"Well, it's at least part of it." He cast his glance back again at the destruction. "Jesus Christ. What got into them?"

"From talking to Peter," Chuck said, "I gather it was about you."

"Me? How could it have been me?"

Chuck rested a hand on his shoulder. "Maybe you should talk to Peter."

"I think I'm a little too mad to talk to Peter."

"If I was going to be mad at anybody, Michael, I think I'd go for Jon."

"I got plenty of mad for both of them." Another sweep of the room. "Christ. It looks like a bomb hit this place. Why should I be more mad at Jon?"

"He evidently told Peter that you had some kind of a hand in Janice's death."

Durbin's head dropped until his chin nearly touched his chest. "How can he think that, my own son? How can anybody who knows me at all . . . ?"

"He followed you last night, Mike. Jon did. When you left here. Over to Liza Sato's."

Durbin turned to face his brother-in-law. "Christ," he said, "not you, too?"

Chuck shook his head. "Not me at all, Michael. I'm just telling you what your son was saying." He motioned to the room. "What started all this."

"I needed to talk to somebody," Durbin said. "I'd leaned on you and Kathy enough. I had to get out of here for a while, that's all."

"You don't have to explain anything to me. As far as I'm concerned, Janice was murdered by Ro Curtlee and that's all there is to it. Look at the paintings, too."

"Jon can't think I'd have done that."

And suddenly a new voice—Peter's, hoarse and choked—from behind them. "He does, Dad. To make it seem more like it was Curtlee."

Durbin turned to see his younger son. He was still wearing his ripped and bloodstained shirt. His face was swollen, his eyes red, his cheeks glistening with tears, his nose flattened and off center, possibly broken. "Peter." Durbin, shocked by his sweet son's battering, spoke more gently than he'd intended. "What the hell?"

"I know. I'm sorry. I don't know what happened. Jon just started talking crazy and I went off on him." He looked past his father at the damage he'd done. "I'm so sorry, Uncle Chuck. I'm so sorry."

"Sorry's a good start," Chuck said, "but I've got to tell you, Peter, you've got a ways yet still to go. Do you know where Jon's gone to?"

Peter shook his head no. "He was staying at Rich's, but I don't know where he is now. And I don't care, either. I hope he never comes back."

"No, you don't hope that. He's just reacting this way because he misses Mom. We all miss Mom. And he's really, really angry about it and doesn't know where to put it so he's taking it out on me. And you. And maybe all of us." Durbin touched his son's arm. "But how did he get this into his head, Peter? Just because I went to see Liza Sato?"

Peter nodded. "He believes you're having some kind of a thing with her. I told him there was no way. You loved Mom."

"I did love your mother, Peter. I loved her so much. I still love her."

"That's what I told him. I said you and Liza were just friends, that's all. And that's true, isn't it? I mean, isn't that completely true?"

"Of course it is," Durbin said. "Completely, one hundred percent true."

Hearing his father's emphatic denial seemed to bring some real relief to the boy. He blew out heavily through his mouth and closed his eyes while he let the answer sink in. "Okay," he said. "Okay, then."

36

Eztli and Ro got home at a little after six o'clock.

Ro had originally wanted to get dropped off again at MoMo's, where he could get some food and drink at the bar until Tiffany got off, but this was Friday night and Eztli was cutting it close getting to the Curtlees' home on time when he knew he had to put on his tuxedo and drive them to the Saint Francis Hotel by eight for a fundraising wine auction of some kind. This had been on Eztli's schedule for the past month and though he got a true rush out of the time he spent with Ro, he also didn't have any nagging ambiguity about who was writing the check every month, and if Cliff and Theresa needed him to be someplace, then that's where he would be.

Stoned, mellow, and buoyed by the positive turn of the afternoon's events with Gloria Serrano, Ro hadn't objected. And so at seven o'clock, Eztli and the three members of the Curtlee family were all gathered in what they called the "little study"—a quiet, book-lined, relatively small room with a fireplace just off the dining room.

Cliff and Theresa in their black-tie garb were sharing a split of Roederer Cristal champagne, sitting hip to hip on the love seat that directly faced the dancing flames of the fire. Ro, on a wing chair catercorner to them, had showered and changed into a blue silk long-sleeved shirt and a pair of khakis. He had his bare feet up on an ottoman, his hands around a large leaded-crystal brandy snifter with a good strong two fingers of Rémy Martin V.S.O.P. Eztli stood in his own formal wear, across from both the parents and from

DAMAGE

Ro, closest to the fire, where he could keep an eye on the one entrance to the room. He hadn't shared any marijuana with Ro on the way up to town, and he wasn't drinking here tonight with the family, either. Since he would be serving double duty—chauffeur and bodyguard—he was carrying a .40 caliber semiautomatic pistol in a shoulder holster under his left armpit, nothing like the weapon that he'd used on Matt Lewis.

Ro was regaling his parents with his good fortune today in locating Gloria. "It was amazing to see, you guys. The change in her, which is I guess what living with guilt can do to you," he was saying. "She was like a different person. She told me she had nothing but remorse for testifying against me last time."

"I should think so," Theresa said. "I always thought, before she told those lies on the stand of course, that she was a nice girl."

"Very nice," Cliff concurred. "And I thought one of the prettiest, really."

"She still is," Eztli said.

"Anyway, bottom line," Ro continued, "and this is the really great part, no way is she going to be testifying again. She even asked me if there was any way she could talk to Tristan and recant some, maybe even all, of what she said last time."

"Ro," Cliff said, "that is fantastic. Really fantastic!"

"But I'm curious. How did you find her?" Theresa asked. "I understood from Tristan that that was turning out to be a little problematic."

"Well, he was using a private eye. I used Ez."

To whom all eyes turned. He shrugged, self-effacing. "I just put the word out in our community. Not much of a deal. There's a network of like-minded people. And really, she wasn't hiding."

"Yes, well, nevertheless, your efforts were a little bit more effective than the attorneys we're paying, now, weren't they?"

Eztli smiled. "We got lucky. But I'll take lucky over smart anytime."

"Hear, hear," Theresa said. "And wasn't she, this Gloria, wasn't she the last one? I mean, the last witness who was set to come to your next trial?"

Ro sipped contentedly at his cognac. "Well, never set, as it turns out. She didn't even realize I'd gotten out of prison."

Theresa's nearly immobile face almost managed to look surprised. "How could she be unaware of that?"

Ro smiled at her. "I don't think she's a big reader of newspapers, Mother. Or watching the news."

"She has three small children," Eztli added. "It looked like they keep her busy."

"Well, that will explain it," Theresa said.

And Cliff added, "So that's pretty much their case, then, am I right?"

"Let's hope," Ro said. "They've got no new witnesses and now pretty much none of the old ones. That's what Tristan has been hoping for all along, and now it looks like that's what we've got."

"So they may not send you back?" Theresa asked.

Ro sipped more cognac, put on a rueful expression. "I don't want to jinx us," he said. "You know they're going to try. I can't see them just giving up. But now there is some real hope."

"Glitsky won't give up," Theresa said. "He's such a nuisance. We've got to find a way to get him transferred into another department or something."

But Cliff was shaking his head. "It's not Glitsky. It's Farrell. If he's got no case, they don't retry. And we can get to him. In fact, I've already gotten to him. Again, thanks to Ez here."

Eztli gave another slight acknowledgment, a tip of the head. "I would think Farrell's pretty well neutralized," he said.

Cliff looked down at his empty champagne flute. "Well," he said, "all this calls for a toast. And just as I've run out of champagne. Ez, you might even have a sip, just for the celebration of it."

"As you wish. I'll ring, sir."

———

Bracco stood outside in a steady drizzle, a full two blocks down the street from the Curtlees' home, waiting for the last two guys of the ten-man team that Lapeer had put together to effect the arrest of Ro Curtlee. He would have already moved the men into positions all around the house except that he wanted to be sure they didn't compromise the element of surprise. And unfortunately the last two guys were coming from downtown, and bringing with them the physical arrest warrant.

A pair of headlights cut through the mist as it turned onto the street a couple of blocks down, and Bracco heaved a sigh of relief as the car pulled up and parked behind the small caravan that had already formed behind Bracco's car at the curb. Unable to calm his nerves, Bracco jogged down and arrived at the car as its driver was just opening his door.

"Warrant?" was about all he could manage to say.

The driver tapped his chest with his knuckles—"Right here"— and from the sound of it, Bracco realized that these guys, too, were already wearing Kevlar, as was the rest of the team.

Nobody taking any chances.

And now everyone was ready. Another wash of relief swept over him. It was time. He counted the men one last time, now all of them having gathered close, ten of them present and accounted for.

"Okay, guys," he said. "Quiet and careful. Let's move it out."

———

Eztli crossed to a small table at the back of the little study that featured a diminishing selection of nuts and hard candies. He picked up the little silver bell, identical to the ones in the kitchen and living room, and gave it a shake, which produced a melodic tinkle.

And which in turn produced one of the uniformed young women from the kitchen—Eztli did not always bother learning their individual names since he had so little interaction with them, and also because they tended to move along to their next posting to one of the Curtlees' acquaintances within a year or so. He thought this one might be named Linda, but it wouldn't do to call her by a name and get it wrong. Eztli prided himself on being unfailingly polite. "Another bottle of the Cristal, please," he said. "The full-size bottle from the refrigerator. Oh, and two more champagne glasses."

She looked over at where the Curtlees sat, let her eyes rest on them for a moment, her face, it seemed to Eztli, fighting against itself to keep an expression of resentment at bay. It was difficult, he knew—he was not entirely immune to some resentment himself—to be constantly aware of the unbridgeable gap between staff and principals.

When her eyes came back to him, he gave her what he hoped was an understanding nod, and she returned it, curtsying as she'd been taught. She then glanced at the nearly empty nut tray and went over to pick it up and carry it back with her. His eyes followed the smooth perfection of her hips as she crossed the dining room and disappeared back into the kitchen, and for an instant he thought he might reconsider his firm lifelong policy of never dating the help. This young woman was certainly pretty enough to make the effort worthwhile.

But he banished that thought as quickly as it had appeared. No good could come of it. Just look what problems Ro had had. Even though that was a lot of years ago, it was still wreaking havoc on his life. There were other women who didn't live under this roof that Eztli could enjoy. It wasn't as though he was hurting in that department.

It didn't take the young woman thirty seconds to reappear with the glasses and the champagne wrapped in a plain white dish towel. Carrying the expensive champagne and the dainty expensive glassware obviously made her nervous—the glasses were clinking dangerously against one another—and she set all of the stuff down on the small table with visible relief that she'd made it without breaking anything. With another little bow, she turned to go back to the kitchen.

Eztli brought the champagne bottle over to Ro's parents. Presenting it for their approval, he got a brisk nod from Cliff. Theresa said, "I believe that will do just fine."

Half listening to the conversation that had now moved along to Sheila Marrenas and her latest column on Leland Crawford's assertion of his vision over the police department and how well it was beginning to work, Eztli went back to the table, removed the foil expertly, then the wire, then turned the bottle carefully while holding the cork in place. With a satisfying little pop, the bottle opened with no spillage. First he poured one of the two glasses for Ro and crossed the room to deliver that. Next he would pour for Cliff and Theresa. Only then would he take care of his own half glass.

He was almost to Ro when, behind him, he became aware of the young woman returning again, this time with the tray of nuts under a silver dome. She set it heavily on the small table, clearing a space for it, and then stood still for a moment, her hands holding both sides of the table, as if she needed to do that to remain standing.

Aware of the unusual hesitation, Eztli turned back to see if everything was all right with her just as she removed the dome and placed it in front of the tray so that it blocked Eztli's view of it. Then she reached down with both hands and lifted an object, and for an instant Eztli found himself confused by something that in this setting was so bizarre and unexpected that it paralyzed him. She was holding the big semiautomatic in both hands, beginning to bring it up.

As the confusion crystallized into a horrified and desperate certainty, Eztli dropped the bottle of champagne from his right hand and, in the same motion, threw Ro's glass over toward the fire.

"Ez!" Cliff jerked at the sudden noise and movement. "What the . . ."

Eztli's right hand was reaching for his own weapon, turning to face her, inadvertently giving her a larger target, but with no other real choice, and by the time he got his hand on the grip, she had brought the gun all the way up, centering it on his chest.

He never heard the first blasting report as the slug hit him just above the heart and threw him backward onto the floor. Then, as though from far away, he did hear and this time felt another shot, a searing pain in his shoulder, and then, all the sounds in the world growing fainter, several more reports in quick succession.

Until finally everything went quiet.

And then dark.

———

Ro didn't believe that this was happening. This wasn't how he was supposed to die.

He had been so relaxed with the weed and the glass of cognac that he felt molded to his chair, slumped down into the cushion, just reaching up to grab his glass when Ez turned and suddenly was looking at Linda, then throwing the drinks down and making a move toward his shoulder holster.

He never got to it.

And she kept pulling the trigger. Another shot hitting Ez—Ro trying to look everyplace at once, with nowhere to run or even duck away to.

Now he heard his mother scream and Linda had fired again at his father, who had been halfway to his feet, and who then went down. Now she was bringing the gun around, just firing away, not really taking time to aim, but pointing straight at his chest and . . .

He felt the first slug go all the way through him from side to side, low in his gut, as the force of it knocked him back and sideways now in the chair.

He couldn't take his eyes off her. She was still pointing the thing at him. He tried to put his hands up, but they didn't seem to want to obey him.

"Don't . . . ," he began.

She pulled the trigger again and it felt as if someone had ripped his right arm off. In the corner of his eye, he saw his mother stand and as he watched, Linda turned to her and fired once, doubling her over before Theresa went down on her knees.

But Linda wasted no time making sure with his mother as she came walking forward now, the gun extended in front of her, pointing right at his face.

He met her eyes.

Through the shock and pain, Ro's brain tried to make sense of any of this. What was her problem? What was the big deal? So, she hadn't been in the mood. He had to fight her a little to finally get it done, but so what? That's what you did. He couldn't believe she wasn't already pretty used to it. She was a big girl. She . . .

He felt the gun pressed high against his left cheek.

"Adios," she said. *"Fucker!"*

37

Glitsky got the call from Bracco, with one of the arrest teams. The teams had been gathering out in front of the mansion on Vallejo Street when they'd heard the shots from inside the house and rushed to the door.

Glitsky had to pull up and park behind rows of other cars and vans nearly two blocks away. It was raining steadily and it seemed impossible to him that such a crowd—of police personnel, curious neighbors, news vans, politicians, and reporters—had developed in such a short time. But then again, the bare fact of what had apparently happened here seemed impossible as well. All these people braving the inclement weather in coats and umbrellas, pressing in against the yellow police tape line they'd strung along the street and across the property line.

Glitsky picked his way through the mass of people, ducked under the police line, and showed his ID to one of the patrolmen standing guard at the bottom of the steps. Once he was safely inside the perimeter, he turned briefly to look behind him.

He estimated there were fifteen black-and-white patrol cars, each with their red and blue lights strobing the night. Somebody had already set up at least one set of kliegs to brighten the place even more. Glitsky counted four television vans, which must have gotten the word even more quickly than he did. Sheila Marrenas, so far unsuccessfully, was trying to bully her way through the line down at the end of the driveway. Leland Crawford was giving an interview to a small knot of television people over by his limo.

Glitsky jogged up the steps and slowed down at the open door, where Bracco was waiting to meet him. "That was fast," the inspector said.

Glitsky nodded. "I was motivated. Where'd it go down?"

Bracco pointed and started walking toward the study at the same moment, Glitsky at his heels. "The chief here yet?" he asked.

"Not yet, no."

"How about CSI?"

"Yep. And we've got the suspect in custody back in the kitchen. One of the maids. Linda Salcedo. She's not giving us any trouble."

"Let's hope we can keep it that way. You got the weapon?"

"Tagged and bagged. It was on the floor where she dropped it."

"She dropped it?"

"Dropped it and answered the doorbell, then showed us where to go. You could still smell the cordite. Craziest thing I've ever seen."

But by then they had reached the arched entrance to a small room, guarded by two other members of what was originally supposed to be the arresting team. Glitsky stopped a half step behind Darrel, and nodded at both of the other men. There was plenty of light from a couple of standing lamps and an overhead chandelier. The study was less than fifteen feet deep, maybe twelve feet wide. It seemed to be filled with bodies.

And even with his vast experience, Glitsky was impressed by the body count in the enclosed place.

The iron smell of blood and, underlying it, something sweet smelling and alcoholic. Glitsky stepped forward so he could take it all in.

The butler lay on his back by the fireplace, his tuxedo coat wide open revealing a shoulder holster with its gun still in it. A red splotch bloomed in a wide circle in the shirt over his heart. Another slug looked like it had taken him in the shoulder, but the one by the heart looked like it had done the job. When Eztli had gone down, he'd knocked over the screen in front of the fireplace, which lay on the floor by his head. On the other side of his head, a bottle of champagne lay on its side. The mirror above the fireplace was shattered, and shards from it littered the floor all around him.

Ro Curtlee sat slumped in an easy chair, literally soaked in blood. He'd taken two or three in the chest and one at really close range high in his left cheek. The force of the shot had canted his head to the right and the entire right side of his shirt was soaked from the exit wound damage, the exit wound annihilation.

The most ghastly image was Cliff Curtlee, who had managed to get up and turn around before he'd been hit, or hit fatally. The shot that had done the most obvious damage had evidently taken him in the side of the throat—his carotid spurting arterial blood over the rug and onto the hardwood of the adjoining dining room floor—but several other rounds had hit him in the side and back, evidently as he tried to get away. From the blood trail, it looked like he kept on crawling through his own blood for a good three or four feet before finally stopping with the shock and trauma of the injuries and bleeding out.

Bracco leaned over Cliff and examined the throat injury with interest. He turned to Glitsky and said, "That's going to leave a mark."

Glitsky took in all of this at a glance, then said to no one in particular, "Where's Mrs. Curtlee?"

One of the crime scene guys looked up from photographing Ro's body in his chair. "Other room," he said.

"Dead?"

In a perfect imitation Munchkin voice from *The Wizard of Oz*, the tech said, "She is not just merely dead, she is really most sincerely dead."

Glitsky, once again reminded of the wisdom of the rule that reporters were not allowed on crime scenes until the techs had finished, turned and saw Vi Lapeer coming through the front door and he moved to intercept her. "Chief," he said. "What you've probably heard is true. They're all dead, the Curtlees and their butler. Shot at close range. We have a suspect subdued and in custody in the next room."

Lapeer slapped her game face on. Taking a steadying breath through her mouth, she set her jaw and started across the dining room toward the archway.

———

At eleven o'clock, the techs were still working in the study. The bodies had been bagged and taken in the coroner's van to the medical examiner's office behind the Hall. Since Bracco spoke excellent Spanish and was already here at the scene, Glitsky assigned the formal investigation of these murders to him, so Bracco had given Linda Salcedo her Miranda warning and a quick preliminary interview and was on his way with her to the detail for a full videotaped statement. Outside, the crowd had eventually mostly dispersed. Neither the mayor nor Sheila Marrenas had ever been admitted to the crime scene, and both had eventually gone away, as had a stoic Vi Lapeer.

Amanda Jenkins had been out at a restaurant with a couple of other assistant DAs and caught the breaking news flash on the television. Now she sat at the dining room table with Glitsky, both of them too wound up to go home.

"So our suspect evidently had heard about the earlier rapes, so she had some type of warning," Glitsky was saying, "but she didn't take it seriously enough."

"You're saying Ro had already done another one of them? Since he got out?"

"No. One of the other workers here had heard the stories and told her she should be on her guard."

"But she wasn't."

"Not enough, anyway. He called her up to his room under the pretext of her cleaning up something last night . . ."

"Last night? He pulled this shit just last night? When he knew we're all over him?"

A brisk nod. "He thought he had us beat. Killing Farrell's dog. Cutting our balls off. Squeezing Lapeer with the mayor. Time to go back and check out the home turf."

"What an asshole. So she was warned about it and still went up?"

Glitsky shrugged. "He'd been home almost a month and never did anything. Last night he called and needed something cleaned up, so she goes to his room and he's naked in bed with a gun on her."

"So she . . . ?"

"She wanted to stay alive."

Jenkins shook her head in disgust. "I'd like to kill him again."

"I hear you."

"What about the shoes?"

"Evidently not an issue this time. I know she didn't mention anything to Darrel."

"Okay, so how'd she get the gun?"

Glitsky's lips turned up slightly. "This is my favorite part," he said. "He just left it in his drawer next to his bed in his room. Loaded. So he goes out with his man, Ez, today and doesn't take it with him. Probably figures that Linda liked it—the sex, not the gun, or the sex with the gun. So today she comes up, makes sure the gun is still there, and waits for her opportunity, which doesn't take long coming."

"But why kill the others? Why isn't she just waiting in his room for him when he comes home?"

"I asked Darrel to ask her that myself. She said it was self-defense. Where she's from, you kill a member of a powerful family, they kill your whole family. She knew if she was going to kill Ro, she had to kill them all."

Jenkins thought about this for a minute. "Knowing the Curtlees, she just might have been right."

"Maybe. Anyway, she knew Ez carried a gun, and so he had to go first. And then she figured Cliff and Theresa, they knew what Ro was doing and had been doing all along and they enabled him. Not her word. So they were part of it, what he was doing, and so the heck with them, too."

"Jesus Christ, though," Amanda said. "I didn't think anybody was that good with a pistol. She killed all four of them?"

"God was on her side."

Amanda sat back, looked up at the ceiling, and closed her eyes for a moment. "I'm going to want to run ballistics on the gun to-night, the murder weapon, to see if it matches the one that killed Matt."

Glitsky nodded. "Probably a good idea."

"And Ez's, too, while I'm at it."

"Whatever you can find," Glitsky said. "I don't think a search warrant is going to be a problem this time around."

———

At the Novio house, the muted jubilation over news of the death of Ro Curtlee was even more restrained than it otherwise might have been because by midnight, Jon Durbin still had not come home. He had not answered his cell phone or responded to text messages, either, even when Michael had Jon's little sister, Allie, text from her phone and beg him to just tell her he was okay.

Now finally all three of the girls were asleep and Peter lay on a couch covered by one of Kathy's comforters, sleeping with the TV on in the family room. The three adults sat in the living room, Chuck and Michael on either end of the couch, Kathy in a lounger, all of them obviously wrecked by the recent and continuing events.

Finally Michael sat up straighter and slapped at his arm of the couch. "That's it," he said, starting to get up, "I'm going to call the police."

Chuck looked over. "And say what?"

"That my son's missing. See if they can go on some kind of lookout for him."

"But he's really not missing," Kathy said softly. "Not any more than he was last night, Michael. He's just confused, trying to sort things out."

"And the police won't be able to find him anyway. Or—check that—they won't look for him," Chuck added. "He's too old and it hasn't been long enough. I don't think they even consider an adult missing anymore unless no one's heard from them in three days."

"Well, that sure gives whoever it is enough time to hide out pretty good, doesn't it?" He slumped back into the cushions. "I just want to talk to him, that's all. I can answer any questions he's got for me. Any of them. I promise."

"Of course you can." Kathy let out an exhausted sigh. "Maybe this news tonight will make a difference to him. They said on the news that the police are closing the Ro Curtlee cases, and that's got to include Janice, wouldn't you think?"

"You would think," Michael said, "but maybe not. Not the way Glitsky's been looking at it. He obviously still thinks it was Ro, but keeps talking about things that don't fit. Which still doesn't mean it was me. I mean, as far as I know, he hasn't done a thing about even looking at her clients."

"I don't know if he can do that," Kathy said. "Isn't there some kind of privilege or something? And besides, why would he want to talk to her clients? Do you know something that points to any of them?"

"Only that she was—" He stopped abruptly.

"What?" Kathy asked. "You were going to say something."

"No." Mike brought his hand up and squeezed at his temples. "Only that I'm so tired. I don't know what I'm saying."

But Kathy persisted. "Was there something you know about one of her patients? Michael? That could be real."

"I don't want anything to be real, Kathy," he said. "I'm sure it was Ro Curtlee. It's just this other stuff muddying the waters for Glitsky."

"But what other stuff?" she persisted.

Chuck finally spoke up. "Mike thinks she was having an affair."

"What? Janice? No way, Mike."

Durbin shrugged. "Yeah, Kathy, I think there was a way."

"Why do you think that?"

"Well." A brittle little laugh. "That's kind of personal, if you know . . ."

"Did you talk about it?"

"No."

"Did she say she was going to be leaving you or anything like that?"

"No." He hesitated, looked to each of them in turn, then spoke to Kathy. "We hadn't had the most intimate last couple of months."

And now she laughed her own brittle laugh. "Ha! If that's it, I think they must be putting something in the water."

Chuck's head came up in a quick spurt of anger. "Kathy!"

She looked right back at him. "What? What if it's the truth?" Then she turned to Durbin. "Like that's a sign you're having an affair? Even happy couples go through some ups and downs like that. It's part of the package." Then, back to her husband, "Isn't that right, Chuck? It doesn't mean your marriage is in trouble. At least, I hope it doesn't."

"She's right, Mike," Chuck said. "She's absolutely right. But going back to the original question, I'd like to know what Glitsky's reservations are," he said. "I mean, it's obvious enough to all of us that Janice was killed by Ro Curtlee and now Ro Curtlee's dead and that ought to be the end of it. Is there something none of us are seeing?"

"Well, this affair, if there was one," Kathy said.

"But even if there was one," Chuck said, "there's nothing that eliminates Ro Curtlee. He had a reason, he slashed the paintings for the same reason, Mike. He wanted to get at you. Even if Janice was having an affair, why would the guy slash your paintings? That had to be Ro. Which means the fire had to be Ro, too. Why don't you tell that to Glitsky next time he asks?"

But all this emotion and discussion, along with the worry over his son, were finally taking their toll. Durbin bowed his head and shook it slowly back and forth. "Let's just hope he doesn't," he said. "Doesn't think he's got a reason to ask. Now, if you guys don't mind, I'm going up to bed."

"I think we should, too." Kathy pushed herself up and looked down at her husband. "Chuck?"

He brought his head up and smiled at her. "Right behind you," he said.

———

"You said call anytime."

"I did," Treya said, "but I'm not sure I meant one o'clock. You're never out until one o'clock."

"Occasionally I am, as you can see. But I can hang up now and call you in the morning."

"Or you can just tell me what time you're getting down here, and then I can go back to sleep and wake up in time to greet you warmly."

"Well, on that . . . I thought you and the kids might want to consider coming back up here, get back to normal life."

She paused for a long beat. "You got your indictment and arrested Ro."

"No. Close, but better."

"What could be better?"

"If one of the maids he raped shot him."

"Are you kidding me?"

"Not even a little."

"He's dead?"

"Completely."

He heard her exhale. "I know I shouldn't be too happy about somebody dying, but . . ."

"There are cases it's warranted. This would be one of them. So, do you want to come home?"

She paused again. "What's the weather like?"

"Beautiful. Forty-five and pouring. What could be nicer?"

"Seventy-eight and sunny, for starters."

"Seventy-eight?"

"Scout's honor. Sixto told the kids we'd take them to the beach tomorrow. Do you realize we've never taken either of them to the beach?"

"I'm not surprised. Why would we?" It was Abe's turn to hesitate. "It's really going to be seventy-eight?"

"If not eighty."

A last pause, and then Glitsky said, "I'm on Southwest, landing in Burbank at eleven fifteen. Maybe you could pick me up?"

"Not impossible," Treya said. "I'll see what I can do."

38

Farrell crossed the threshold from the hallway inside to his outer office and stopped in his tracks. He broke a genuine smile, his hands outstretched with more than a bit of theatricality. "The sun shines, my secretary returns, Ro Curtlee is off to that big appellate court in the sky. Could life get any better?"

At her desk, Treya rose out of her chair. "There are a couple of bear claws on your table," she said. "Would that do?"

"It's a good start, anyway. Very nice. Thank you."

"You're welcome. They're by way of an apology. I'm sorry about the absences, just taking off like I did. I didn't mean to leave you in the lurch, but . . ."

He waved that off. "No explanation necessary, Treya." His expression sobered. "I should have taken it more seriously myself. Maybe sent Gert down to be with you."

"I'm so sorry about that."

"Me, too." His smile didn't quite take. "I try to console myself that she was some kind of a martyr to the cause. Cliff, that son of a bitch, killed her to try to scare me off, and it almost worked. Instead, much to my own surprise, it kicked me in the ass and got me moving. Although in the end, I guess, it didn't matter one way or the other."

"No. It mattered. Either way, it was going to end Friday night. You just provided the insurance."

"Maybe. That's another nice spin on it. But if somebody told me I could trade Gert's life for Ro's, I'm not sure I would have done it. Even though she was just an animal . . ."

"So was he."

"Well, there you go." Changing gears, he pointed toward his office. "Anything else I should know about in there, besides the bear claws?"

Treya glanced down at the book she kept next to her computer. "Vi Lapeer wanted to have a talk with you when you got in. Also Mr. Crawford."

"Himself?"

"In person. After that," Treya continued, "nothing else till ten, when you swear in the two new ADAs. Their names are in your folder. Then at noon, lunch with the Odd Fellows and a few words on disaster preparedness."

Farrell chortled. "My specialty."

"Don't worry. I got the talking points from the IO." This was the information office. "Again, it's all in the folder. Just don't forget the folder and you're golden. You want a cup of coffee?"

"A cup of coffee would be wonderful. And, Treya?"

"Sir?"

"Good to have you back."

———

Glitsky said, "I think I've got a vitamin D overdose, or hangover, or whatever you'd call it."

Dismas Hardy had a court appointment on this Monday morning, but things were dragging downstairs in the departments, and his hearing wasn't going to be called anytime soon. So he dropped in at Glitsky's office to share some peanuts and abuse with his friend. "You can't get a vitamin D overdose. And in my extensive research into hangovers, I haven't run across that one. What's it feel like?"

"Weird. It's like I'm almost, I don't know, happy, I guess."

"Wow." Hardy cracked a peanut. "That *would* be weird. And it's neat how you qualified the living shit out of it. Almost, you guess, you don't know. Bar the door, Katie, Glitsky's on a roll."

Glitsky ignored the derision. "I think it was the beach. All that sunshine."

"Hey, the sun is shining here, too."

Glitsky, with a dour look, glanced up and over at the high windows in his office. "Yeah, but here it's only fifty-two degrees. Down there it was eighty-two. That's thirty degrees difference."

"He excels at math, too. But it's a rare treat to see you even almost happy, I must say. You think it might also have something to do with the Curtlees?"

Glitsky chewed his own peanut. "I'm not ruling that out."

"So how many cases did that clear for you?"

"Well, not including the retrial, at least Felicia Nuñez and Matt Lewis and Janice Durbin. To say nothing of Gert, Wes's dog. Plus the damage Ro will never get a chance to do to Gloria Gonzalvez or her kids or my kids or anybody else."

Hardy hesitated for a minute. "Not to pick nits," he said, "but last time we talked, you had a small problem with Janice Durbin."

"Not really." Glitsky shook his head. "Mostly logistical. If we couldn't prove it to the grand jury. And now there's no need."

"Okay," Hardy said.

"Okay what?"

"Nothing." Another peanut. "I don't want to be the proximate cause of you lapsing back into your traditional funk."

"No chance. Right now I'm too high on life, too hooked on a feelin'."

Hardy sat back, grinning. "If you break into song, I swear to God I'm calling the paramedics."

"B. J. Thomas," Glitsky said.

"I know who it was. 'Raindrops,' 'Good Time Charlie.' I know every song the guy's ever sung."

"Of course you do. With your eidetic memory, I'd expect nothing less."

"Okay, then. With my eidetic memory, I need to tell you that I remember Ro Curtlee had apparent alibis both for Janice and Matt. That's not logistical, as you put it. That's factual."

"Well, then we'll never know for absolute sure, because his parents were it for Durbin, and his butler was it for Lewis. All three of them being dead, I choose to believe both alibis would fall apart under questioning. Sometimes you just take a free gift from the Almighty, bow your head, and say 'Thank you, Lord.' These cases are done, Diz, all closed up. And more power to 'em. That's what I'm sayin', know what I'm sayin'?"

"I'm not arguing," Hardy said. "You know best." He broke another grin. "As the great bass player Ray Brown once said: 'I just came to town to help with the fuckin'.' "

———

Amanda Jenkins felt about as attractive as a turnip.

She hadn't slept more than three hours at any stretch since she'd heard about Matt, and the past weekend—in spite of the apparent closure and cosmic justice represented by the deaths of the Curtlees and their butler— had been more grueling still. She had dated him for more than a year, but she had never met Matt's parents or his three sisters or his older brother. Nevertheless, on Saturday she'd been included in the extended family for the huge funeral Mass at Saints Peter and Paul at Washington Square, and then the burial down in Colma, after which she'd been seated between his mother, Nan, and his sister Paula at the reception at Fior d'Italia.

That had gone on until seven or so, and then she and Nan—by now her best friend—had gone out on an old-fashioned roaring drunk around North Beach, where they hooked up with some other assistant DAs and cops who'd also been at the funeral. In spite of the alcohol, or maybe because of it, she woke up before dawn yesterday, Sunday, and cried pretty much nonstop until the late afternoon, when her crushing hangover finally began to fade after a two-hour doze. She had moderated the drinking somewhat last night, ate some Chinese at home and then didn't fall asleep again until three A.M.

So when she got to the police lab at nine thirty, she knew she wasn't at or even near her physical peak. Still, you had to play the cards you got dealt, and she knew that her aces were her legs, so it would be foolish not to play them. She wore her shortest mini-skirt, dark green, under a severely plunging green pullover sweater. And three-inch heels. Checking herself in her mirror before she went out, she was reasonably certain that nobody was going to spend much time noticing the pallor of her face, the sag in her cheeks, the red in her eyes.

She'd handed in the request early Saturday morning, to one of the CSI guys, who promised he'd take it out to the lab as part of their general delivery. Glitsky had been right and there had been no legal issue at all with serving a search warrant at the Curtlee mansion. Amanda was still there, going on two o'clock in the morning, when they found the safe in Eztli's room and broke into it. What they found inside brought to six the number of handguns in the house—the Curtlee/Eztli murder weapon, the gun under Eztli's armpit, an S&W .357 in his safe, and three other pistols in another unlocked safe in the headboard of the Curtlees' bed. Four of the weapons were .40 caliber and could have been the weapon used to kill Matt Lewis.

For some reason, Amanda had become fixated on getting all the details right about Matt's murder. She thought she knew that Ro had killed him, but somehow it had become very important to her to make absolutely sure, if only so that it might help her better understand, although to understand precisely what was something she could not have elucidated.

From Linda Salcedo's statement, the murder weapon in Friday night's massacre had been Ro's personal gun, so what Amanda had requested was that the lab conduct a ballistics test with a bullet from that gun against the bullet that had killed Matt. Since she'd marked it as high priority and rush, she'd hoped to have it by first thing Monday morning, assumed that someone would have pulled some overtime to get it.

When she'd called at eight, hoping to get some results, they hadn't even started yet. When she got the name of the ballistics tech, Vincent J. Abbatiello, and realized that it was a guy who sounded on the phone to be about in his late twenties, probably straight if he was a cop, she'd reached for her miniskirt.

Now Abbatiello had invited her back with him, showing off the still relatively new lab in the department's Building 606 facility in Hunters Point Naval Shipyard with ill-concealed pride. This was an enormous and modern structure, a far cry from the tiny and cramped lab of the past. Amanda oohed and aahed her way along with him, and by the time they reached his area, what she wanted was his first priority.

Given that no one had seen fit to get to it over the weekend, Amanda was amazed at how little time it took. The lab really had modernized its capabilities, and the shooting and computer analysis of ballistics results took no more than five minutes per test, including shooting the gun and retrieving the bullet to test against the standard.

Fighting her nerves and the residual alcohol, the tension while she waited on the first test—with Ro's gun, a Smith & Wesson Military and Police semiautomatic 9 mm—was nearly unbearable. She sat next to the microscope that Abbatiello used and while he calibrated the machine, she had to lean over, her hands over her stomach. And the result of this first test was obvious, although not in the way she hoped. It was clearly a mismatch.

"Oh God," she said to Abbatiello. "How could that be?"

"It's all right. We got three more tries."

They got it on the second one.

———

Glitsky was down on the third floor in Amanda's office, leaning back against one of the counters with the door closed behind him. "Doesn't mean it wasn't Ro," he said.

"But it was this guy Ez's gun. I mean, it was in his safe. It's registered to him. He's got a carry permit. And while we're at it, tell me, would you, how in the world does that happen? How's a guy like this get a carry permit?"

"He's a citizen, right? Naturalized, but even so. He works in security. He's got no criminal record. But mostly, Cliff Curtlee is behind him pulling strings with just a tiny bit of influence. No problem."

"So here's the problem with that. I don't see him letting Ro shoot his gun. I don't know if I see anybody letting Ro even hold a gun, much less shoot it. He might point it back at you and pull the trigger just for jollies."

"He might." Glitsky chewed his cheek. "Any of Ro's prints on the gun itself?"

"No."

"Any of this other guy?"

"Several."

"Hm."

"So what's it mean, Abe? If Ro didn't shoot him . . ."

"For what it's worth, I think Ro probably shot him."

"I know. But what if he didn't? I mean, then what would that have all been about?" She was back on the verge of tears.

Glitsky couldn't offer much in the way of solace. "Look," he said, "whoever actually pulled the trigger, Ro was responsible for it. He's responsible for all of this."

———

Glitsky's vitamin D overdose, if that's what it was, had worn off completely by the time he stopped in front of Darrel Bracco's desk out in the middle of the homicide detail. His inspector was filling in an administrative report of some kind, engrossed in it, when Glitsky put a haunch on the corner of his desk, sat, and said, "I don't even want to start to tell you how much I don't want to ask you this question."

Bracco looked up. "Then don't."

"Yeah, but here's the deal. This morning I come in to work and the world is a rosy place. Ro Curtlee is out of our hair forever. All of his cases are closed. There's a high degree of certainty about all of this, right?"

"Right. As in none."

"Right. So then Amanda Jenkins gets into work this morning and she's been down at the lab doing ballistics on the bullet that killed her boyfriend."

"Okay."

"Actually not so okay. That bullet didn't in fact come from Ro's gun. It came from the bodyguard's gun."

Bracco clasped his hands behind his head. "Doesn't mean Ro wasn't shooting it."

"That's what I said, too. It doesn't mean Ro didn't shoot it. But you know what it does mean? It means it wasn't *definitely* Ro. It might have been the other guy, the butler."

Bracco snapped his fingers. "That's why he offered to take a polygraph. The son of a bitch would've passed it, too." He broke a sudden grin. "But here's the good news. Fourteen years a cop and I finally get to say 'the butler did it.' How cool is that?"

"I don't want it to have been the butler, so not very cool at all."

"I wouldn't worry about it, Abe. It probably was Ro. What does it matter anyway? Anybody it matters to is dead."

"Not true. It matters to me."

"Why?"

"Because I was completely and absolutely certain that Ro had killed Matt Lewis. I mean, he had motive. He had opportunity. He had the means. No question, he did it. Now there is doubt. Maybe not a lot of it, but real honest-to-God doubt. He might not have done it."

"But again, Abe, so what? Why does it matter now?"

"It matters now because now I'm starting to have doubts about the other case I was equally certain about. Janice Durbin."

"No," Bracco said. "There's no doubt there. With the shoes and the fire and then the paintings getting slashed. That was definitely Ro."

"Right," Glitsky said. "Except if he wasn't there."

"But he was."

"Well, remember your talk with him at Denardi's office, where he essentially admitted to killing Matt Lewis, when it turns out maybe not after all?"

"Sure. But I still think he pulled that trigger."

"Well, think it all you want, but he also in that same interview gave us an alibi for the morning of Janice Durbin's murder. You remember that?"

"Of course. His parents, the butler, and the maid."

"The maid," Glitsky said. "That would be Linda Salcedo, wouldn't it?"

Bracco sat all the way back in his chair; his eyes had closed. "This was the thing you didn't want to ask me."

" 'Didn't want' isn't strong enough."

"Then I'll say it again. Don't."

"I've got to. She's the last person in the world who'd want to give Ro an alibi for anything. She hasn't been to court yet and doesn't have a lawyer. I want you to go over to the jail and see if she'll talk to you. Ask her if she remembers any time Ro went out early in the last couple of weeks. She's already told us he's a late sleeper. If she corroborates his alibi . . . if he really couldn't have been there . . ."

"He was there, Abe, at Durbin's. He had to have been there."

"Yeah, I know. But it would be better if we made sure. Way better."

39

Jon Durbin got called out of his English class at eleven fifteen and was asked to report to the principal's office. When he got there and gave his name, the secretary instructed Jon to go to one of the counseling rooms down a short hallway off the main lobby. His stomach doing cartwheels and his head light—*what else could have happened now?*—he got down to the third doorway on his right and knocked once.

The door opened away from him and he stepped inside, not seeing his father until the door was nearly closed behind him. Jon looked from side to side in anger and frustration, trapped. "I don't have to stay here. Let me out."

Michael Durbin stood his ground, holding the door closed behind him. "I wanted to have a few words with you," he said, "after which you're free to go."

"I'm free to go now. I've got nothing to say to you."

"Well, that makes one of us. I've got something to say to you, short and sweet. I did not kill your mother. I don't know where you got that idea . . ."

"You don't? You don't think we all heard you fighting all the time?"

"It wasn't all the time. We were having some issues. That's what parents do sometimes. I did not kill her. We were trying to work things out so we could stay together. We got a little vocal from time to time."

"Ha. A little?"

"So what, Jon? Really, so what? The issues were serious. Okay?"

"I know what the issues were. Or rather, the main issue."

"You do? Maybe you could tell me, then."

"You and Liza, that's what. How's that?"

"Well, that's just completely wrong, is how that is." Michael's arms were crossed over his chest—protecting the door, protecting himself—and now he dropped them to his sides. "You think we could sit down a minute?"

The room held a table and four chairs. Jon hesitated, then finally sidestepped over to the nearest chair and lowered himself into it. His father pulled another chair from where it sat against the wall over to him. He wasn't going to leave an open shot at the door to his son. Now, though, seated in front of it, he came forward with his elbows on his knees and raised his eyes directly to Jon's. "I don't know how I'm going to convince you of this, but Liza is a friend of mine and that's all she is. That's all she has ever been."

"Yeah, right. You went over there the night after Mom's service. Are you gonna deny that, too?"

"No. I went there. I was in pain, Jon. I'm still in pain. I needed to talk to somebody and felt I'd dumped enough on Chuck and Kathy. I knew Liza would listen. Why is that so hard for you to understand? I'd think that you, of all people, would get it. You know who I am. You've always known who I am."

Michael's even tone was puncturing Jon's bubble of hostility. He sat back in his chair, hands folded in his lap, studying the floor. Finally he looked up. "Well, then, what was all the fighting about? With you and Mom?"

"I don't know which fights you're talking about exactly, but some of them were probably about money. Your mother wanted a bigger house, like Chuck and Kathy's. She wanted me to open another store if I could. I didn't want to do that. If anything, I wanted to work less and maybe get back to my painting. And that's the other thing; do you really believe I cut up my paintings?"

"I don't know. If it was the only way to get the cops off you."

"Jesus." Michael dropped his head and wagged it from side to side. "I don't know how I've failed you so badly that you could think I'd do any of this. I didn't, I swear to you. No Liza, no slashed paintings, no hurting your mother in any way."

"Then why couldn't you even say where you were that morning?"

"I was driving to work, thinking about work, about making more money, worried about your mother and me, and about Ro Curtlee being out of jail. I wasn't paying any attention to the drive, or the delays. Do you remember all the details about coming in to school today?"

"So who killed her, then?"

"Ro Curtlee killed her, Jon. I was the main reason he did all that time in prison, and he killed her and slashed my paintings to punish me. Why doesn't this make sense to you?"

"Because, Dad, he had a goddamn broken arm. How about that? It was all in the papers about the police breaking his arm when they arrested him. You don't strangle somebody if you've got a broken arm, not somebody like Mom anyway. She was strong, you know? She could still beat Peter at arm wrestling. So it just couldn't happen. And then who's that leave?" He slammed his palm flat against the surface of the table next to him, eyes filled with rage and confusion. "You don't think I haven't thought enough about this? You think I want to believe that my father . . . that he'd do this and so fuck up all our lives? So if it's not Ro Curtlee, who's that leave, huh? Especially when you can't remember what you did that morning . . ."

"I did remember! I do remember. It just didn't come to me when it should have."

"Don't you hear yourself? That is so fucking lame . . ."

"It's what it was, Jon. It's just what it was." Afraid that he was losing him again, and maybe for the last time, Michael came forward in his chair. "Listen," he said, "listen." Urgently, quietly. "You're not going to want to hear this, but it wasn't me having an affair."

"Are you saying it was Mom?"

"Your mother, yes."

"Bullshit."

"No. True. Just so you know somebody else is in the picture."

"Who?"

"We don't know. Inspector Glitsky doesn't know. Maybe one of her patients. But the bad news about that is that with Ro dead, Glitsky's not going to be looking very hard anymore. He thinks it was Ro."

"He can't think that. It's too damn convenient and beyond that, it doesn't make any sense."

"He thinks it does. But the bottom line is we may never know who killed her. And that just kills *me*, but it might be true." He reached a hand across and touched his son's knee. "Come back home, Jon. Please."

Jon's mouth stayed tight, his posture rigid, not committing to anything. Tears pooled in the corners of his eyes and overflowed.

"Where have you been staying, anyway?"

"Rich's."

"They said you weren't there."

"I know."

Michael's frustration with Rich's family forced a breath out of him. "Well, we're moving out of Chuck and Kathy's and into a motel on Wednesday. I think it's time we started trying getting along again as a family. Do you think you could do that?"

Angrily Jon brushed away where his tears had wet his cheeks. "I don't know, Dad. All I know is I want to kill whoever killed her."

"I do, too, Jon. I do, too. And I swear to God, that wasn't me. It wasn't me. I need you to believe me. Do you think you can do that?"

Jon slumped back and crossed his arms, his face set in a mask. After a few long beats, Michael realized that this was the best he was going to get from his son today, and he stood up, laid a hand gently on his shoulder, and walked out the door.

———

Darrel Bracco phrased his questions to Linda Salcedo in such a way that she had no idea he was inquiring as to the alibi of Ro Curtlee on the morning of Janice Durbin's death. He let her believe he was getting general background about daily life in the Curtlee mansion, and she had been unwaveringly certain: Since he'd been released on bail the first time, and except for when he'd been in police custody and on one other morning last week, Ro Curtlee had spent every night in his bedroom, and had never gotten up before nine or nine thirty in the morning. Linda remembered specifically because she herself was up at six thirty, starting her cleaning upstairs before coming down to help with breakfast. She passed directly in front of Ro's room every morning, knocking quietly, then opening the door a crack to look in and see if he'd gotten up so that she could clean up in that room and make the bed. But no, he'd been in there every day. Definitely. And had appeared downstairs either during or after the Curtlees' having their breakfast.

This was not the news Glitsky wanted to hear.

After Bracco left his office, Glitsky sat in a blue funk for nearly a half hour. Finally he got up and went around his desk to the whiteboard where he kept his list of active cases and inspector assignments. In the clean white space that only this morning had held the name Felicia Nuñez, he wrote the name Janice Durbin in large block letters, and then across from it in the empty rectangle on the right—GLITSKY.

———

It was going to be a long, slow haul getting a special master appointed by a judge to go through the patient files in Janice Durbin's office and try to find evidence of a carnal relationship between the psychiatrist and someone who was seeing her professionally. It could take weeks, even months, and still in the end yield nothing— for the truth remained that there was a whole universe of men and even women who might have been intimately involved with Janice Durbin, and none of them her patients.

And that was if, in fact, it had not been Michael Durbin who'd been having the affair, contracted chlamydia, and killed his wife— perhaps even by accident—when she'd become infected and fought with him over it. Of course, to believe that Michael Durbin had killed his wife, Glitsky would have to believe that he'd also slashed his own works of art, but this was just the sort of almost unfathomable subterfuge he might in fact expect from a desperate killer.

In any event, he'd already let too much time go by because of his insistence upon the guilt of Ro Curtlee. This was the eleventh day after Janice's death, and to say that the trail had gone cold was a significant understatement.

At 2:40, having spent an hour on his paperwork for a search warrant and special master request, Glitsky found himself in the hallway of the block-long, low-rise stucco professional building about midway between the Stonestown Mall and San Francisco State University where Janice Durbin had had her office. It was a relatively modern building with no apparent frills. Janice had practiced in suite 204, just across from the elevator on the second floor, and Glitsky now stood outside of that suite, in the hallway, peering into it through the half-open gray venetian blinds. Unless he was missing something, and he didn't think he was, he could see the entire office.

There was no reception area, simply a couple of functional couches, one along the right wall and one under the wide, rectangular window—its blinds, too, half open—that made up most of the back wall. On the left, a low dark wood credenza looked like it probably held her files. Facing the two couches was a large red-leather lounge chair, with a telephone table and a floor lamp next to it. A large purple beanbag chair sat in the far corner. Some framed pictures hung on the walls on either side, but the glare from the outside window kept him from seeing what kind of art she'd hung there.

It wouldn't matter too much, he thought. The place was clean, uncluttered, basic.

"Can I help you?"

Glitsky straightened and turned to face an attractive, professionally dressed, heavyset black woman who looked to be somewhere in her late twenties. Introducing himself and proffering his badge, he said, "As you may know, Dr. Durbin was murdered a little over a week ago. I was hoping to talk to some of her neighbors in this building, see if somebody might be able to throw some light on the investigation."

"In what way?"

"In any way, really. We haven't gotten very far yet. Did you know Dr. Durbin?"

"Not exactly. Just, you know, in the ladies', or passing in the hallway. I couldn't believe when we heard what happened. Nobody could. You never think that kind of thing could happen to somebody you know. Or like her."

"How was she, then?"

"Oh, you know. Polite, sweet, classy, down-to-earth. Just a regular person."

"Do you know if she had any particular friends here in this building? People she hung out with?"

"Not really, no. Not saying she didn't, just if she did I didn't know about it. It's not like we're all one big office here, as you probably figured out already. Everybody's got their own, mostly. I'm with Bayview Security, down at the end there at two-oh-seven. Although Dr. Mitchell downstairs, he's a dentist actually. He's got his own big triple suite. But he's about the biggest. Lots of equipment, you know. Probably the main reason the building needs a security service, although we're here for everybody."

"Well, thank you," Glitsky said. "Maybe I'll just knock on a few doors. Would that be all right with you?"

"You go ahead," she said. "Good luck to you."

———

Starting at 201 on the opposite side of the hall, Glitsky worked his way quickly down to 215, then started up Janice Durbin's side, which faced west over the back parking lot. As he'd been warned, there wasn't much in the way of information. Six of the offices housed therapists or counselors of one kind or another, and two of those were in session on his first pass, but none of the other four, nor the people in the insurance office in 203, knew Janice any more than the first woman he'd met in the hallway.

It was the same on Janice's side until he got to 208, a Pilates studio. Glitsky almost gave it a pass, figuring that it would be a room where people just showed up as they would at a gym, willy-nilly. He didn't even know if a specific tenant ran the place. In the end, though, being thorough, he knocked.

Even with no discernible makeup and a light sheen from sweating, the woman who opened the door nearly tied his tongue in knots. Clad only in a red leotard, she wore her blond hair shoulder length, held back with a red headband. It showed off the broad, fair forehead over eyes of pure jade. Perhaps in her early forties, she had trace lines at the corners of those distinctive eyes, but otherwise her face might have belonged to a twenty-year-old. "Hi," she said, extending her hand. "I'm Holly."

"Hello." Glitsky shook her hand, showed his badge, kept it simple. "I'm Abe Glitsky, with San Francisco homicide. Can you answer a few questions?"

She cast a glance back over her shoulder at the obviously empty studio and shrugged. "Sure. This must be about Janice, right?" And then suddenly her incredible eyes flashed. "That fucker."

The vehemence surprised Glitsky. "You mean Dr. Durbin?"

"No, no, no." Hands waving in front of her face. "Of course I don't mean Janice. I mean that fucker who killed her."

"So you knew her?"

"Yes. I mean, not that we'd been friends a long time—I just started the studio here two months ago—but she was . . . I thought we were going to be friends forever, you know how that is. You meet somebody, wham, right?"

"Actually not too often," Glitsky said.

"No. I know what you mean. Not too darned often."

"So you felt you were getting to know her well?"

She nodded, now dead somber. "I thought she was starting to be my best friend. Some days she'd get an hour or two between appointments and she'd come down here, and as you can see, it gets a little slow here, too. So we'd just talk."

"What about?"

"Everything. Kids, staying in shape, getting old, running your own business, books, movies. You name it, we talked about it."

"Men?"

She cocked her head to one side. "Sure."

"Not just her husband?"

"Not always, no." Shifting her weight from one foot to the other, she added, "I guess what you want to know is was she seeing someone else. She was."

"One of her patients, did she say?"

"No. I mean, yes, she did say. No, not one of her patients."

"You're sure?"

"Unless she was lying to me, which she wasn't."

"So who was he? Did you ever meet him? Or see him?"

"No."

"Did she ever mention him by name?"

"No. She really wasn't comfortable talking about it. It was like she didn't want it to be happening, but she didn't know how she could stop. She wasn't really proud of it."

"So she wanted it to stop?"

"I don't know. I don't think so, really. She was just mostly worried that she'd get caught. She didn't want to lose her family life. And her husband. But she was infatuated with the guy, even though she was pretty sure he was a player."

"A player?"

"You know. Lots of partners. A player."

"Lots of partners? Where would he get lots of partners?"

The question clearly amused her. "Hello? A straight guy in San Francisco? Finding partners isn't your problem, trust me. You look a little frustrated."

Glitsky nodded. "I am. If this guy wasn't one of her patients, I've got basically no place to start looking for him. He could be anywhere."

"You think he's the guy who killed her?"

"I think he might have a motive, or given her husband one. Either way, I'd like to find him. Do you know where they hooked up? Some motel, maybe? An apartment?"

"Why?"

"If he used a credit card, we got him. If he paid cash, he had to show an ID and they keep it on file. I'm grasping at straws here."

After a small silence, she said, "If it's any help, Janice told me he came by here a few times after hours. Maybe somebody would have seen him then."

"I'll be sure to ask," Glitsky said. And then, berating himself for not getting to any of this much earlier, he thanked Holly and continued on his door-to-door down the hallway. In the end, he'd spoken to a living person in every one of the twenty-two businesses in the building, and except for Holly, no one had known Janice Durbin as other than a professional acquaintance.

40

Waiting for Michael Durbin to get back to the Novios' after his day of work, Glitsky sat alone for the moment at the dining room table with a cup of tea that Kathy had brewed for him. Then she appeared in the doorway leading to the kitchen with a platter that held a plate of cookies and a china cup of coffee on a matching saucer. Glitsky watched her place the tray down on the table. Sitting across from him, she picked up her cup and saucer as though afraid that it would shatter.

"How are you holding up?" Glitsky asked her gently.

She gave him a weak smile. "Is it that obvious? Every minute I feel like I'm going to break. She wasn't only my sister, you know. She was my best friend."

"Have you thought about talking to somebody?"

"A grief counselor, you mean?" She shook her head. "I've had a couple of my other friends recommend that. Maybe I should look into it. Although something tells me that what it's going to take, mostly, is time. Which right now seems to have stopped moving, so it feels kind of hard to depend on."

"It can seem like that, I know."

She lifted her cup, put it back down. "That sounds like experience talking."

He nodded. "My first wife," he said. "Cancer."

"I'm sorry."

Glitsky shrugged. "It was a long time ago."

"It sounds like it still hurts."

"There are moments. Mostly, though, you remember the good times."

"The good times. Sometimes you feel like they're never going to come back. Like it's completely impossible."

"I know."

"I mean, when I think of how it was even so recently. Here we are, me and Chuck and the girls, sitting here around this table, no more than a month ago. Everybody getting along, everybody laughing and loving one another. And here I am, about to turn forty next week, and Chuck made up this song they were all going to sing at my big old monster birthday party we were going to have. 'Old, old, really old,' or something like that, the chorus, you know. 'Really, really, really old.' Then the girls each wrote their own verse, just cruel and witty and funny as hell. We were all cracking up. And now I see the girls all just so sad, and me and Chuck in this awful funk." She stared across at him. "The idea that we could ever have a time like that again, carefree and happy, it just doesn't seem possible." Suddenly she straightened up, dabbing at her eyes with her napkin. "I'm sorry," she said. "You don't need to hear this."

"It's fine," he said. "It's part of it."

"I don't know how you do it." She brought her coffee up and sipped at it. "All the victims and their families. They're all like us a little, aren't they?"

"A little. Everybody deals with it in their own way, but it's never easy."

"That must be good for your motivation. In your job, I mean. The pain of the victims."

Glitsky felt the impulse to smile and resisted it. "It's a factor," he said.

They both went to their drinks and sipped. "Can I ask you another question?" Kathy asked.

"I don't know that you've asked even one yet, but go ahead."

"What are you here to talk to Michael about? I thought it was pretty clear that this, that Janice, was Ro Curtlee."

Glitsky killed a couple of seconds with his tea. Then, "There are some unresolved issues."

"Like what?" She brought her hand up to her mouth. "You mean it might not have been Ro? You can't think it was Michael, do you?"

"Not necessarily. I've got some questions for him, that's all."

She put her arms out on the table. "He didn't do this, Inspector. You don't know him. He couldn't have. He loved Janice."

"All right."

"That's not really an answer."

"I'm sorry," Glitsky said. "I don't really have a better one."

———

"She had chlamydia," Glitsky said.

They were in the library/office, the door closed to keep them out of earshot of the rest of the household. Glitsky half leaned, half sat against Chuck's desk while Michael sat at one end of the leather couch, his feet up on the coffee table.

"What?" And now he brought them down as he came forward to the edge of the couch. "What does that mean?"

"It's a sexually transmitted—"

"No, no. I know what chlamydia is. You're saying that Janice had it?"

"You didn't know this?"

"No. How would I—?"

"If we subpoena your medical records, we wouldn't find that you'd had yourself treated for chlamydia?"

"Absolutely not. How did you find this out?"

"The autopsy."

"Why didn't you tell me?"

"At the time, we thought it might save you from some pain. That's when we thought Ro Curtlee had killed her."

"You don't still think that?"

"Not so much. His alibi stands up. He wasn't there."

"I wasn't, either."

"That's what you've said. Did Janice tell you she had an STD?"

"No. I've told you. We hadn't had sex for two months. Which is one reason why I thought she was having an affair. So now I know why the sex stopped, don't I? I would have gotten the chlamydia, and then would have known for sure, wouldn't I?"

"And knowing for sure about that, and knowing all about how Ro Curtlee set up his victims, and also knowing that he was out on bail . . . if you were going to make it look like him, you should have gotten in touch with Ro and made sure he didn't have a solid alibi. Maybe invited him to come by your house on some pretext, planted something to look like he'd been there . . ." Glitsky stared down at him, waiting.

Michael Durbin met his gaze. "You know, Lieutenant, I agreed to meet you voluntarily tonight, but I've got to tell you, I'm not going to listen to this. I'm trying to keep my family together and deal with the tragedy of my wife's death, and I just don't have the energy to argue with you anymore about it. If you're going to arrest me, find some evidence and take me downtown. Otherwise, get the hell out of my face so I can go back to trying to live my life and make it worth something."

———

At dinner, all eight of the extended family about to start digging into the huge platter of spaghetti and meatballs at the big table, Michael clinked his wineglass and drew a shaky breath. "First," he said, "before we move out of here on Wednesday, all of us Durbins want to thank all of you Novios for your incredible generosity in letting us share your home these past ten days. It makes us realize that this is what family is all about. Hanging in there together when the times are hardest.

"Second," he went on, "here's to Jon for coming back to us."

Michael looked at his oldest son. "I know you've still got reservations, but I'm confident they're all going to get resolved. I want to thank you for putting your trust back in me."

Michael held Jon's eye, knowing that this little speech was mostly for the benefit of Peter and the girls, to calm the waters. Jon didn't look exactly like he was sold on his father's story, but for the moment he was giving it the benefit of the doubt, and Michael felt that was good enough—in any event, it was all he was going to get. His glance went over to Peter. "And to both of you boys for burying the hatchet."

"And finally," Kathy put in, "can I just say? Here's to Janice. We will always love you and miss you."

"Hear, hear," Chuck intoned and tipped his glass.

"And now," Kathy said. "Let's start passing the food before it gets cold."

But the pasta platter hadn't even gone halfway around the table when Jon spoke up. "So, Dad, what did Glitsky want to talk to you about?"

Michael made a face. "He's frustrated that he can't seem to put Ro Curtlee at our house that morning."

"Why not?" Chuck asked.

"Well, evidently his housekeeper says he was at home and Glitsky believes her. So now he needs something he can point at and prove to shut up his critics. He's taking a lot of flak about Ro, that he blamed everything on him without any real evidence to back him up."

"And how are you going to make any difference about that?" Jon asked.

"I can't," Michael said. "He's got the same problem with me, but it seems to me like he's getting desperate. Like he's got to have a different story to tell pretty soon or he's in big trouble himself." He put his fork down. "In fact," he went on, "I was hoping to not get into this discussion, but I might as well say it. I don't think it's entirely out of the question that Glitsky might decide to arrest me."

"Daddy, no!" Allie cried. She jumped up out of her chair and came around to put her arms around her father. "How can he do that? You didn't do anything."

"That's right. I didn't do anything, so there's no way he can prove that I did, but we'll need to all stand together"—he looked from Jon to Peter—"especially you kids, if he does come after me."

"You don't really believe he'll do that, do you?" Kathy asked.

"I don't see how he can with no evidence. But he was planning on arresting Ro with just about as much. I don't know what he's going to do. I doubt even if he does. But it would be a good idea if we were a little prepared."

"The power of the police," Chuck said, "it's scary."

———

Michael and Chuck sat at the kitchen counter with the remains of their wine while Kathy did the dishes. The kids had dispersed back into the house to start packing for the move on Wednesday and to start their homework. The talk about his possible, if improbable, arrest had seemed to grow weightier on Michael throughout dinner, and he was now on his sixth glass of wine, staring into the glass.

"I don't know what I'd do with the kids," he was saying.

"Don't be silly," Kathy replied. "You know we'd take them again."

A bitter laugh. "Just what you guys need. Five kids instead of two."

"We'd take them in a minute, Michael," Chuck said. "But it's not going to happen."

"I'm glad you're so sure."

"You said it yourself. He can't have any evidence against you since you didn't do anything. No evidence, no trial."

"Yeah, but even if I'm arrested, all that time before the trial I'm in jail."

Kathy jumped in at that. "We'd bail you out, Michael."

"Thank you, but only if you could."

"Well," Chuck said, "that's putting the cart way before the horse at this point. I don't believe Glitsky's anywhere near arresting you."

"I was with him today, Chuck. I heard him. He's closer than you think. And forget about me, what would that do to the kids? Jon already thinks it might have been me. If I lost all of them over this . . ." He picked up his glass and took a drink. "I don't know what I'd do. I couldn't let them see me go through it."

"Sure you could," Kathy said. "You'd fight it. We'd all fight it."

"I don't know if it would be worth it."

"Of course it would." Kathy came around the edge of the counter and picked up Michael's still half-full glass, then kissed him on the cheek, and went back around to the sink. She poured out the wine. "It's obvious that this red stuff isn't helping your state of mind at the moment. First, nobody's going to arrest you. And if they do, we're all on your side to get you back out. Okay? You hear me?"

"Okay." He let out a deep sigh. "I'm just so tired. Tired of the suspicion, tired of my son's doubts, tired of Glitsky and of living without Janice. Of living, period."

"Don't say that, Michael."

He looked up at her with an unfocused, bleary-eyed gaze. "Oh, okay, then," he said. "I won't."

———

With a stifled cry, Glitsky jerked and sat up straight in bed, his hand over his heart. His breathing came in heavy gasps.

Beside him, Treya was immediately awake, one hand on his back, the other reaching around to rest over his heart. "Babe, what is it? Are you all right?"

He shook his head from side to side and kept taking heavy breaths.

"Abe! Answer me. Is it your heart again? Should I call nine-one-one?"

He finally got out some words. "No. No, I'm okay. I'm okay." He took another enormous breath and let it out completely. "I've just got to get up." Starting to rise.

"No, you don't. Just stay here. Lie back down."

"I can't."

"Yes, you darn well can. Calm down."

But he stayed in a seated position. Gradually he brought a hand up and covered where his wife still had her hand pressed against his heart. "Okay," he said again, as if to himself. "Okay."

Treya whispered. "So what was that if it wasn't a heart attack? A nightmare?"

"Not a nightmare," Glitsky said. "I wasn't asleep."

"So what is it?"

"Janice Durbin," he said. "Just another something I missed, but this one could be real." He turned back to her. "I've got to get up."

"Abe, it's the middle of the night. What are you going to do?"

"I don't know, but sleep's out of the question."

41

He was waiting in the spacious back parking lot to Janice Durbin's office building and saw the African American woman he'd met before get out of her own car at a few minutes before eight. Summoning all of the patience he possessed, Glitsky gave her another ten minutes to let her get settled, and then he went to the door and into the building, heading upstairs again to suite 207.

She recognized him right away, greeting him with a warm smile. "But I'm sorry, I don't remember your name."

"Glitsky," he told her. "Lieutenant Abe Glitsky."

"And I'm Roberta. So what can I do for you, Lieutenant Abe Glitsky?"

"Well, you'll remember yesterday I was asking about who in the building might have known or been close to Janice Durbin. It turns out that might not have been the right question. I talked to Holly down the hall and she told me that Janice had admitted to her that she was seeing someone outside of her marriage, and that that person had apparently come by here to this building after hours, maybe several times. So I noticed you seem to have video cameras mounted over the doors and I wonder if one of them might have picked up a picture of either this guy or his car."

Roberta scrunched up her face in disappointment. "This would have been more than a week ago, then, wouldn't it?"

"Right. At least eleven days, maybe a lot more."

She tsked. "I'm sorry, but I don't think you're going to be in luck.

We're on a seven-day cycle on this building and most of the others we monitor. If we're going to need to identify somebody, usually we know the next day, if you know what I mean. When the robbery or vandalism is reported. Three days at the most, if it's over a weekend. You're sure it would have been that long ago?"

"At least, I'm afraid." Glitsky's mouth tightened in frustration. "Would you mind telling me how else you monitor the building? I notice you've got alarms at the doors. People punch in a code when they go in or out?"

"Right. But that's only for off-hours. Normal business hours, we're wide-open." Roberta suddenly perked up, snapping her fingers. "But wait, here's something else, maybe." She got up from behind her desk and walked over to a bank of filing cabinets against Glitsky's right-hand wall. "We've got a nighttime drive-by service every two hours from six P.M. to eight A.M. That's every night. Physical inspection of the building and parking lot. Patients and clients and tenants are welcome to use the lot whenever they need to, but generally at night it's pretty empty. And if it's a non-tenant car, they make a note of it—license number, make, and model. Or they're supposed to." She reached into the file and pulled out two relatively thin binders. "Here's the hard-copy reports from January and last December. February's probably still out with the unit. You're welcome to look at them."

———

At a quarter to four that afternoon, Novio turned his cell phone on as soon as he got back to his office from his last class. "Chuck. It's Michael," he heard. Durbin's voice on his voice mail was hoarse with emotion. "Please call me as soon as you get this. It's urgent."

Frowning at the tension in his brother-in-law's voice, he hit the "call back" graphic on his iPhone and waited for the connection.

It came before the end of the first ring. "Chuck. Thank God. Where are you?"

"My office. Just finishing up."

"Can you meet me at Janice's right away?"

"Janice's office?"

"Yeah."

"Sure. What's wrong?"

"Everything. I just talked to Glitsky. I think he's coming down to your house to arrest me. I had to get out of there. I'm not going to jail." A pause. "I've got my shotgun with me."

Novio swore. Then, "Don't do anything stupid, Michael. I'll be right there. Hang tight."

———

Less than ten minutes later, Chuck knocked on Janice's office door.

"Come on in."

Michael sat back, his hands clasped in his lap, at one end of the couch that was under the window. His face looked pasty, drawn with fatigue and stress. His shotgun lay on the top of the file cabinets next to him, the barrels broken open, the brass backs of the shells visible in them.

The weapon was loaded.

Chuck's eyes went quickly from Michael over to the shotgun, then back to Michael. Carefully he closed the door after him, then turned back. "What are you doing?" he said, motioning toward the gun. "What's that thing doing here?"

"I told you I'm not going to jail, Chuck."

"Of course you're not."

"No. I mean I *really* wasn't going to jail. If Glitsky was coming down for me, I wasn't going to give him the satisfaction. I wasn't going to let him put the kids through the whole ordeal of a trial, with me a murder suspect."

"The kids would be fine through it, Michael. They'd be way worse if you weren't there for them at all."

"I'm not sure that's true."

"Well, I'm telling you it is." Chuck half turned and lowered himself down onto the front edge of the leather lounge chair. "We'll get you the best lawyer in town and . . ."

But Michael was holding up a hand, shaking his head no. "That's not happening. In fact, none of this is happening."

"None of what? What do you mean?"

"I mean I came down here thinking it would be a good place to end things, you know? A little symmetry. Janice betrayed me and I splash my brains all over her office. You see what I'm saying?"

"There's no reason to end things, Michael. If you didn't do it . . ."

"What do you mean, *if* I didn't do it?" Michael moved up to the front edge of the couch, his voice raspy. "You of all people know goddamn well I didn't do it. And you know why you know that?"

"No, I don't." Chuck was the picture of rational calm and concern for his brother-in-law. "Except that I believe you if you say it wasn't you."

Michael all but collapsed back on the couch. "God, you're good," he said.

Like an inquisitive bird, Chuck cocked his head to one side. "What are you talking about, Michael? Good at what?"

Regaining his composure, Michael straightened up. "Maybe it was actually getting close to thinking I was going to end my life over this, Chuck. What a goddamn waste that would be when I knew I was innocent. So while I was sitting here trying to rationalize myself out of it, my brain must have gone into high gear and I remembered something you said."

"Something I said?"

Michael nodded. "That first weekend after Janice was killed. You told me that Glitsky had asked you about all these cell phone calls to and from you on Janice's phone, and you'd told him that you were both planning a surprise party for Kathy's birthday, that was the reason for them. You remember that?"

"Sure."

"Well, the thing is, Chuck, you in fact weren't planning a surprise party for Kathy. Janice wasn't planning a surprise party for
Kathy."

Chuck put on a rueful expression. "I know," he said. "She found
out about it and we had to cancel the surprise part. I don't see
anything sinister in that. I wasn't hiding anything."

"No? That's funny, because once I started thinking about those
phone calls, that it might have been you who was having the affair
with Janice . . ."

Stung with a cattle prod, Chuck held up both hands. "Whoa.
You're out of your mind, Michael. Janice and I didn't—"

Michael cut him off. "So I started thinking you two must have
been meeting all those nights she told me she was out with her
patients and you were at school, working late. And where would
those meetings have been? Probably right here. And since I was
down here anyway, I went to the security office, just down the
hall, just a couple of hours ago. Did you know they keep track of
the nontenant cars that are parked here at night? Hard-copy records, Chuck. With license plate numbers. How about that? So are
you going to try to tell me you were visiting somebody else in this
building all those times? Or maybe you had become one of Janice's
patients? And you certainly got here fast enough when I called you
today, didn't you? No directions needed."

Both men were breathing hard in the tense silence. After a long
moment, something went out of Chuck's shoulders. "We didn't
plan it, Michael," he said. "It was just one of those things that happened. We were trying to stop. We didn't want it to hurt anybody
in the families. I am so, so sorry."

Crushed by the enormity of this admission, Michael hung his
head. When he looked up again, he asked in a hoarse whisper. "So
why did you have to kill her?"

Chuck's eyes went wide as if he couldn't believe the accusation.

"Michael, I didn't kill her. I swear to God. I had no reason to kill her. I loved her."

"You loved her, but you were fucking someone else, too?"

"I wasn't . . ."

"Chuck, she had chlamydia. She didn't get it from a toilet seat and she didn't get it from me. You gave it to her. So who gave it to you? One of your students?"

Chuck held Michael's gaze until it became too much for him, and this time it was Chuck who hung his head, letting out a deep sigh. Looking back up, he saw that Michael was wiping tears from his eyes. Suddenly as quick as the strike of a snake, he bolted from the chair and reached out across the small room, getting his hands on the shotgun, snapping the barrels shut, and bringing it to bear on Michael's chest.

"You fucking idiot," he said. "You stupid, meddling fool." He let out a one-note bitter laugh. "You and Janice deserve each other. You want to know what happened? One of my students happened to go to her for counseling, fed her a load of shit about being exploited."

Novio kept talking, working himself up. "All they wanted was their fucking As, you know. They were happy as hell to trade a little tail for it. But Janice thought that was *wrong*. That wasn't just fucking. That was taking advantage of the poor students."

His knuckles were growing white holding the shotgun. "So now it's not just being mad at me, it's a moral crusade. And do you know what she was going to do? She was going to go not just to Kathy, but to the school, the dean. You hear that?"

"Sure. I hear it."

"Well, that would have been it for me. *You get it?* Turns out the little bitch was seventeen. Like I knew."

Lowering his voice, he drove in the last nail. "And that's statutory rape, my friend. Janice was going to call the cops and have them put me in jail. She wouldn't even admit it was personal. She kept saying that as a therapist, she was mandated to report sexual abuse."

Michael sat back on the couch, his eyes trained on the twin barrels. "So what are you going to do now? Kill me, too?"

Chuck let out another humorless laugh. "Me? I'm not going to do anything. I'm afraid I'm going to have not gotten here fast enough. I was just coming through the door when my poor brother-in-law, thinking he was about to get arrested for killing his wife, blew himself away."

Chuck advanced a step. "And, by the way, thanks for the tip about there being no good forensic record with a shotgun." Coming closer, now within a couple of feet, he cocked back both hammers and went down to one knee. "I like this lower angle," he said. "Like you put the thing up to your own throat."

And he pulled both triggers.

———

Glitsky had started to lead Bracco and the three other inspectors in their charge to the door of Janice Durbin's office before they heard the pop and came barreling in with their weapons drawn.

"Throw down the gun and put up your hands!" Glitsky yelled. "The gun!"

Chuck Novio dropped the shotgun to the floor with a heavy thud. He stood there, staring down at an unharmed Michael Durbin as though he were looking at a ghost. "What the hell?"

Pairs of strong hands took each of his arms, jerked them back behind his back, and fastened them together with handcuffs.

Glitsky was already around Novio next to Durbin on the couch, looking for signs of burns or other damage.

"I think I'm okay," Durbin said. "Maybe a little deaf."

"You did good," Glitsky said. "You did amazing."

Behind them, Bracco was telling Chuck Novio that he was under arrest, that he had the right to remain silent, that anything he said could and would be used against him.

Glitsky turned back to Durbin. "Sorry we didn't get in sooner. We thought he'd give a little more warning but he moved too fast. But the good news is you're okay and we got it all. Quite a confession."

As the inspectors marched Novio out of the room and down to the waiting car, Durbin tried to get to his feet, but found that he didn't have the strength. "I've just got to sit here a minute, Lieutenant," he said. "I can't seem to get my legs to work. I feel like I might faint. Jesus Christ. Poor Kathy. Those poor girls."

"Take a deep breath," Glitsky said. "Put your head down between your knees. You'll get all the time you need to think about it later. For the time being, though, you're a bona fide hero."

"I don't feel anything like a hero."

"Well, join the club," Glitsky said. "Most of 'em don't."

42

"There was no evidence," Glitsky said. "Even after I thought it probably was him, I needed evidence. I had to trick him."

He was in a booth at Lou the Greek's two days later. It was after the lunch hour, and hence there was no pressure to order the special (yeanling clay bowl for the second time in two weeks), so Abe was drinking iced tea. Across the table, Vi Lapeer and Amanda Jenkins sipped their Diet Cokes. It wasn't altogether a casual meeting. Lapeer had come up to Glitsky's office needing to understand why he'd done what he'd done so that she could go and defend it to Leland Crawford, while Jenkins—who'd drawn the prosecution case against Chuck Novio—simply wanted to get all the information she could on general principles.

"But what made you even think of him in the first place?" Lapeer asked.

"Well, I didn't remember it right away, in fact almost not at all, but he told me a lie. The very first time I talked to him, I asked him about him being all over Janice's cell phone, and he said he and Janice were planning a surprise party for his wife. But later his wife, Kathy, was telling me about how they were all planning for her big monster blowout fortieth birthday party. She was in on it, so it wasn't a surprise, now, was it? Luckily the contradiction came back to me."

Lapeer still didn't like it. "And on that one lie, Abe, you risk a citizen's life?"

"Well, two things. First it wasn't just the one lie. The lie got me to wondering about Novio and Janice, which led to his car in her parking lot."

"Still a long way from murder."

"Granted. And I wouldn't have risked any life on it, civilian or otherwise, if that was all I had. But it wasn't. Once I was up and had Novio on my mind, and I admit I was desperate with Mr. Crawford and the Curtlees and all that, I surfed the Web about half the night. Novio's got about fifteen thousand hits on Google."

"Thousand?" Jenkins asked.

Glitsky nodded, sipped his tea. "So naturally I just found what I wanted in five minutes or so."

Jenkins stared at him. "You're kidding."

"Yes," Glitsky said. "It was more like three hours, and even then it was lucky."

"I'm sorry, Abe, but what were you looking for?" Lapeer asked.

"Anything, nothing, I didn't know. All I know is that if somebody lies to me during an investigation, there's usually a reason. And his lie was deliberate around a woman who I knew was having an affair."

Jenkins got him back on point. "So what'd you find?"

"A couple of articles in a small New England newspaper in 1995 about this scandal they evidently were having where Novio was named as one of the professors who was selling grades for sex. The second article just said that all the charges had been withdrawn and a settlement reached."

Jenkins nodded. "They hushed it up, paid off the girl, and shipped him out to San Francisco with great recommendations."

"That's what I think," Glitsky said. He chewed some of his ice. "So, Chief, I had Janice's affair, Novio's past sex with coeds, the chlamydia, and the lie. So I went to Janice's office and found out he'd been parking there after hours, basically your smoking gun.

So I had the affair with Janice, but still no evidence and no murder."

"Okay," Lapeer said. "This is where it gets squirrelly. So then you go to Michael Durbin? Why him?"

"His wife was the victim, Chief. He wanted to catch the killer, no matter who it was. You want to know the truth, I came up with the wire idea, okay, but he's the one who came up with the shotgun, which was just brilliant. And remember, Novio would never have admitted any part of this if we interrogated him, even if we had him dead to rights on the affair. To get him to talk about the murder, it had to be with someone he didn't suspect."

"But it could have killed him, Durbin."

Glitsky shook his head. "Not really. Not even probably. Not with empty shells in the shotgun. At the worst, he could have maybe gotten burned."

"Badly burned. And sued the city for a zillion dollars."

"True." He met the chief's eyes. "Entirely possible, but to tell you the truth, I didn't much care about that. And Michael wasn't going to do that anyway. I knew the guy was a justice freak from the Curtlee trial. He'd do what it took and take the consequences. He was all the way on board when he realized about Novio and Janice. Devastated, but on board."

"So," Amanda continued, "to go back to the beginning. What got Novio thinking about this? Ro getting out?"

"Exactly," Glitsky said. "Janice had just told Novio what she was going to do to him. She just didn't make up her mind fast enough to actually expose him. And the hesitation—maybe a couple of days, a week at most—that's what killed her. Because Chuckie boy thinks he's ruined and he's going to jail, and he's probably right. Meanwhile, just at this time, Ro gets out and burns up Felicia Nuñez's apartment. Novio knows the connection between Ro and Durbin, and comes up with this great idea. Make it look like Ro did it! And hey, while we're at it, slash the paintings. That would be Ro all over." Glitsky's face went sour. "And I almost helped him get away with it."

Lapeer reached a hand across the table and touched his. "That's a big 'almost,' Abe. I wouldn't get yourself too wrapped up in it. And meanwhile, if this whole thing comes up in shall we say loftier surroundings, which it will, you're comfortable with me saying Michael Durbin got into this because he volunteered?"

Glitsky gave a measured nod, thought a minute, then nodded again. "That would not be inaccurate," he said.

Since the slaughter last Friday, the *Courier*'s offices had been in a state of upheaval. Cliff and Theresa Curtlee had been hands-on managers, and without their presence, the ship was rudderless and Marrenas felt it keenly. The office manager was already engaged in a three-way power struggle with the managing editor and the head of sales; the stock had plummeted, and rumors of a hostile takeover by the McClatchy Group had put everyone on edge.

The past four columns by Heinous Marrenas had eulogized the Curtlees and their legacy, such as it was. Beyond that, she'd made as much hay as she could blasting the police department and the district attorney for their unscrupulous persecution of Ro Curtlee, a man who was "guilty of nothing more than coming from a family who had dared to take on the city's entrenched law enforcement establishment while it trotted out every trick in the book in a concerted effort to deny him his civil rights."

With her network of informers at the Hall of Justice, by last Monday morning she'd discovered that Ro Curtlee had in fact not murdered Janice Durbin. And for her it was but a short and seemingly logical extrapolation to conclude that he'd had nothing to do with the other murders either.

Now she was in the middle of her Friday column, in which she was well on the way to characterizing the murderous actions of Linda Salcedo at the Curtlee mansion as the work of a low-intelligence, disgruntled domestic employee. It was shaping up to be the kind of emotional broadside she was best at, and she was wrestling with her prose when suddenly the door to her office opened and a man came in like a blast of angry wind.

Who let this man in? What was going on in the front office that he hadn't been stopped?

Standing up, whirling to face him, her hands went to the phone to call security and her eyes flashed in fury over the invasion of her privacy. "What the hell . . ." But in the next second, she recognized him. She replaced the phone's headpiece and leaned forward over her desk, her weight on her hands and arms. "You're Michael Durbin."

"That's right." Durbin wore jeans and a windbreaker and carried a large cloth book bag from the San Francisco Mystery Bookstore over his shoulders. "How are you doing this morning?"

"I'm fine," she said, "but as you can see, I'm in the middle of a column. Normally I don't take appointments until my column's done for the day." *Heads are going to roll over this,* Marrenas was thinking. *Whoever let this clown into the building.* Forcing on a patient smile, she said, "But since you're already here, I can probably spare a couple of minutes. What can I do for you? Do you want to take a seat?"

"That would be nice, thanks." He pulled around the cafeteria chair from the side of her desk.

When he'd gotten seated, Marrenas sat back down, too. "Well?"

Durbin pursed his lips, took in a breath. "Well, Sheila—do you mind if I call you Sheila?—I noticed that the past few days you've been going out of your way to clear the name of Ro Curtlee, bringing out all the facts of the police investigation and so on."

"Right. That's what I . . ."

Durbin held up a hand, stopping her. "I'm very familiar with what you do, Sheila, as you know. More familiar than most. What

I'm down here for today is to tell you about the damage you do, to let you know how close you came to destroying me and my family, and to let you know that we've come out of it stronger and better."

"Well, I'm glad to see . . ."

Durbin stopped her again. "Please. You and your poisonous column came a long way toward convincing my boy Jon that his father was capable of murdering his mother."

Marrenas shifted her gaze. "I'm very sorry about that. I was going on the facts as I knew them at the time. For the record, I didn't print anything that was factually wrong, so if you're entertaining a lawsuit, forget about it."

"I'm sure that's how you justify your hatchet jobs to yourself. Select the facts you need for your own purposes, ignore context, and avoid responsibility."

Marrenas huffed in self-righteousness. "I'm not an irresponsible journalist, Mr. Durbin. I'm an investigative reporter." She gestured to the walls around her office, the plaques for her awards and achievements. "They don't give these things out in Cracker Jack boxes, you know."

"No, I'm sure they don't. But let me give you a couple of facts. Feel free to take notes if you want. First, of course, the most important fact—I didn't kill my wife. Second, I love my children. Third, since I didn't kill Janice, the alleged affair that I had with my good friend Liza Sato could not have been the motive for that murder, now, could it? And as for her sticking up for me at our workplace, that was the simple loyalty of a friend, not an example of collusion to help me with a cover-up. Are you getting all this?"

Marrenas gave him a dismissive shrug.

Durbin went on, "Finally, here's some excellent news about my plans for the future. I'm going to take Janice's life insurance and enough from the fire to build a new house. I'm going to resurrect my career as a painter, the career you helped destroy for me ten years ago. How does that sound to you?"

"Good," Marrenas said, her eyes frankly nervous now, flitting back and forth between Durbin and the door behind him. "That sounds good. I'm very glad to see that things will work out for you. But I really have to insist you leave now."

Durbin shifted his weight in his chair. "Fine, but I want you to know that I'll still have enough cash left over so that if I ever see my name in your column again, I'm going to pay someone to hunt you down and kill you like the vermin you are."

Staggered by the verbal assault, she could do nothing but stare at him.

"Unless, of course," Durbin said, "I don't think you're taking me seriously. In which case, maybe I'll just do it myself right now."

Durbin reached into his book bag and brought out a small handgun.

Marrenas's eyes went wide with panic. She put her hands out in front of her. "Oh my God, don't. No, please. Oh God, I just peed my pants. I'm so sorry. I didn't mean to hurt anyone. I was just trying to do the best job I could. Please. Please, don't . . ."

Durbin allowed himself a small, tight smile. "Good," he said. "I appear to have your undivided attention. I'm going to quote a famous line from *The Graduate*, Sheila. You ready for it? 'Plastics.'" He reached out and placed the toy gun on the front edge of her desk. "Keep it as a souvenir to remember me by," he said. "And don't even think about calling the police. After all, what harm could I have done with a plastic gun? And I can practically guarantee that they might just agree with the position you took in your column on Ro Curtlee—that threatening people really isn't a big deal. But never forget what I told you. If my name ever appears in your column again, I will have you killed. Now"—he smiled at her—"have yourself a nice day."

43

Frannie Hardy came back into their house on Sunday morning just as her husband, Dismas, was sitting down to the hash and egg breakfast he'd cooked up in the ten-pound cast-iron pan he kept hanging from a marlin hook over their stove. "Where have you been?" he asked her. "I was thinking about getting worried."

"That's what I love about you," she said. "That 'almost worried' quality."

"I'm pacing myself," Hardy said. "You don't want to get too worked up and worry unnecessarily." He pointed down at his plate. "You want some of this? I've got plenty."

"No. You go ahead." She sat down across from him.

"Where were you anyway?" he asked. "And don't say something impossible like the Galápagos Islands or the Ukraine or someplace."

She said, "I went to church."

"I told you, no kidding around."

"I'm not kidding. I went to church. I could even tell you the specific one if you want."

Hardy put down his fork and looked across at her. "Not that it's not a fine thing to do, especially here on a Sunday morning and all, but now I am a little worried. Is everything all right?"

"Everything's fine. Us, health, kids, all good."

"But . . . ?"

"But remember the other night when you and Abe were sitting

here doing the postmortem on all this madness with Ro Curtlee? And he was telling you how it had all begun this time around with the burning death of this poor woman Felicia Nuñez, who'd evidently been one of his first victims, too?"

"I remember it all too well. What about her?"

"Well, for some reason I couldn't get the idea of her out of my mind. I mean, here's this young girl comes up to this country full of hope from Guatemala. She gets raped by her bosses' son, does the right thing and testifies against him, then goes to work in a dry cleaners, lives alone, probably never has a boyfriend, maybe because of shame about the rape. And finally Ro gets out of jail and basically the first thing he does is kill her and burn her body." Frannie grabbed Hardy's napkin and dabbed at the corners of her eyes. "It's just so unfair, so unbearable."

"Hey." Hardy got up and came around the table, put his arm around her. "Hey." More gently. He kissed the top of her head and she leaned into him.

After a minute, she sighed. "I don't know why, but it just came to me sometime in the middle of last night that Abe said there really was nobody to mourn for her. Nobody even to come and get her body, and it just struck me as so, so sad. So I decided I'd go down to the church and light a candle and say a prayer for her. I know it's such a small thing and it's probably just superstitious and silly, but I just thought . . ."

Hardy said, "It's a beautiful thing, Fran. You are a beautiful person."

"Well, not really so much, but . . . at least it was something for somebody who never had anything, not even a tiny chance. Do you know what I'm saying? I felt like I had to do something. So she could maybe at least, if there is such a thing, rest in peace. You know?"

Hardy tightened his arm across his wife's shoulders. "Amen," he said.

JOHN LESCROART

———

Since the present they'd bought for Zachary Glitsky's fourth birthday was a relatively bulky electric piano keyboard, Hardy wound
up dropping Frannie off early that Sunday afternoon at the bottom
of the steps to Glitsky's door, after which he continued to drive
around looking for a place to park. When he finally made it to the
front door, Hardy rang the doorbell, heard footsteps approaching
inside, and then Glitsky's voice. "Who is it?"

"The Easter Bunny," Hardy said.

"You're a few weeks early."

"I'm getting a jump on the holiday. Get it? Jump?"

"Good one," Glitsky said.

"Are you going to open the door?"

"If you say please."

———

Nearly ten minutes later, Hardy was still sitting on the top step
outside when Wes Farrell and Sam Duncan appeared at the bottom of the stairs.

Farrell was carrying a small gift-wrapped box. He looked up to
see his former partner cooling his heels in jeans and a button-
down shirt. "Hey, Diz. What are you doing out here? Isn't Abe
home? Isn't this where the party's supposed to be?"

"He's home all right." Hardy stood up, shook hands with Farrell,
gave Sam a hug. "He's being immature. Let's see if he'll open the
door for you." And Hardy reached out and rang the doorbell. Again
he heard the footsteps coming up to the inside of the door. "Who
is it?"

"Don't say the Easter Bunny," Hardy whispered.

Farrell gave Hardy a quizzical look. "I'll resist the temptation."
Then, to the door, "Wes Farrell, district attorney," he said.

"He loves to say that," Sam said. "Makes him sound like an action hero."

"Hey!" Farrell said. "I am an action hero."

392

The door opened. Smiles and greetings, finally Glitsky looking around Wes and Sam and saying with apparent surprise, "Hey Diz, when did you get here?"

"Just now with the rest of the party."

Frannie appeared from the kitchen, coming up behind Glitsky. When she saw Hardy, she said, "Hey, babe. I was starting to get worried. How far away did you have to park?"

"Couple of miles," Hardy said.

Twenty minutes later, the three men stood in a knot over in the far corner of Glitsky's backyard while six women, Glitsky's father, Nat, and a gaggle of kids were deeply involved in a cutthroat game of Pin the Tail on the Donkey.

"You're damn right there's no bail on Novio," Farrell was saying.

"On what possible legal basis?" Hardy asked.

"Lying in wait. Makes it special circumstances."

"He was lying in wait at her house?"

"That's my position."

"For how long was he lying in wait?"

"Long enough," Glitsky said.

"That's a perfect cop answer," Hardy said. "But how do you know he didn't just knock at the door, knowing Durbin had gone off to work, and come on in like he had a hundred times before?"

"No, this day was different. Abe interrogated him personally and he admitted to lying in wait. Unequivocally."

"You tricked him."

"I wouldn't have done that," Glitsky said. "That would have been unethical."

Hardy looked from one of them to the other. "You gentlemen better be careful you don't give this guy grounds for appeal. That's all I'm saying."

"Duly noted," Farrell said. "But I'm not going to let a possible appeal affect the vigor of my prosecutions. That's what the people elected me for, and that's the way I'm going to run the show from here on out."

"Spoken like a true DA at last," Hardy said.

Farrell seemed to consider that for a moment. "Damn straight," he said. "That's exactly what I am."

———

All the other presents were opened. Farrell picked up his box and crossed the living room where Zachary sat surrounded by the day's booty—the portable piano, a football, a Game Boy box that Abe was clearly not all that pleased with, several books, the latest Disney DVD. "Here you go, Zack. Uncle Wes saved the best for last."

Zachary untied the bow, pulled off the ribbon, and ripped off the wrapping paper. Seeing the shape and size of the box underneath, Sam turned to Wes and said, "You didn't."

"He'll love it," Wes said. "Guaranteed. Go ahead, bud, take it out and wear it proudly."

Zachary couldn't read yet, which was probably just as well.

The T-shirt read, LOCK UP YOUR DAUGHTERS.

ACKNOWLEDGMENTS

Some books are more works of the imagination and spirit than are others, and this book falls into that category for me. While I generally have to do a great deal of research to get comfortable with legal details, criminal procedure, and other plot elements of my work, in this novel those elements were reasonably familiar to me from the outset. Accordingly, once I had settled upon the basic idea of this book, I set myself directly to the task of writing it, thinking I would interview acquaintances and sources as problems arose in the text. Much to my surprise, those problems for the most part did not arise. Aside from my usual dependence upon the legal expertise of my great friend Al Giannini, I did not have to seek very much other technical advice to make this story real and believable.

This fortuitous circumstance did not come about purely or even mostly by accident, however. When I first starting flirting with the ideas that would become *Damage*, I sent a preliminary outline of the proposed book to my agent, Barney Karpfinger, and a copy to my editor at Dutton, Ben Sevier. Both of these gentlemen, keen from the outset on the basic idea for the book, spent the better part of a couple of weeks patiently helping me to iron out potential problems and roadblocks with the plot. In all, I believe I completed four complete iterations of the outline, and through the intelligence and efforts of Barney and Ben, by the time I was ready to start putting words on the page, I had a crystal clear vision of what the book would look and feel like, and how I would try to realize this vision. So a special thanks to you both, Barney and Ben—without your diligence, brains, and enthusiasm, *Damage* would not exist today.

All of that said, an area where I did need some technical insight was the question of how a person goes, and stays, missing. For assistance in this matter, I'd like to thank Private Investigator Marcel Myres of Submar Investigations.

Of course, just because I didn't need too much technical help with this book doesn't mean that a host of friends and relatives didn't contribute to making the writing experience more fruitful and pleasant. This list includes: my siblings, Michael, Emmett, Lorraine, and Kathy; Don Matheson; Frank Seidl; Max Byrd; Tom Hedtke; Bob Zaro; Facebook Guru Aryn DeSantis; Web Master Maddee James; and Andy Jalakas. Day to day, my assistant, Anita Boone, makes things go smoothly and happily along in my workplace—I couldn't write these books without her invaluable, cheerful, and continuing assistance because I would spend all my time gnashing my teeth over logistical details and office records and housekeeping that Anita masters without breaking a sweat. My daughter, Justine, and my son, Jack, also continue to inform my plots, themes, and life with cool ideas and unexpected perspectives.

I'm most grateful for the help of my personal proofreader/editors: Karen Hlavacek, Peggy Nauts, and Doug Kelly.

Several people have generously contributed to charitable organizations by purchasing the right to name a character in this book. These people and their respective organizations are: Ritz Naygrow, Stacey Leung-Crawford, and Leland M. Crawford (The Sacramento Library Foundation); Vincent J. Abbatiello (Brenda Novak's Annual Online Auction to Benefit Diabetes Research); Trisha Stanionis (Yolo Family Service Agency); Gladys Mueller (Notre Dame de Namur University); and Mike and Tina Moylan (University of California, Davis).

A book's very life ultimately depends upon its publisher, and I remain extremely fortunate and proud to be a member of the Dutton family—an incredibly intelligent, dedicated, hardworking, efficient team that also manages to be filled with people who know how to have fun while being creative and talented. Specifically, I'd like to thank publisher Brian Tart, the marketing team of Christine Ball and Carrie Swetonic, Melissa Miller, Jessica Horvath, Susan Schwartz, Rachael Hicks, Signet/NAL paperback publisher Kara Welsh, Phil Budnick, Rick Pascocello, and the brilliant cover designer Rich Hasselberger.

Finally, I very much like to hear from my readers, and invite all of you to please visit me at my Web site, www.johnlescroart.com, with comments, questions, or interests. Also, if you are on Facebook, please join me (and become a fan) there.

ABOUT THE AUTHOR

John Lescroart is *The New York Times* bestselling author of twenty-one previous novels, including *Treasure Hunt*, *A Plague of Secrets*, *Betrayal*, *The Suspect*, *The Hunt Club*, *The Motive*, *The Second Chair*, *The First Law*, *The Oath*, *The Hearing*, and *Nothing But the Truth*. He lives in northern California.